John H. Stevens, Marshall Robinson

Personal Recollections of Minnesota and its People

and early history of Minneapolis

John H. Stevens, Marshall Robinson

Personal Recollections of Minnesota and its People
and early history of Minneapolis

ISBN/EAN: 9783337288501

Printed in Europe, USA, Canada, Australia, Japan

Cover: Foto ©Andreas Hilbeck / pixelio.de

More available books at **www.hansebooks.com**

OF

MINNESOTA AND ITS PEOPLE,

AND

EARLY HISTORY OF MINNEAPOLIS.

BY

JOHN H. STEVENS.

WITH BIOGRAPHICAL MEMORANDA AND LETTERS
TO COL. JOHN H. STEVENS, SELECTED
BY MARSHALL ROBINSON.

MINNEAPOLIS, MINN.
1890.

INTRODUCTORY.

I essay to write something of my personal recollections and present knowledge of Minnesota and its people. Living alone, as to white men, on the west bank of the Falls of St. Anthony, I preempted a part of the present site of Minneapolis. I have witnessed wonderful transformations. With such aid as I can command, I commence the relation I have long contemplated, as one of love and legacy to such patient and charitable readers as I may have. A multitude of loved ones have gone before, but many remain. In spirit they are equally present and in view. Heroes of the past, brave men of the present, many of them were, and are. Blessed is their memory, and their presence.

TABLE OF SOME OF THE CONTENTS.

CHAPTER I.

On returning from Mexico to my Wisconsin home in 1848, with impaired health, I thought of returning to a claim I made in Texas in 1846. During a military march in the fall of 1846 from Matamoras to a point on the plains some forty miles east of that city into Texas, the command lost its bearings on the prairie, through the carelessness of the guide, and in seeking water and a place to camp, after a march of two days, on the second night a light was seen in the distance which evidently indicated the presence of either a settlement of whites or a Comanche camp. The latter would not be a desirable event, but after so long a march over an unbroken wilderness it was decided best to approach the signs of habitation. About midnight the place was reached and it was found that three men had taken claims on the banks of a small stream which drained that part of Texas, where both mesquite trees and grass were abundant. The owners of these claims were from New Orleans where, as clerks, they had saved considerable money. They had concluded to unite their earnings and become planters in southwestern Texas. They purchased a few negroes and mules, supplied themselves with provisions and agricultural implements, and wandered through the wilds of Texas in search of land suitable for planting, and located in what they thought the most desirable place. Upon a hasty examination of the neighborhood the next morning, I decided to take an adjoining claim, and employed them to make improvements on it for me, with a full intention of making it a permanent home after the war.

1

I had made up my mind to reach this point as soon as I
could close my business in Wisconsin and Illinois.

The morning after the election of General Taylor to the
Presidency, in company with General Henry Dodge, who
was on his way to Washington to take his seat as United
States Senator from Wisconsin, I left Mineral Point for
Galena as a starting point for my proposed new home in
Texas.

A CHANGE IN MY PLANS.

Early as it was in November, we were met by one of the
most fearful snow and wind storms that ever swept over
the Northwest. The result was that we were snowed in at
Hazel Green, a little hamlet a few miles east of Galena, and
were obliged to remain there two days. Upon our arrival at
Galena the roads between that place and Chicago were still
impassable. Governor Dodge concluded to go by way of St.
Louis, while I remained waiting for one of Frink & Walker's
stages to make the trip to Chicago. While thus waiting at
the old American House for the roads to become passable, the
Prairie du Chien stage from the north arrived, one evening,
having for one of its passengers no less a personage than
John Catlin, the former Secretary of the Territory of Wisconsin. When that Territory became a State, in 1848, it left
Mr. Catlin acting governor of the portion of the old Territory
not included in the new boundaries of the State ; hence Mr.
Catlin had just returned from the Upper Mississippi, after an
official visit. Among other duties he had authorized the
election of a Delegate to Congress.

ATTENTION DIRECTED TO MINNESOTA.

From Mr. Catlin I first learned it was expected that a new
Territory would be organized by Congress at the coming session, which would include the Falls of St. Anthony, and its
name would be Minnesota ; that the result of the election
was in favor of Henry H. Sibley as Delegate from the proposed new Territory.

Learning that I was on my way to Texas in consequence of
serious lung difficulties, Mr. Catlin strongly urged me to give

up Texas and try Minnesota, as it was well known, he said, to be the best climate in the world for such invalids. He urged me so strongly in this matter, and said so much in favor of the new country that I became half inclined to retire to my farm near Rockford, Illinois, for the winter, with a view of visiting Minnesota before I returned to Texas. Delayed by the storm, and dreading the long winter journey which must be accomplished mostly by land, I finally concluded to abandon, at least for the time being, the journey to Texas, and in the mean time would seek more information in regard to Minnesota.

THE WONDERLAND OF THE NORTHWEST.

After being settled for the winter, I made diligent inquiries about this new Wonderland of the Northwest. I wrote to my friend Lieutenant Governor Timothy Burns of Wisconsin. Governor Burns and myself had for years been intimately associated in the mining region around Mineral Point. He had traveled extensively through the Territory. Here is an answer to one of my letters :

LETTER FROM GOVERNOR BURNS.

Madison, February 4th, 1849.
My Dear Sir : In answer to yours of the 20th of January making inquiries of me about the Territory of Minnesota, I would state that I think there will be a great deal of business there next summer. Besides the agricultural and lumbering advantages it possesses, our Government pays off some four or five tribes of Indians, with three or four companies of United States troops, which necessarily causes a great amount of money to be put in circulation there annually. In addition to these resources, the country is very well adapted to farming purposes. The soil and location of the country is excellent, and St. Paul, in my opinion, will soon be a place of considerable importance. The whole business of the people of the Red River of the North is now transacted at St. Paul, which is very considerable in itself. In conclusion, I think it a very good country. Yours truly, TIMOTHY BURNS.

PREPARING TO VISIT MINNESOTA.

In a subsequent letter Governor Burns informed me that upon the opening of navigation he should make a visit to the

upper country as far as the Falls of St. Croix, and I agreed to
meet him at Galena to accompany him on the journey. The
result was the abandonment of my Texas claim, though at
first I did not observe all the attractions of the country. We
intended to have left on the first boat, but on arriving at
Galena we found that three or four steamers had preceded us.

MY FIRST BILL OF GOODS.

Governor Burns suggested that I should lay in a supply of
stores, as hotels and boarding houses were scarce where we
were going, and being a novice in such matters, I purchased
from B. H. Campbell, through J. R. Jones, at Galena, the
following :

One barrel of pork - -	$9 50
Two hundred pounds of ham - -	8 00
Ten pounds of coffee - -	1 00
One pound of tea - -	1 00
Fourteen pounds of sugar - -	1 00
One-half sack of salt - -	50
Pepper, spices - - -	30
Four and one-half pounds of Tobacco -	1 67
One barrel of whiskey - - -	6 48

It will be observed that these necessaries of life were
cheap in those days. These merchants had not become the
prominent and · illustrious politicians which they were a few
years later.

EN ROUTE FOR MINNESOTA.

On the 20th day of April the good old steamer Dr. Franklin, Captain Pres Lodwick, with Captain Russell Blakely
in the office, entered Fever river and landed at Galena. On
going aboard to secure a passage to St. Paul we found the
cabin full of passengers. Among them were Hon. Henry H.
Sibley, Hon. Henry M. Rice and his bride, the late Joseph
McAlpine so long the book-keeper of the old St. Anthony
Mill Company, and several others who have since become
prominent citizens of Minnesota. Messrs. Sibley and Rice
were returning from Washington, where they had put in a
good winters work in behalf of the Territory. Governor

Sibley had been admitted during the session as a Delegate in Congress, and had made many friends in Washington. Mr. Rice was no less active than Governor Sibley during the session, and to the united efforts of these gentlemen, with those of the late Franklin Steele, who spent a considerable portion of the winter of 1849 at the seat of Government, is Minnesota indebted for the early organization of the Territory.

PROMINENT ORGANIZERS OF THE TERRITORY.

No country was ever more fortunate than Minnesota in containing such honest, able men as the three above named. The steamer laid all day at the levee in Galena, and only started on her northern journey after dark, hence we passed old Julian Du Buque's town during the night. We reached Prairie du Chien early in the forenoon of the next day, where a portion of the old Sixth Infantry was stationed at Fort Crawford. I recognized, and was cordially greeted by, many of the officers of the Sixth Infantry, with whom I had been quartered at the Convent of San Fernando, in the City of Mexico. Among them were Dr. McLaren the Surgeon, Lieut. Winfield S. Hancock, and several others whose names have since become known all over the world for their gallant deeds of patriotism during the War for the Union. Dr. McLaren was a brother-in-law of the late Adjutant General Townsend of the United States Army. His removal to Fort Snelling soon after I saw him at Fort Crawford made him one of the pioneers of Minnesota. We remained at Prairie du Chien several hours, which afforded the passengers an opportunity to take a good survey of the ancient town. We met Douseman, Brisbois, Fenton, Brunson, Savage, and several others. We missed the familiar face of a good old friend, Thomas P. Burnett, who had, while a member of the then recent Constitutional Convention of Wisconsin, passed over the silent river—where all those citizens of Prairie du Chien whom I have mentioned have since joined him on the other shore.

TOWNS AND SETTLERS ALONG THE WAY.

There were no towns of importance in those days on either side of the river between Dubuque and Prairie du Chien.

A German colony had recently landed and founded a town called Guttenberg, on the Iowa side. McGregor, just opposite Prairie du Chien, contained only a wareroom and a house or two. Cassville was a mining hamlet on the Wisconsin side, supported mostly by the mineral in the neighborhood. Since more attention has been given to the agricultural resources of the country, there is no reason why these old Wisconsin mining towns on and near the banks of the river in Grant and other counties should not become places of moment, for a better soil for farming purposes never laid " out of doors".

From Prairie du Chien up to the Bad Axe there were few if any white settlers—if we except the Indian traders and wood choppers. Once in a while we found a squaw man who had a small patch of vegetables—which was worked by a poor Indian wife.

BLACK HAWK BATTLE GROUND.

There were several Eastern passengers on board who, as well as the others, were much interested in looking at the neighborhood in the vicinity of the junction of the Bad Axe with the Mississippi. The location had become famous as the place of the defeat of the Sauk Chief Black Hawk by our troops under General Dodge and General Atkinson, August 1, 1832. The Indians were dreadfully whipped. Black Hawk said, when taken prisoner, that his warriors fell around him like hail. He claimed that his evil day had come. The sun, he added, rose clear on the morning of that eventful day, but at night it looked like a ball of fire and sank in a black cloud. It was, he continued, the last sun that shone on Black Hawk. During our stay at the mouth of the Bad Axe much sympathy was expressed for the Indians. Doubtless this was one of the most disastrous battles to them known in the history of the Indian war with the United States, as it ended in the total destruction of most of the followers of Black Hawk.

From the Bad Axe the Dr. Franklin made but few landings until we reached La Crosse, which at that time contained but

a few houses. I was introduced by Governor Burns to a Mr.
Levy as the pioneer of the village. I also met at La Crosse
Hon. Nathan Myrick, who subsequently became one of the
most prominent citizens of Minnesota. He was also a pioneer
of the place. A village had just been commenced on the Iowa
side, on the banks of the river, in Allamakee county, under
the auspices of John Hanney, since known as Lansing.
With the exception of a warehouse it was a paper town.
There was no Brownsville or La Crescent at that time on the
Minnesota side of the Mississippi. The fact that La Crosse
was the center of a considerable trade in fur with the Indians,
as well as a depot for the lumber trade on some of the streams
entering the Mississippi, warranted the belief that it would
eventually expand into a city of considerable proportions.
This induced Governor Burns to make a large investment in
the embryo village.

FROM LA CROSSE TO ST. PAUL.

From La Crosse to St. Paul the landings became more frequent. Lumbermen and Indian traders were more numerous.
At one point under the bluffs the boat landed to take on
several hundred bushels of potatoes, the product of land cultivated by a man by the name of Reed. Mr. Reed had sold
the potatoes to a house in St. Paul. He informed me that
this was his first shipment of farm products north, and he
thought the first of a similar character between Lake Pepin
and the upper Iowa river. Heretofore, he said, most of the
agricultural products required for the upper country were
raised between Dubuque and St. Louis. I think Mr. Reed
was an Irishman, with a mixed blooded woman for his wife,
and had lived under the bluff for a great many years in a kind
of voluntary retirement. He seemed to be much pleased that
a market had been opened at St. Paul and Stillwater for his
surplus products. Nelson's Landing at that time was a depot
for lumber. There was no Winona. I think the landing was
known as Wabasha prairie. The only business—small at
that—was the Indian trade. At Wabasha large groups of
Indians were seen. Early traders with the natives had made
this a point for many years. Hon. Alex. Bailey was at that
time the representative of the Fur Company at Wabasha.

Oliver Cratt, A. Rocque, and several other Canadian French-
men, were residents of the village. Hon. James Wells, an
old trader, had a store at the foot of the Lake. They were
mostly employed by the Fur Company and the United States
Agent of the Indians. Reed's Landing, just above Wabasha,
was at that time one of the most important trading points on
the river. The numerous logging camps up the Chippewa
river, in Wisconsin, had all their outfits stored and reshipped
from this point, which made business lively, especially every
fall and spring. Mr. Richards had a store house at Maiden
Rock, on the right bank of Lake Pepin, which was a place of
much interest to the passengers. It is about five hundred
feet high, and the location of a sad legend of the natives.

AN INDIAN ROMANCE.

Winona, an Indian maiden, was commanded by her father,
a prominent Chief, to marry a favorite brave, but the girl had
made choice of another for her husband. Rather than comply with her father's wishes, she threw herself from the rock,
and was instantly killed.

Lake City was not in existence as we passed Lake Pepin,
and there was no town or landing-place on the eastern banks
of the Lake until we reached Wacouta, at the head of the
Lake, at which point an Indian trader or two had goods to
sell to the Indians. Red Wing was the seat of an Indian
colony. I think only a few whites resided there at the time.
I only remember John Bush, the Indian farmer, and Rev. Mr.
Hancock, the missionary. Probably there were others that
I did not see. It was, and had been for a long time, a favorite
resort for Indians, and I believe they love to linger in the
bottoms, near that city, to this day. Prescott, on the Wisconsin side, attracted considerable attention in consequence of
its beautiful location. There were but few buildings, aside
from the necessary warehouses, but many of my fellow-
passengers predicted a flourishing town in the near future.
That was before the days of Hudson, which place has sprung
up since, and has reaped many of the benefits that naturally
belonged to Prescott. We thought the more of Prescott
because it was named after that philanthropist, the late Philander Prescott, who was so wantonly murdered by the

Dakotas, below Redwood, during the Indian outbreak, on the 19th day of August, 1862.

On the steamer leaving Prescott, the next landing was at Point Douglas, a trading post of some consequence in the early days of the Territory. Two of its early traders, Messrs. Burris and Hertzell, had accumulated quite a competency, even at that early day. The village had the advantage of the trade of the pioneer farmers residing on the fertile lands bordering on both the Mississippi and St. Croix. Other towns have sprung up since, and the trade of the Indians has passed away. Point Douglas has not made the growth that all the passengers on the steamer Dr. Franklin expected on that pleasant April day in 1849.

Our next call was at Oliver's Grove, now Hastings. A few Indian traders came aboard with packages of fur destined for Mendota. Oliver's Grove was so called from a Lieut. Oliver, who, at an early day, had charge of Government stores destined for the St. Peters camp, that were landed there in consequence of the close of navigation. There were no permanent residents there then, though the late Hon. Joseph R. Brown had a trading post there as early as 1828. It was considered an excellent point for trading with the Indians. I do not think there was a soul on board who could for a moment have thought that a large and flourishing town would be built up so rapidly in less than a decade.

LITTLE CROW'S VILLAGE—MISSIONARY WILLIAMSON.

Kaposia, or Little Crow's Village, was the next and last landing before we reached St. Paul. This was the residence of Rev. Dr. Williamson, so long a missionary among the Dakotas. A large band of Indians of both sexes came down to the levee to see the strangers on board the boat. Presently the venerable missionary came aboard and took passage for St. Paul. He was warmly greeted by Governor Sibley, Mr. Rice, and other early settlers, who were passengers. On being introduced to him by Governor Sibley, he asked if I was a relative of the missionary, Rev. J. D. Stevens, who arrived at Fort Snelling in September 1829, and who preached to Good Road's division of the Dakotas at Lake Calhoun so long, long ago. Dr. Williamson gave a warm welcome to his

new friends who were on the boat. He said the country
would not disappoint earnest men who were willing to farm
or to follow any other legitimate business. Of course it was
new, but it had a rich future, and as soon as its rare resources
were known it would become populous. People could not
afford to lead an idle life here ; that owing to its peculiar
climate and surroundings they would prefer to keep busy.
This was the commencement of a life-long friendship between
Dr. Williamson and myself, and I consider it one of the
fortunate events of my life. The friendship of such a man is
worth more than silver or gold.

FIRST SIGHT OF ST. PAUL.

We were soon in sight of the new Wonder of the Western
World, as it was before the day of booming Western towns ;
and as every place had to stand on its own merit, we had not
read or heard very much in regard to it. There was no paper
yet printed in St. Paul, nor anywhere in the Territory, though
James M. Goodhue had arrived with his printing outfit on the
18th, and ten days from that time the first paper, the Pioneer,
made its appearance. On landing, April 24th, we found the
town something more than a frontier trading station. I
secured a home for the time being, and a good one, too, with
J. W. Bass, a son-in-law of the early Wisconsin pioneer,
Rev. Dr. A. Brunson, and a brother-in-law of the lamented
Judge Thomas P. Burnett. Mr. Bass assigned me one of the
best rooms in his house, which I shared the next day on the
arrival of another boat, with a gentleman also from the lead
mines in Wisconsin, Dr. David Day, who has since occupied
high trusts in the Territory and State. Dr. Day, like myself,
was suffering from lung difficulties ; he could scarcely walk
up the bluff from the old landing ; so it may be presumed
that we made peaceable bedfellows. In any event it made us
friends, and the climate—not medicine—made us both strong,
healthy men.

OLD ST. PAUL.

I do not suppose St. Paul had, on that 24th day of April,
more than thirty-five or forty buildings, and it was claimed
that from 1838, when Pierre Parrant, the first settler, followed

the same year by Messrs. Abram Perry, Edward Phelan, William Evans, Benj. and Pierre Gervais and a Mr. Johnson, up to the end of December 31, 1848, there had been only about ninety-five heads of families settled within the limits of St. Paul proper. In 1839 Dennis Cherrier and Vital Guerin, with four others, were all the additions received, while in 1840 there were only three, which included that excellent man Rev. A. Ravoux, Rev. Lucian Galtier and Joseph Rondo. In 1841 there was only two—Pierre and Sever Bottineau, of the early explorers—and both of them had moved to St. Anthony in 1849. In 1842, Hon. Henry Jackson, Sergeant Richard W. Mortimer, and four others, were all the additions to the place. In 1843 the village received real, solid, substantial and lasting encouragement by the arrival of such men as Hon. John R. Irvine, William Hartshorn, A. L. Larpenteur, Hon. D. T. Sloan, James W. Simpson, and fourteen others, many of them men of much merit ; but in 1844 there were only five who made St. Paul their home ; yet small as their numbers were, it included such enterprising men as Captain Louis Roberts, Charles Bazelle and Hon. William Dugas. Captain Roberts and Mr. Bazelle were worth scores of common men in building up a new country. The year 1845 did better in numbers, though there were only twelve fresh arrivals, but they included such well known men as Charles Cavileer, Augustus and David B. Freeman, and Jesse H. Pomeroy ; while in 1846 Hon. James M. Boal, William H. Randall, William Randall, Jr., and seven others, selected a residence in St. Paul. In 1847 Hon. William Henry Forbes moved down from Mendota, and J. W. Bass and his brother-in-law Hon. Benj. W. Brunson, Hon. John Banfil, Hon. Parsons K. Johnson, and Hon. Simeon P. Folsom, came up from the lead mines. Miss Harriet E. Bishop, the pioneer school teacher, ex-sheriff C. P. V. Lull, Daniel Hopkins, the merchant, and four others—making thirteen in all, cast their lots in the new village.

PRE-TERRITORIAL SETTLERS.

The next and last year before the organization of the Territory, the pre-territorial settlers numbered thirty. Among them were Hon. Henry M. Rice, A. H. Cavender, Rev. B. F. Hoyt, Hon. William H. Nobles, David Lambert, W. C· Morrison, Nathan Myrick, Major E. A. C. Hatch, Hon. William Freeborn, Lott Moffatt, Hon. B. W. Lott, Hon. David Olmstead—all historical names— with seventeen others, many of them men full of energy and enterprise. It will be seen by the above that St. Paul, at the commencement of 1849, could not have been a very populous city, but there were men, who were residents, of the very best business habits, of strict integrity, and who were capable of surmounting every obstacle that came before them. It is true the majority were easy-going, but honest, and in some instances frugal. Many of these early settlers were discharged soldiers from Fort Snelling. Others—especially the French Canadians—had been employed for years with the Fur Company. As a general rule the French population were contented, and were not inclined to be over-ambitious in relation to making money ; but it must be remembered that the wants of the people were not what they became at a later period. During the short period that I remained in St. Paul, every boat that arrived was crowded with passengers. The same may be said of the boats during that entire season. The boats of 1850, and for several years thereafter, were full of people coming to make Minnesota their home.

SEEKING CLAIMS.

A colony of some twelve persons from Rock River had preceded me to St. Paul. They were neighbors and acquaintances of mine. They could find no desirable claims in the immediate vicinity of the village, and after consultation it was determined to proceed up the Mississippi in search of Government lands. The impression, previous to leaving home, was that the portion of the Territory west of the Mississippi was open to settlers ; but it still belonged to the Indians. The report had gone abroad that this land west of the river was greatly superior to that on the east side—which was true. As only Indian traders and squaw men could get a foothold in the Indian Territory, we concluded to explore the upper Mississippi country.

CHAPTER II.

Leaving St. Paul with plenty of stores and a good camping outfit, we arrived at old St. Anthony about noon on Friday, April 27th, 1849. There was no place where one could get accommodations for man or beast; but we were told that up the river, a few miles further, we could get a good place to stop over with John Banfil, who kept a hotel at Coon Creek. This we found to be true; but we did not like to fast until we should get there. Some one told us to try the old mess-house; it might be by making terms with the cook we could get a dish of pork and beans, and a cup of coffee. We wanted to take a good look at the Falls. We had discovered that a tenderfoot, some way, contracted a pretty good appetite upon, or soon after, his advent into Minnesota; so we wandered to the old mess-house, which stood on the bank of the river at the east end of the present bridge on Central avenue; and after the hands engaged in building the mill had finished their meal, we took what was left, with thankful hearts and diminished funds. Little did we think, on that day, that our future home, for many long years, was to be in the vicinity of that old mess-house.

We found that the principal Falls were on the west bank of the river. Messrs. Franklin Steele and Godfrey had their saw mill completed, which had been commenced in the Autumn of 1847. This was a great convenience to the new Canada people, as well as to the new-comers in both St. Paul and St. Anthony. Previously the lumber for building had to be hewn out of tamarac and hard wood, or hauled overland from the St. Croix country. The army officers stationed at Fort Snelling, in an early day, made strenuous efforts to get hold of real estate around the Falls. In most instances the few citizens then residents of the country got the advantage over them, and obtained the prize. At a later period, however, several of the army officers became interested in choice lands on the west bank of the river, which were included in the military reservation. They held the winning cards, from the fact that claims could only be held by their permission.

FIRST PERMANENT CLAIM AT THE FALLS.

At the time of my first visit to the Falls I learned, from unquestionable authority, that Franklin Steele made the first permanent claim in St. Anthony, that was recognized in 1838. At that time he was Sutler at Fort Snelling. Major Plympton, of the Fifth U. S. Infantry, made a claim, in 1836, and built a log house on it. This was the same claim afterwards made by Mr. Steele. The next year, Sergeant Carpenter of Company A of the same regiment, made a claim immediately north of Major Plympton's. As the lands belonged to the Indians, the claims were of no value.

THE CHIPPEWA INDIANS SELL THEIR LANDS.

On the 18th day of June, 1838, it became known at Fort Snelling that the Chippewas had sold to the General Government all their lands between the Mississippi and the St. Croix, which of course included the east bank of the Falls of St. Anthony. Then Mr. Steele, by dint of great perseverance, obtained his original claim by virtue of making the first settlement after the land was ceded. He accomplished this over all competition, including that of Captain Martin Scott of the Fifth Infantry. Captain Scott was killed at the battle of Molino del Rey, in Mexico, on the 7th of September, 1847. He was born in Vermont, and was considered one of the best officers in the Army. Of course, under the land-laws, officers of the Army could not hold claims, because of their incapacity to pre-empt them. Mr. Steele secured the services of an old voyager, named La Grue, to live on the claim; but while absent from home, La Grue's cabin was destroyed by fire, and his wife was burned to death in it. He immediately left the country and was never heard from. Mr. Steele then built a commodious log house in place of the one that was destroyed, and placed a well known voyageur, Charles Laundry, in it to hold his claim. During his absence from the house an old discharged soldier, James Mink, jumped the claim, got possession of the house, and Mr. Steele was obliged to buy him off at pretty round figures. Then Mr. Steele hired Joseph Reach to occupy his place. He was faithful to the end, and in 1847 Mr. Steele secured a deed from the United States for the claim, paying a dollar and a quarter an acre. At the same time he purchased Nicollet Island at the same cost per acre. Charles Laundry died early in the fifties, near Bottineau Prairie, and Mr. Reach died about the same time at his home in the northern part of St. Anthony. In 1838 Carpenter sold his claim to a soldier by the name of Brown. In May, 1840, Brown disposed of it to Peter Quinn. Mr. Quinn fell a victim to the treachery of the Indians, on the Minnesota river, on the 20th of August, 1862. Mr. Quinn came at a very early day to the St. Peter country from the Coast of Labrador. He was an honest, warm-hearted man and, I think, a native of Ireland. He was for many years employed in the Indian Department of the Territory. His widow and daughter are now residing in St. Paul. He has two sons living. His eldest son, occupying a high position in the Northwestern Territory, was killed during the Riel Rebellion in Northwestern Canada. In 1845 Mr. Quinn sold his claim to his son-in-law, Mr. Findlay, and R. P. Russell. The next year, May 9th, they sold it to Pierre Bottineau, who at that time was a resident of St. Paul.

Another claim was made, by Mr. Pettijohn, as early as 1842, on the land now belonging to the University and other parties. Afterwards Mr. Bottineau obtained it, but it eventually fell into the hands of Calvin A. Tuttle, who purchased it from the Government. Joseph Rondo, of St. Paul, partly made and partly jumped Carpenter's old claim near Boom Island, in 1843, but when Bottineau came in possession of the Carpenter land, he soon disposed of Rondo, who went back to St. Paul in disgust. By purchase and otherwise Mr. Steele and Mr.

Bottineau, in 1845, held all the land from above Boom Island down to near the Tuttle place. I find that one Baptise Turpin, a half-breed from the north, lived on the Pettijohn claim in 1845. He held it for Mr. Bottineau. This year two brothers, Pascal and Sauverre St. Martin, made claims down the river from the Pettijohn claim. The land became the property of William A. Cheever and Judge B. B. Meeker. Here, then, we have all the actual residents of the east bank of the Falls of St. Anthony up to and including the year 1845.

Charles Wilson, a discharged soldier, long employed by Mr. Steele as a teamster, was off and on at St. Anthony after 1845. He died at Fort Snelling the early autumn of 1849. He could hardly, however, be called a resident; and yet, perhaps, he was more than a visitor; but his home proper was, after his discharge from the Army, always at the Fort.

Mr. Bottineau, his two brothers Severre and Charles, and his brother-in-law Louis Desjarlais, Joseph Reach and family, and their employees, were the occupants of St. Anthony until early in 1847, when operations were commenced for building the mill. The services of Ard Godfrey, a prominent mill-wright from the Penobscot river, Maine, were secured as overseer of the mill. William A. Cheever, of Boston, Calvin A. Tuttle, John Rollins, Luther Patch, Edward Patch, Sumner W. Farnham, Caleb D. Dorr, Robert W. Cummings, Charles W. Stimpson, John McDonald, Samuel Ferrald and David Stanchfield, became identified with the place. W. R. Marshall, J. M. Marshall and R. P. Russell, were also more or less in the village during the year. Mr. Russell had been a resident at Fort Snelling since 1840, and frequently made St. Anthony a semi-home; and in 1848 he became a resident in earnest by settling down and marrying Miss Marian Patch, and soon after became the pioneer merchant of the village, though he had previously sent a small stock of goods to various parties in St. Anthony to trade with the Indians and the few whites in that vicinity. The additions to the population in 1848 were Sherman Huse, Edgar Folsom, Elias H. Connor, Joseph Potvin, Silas M. Farnham, Bernard Cloutier, Washington Getchell, A. D. Foster, Charles W. Stinson, and a few others.

Many of these gentlemen became permanent residents ; all, and those who came before, have been useful and respected citizens. In looking over the list of the old settlers of pre-Territorial days in Minnesota, it is gratifying to observe the fact that not a single one of them was ever presented on a criminal charge—which shows that they were men of good moral character.

EXPEDITION TO COON CREEK.

About 3 o'clock in the afternoon our expedition left for Coon Creek. The farmers in our ranks objected to the quality of the soil from St. Anthony on the route because of the quantity of sand in it ; but as none of it had ever been cultivated, of course we could not judge of its productiveness. Arriving at Banfil's a little after dark, weary after the day's walk, Mrs. Banfil seated us at the supper table, which was filled with wholesome food. One of the party thought it the best meal he had partaken since he had left the old American House in Galena which was praise indeed when we consider the excellent tables on the upper Mississippi steamers in the old colony days, as well as of mine host, J. W. Bass of the primitive Merchants' Hotel of St. Paul. Mr. Banfil landed in St. Paul in 1847, and made a claim at Coon Creek, which was considered a good place for a hotel, securing all the travel from St. Paul to Fort Gaines, the Indian agencies on the Upper Mississippi, and those engaged in the Indian trade in the Northwest.

AT THE MOUTH OF RUM RIVER.

After a comfortable night's rest and a good breakfast we continued our journey, arriving at Rum river about noon, where we found a solitary cabin occupied by Mr. Dahl, who was holding down the claim for Louis Roberts of St. Paul. In order to make the enterprise pay, Captain Roberts had established a ferry, and Mr. Dahl acted as ferryman. With the exception of the cabin, there was not a house, a chick or child, where the proud city of Anoka stands to-day. Inquiring for a good camping-place where we could remain for a few days, to explore the country, Mr. Dahl directed us to a point a mile or so above the ferry, on the banks of the Mississippi.

2

known as the Big Island, which had everything desirable for camping purposes. There was wood, water and, at the proper season of the year, good grass. At Big Island we prepared a temporary home, and commenced keeping bachelors' hall. The next day being Sunday, a portion of the expedition remained in camp. Others followed the margin of the river to the junction of Rum river with the Mississippi, hunting bottom lands and hay meadows, but found none that were satisfactory.

MISSIONARY FRED. AYER.

Observing that a tent had been pitched since we left the previous evening, and seeing a wagon, and a span of horses feeding on the banks of the river, we made a call—Sunday as it was—on the new-comers, and found that the occupants of the tent were the Rev. Fred. Ayer and one of his sons, who were on their way to what is now known as Belle Prairie, to establish a mission for the Chippewa Indians. We were greatly interested in Mr. Ayer's account of his long missionary labors with the Indians.

In 1830 Mr. Ayer, who was then stationed at Mackinaw, was sent to La Pointe to examine the Lake Superior region to report in regard to the propriety of establishing a post for missionary work on or near the great "unsalted sea". He returned to Mackinaw the same year, but the next year, in company with Rev. Sherman Hall, he returned to La Pointe and established a school for Indian children, and was by Mr. Hall selected as its principal teacher. In 1832 he was sent from La Pointe to open a kindred work at Sandy Lake ; · and the next year in September, he was transferred to Yellow Lake for the beginning of a mission station. Mr. Ayer was for a time, I think, stationed at Pokegema Lake, a beautiful sheet of water some five miles long by one mile wide ; and also on Snake river some twenty miles from where it empties into the St. Croix. When I saw him his hair had become gray in missionary work. I think in addition to the places I have mentioned, Mr. Ayer had done missionary work in various parts of the Indian country. The next morning we saw him passing our camp at Big Island, and shook hands with him. From that day to his death I heard and read of his good deeds at Belle Prairie and elsewhere. In 1865 he went to Atlanta, Georgia, in the employ of the Freedmen's Bureau, and died and was buried in that city in 1867. His life was one of great self-sacrifice and usefulness.

THE COLONY SCHEME ABANDONED.

As the explorers came into camp it became evident that we could not establish a colony in the portion of the territory we were visiting, as they all protested against locating where there was such light soil. We had lived in Illinois where there was a deep black soil, and we wanted to find that in Minnesota ; but we looked in vain for it on the east bank of the river. We accidentally discovered that a small piece of land had been cultivated with corn, beans, and potatoes the previous year, just above the camping ground, and looking around we found the product of the land concealed in an old stack which was covered with brush, and were surprised to see such large ears of corn. Upon this discovery I made up my mind that the soil might be light, but if it produced such corn it was good enough for me ; and after returning to St. Paul I hunted up the owner of the claim, William Noot, who resided on the Fort Snelling reservation, and purchased his right for $200 ; but before I got ready to occupy it, some one jumped the claim ; so I lost not only the claim, but my two hundred dollars. This was my first venture in Minnesota soil. I found it was necessary to enter land as soon as it was in market ; for mere claims to land could not be depended upon.

Procuring an old Indian canoe, we crossed the Mississippi and made a journey of several miles into the interior west of the river. Here we found the quality of soil we wanted ; but as all the land west of the river from the Iowa line to the Canadian provinces belonged to the Indians, we could not obtain it ; and the result was that all the members of the party, except myself and one other, determined to abandon the country and seek homes elsewhere. This intention was carried out.

CHAPTER III.

Returning to St. Paul by way of Crow river, Fort Snelling, and Mendota, we had an excellent opportunity to see the new country along the route before its appearance had been changed by the hands of white men. We were all in love with it, and wondered how it was possible there could be such a difference in the quality of the soil from the other side of the river.

We found a band of Winnebagos encamped on Crow river. They came down from Long Prairie to hunt and fish on the neutral lands between the Dakotas and Ojibways. I was acquainted with some of the Winnebagoes when they lived in the lower country. They expressed their dissatisfaction with the Long Prairie country, and their determination to abandon it as soon as possible; which resolution they carried into execution a year or two afterwards.

At this time the neutral lands were full of game, and the numerous lakes and streams were alive with fish. We followed the old Indian trail from the mouth of Crow River to the western bank of the Falls of St. Anthony. It was an unbroken, beautiful wilderness. With the exception of the old military building on the bank opposite Spirit Island, there was not and, for aught I know, never had been a house or a sign of habitation from Crow river to a mile or two below Minnehaha.

The scenery was picturesque, with woodland, prairie, and oak-openings. Cold springs, silvery lakes, and clear streams abounded. Except the military reservation, from what is now known as Bassett's creek to the mouth of St. Peter river, the

SAINT ANTHONY FALLS OF OLD.

land all belonged to the Indians, and we were trespassers in walking over it.

We were particularly charmed with the lay of the land on the west bank of the Falls which the present site of Minneapolis includes. A few Indians belonging to Good Road's band had their tepees up, and were living temporarily in them, in the oak-openings on the hill a little west of the landing of the old ferry. There was an eagle's nest in a tall cedar on Spirit Island, and the birds that occupied it seemed to dispute our right to visit the crags below the Falls.

We started up a number of large timber wolves —old hoary fellows, wandering in the vicinity—that had grown fat, bold, and vicious in feeding for years upon the offal of the old military slaughter-houses that were in the neighborhood.

Many government mule-wagons from Fort Snelling, loaded with supplies for Fort Gaines, were fording the broad, smooth river, near the brink of the trembling Falls, where the dark water turned white, and with a roar leaped into the boiling depth, and gurgled on its rapid way to the Gulf of Mexico.

The banks of the river above the Falls were skirted with a few pines, some white birch, many hard maples, and several elms, with many native grape-vines climbing over them, which formed fine bowers up to the first creek above the Falls. The table-land back from the river was covered with oak. There were some thickets of hazel and prickly pear. On the second bench, a little below the Falls, from a quarter to a half mile back, there was a dense growth of poplar that had escaped the annual prairie fires. These trees were very pretty, on that spring day, with the foliage just bursting from the buds.

Here and there were fine rolling prairies of a few acres in extent, in the immediate neighborhood of the Falls ; but toward Minnehaha the prairies were two or three miles long, and extended to Lake Calhoun and Lake Harriet. Near the Falls was a deep slough of two or three acres. It was seemingly bottomless. This and a few deep ravines and grassy ponds were the only things to mar the beauty of the scene around the Falls.

On the old road from the west-side landing to the rapids

where teams crossed the river was a fine large spring with a copious flow of clear cold water. From appearances it seemed to be a place of summer resort for Indians and soldiers. Large linden-trees with wide-spreading branches made a grateful shade. In after years the water of the spring was much used by the early settlers. Picnic parties were common in those days from Fort Snelling. The officers with ladies would come up and spend the long, hot days in the shade of the trees and drink the cool spring water.

From 1821 for many years all the beef cattle required for the Fort were pastured, wintered, and slaughtered near the old government buildings. For this reason the locality appeared more like a New England pasture than a wilderness.

On the way to Fort Snelling was a lone tree about half way to Little Falls creek. It was a species of poplar, and had escaped the prairie fires. Its trunk was full of bullet holes, said to have been made during a battle between the Chippewas and Dakotas. This was the only landmark then on the prairie between Minnehaha Falls and the west bank of the Falls of St. Anthony. It was far from being a pretty tree, but it served an excellent purpose during the winter months when the Indian trail was covered with snow, as a guide to the few travelers who passed over the lonely prairie. It disappeared long since, but there is not a pioneer who had occasion to use the old trail in the winter but will hold it in grateful remembrance.

LITTLE FALLS.

Arriving at Minnehaha creek, we waded through its silvery waters and encamped for the night near the Falls. We had for company several Winnebagoes who had put up their wigwams for a few day's rest. They had been on a visit to their old home in Wisconsin and Iowa, and were on their way back to Long Prairie. The Indians seemed to be as enthusiastic over the beautiful Little Falls as we were. Early the next morning we left for St. Paul.

FORT SNELLING TO ST. PAUL.

Passing Fort Snelling, we crossed the St. Peter river on

the government ferry and went through Mendota without calling. We followed the west bank of the Mississippi, frequently through mire, to a point west of St. Paul. We were fortunate enough to secure the services of a Dakota Indian to cross to the village, where we were safely landed in our old room again, with Dr. Day, at the Merchants.

DISBANDING OF THE PARTY.

After a consultation among the members of the colony, it was determined to abandon the scheme of looking further for lands, for the present, and all, except two, took passage on the first boat for the lower country. In the meantime it would not answer to be idle while waiting for a treaty with the Indians, who were willing, if not anxious, to sell their lands west of the Mississippi.

EAST AND WEST OF THE MISSISSIPPI.

Though much good land could be found between the Mississippi river and the St. Croix, the report had gone abroad that there was too much sand in the soil east of the river, and that it never could be made good farming land—which is not true. Yet the old saying was pretty well illustrated, that to give a dog a bad name, no one will believe he is a good dog; but for all that he may be one of the best of dogs. Be that as it may, the east side suffered greatly in an early day from these reports. It should have been determined in this way : while the country east of the river is pretty good, that on the west side, as a general rule, is better.

CHAPTER IV

Meeting Mr. Sibley early in May, he said the business of
Mr. Franklin Steele, at Fort Snelling, required some one to
take charge of it; that Mr. Steele was in the East, and was
expected home soon. On the return of that gentleman I
entered into close business relations with him, which were
continued through his lifetime. A more enterprising, honorable, and popular man never lived in the Northwest. He
was born of distinguished parentage in 1813, in Chester
county, Pennsylvania. His father, General James Steele,
was of Scotch descent. One of his ancestors, General Archi-
bald Steele, served under General Montgomery in the expedition against Quebec. He became Deputy Quartermaster-
General of the troops in the western division of the Army in
Pennsylvania. Another ancestor, John Steele, was an officer
in the Revolutionary Army. A letter is preserved which he
wrote to his brother, dated Morristown, New Jersey, June 14,
1787, in which he says : "I at present enjoy myself incompar-
"ably well, in the family of Mrs. Washington, whose guard I
"have had the honor to command since the absence of the
"General and the rest of the family, which is now six or
"seven days. I am happy in the importance of my charge,
"as well as in the presence of the most amiable woman on
"earth, and whose character, should I attempt to describe,
"I could not do justice to; but will only say that I think it
"unexceptionable."

At the commencement of my acquaintance with Mr. Steele
he was the foremost business man in this part of the North-

LITTLE FALLS OF OLD NOW MINNEHAHA.

As one sees the Minnehaha, gleaming, glancing thro' the forest.

In the land of the Dakotas,
Where the Falls of Minnehaha
Flash and gleam among the
    oak trees,
Laugh and leap into the valley.

And he journeyed without
    resting,
Till he heard the cataract's
    laughter,
Heard the Falls of Minnehaha
Calling to him thro' the silence,

"Pleasant is the sound !" he
    murmured,
"Pleasant is the voice that
    calls me !"
Would he come again for
    arrows
To the Falls of Minnehaha ?
Heard the Falls of Minnehaha
Calling to them from afar off :
Fare thee well, O Minnehaha !
    [Longfellow's Hiawatha.

west.   His numerous enterprises were distributed from the
head of Lake Superior to the Iowa line, and from the Mississippi to the Missouri.   Gentlemanly and generous, every
member of the community was his friend.   He was a philanthropist—a lover of men.   His principal business office was
at Fort Snelling, where he occupied the position of sutler.
His pleasant home was just outside the walls of the Fort,
where his accomplished wife presided.

OFFICERS AT FORT SNELLING.

On my arrival at the Fort, in May, 1849, that post was
under the command of Brevet-Major Samuel Woods, Captain
of Company E, Sixth Infantry.   Major Woods married Miss
Clayborne Barney, the youngest sister of Mrs. Franklin
Steele.   She was a lady of rare merit.   She and her three
children died of cholera at Fort Riley, Kansas, in 1854.   They
are quietly resting in the beautiful Lakewood cemetery on the
borders of Lake Calhoun.

The other officers at Fort Snelling at that time were Captain
James Monroe, Company K, Sixth Infantry ; Captain Simon B.
Buckner, Company C ; Lieutenants I. W. T. Gardiner and
Castor, Company D, Second Regiment U. S. Dragoons ;
Lieutenants A. D. Nelson and Page.   Dr. Martin, father-in-
law of Captain Monroe, was the Surgeon, and Rev. Dr. E. G.
Gear, Chaplain.

Early in June Lieutenant-Colonel Gustavus Loomis arrived
and assumed command.   Captains R. W. Kirkham and Wetmore, and Surgeon A. N. McLaren, also arrived in June.
Soon after Colonel Loomis assumed command at Fort Snelling
Captain John Pope of the Topographical Engineers—now
Major-General Pope—and Dr. Sikes, arrived en route to the
boundary line.   The expedition was to be under the command
of Major Woods, accompanied by Company E, Lieutenant
Nelson, and Company D, Lieutenant Gardiner.   The command
left Fort Snelling on their march June 6th, and returned in
September.

WHAT BECAME OF THE OLD COMMAND.

Few of the officers stationed at Fort Snelling at that time
are now alive, and of the soldiers who were included in the

command I only know of four who survive, viz: James Brown,
Valentine and Charles Haeg, and Mr. Geo. W. Gellenbeck of
Shakopee, Scott county.   One of the members of the old band,
old-settler M. N. Kellogg, still lives in St. Paul.   Colonel
Loomis died March 5th, 1872, at Stafford, Connecticut, aged
83 years.   He was a man of much moment, a friend of the
early missionaries, and a Christian gentleman who delighted
in good works.

Lieut. Paige soon after left the army and died in Massachusetts.

Lieut. Castor married the widow of Lieut. Whitehorn, and
lived but a few years.   Mrs. Whitehorn was the daughter of
Rev. Dr. Gear.

Lieut. Gardiner became an officer of high rank, and died
during the late civil war.

Captain Wetmore, who married a beautiful Mexican lady,
retired from the army in 1850, and only lived a short time.
He died in St. Louis.

Captain Monroe was a colonel during the civil war, and was
killed in battle.

Captain Buckner left the army, in 1854, to superintend his
wife's large estate in Chicago, which was left her by her
father, Major Kingsbury.   The lady lived only a few years
afterwards.   Her husband became a confederate general, and
is now governor of Kentucky.

Major Woods was transferred to the paymaster's department, and has long lived in California.

Captain Kirkham became assistant quartermaster-general,
from which service he retired, a few years ago, and now
resides in Oakland, California.

Dr. McLaren became assistant surgeon-general, and died
in Washington after the war.   Dr. Martin was an old man in
1849.   He died in Pennsylvania not long after leaving Fort
Snelling.   Rev. Dr. Gear was transferred from Fort Snelling
to Fort Ripley.   He retired from the chaplaincy, and died
in Minneapolis.

Having been quartered with the Sixth infantry in the
convent of San Fernando, in the City of Mexico, in the fall
of 1847, it was a pleasure to meet a portion of the old regiment again at Fort Snelling.   At that time it did not seem

that the City of Mexico was much further removed from the center of civilization in the United States than Fort Snelling. The change from the tropical South to the hyperborean regions of the North had a beneficial effect on the health of the command. The climate did what the surgeons failed to do with Uncle Sam's medicine—it banished malaria and other diseases incident to the South, contracted in Mexico, from the members of the regiment. As Fort Snelling is the fountainhead of the early history of the Northwest, it has become classic with interesting events of the long past. Many of them have never been published. I shall refer to the grand old fortress again, and at more length, in the pages of this humble offering.

IN BUSINESS.

Having got down to business, in examining the journals and ledgers of Mr. Steele, the posting of which was under my supervision, it was demonstrated that his extensive business was in a most satisfactory condition. His mills at the Falls were completed, and his trade was profitable.

A NEW DEPARTURE.

On the morning of the 10th of June, 1849, Mr. Steele came into his counting-room, in the rear of the sutler's store, and asked if I could spare the day to accompany him to the Falls of St. Anthony. He added that he had an object in view, which might possibly be of advantage to me. Having decided to go with him, I did not inquire, at the time, in relation to the proposed visit.

CHAPTER V.

On the way up to the Falls with Mr. Steele he said that, from the best information he could get, the military reservation of Fort Snelling would soon be reduced in size; that many valuable claims could be secured on it, provided the Secretary of War would grant permission to occupy them ; that Hon. Robert Smith, M. C. from the Alton district, Illinois, had secured such a permit to hold the old government property, which included the west bank of the Falls ; that the claim immediately north of Mr. Smith's was equally as desirable, and he thought, if I wished, there would be no difficulty in obtaining War Secretary Marcy's approval of its occupation.

MY CLAIM AT THE FALLS.

During the journey up to the Falls we completed our plans and marked out the claim that became my home for many years. I readily obtained permission from the Secretary of War to hold the claim, but was under bonds to maintain a free ferry for the crossing of government troops. There was constant communication between the government forces at Fort Snelling and Fort Ripley. Thus, through the engagement with Mr. Steele, I became an occupant of the land that I had so much admired a few weeks before on the occasion of my first visit to the Falls. Had any one intimated such a thing as possible at that time I should have considered it the most visionary of all earthly matters. The idea of such a result did not enter my mind at my first visit. There, on the bank of the river, just above the rapids, I commenced building my humble house, to which, when finished, I brought my wife as a bride, and in it my first children were born, the eldest being the first-born child in Minneapolis proper.

Under that primitive roof many important historical events occurred ; among them the organization of the county of Hennepin, and election of the first officers of the county. Indian councils were held in it.

SOME OF MY INDIAN GUESTS.

Little Crow, Good Road, Gray Eagle, Shakopee, and other Dakota chiefs, held consultation with the government agents, Major Richard Murphy and Major McLean, in that house ; while the Winnebagoes, when residents of the upper country, seemed to think they had a pre-emption right on their old down-country friend, when making portage around the Falls. Hole-in-the-Day and his Chippewa braves frequently dropped in. The nearer the dinner hour the better it suited the different tribes to make their call. A barrel or two of crackers, and a good supply of salt pork, was a special delight to the red brothers. It was thought advisable that these Indian luxuries should always be on hand, and ready for any emergency. They prevented depredations on the garden, growing crops, and stock. If the Dakotas did not always respect the property of the missionaries—such men as Dr. Williamson, Dr. Riggs, and Rev. M. N. Adams it could hardly be expected that they would exhibit any greater respect for the possessions of a man who lived almost alone on the borders of their territory.

The United States judges in the Federal court frequently sat "in chambers" in the small parlor of the old house, and decided questions of law that were brought before them— much to the disgust of the officers at Fort Snelling. Sometimes soldiers would be brought before a Federal judge in relation to the legality of their enlistment. At one time when Judge Chatfield occupied the bench, he ordered Colonel Lee, the commanding officer at the Fort, to discharge from the army two privates who had enlisted before they were twenty-one years old, without the consent of their parents.

Then again the pioneer ministers of the gospel would hold meetings on Sundays, and sometimes on week days, in the lone house. The congregation would consist pretty much of my family and those employed to work for Mr. Steele and myself.

Once in a while this old house would be honored with the presence of politicians. For instance, when the fourth legislature met in St. Paul, on the 5th of January, 1853, the house failed to secure a majority of votes for any one man for speaker. Two or three weeks were spent in voting without choice. Many of the members became almost discouraged. When it adjourned, one Saturday, without an election, the Whig members held a caucus, at which it was decided to invite all the Whig members of both houses to be at the little dwelling under the hill, up at the Falls, on Sunday, to see if measures could not be devised for the election of a speaker, and to effect an organization. They all came. There was Dr. Day, Hon. John D. Ludden, Hon. Justus C. Ramsey, Colonel N. Greene Wilcox, and others, of the house ; and Hon. Martin McLeod, D. B. Loomis, Geo. W. Farrington, L. A. Babcock, and N. W. Kittson of the territorial senate. Messrs. Bass, Brunson, J. P. Owens, and other prominent citizens of St. Paul, accompanied them. Suffice to say, a programme was arranged, and on the morrow, at the opening of the session, the dead-lock was broken, and Dr. David Day was elected speaker.

ANOTHER GOOD SERVICE IN THE ANCIENT BUILDING.

In the early days, after the lands could be occupied by the settlers, the different religious denominations held meetings in the winter. The result was many conversions. Our good friends, the Baptists, with old Father Cressey, and the respected elders Palmer and Russell, were there, and through their influence a revival of much moment occurred. The house being close to the bank of the river, it was used for the reception of the members after baptisms, on the cold Sundays. It happened, one winter, that almost every Sunday when these solemn rites were observed, the mercury fell to nearly forty degrees. A hole of sufficient size was made in the ice to admit the clergyman and a candidate for baptism, when the immersion would take place. The parties would come out of the river almost covered with a sheet of ice, when they were hurried into the house for a change of clothing. There was always a good fire in the few rooms on these interesting occasions—especially for the benefit of the new-made Christians. There never was the least cold taken by any of those who were immersed during those extremely cold days.

The lowly dwelling was frequently honored with the presence of distinguished visitors. One early autumn the Swedish authoress, Miss Fredericka Bremer, was entertained for a brief period. Another summer the authoresses, Miss Clark and Mrs. E. F. Ellet, made the household glad by a sojourn of a day or two. Military men of high rank frequently made it their home. From there Governor Isaac Ives Stevens started on his extraordinary trip to the Pacific.

The first agricultural society in the Territory was organized there, the first singing-school held, and the first lyceum matured. Marriages were solemnized—the most interesting of which, to my family, was that of Mr. Marshall Robinson to Miss Mary E. Miller, the youngest sister of Mrs. Stevens. Miss Miller was the first public-school teacher in the pioneer settlement. The organization of the first school-district on the west side, under the laws of the Territory, was completed in the house, and Messrs. Edward Murphy, Judge F. R. E. Cornell, and John H. Stevens were elected trustees.

The name of the place was first proposed to the county commissioners by Mr. Chas. Hoag, while those officers were in session in the parlor. The name was promptly confirmed by the board. At a previous session the name of Albion had been agreed upon. The name Minneapolis is derived from the classic Greek and the wild Dakota languages.

The first justices of the precinct and the first officers of the county were sworn into office under its humble roof. Its diminutive walls protected many a poor wanderer far from home and friends. Its site was on a small portion of the grounds occupied by the union depot near the end of the suspension-bridge. The house is in a good state of preservation on Sixteenth avenue south between Fourth and Fifth sts.

CHAPTER VI.

The summer of 1849 at Fort Snelling passed quietly. The last of May the governor and other officers appointed by the President for the territory arrived and, on June 1st at St. Paul, assumed the duties of their high trusts. The governor, Alexander Ramsey, frequently called at the Fort, and made many friends.

Emigration was the great staple during the year, and St. Paul received the lion's share of it.

EDITOR GOODHUE.

The village was fortunate in its pioneer editor, Colonel James M. Goodhue, who wielded a pen equal to any writer on the continent. I had known him in Wisconsin, and was proud to class him among my friends. He was faithful to the whole territory but, as a matter of course, he saw more favorable prospects for the future of St. Paul than for other portions of the territory. This is not to be wondered at; it was his home. In the fall he wrote to me these playful, characteristic lines : "The election has gone—all right enough, of "course. I have done my duty as drummer. If our folks did "not choose to fight and conquer, it was their own fault. Tell "Steele that as the organ, I have to grind for the organization, "whatever it may be. But he understands that. Whatever "comes up as regular, I have to conjugate through all modes "and tenses—and class everything else as 'irregular, defective "or redundant'—until after election. I shall try to come up "on the first ice. Yours truly."

CHAPLAIN GEAR.

Fort Snelling was favored in having an efficient chaplain. In July, 1848, while on board a steamer en route from

Chicago to Buffalo, I had as a fellow-passenger Rev. Dr. E. G. Gear, who was the chaplain in question. He was making a pilgrimage to the scenes of his early eastern labors, and to visit the churches he had ministered to so faithfully in early life. He had many years ago abandoned these comparatively easy places for the life of a clergyman in the wild northwest which, at that period, contained but few whites; yet among them were men of rare ability. At that early day Dr. Gear was of the opinion that many of the settlers did not select the northwest for homes from choice, but drifted here from various causes; some came in the army, many in the Indian trade, others prospecting for lumber, while a few were attracted by the beneficial influence of the climate.

Agriculture was then in its infancy and at a low ebb north of the Iowa line. Dr. Gear thought the indications were that most of what is now Minnesota would suffer from a lack of sufficient moisture in the atmosphere to mature the crops. There was a possibility that a large portion of the northwest would, for a long time, be occupied only by Indians.

Dr. Gear's life and labors at Fort Snelling brought him in contact with all the prominent residents and tourists of the upper Mississippi of two-score years ago and, being a close observer of men, he seldom made a mistake in estimating their worth. He belonged to an old New England family of Puritans, and though an Episcopalian, he retained all the characteristics of his ancestors in relation to the stern duties of life. A man incapable of knowingly doing the slightest injustice to any one, he could not countenance a fault in others. He was greatly pleased with the immigration of 1849, so different from that of previous years--not superior in ability or morality, but the men were in many instances accompanied by their families, and had come to stay.

Dr. Gear was born in Connecticut, September 1793, and was ordained to the ministry by Bishop Hobart of New York. In 1835, he was sent as a missionary to Galena, Illinois. Three years later, through the influence of General Brooke and other high officers in the army, he was appointed chaplain at Fort Snelling and assumed his duties as such at that place in the spring of 1839. He had an interesting family. Most
3

of his daughters married army officers. His only son, Hon. John H. Gear, was for several years governor of Iowa. He is at this time a member of congress from that state. After Dr. Gear retired from the chaplaincy he lived at Minneapolis, in which city his death occurred on the 13th of October, 1873, at the age of eighty years. His honored remains quietly rest in the beautiful Lakewood cemetery. His death was a great loss to the people of the northwest. His aged widow and two daughters are residents of this city.

A TRIBUTE TO THE NOBLE MEN WHO HAVE PASSED AWAY.

People of the present day may not properly appreciate the good works of those of a past generation ; but it is a pleasure to those who have outlived their former friends and associates to speak of those with whom they were intimate, and bear witness to the present generation of the great moral worth of those who have crossed the silent river. The pioneers of Minnesota, as a class, were men of great merit—more so than in many other states—equal to the stern pilgrims and their descendants ; perhaps because there was a mixture of all races, uniting the best blood in the world, which could not fail to accomplish wonders.

Every one seemed pleased with the new officers, and the territory was started under the most favorable auspices.

PIONEER CELEBRATION OF THE FOURTH OF JULY IN ST. PAUL.

The Fourth of July was observed all through the territory, but the chief attraction was in St. Paul, when St. Anthony, Stillwater, and other hamlets, joined the St. Paulites in the celebration. Sauk Rapids furnished the orator, the newly-appointed Judge B. B. Meeker ; St. Paul the reader of the Declaration of Independence, Billy Phillips ; Fort Snelling the chaplain, Rev. Dr. Gear, and also the marshal, Franklin Steele. Unquestionably Mr. Steele was as fine a specimen of manhood as any state ever produced. Tall, well-proportioned, pleasing, courteous, gentlemanly, an accomplished rider—no wonder that upon a fine horse on this occasion he attracted universal attention and admiration. It was said, at the time, that this was the most successful celebration ever held in the northwest. It requires lots of people to make a successful celebration. They had them in St. Paul that day. Many of them were newly-arrived immigrants.

FROM THE RED RIVER OF THE NORTH.

The Red-river caravan arrived soon after the celebration of the Fourth. Our old friend, Hon. Norman W. Kittson, was with the company. This train brought in an immense quantity of furs, pemmican, dried buffalo-tongue, and all the products of the great northwest. Lively times we had for the next four weeks! Buffalo-robes, martin, fisher, otter, muskrat, fox, badger, bear, wolf, wild-cat, lynx, beaver, and all other kinds of fur incident to a high northern latitude, was brought from the extreme north to exchange for merchandise or cash. Whole cart-loads of the handiwork of the squaws were in the train. There were moccasins, gloves and mittens, worked in every conceivable manner. Beads, porcupine-quills, and birds' feathers, were worked into them. These rare articles proved that the native women of the extreme north possessed artistic taste. It plainly indicated that they had instructors superior to the savages.

The arrival of these Red-river carts, so called, added much to the life and trade of the territory. This was the beginning of the wholesale trade of St. Paul. "Tall oaks from little acorns grow." Many of these small traders who accompanied the train brought considerable money with them, which they paid for goods. It was the "coin of the realm", mostly British sovereigns. It was seldom that an American dollar, half-dollar or a quarter, half or whole eagle, came into the possession of these Red-river merchants. The transportation of the products from the far north by the Red-river carts, cost but little. A solitary ox was harnessed to a cart, and one man had charge of several oxen. The teams were fed exclusively on grass. The carts were made wholly of wood, the harness of raw-hide—everything being of the utmost simplicity, and of little expense. Not a bit of iron about the carts : not a buckle about the harness !

CHAPTER VII.

During the season of 1849 several changes were made in the command at the Fort. Brevet-Major Lewis A. Armistead, first lieutenant of company E, arrived and assumed command of the company. Major Armistead was a son of a famous general in the army. A Virginian by birth, he followed the destinies of his state in the war of the rebellion, became an officer of high rank in the confederate army, and was killed in Pickett's celebrated charge at Gettysburg. General Armistead, near the close of the charge placed his hat on his sword, rallied what men he could, and rushed on to the conflict, where he fell pierced with bullets.

Another arrival early in October was that of Brevet-second-lieutenant Richard W. Johnson, assigned to company C. Lieutenant Johnson was just from West Point. He was the youngest officer at the Fort. Full of bright hopes and anticipations, his presence added much to the interesting events that always occur in garrison life. There is nothing that causes young officers to be so completely contented with their work, when first assigned to duty, (usually at some distant frontier post,) after graduating at West Point, as the society of beautiful and accomplished young ladies. The vicinity of the Fort, during Lieutenant Johnson's first year at that place was particularly fortunate in this respect. He became engaged to, and eventually married, one of the most charming of them—Miss Rachel Steele, a sister of Franklin Steele and of Mrs. General Sibley and of Mrs. Dr. Potts. Lieutenant Johnson's promotion in the army was rapid. He passed through all the different grades of rank, and retired in consequence of severe wounds received in battle, with the rank of major-general. Minnesotians are proud of his record, as he is identified with us. Since he retired from the army he has been one of our best citizens. His home is in St. Paul. Having led an eventful and useful life, he is now reaping the fruits of his labor, honored by the whole community.

The first general election after the organization of the territory was held in August. Hon. H. H. Sibley was elected territorial delegate to congress. The few citizens at Fort Snelling went to Mendota to vote. Hon. Martin McLeod, of Lac-qui-parle, was honored, on the occasion, with a seat in the upper house of the legislature ; and the respected Dakota missionary, Rev. G. H. Pond, and Alex. Bailey, were elected delegates to the lower house.

In June, Colonel James Hughes arrived in St. Paul, from the east, with an outfit for a first-class weekly newspaper. He soon disposed of his interest in it to Major N. McLean and Colonel John P. Owens, who issued the Chronicle and Register—a rival to the Pioneer.

A United States court was held August 20th, 1849, in the old government mill on the west bank of the Falls of St. Anthony. Judge B. B. Meeker presided. The jurisdiction of the court covered many thousand square miles of territory. Franklin Steele was foreman of the grand jury. After a session of two days, the court adjourned without transacting any business. This was the first court ever held in what is now Minneapolis. Thirty-nine years after this event there are four district judges almost constantly in session at the court-house, a few blocks distant from where the first court was held, beside two municipal judges who hold daily sessions, and all are crowded with business. To the best of my knowledge, there is not a member of the first court held in that old mill alive to-day. The judge and all the jury have crossed the silent river.

Judge Meeker was born in Connecticut, on the 13th of March, 1813, and died in Milwaukee, Wisconsin, while on his way east, February 3, 1873, aged sixty years. Previous to his appointment as one of the judges in Minnesota, he had for some years resided in Kentucky, and was appointed from that state. He was closely identified with Minnesota during his residence here, and largely contributed to its prosperity.

The county of Meeker took its name from him. He was a member of the constitutional convention which was held in St. Paul in 1857. Although never married, he took a great interest in the schools of the State and labored incessantly for their benefit. He was fond of agricultural and horticultural pursuits. He purchased and worked a farm just below and bordering on old St. Anthony. He was a good lawyer, an honest judge, a valuable citizen, unusually respected, and his death was regretted by the community.

VISIT OF MRS. SNELLING TO THE FORT.

One of the most interesting events of the summer at Fort Snelling, in 1849, was the arrival of Mrs. Abigail Hunt Snelling, widow of Colonel Josiah Snelling, from whom the Fort derived its name, and who commanded the troops during its erection. Mrs. Snelling was the mother of the second white child born in what is now Minnesota. The parentage of the first white child born in the territory was a soldier and his wife. The wife was a laundress who accompanied Colonel Leavenworth's command, and the little one was born soon after the arrival of the troops near the junction of the St. Peter river with the Mississippi, early in September, 1819.

Mrs. Snelling was a daughter of an army officer, Colonel Hunt. She was fifty-one years old at the time of her visit to the Fort, but had been a widow many years. She was with her husband when he commenced building the Fort in 1820, when only twenty-three years of age. Mrs. Snelling remained some time at the Fort, the guest of the commanding officer, Colonel Loomis. On her first visit with Colonel Loomis after her arrival, to the cemetery which contained the grave of her little girl who was gently laid to rest so many years before, she was greatly overcome with grief, and could not be comforted. The little grave had been well cared for; the sod upon it was green, the little stone monument was in place, with the loved letters E. S. as plain as on the day the memorial of love was placed over the precious remains so many long years ago. The sad scenes attendant upon the sickness and death of the dear little one, "in life's early march, when her bosom was young", were all brought back

to the fond mother as vividly as they were more than a score
of years previously.

The whole garrison, and the citizens around the Fort,
endeavored to make Mrs. Snelling's visit pleasant. In leaving
the grand old fortress which her husband built, she gratefully
tendered her thanks to those who had contributed to her
comfort during her visit to her early home.

REV. E. D. NEILL.

After Colonel Loomis assumed command in 1849 he frequently invited the different ministers of the gospel to occupy
Dr. Gear's pulpit in the little chapel, when it was not filled
by the doctor himself. Rev. E. D. Neill, then a young man,
who had just come to St. Paul, gave us an occasional sermon.
He was a great favorite with Colonel Loomis and the rank
and file of the old Sixth Infantry. One pleasant mid-summer
Sunday we were greatly alarmed when informed that Mr.
Neill, who was accompanied by Mrs. Neill, while on his way
to preach to us had, in consequence of an accident, fallen
over the precipice on the opposite side of the river from the
Fort. Fortunately they received but little injury. As usual
Mr. Neill gave us a useful and instructive sermon. The next
day Colonel Loomis came to Philander Prescott and myself
and said he had taxed himself twenty dollars, Mr. Prescott
ten, and myself five, to be handed to Mr. Neill as a small
"thanksgiving token" for the providential escape of his wife
and himself when thrown from the carriage the previous day.
We accordingly waited upon Mr. and Mrs. Neill, who were at
Colonel Loomis' headquarters, but Mr. Neill would only
accept the small tribute as a bestowal to the American Board
of Missions, under whose auspices he was preaching the
gospel in the then far-northwest.

Minnesota was peculiarly fortunate in the advent of many
of its early settlers ; but to no one is the state more indebted
for a combination of everything that is desirable in one person, than to Mr. Neill. As a Christian minister, writer,
patriot, and philanthropist, his name will be handed down to
future generations, and his memory will be ever revered by
those who have the good of the world at heart. To him we are
greatly indebted for perfecting our system of common schools.

Once in a while Dr. Williamson was with us. He had been
so long a missionary with the Indians that his style of preaching was different from that of most sermonizers of the day.
His language was so simple that every one could readily
understand what he said. His sermons were mostly composed
of words of one syllable—but they were always effective.

Major R. G. Murphy was the United States Indian Agent
at Fort Snelling in 1849. He was a native of Tennessee, but
had been a resident of Pinckneyville, in southern Illinois,
from boyhood. He was a member of the Baptist church—
and a democrat of the firmest type ; a man of strong preju-
dices, but thoroughly honest. He made a good agent for the
Dakotas. Their interests were looked after and righteously
cared for. No trader was suffered to take advantage of them.

Most of the Indian tribes on the continent are improvident.
The Dakotas are perhaps more so than many others. If
their hunger is satisfied to-day, they are likely to neglect to
provide that which will be necessary for their stomachs to-
morrow. Major Murphy had been brought up to observe the
rule that it is necessary to look out for the future needful
supply of the wants of the "inner man", and he could not
understand why his Indians should neglect such an important
requisite that they might not suffer from hunger. He found
it quite impossible to instill into them the habits or principles
of economy, and as a result the agency was besieged daily by
a lot of beggars for bread and meat.

Having from boyhood lived on the frontier, which was more
or less traversed by the Winnebagoes, Sacs and Foxes, Pottawatomies, Chippeways and other tribes, I found the Dakotas
more given to fault-finding than any other tribe. In fact
they gave their agent but little rest. In those early days the
office was anything but a pleasant one. In order to better
their condition, Indians must be taught the important lesson
that manual labor is not degrading. When they shall be
convinced of this, it will not be a great task to civilize them.
They must be brought to the knowledge that to hold the plow
is an honorable as well as a necessary occupation. The idea
that "the only good Indian is a dead Indian", is simply
absurd. There is a blossom in the wilderness of the heart of
almost every Indian. Yet when aroused the red man is
capable of committing the most horrible outrages.

CHAPTER VIII.

In 1849 there were only two garrisons in the territory—Fort Snelling and Fort Ripley. The latter was first called Gaines, but was changed to Ripley. It was commanded by Captain J. B. F. Todd, Co. A of the Sixth. Previous to the advent of the Winnebagoes at Long Prairie the military post in the extreme upper valley of the Mississippi was ample for the protection of the white and red population. Fort Ripley was commenced in the fall of 1848, and finished the next yea

Captain Todd was a cousin of Mrs. Abraham Lincoln. He was transferred from Fort Ripley to the Missouri, and was one of the founders of Yankton, for some time the capital of Dakota. He retired from the army, and was twice elected a delegate to congress from Dakota. On the breaking out of the rebellion he was made a general in the army, and died during the war. A county in Minnesota takes its name from General Todd.

Captain Dana, another officer at Fort Ripley, rose also to the rank of major-general during the war. Brevet-Captain Geo. W. Long, at one time military secretary to General Scott, was lieutenant in Captain Todd's company. He became a confederate general, but did not survive the war. All of these officers were frequent visitors at Fort Snelling during the year 1849.

RETURN OF THE RED RIVER EXPEDITION.

The command of Major Woods returned from the Red river expedition early in October. The object of the expedi-

tion was to establish the exact boundary line between Minnesota and Canada ; to set monuments thereon ; to locate the
site of a military post on or near the line ; to gather information in regard to the prospective agricultural resources of the
valley of the Red river of the North, and the country between
the Fort and the northwest, and to make a thorough topographical survey of the whole country. The report of Captain
Pope contained so much valuable information in regard to
the new country that it was deemed necessary by congress to
publish it. The command during the long and tedious journey had excellent health, and enjoyed rare sport in hunting
buffalo, several herds of which they found. Lightning struck
Lieutenant Nelson's tent one night while encamped on the
borders of a lake in the northern portion of the territory.
He received a serious injury therefrom, and did not entirely
recover from the stroke for many years.

FIRST SESSION OF THE TERRITORIAL LEGISLATURE.

The first legislature of the territory convened in St. Paul
on the 3d of September, in the old Central hotel, where Governor Ramsey delivered his message. Some nine counties
were created, viz : Istaska, Waubashaw, Dahkotah, Wahnah-
tah, Mahkakto, Pembina, Washington, Ramsey, and Benton.
The names of many of these counties have been changed by
legislation. Some have been blotted out altogether ; while a
decided improvement in the spelling of all of them of Indian
origin has been made. Hon. David Olmstead, of Long Prairie,
was elected president of the council, and Hon. Joseph W.
Furber was elected speaker of the house.

NEGOTIATIONS WITH THE INDIANS.

There was a great gathering of the Indians in October on
the flats between the St. Peter or Minnesota river and the
trading posts at Mendota. They had concentrated to meet
Governor Ramsey, and ex-Governor Chambers of Iowa, who
had been appointed commissioners, on the part of the government, to make a treaty in relation to ceding their lands west
of the Mississippi. The proposed treaty was a failure in consequence of the absence of a majority of the Indians ; but the

half-breed tract, so called, bordering on Lake Pepin, was secured.

FORMATION OF A LITERARY SOCIETY.

The St. Anthony Library Association, incorporated by an act of the legislature, late in the fall inaugurated a series of lectures. Rev. E. D. Neill, Rev. Dr. Gear, Hon. Wm. R. Marshall, and Lieutenant R. W. Johnson, among others, lectured before the association.

During the season of 1849 St. Anthony made great progress in the erection of houses, and in other improvements. Most of the immigration was from Maine. The people brought their habits of industry and economy with them ; nor did they leave behind their fondness for reading, and for attending church. The people at that early day set a good example to their contemporaries in other portions of the new northwest.

PHILANDER PRESCOTT.

During the year I boarded with the United States Indian interpreter, Philander Prescott, whose residence was just outside of the Fort and next to that of the Indian Agent. Mr. Prescott came up with the troops in 1819, as a clerk for the sutler. He soon became a trader among the Indians, and was a member of the Columbia Fur Company. Like many of the early traders, he purchased a Dakota girl for his wife. She accompanied him in visiting his numerous trading outfits, where he exchanged goods for furs. Children were born to him. He became dissatisfied with his northwestern possessions. He had never married the Indian woman except in the Indian fashion : that is, he gave a pony and some goods for her to her parents. It did not seem difficult or cruel to abandon her. Other traders left their wives and children— why should not he ? She was abundantly able to care for herself, his and her children, for their wants were few ; and she had well-to-do relatives Indians of course, but Indians are fond of their kith and kin. He had made some money ; he would sell his interests and make more ; then he would leave all and go south to Texas or some other place, and start anew without incumbrances —wife, child, or chick. He made his way down the Mississippi, traversed Texas and

Louisiana, visited the Choctaw, Creek, and Chickasaw Indians, but found poor prospects for starting a new business in the lower country. He spent two or three years in hunting and traveling. It is probable that, discouraged, once in a while he indulged in fire-water to a greater extent than was for his good.

A SPIRITUAL AWAKENING.

While Mr. Prescott was near the head-waters of the Sabine river, he visited a religious protracted-meeting, which was attended pretty much by Crackers. He became, through the influence of the preacher, a changed man. Although several thousand miles away from the Dakota wife and children that he had abandoned—who were wandering with the mother's tribe over the plains—he determined to return to them at once, and do what he should have done at first—marry the woman according to the rules of Christianity. After a long journey he landed at the St. Peter agency, when he found that the mother of his children was away beyond the coteaus in the buffalo range of the Missouri valley. With his pack on his back he started in search of her. It was mid-summer when he found her. Poor Indian woman that she was, she was overjoyed to see him, but could not understand why he would not live with her any more as his wife, until after a long journey should be made to find a regularly ordained minister of the gospel, and they should be married in the same manner as the white folks. After urging, coaxing, and praying, he persuaded her to leave her people and, with her children, the broad prairies were crossed, the home of a missionary was found, the solemn marriage rites were performed, and at the same time and by the same holy ordinance his children were made legitimate.

Mr. Prescott has often spoken to me of the great privation and suffering that attended this (to him) sacred pilgrimage. That Indian woman was an excellent housekeeper, fond of her domestic duties, an affectionate wife, and a good mother. It could not well be otherwise when we consider that she had a noble, Christian husband. Her hospitable house was always full of people. It was the only roof at Fort Snelling that afforded a stopping-place for travelers and strangers.

CHAPTER IX.

At the period mentioned in the last chapter, the eldest daughter of Mr. and Mrs. Philander Prescott had grown to womanhood. Her father had sent her abroad for an education. She was like a bird about the old stone building, singing and making everyone happy. I never wondered that her father so fondly loved her.

A young man of excellent character from Illinois was employed around the missionary grounds and the Indian farms. He was a Christian man; she was a Christian girl. His heart yearned for her; his life needed her; she alone could be its strength, its beauty, its crown. It was the same old, old story, but ever new— the story Adam first told to Eve in the world's fresh morning, among the first fair flowers and the harmonies of Eden the story that man has told to woman ever since: as sweet, as solemn, as all-consecrating and all-comprehending now as when it was first whispered under skies which no storm-cloud had ever darkened. The result was that one evening, just at the close of the old year and the beginning of the new, there was a large gathering at the old weather-beaten homestead. There were officers of high rank in the army, in full uniform, with their wives; officers holding high trusts in civil positions, with their wives and daughters; gentlemen, with their ladies, in full evening costume; and men and women whose fathers were white and mothers were red; Dakota relatives and friends of the bride in their blankets -making in all about as curious an assembly, as unique a gathering, as ever attended a wedding feast, and one that, as Rev. Mr. Neill (who officiated on the occasion) says, "could only be seen on the outposts of civilization."

AT THE MARRIAGE FEAST.

A varied feast followed the wedding ceremony—one which pleased the white people, and delighted the red guests. The father was seemingly the happiest man in the territory that night—scarcely excepting the groom. What a shadow of the memory of the past was thrown over the father of the bride that eventful evening! None of us could persuade the mother to appear in the parlor during the marriage cere- mony, but immediately afterwards she waited on the guests, and was doubtless as pleased as was her husband that her daughter was wedded to a white Christian. The bride's Indian uncles, aunts, and cousins were present, wrapped in their blankets, and viewed the ceremony with seemingly cold, weary, and stolid countenances, through the parlor doors.

OTHER INCIDENTS AND CHARACTERS AT THE FORT.

During September there were two deaths at Fort Snelling. One of them was that of an old discharged soldier, Charles Wilson, formerly of the First infantry, who had been in the employment of Mr. Steele for several years. Previous to the death of his wife, he had lived in St. Anthony, holding a claim for its owner. It is said, on pretty good authority, that he was the first actual white resident of the eastern bank of the Falls, and I am inclined to think that the assertion is true. He was a faithful man, a native of Maryland, and in early life enlisted in the army, served many years in it, and was discharged at Fort Snelling, when he took charge of the teams necessary for the use of the sutler's store. He always forded the Mississippi river, with his teams, at the Falls just above the precipice. When the dam was built, on the east side, it became necessary to have a ferry, as the old roadway from the east side of the island to the main shore was occu- pied by the dam. He never became reconciled to the idea of the public highway, as he called it, being obstructed in the manner that it was, and lamented the signs of civilization and improvement. Wilson was a man of ability, but some strange misfortune befell him in his early days, which clouded his whole life.

A SQUAW-MAN.

Wilson's only son became a squaw man, whose services were in great demand as a violinist during the winter. He became dissipated, married an Indian woman, and adopted all the Indian habits—breech-clout, blanket and all ! The last that I saw of him was in the valley of the Minnesota, moving with Good Road's band, to which tribe his wife belonged, up the river. He had one of his little pappooses on his back, trudging along, and relieving, for the time being, the mother of some of her many burdens. Poor Wilson !

DEATH OF AN UNKNOWN MAN—HIS SECRET UNREVEALED.

About the time of Charles Wilson's death, an eastern man was taken sick at Mr. Prescott's. Everything possible was done for him. Dr. McLaren, the surgeon at the Fort, was in constant attendance, but his patient only lived for a few days. Every effort was made to find out where his friends lived, but without success. Far from home and relatives, he died among strangers, but they were friendly and gave him a Christian burial out at the citizens' cemetery on Morgan's Bluff. His secret as to his identity was sealed with his expiring breath beyond the penetration of mortal man.

DEPENDENCE UPON THE LOWER COUNTRY.

The steamers during the fall of 1849 were taxed to their utmost capacity in handling the large amount of freight necessary to be brought into the new territory for the use of the old as well as the new settlers. It should be remembered that at that time Minnesota was not producing agricultural products. With the exception of what was raised by the little colony of farmers who resided in Washington county, everything consumed by the people had to be brought up the river from Illinois, Iowa, and Missouri. Even the grain necessary to be fed to the horses was secured in the lower country. Vast quantities of provisions were imported into the territory.

Whole cargoes of flour and pork were shipped from Galena, St. Louis, Quincy, Hannibal, and Dubuque. Sugar, tea, coffee, and molasses—the luxuries of life—were brought in less quantities. Whisky was deemed almost a necessity.

The territory was almost completely drained of money to pay the freight bills due to the steamboats. It was a real relief to the merchants when the smoke of the last steamer of the season disappeared down stream, as their purses could only be replenished after navigation closed.

During the month of June several of the missionaries among the Dakotas gathered at the St. Peter agency at Fort Snelling. It was at this meeting that I first became acquainted with Dr. Stephen R. Riggs and Rev. Moses N. Adams. I had met Rev. Gideon H. Pond a few days previous to the general attendance at the agency. His brother, Rev. Samuel W. Pond, preached the annual sermon in Mr. Prescott's house on Sunday. Major Murphy, the Indian agent, pronounced it the best religious discourse he ever heard—not the most learned, but for the occasion the most appropriate.

June also brought most of the Indian traders to Fort Snelling and Mendota. Among them were Hon. Martin McLeod, Hon. N. W. Kittson, and Hon. Joseph R. Brown—though the last named was at that time more engaged in the lumber trade.

There were many old settlers and pioneers in the vicinity of Fort Snelling and Mendota. Some of them were men of great merit : such as Hon. Samuel J. Findley, Peter Quinn, John B. Faribault who was a Canadian of French descent, Hazen Moores who was an Indian farmer for Black Dog's village, Francis Gammel who was the ferryman at St. Peter river, Victor Chatel the blacksmith for the Lake Calhoun and Lake Harriet band of Indians, and Hypolite Dupuy who was Governor Sibley's bookkeeper. Many of these were in the employ of the Fur company and the Indian department. A venerable man by the name of Edwards, and his wife who was a mixed blood of Indian, negro, and white, were employed at the agency, the latter being Major Murphy's housekeeper. Among the men at Mendota at that time, of great influence, was Rev. A. Ravoux, pastor of the Catholic church at that place. Father Ravoux came to this country at an early day and labored on the Minnesota river at Chaska for the good of the Indians.

CHAPTER X.

Game was plenty in those early times in Minnesota. Indians were plenty too ; but some way the more Indians the more game. At the proper season of the year elk- buffalo- and bear-steaks, could be obtained at very reasonable rates, while there seemed no end of wild geese and ducks in the fall and spring. Prairie-chickens were abundant, but there were few quails. Mr. Steele tried the experiment of introducing quails into the country. He had a large number of them brought up the river in the fall. They were taken out to Morgan's bluff, some two miles from the Fort, and given their liberty. At the same time he deposited wheat, oats, and corn, in the immediate vicinity, so that they would not suffer for the want of food. The birds seemed to go through the first winter in good condition, but in the spring of the second year there were none left ; they all perished during the extreme cold winter months. As there was no grain raised in the country it was thought by many that they starved to death ; but it was evidently too cold for them. Probably if there had been grain-stacks or fields of cornstalks in the neighborhood, for them to winter in—which would have afforded not only protection, but food – the result might have been different. Yet since the country has become so thickly settled, and every protection has been afforded them, quails have never become plenty. The Indians claimed they never would become numerous, because of the extreme cold.

Partridges were found in great abundance in the wooded and brush lands. The wild pigeons were the most numerous

4

of all birds. The sky would for days, at certain hours, be
almost obscured by them. For several years they were taken
in great numbers in nets. Strange to say, they have almost
disappeared from their old visiting-places. They do not now
even fly over the state. It is singular what has become of
them.

Fish then, as now, were caught in great numbers. The
New England speckled trout sported in many of the clear
streams in southern Minnesota.

Most of the large game disappeared with the departure of
the Indians. It was by no means a difficult task, in the early
fifties, to obtain all the meat necessary for one's household,
from the fruits of the chase. Wild bees, too, were abundant
in the portion of the country known as the "big woods"; but
with the disappearance of the shadow of the tall oak, the
wild, busy bee is a thing of the past.

Most of the valuable fur-bearing animals—the great staple
of pre-territorial times—are gone too. A family of otter had
a real nice home in what is now known as Bassett's creek,
where Fourth street crosses it in this city, when I lived alone
on the bank of the river where the Union depot is built. In
fact they were resident there some years afterwards. The
cowardly wolves, but in greatly reduced numbers, still
remain. They appear to be too mean to follow the Indian.
The bear is still found, but not one where there were ten
forty years ago.

There are many more birds here now than there were in
those days. The meadow-lark, the bobolink, the blue-bird,
the robin, and several other feathered songsters, followed the
whites to their new home; while the eagle went with the
red-men; yet the owls and hawks, in limited numbers, are
here yet. The black-bird is an emigrant, following the pioneer, sharing and devouring the seed that is sown and the
grain that is raised. It is pretty well demonstrated that all
the desirable birds—in this part of the northwest, at least—
if we except those of migratory habits—are fond of frequent-
ing the haunts of civilized man. While many varieties are
found in unsettled portions of the continent, our favorites,
such as robins and blue-birds, are partial to the homes and
surroundings of white men.

S.W. POND.

S.R. RIGGS. in 1852

G.H. POND.

MRS. M.L. RIGGS. 1880

THO. S. WILLIAMSON.

W.T. BOUTWELL.

THE EARLY MISSIONARIES TO THE INDIANS IN MINNESOTA.

CHAPTER XI.

Frequently on Sundays, in 1849, after the morning service in the little chapel at Fort Snelling, Colonel Loomis would• suggest that we go, so soon as we had lunched, to the Oak Grove mission, and listen to the usually excellent afternoon sermon by Rev. G. H. Pond. The colder the weather the more anxious the colonel would be to make the trip. The distance was at least ten miles on the ice. He would not have a driver, nor use on such occasions a team belonging to the government, but had his own sleigh and drove his own horses. In the forenoon Mr. Pond usually preached to the Indians in their own language, and in the afternoon to the whites who, besides his own family, were mostly employed in the interest of the Indians. These meetings were held in Mr. Pond's parlors. It mattered not if there were half-a-dozen present or a full house - he preached in the same earnest manner for the welfare of his fellow-men.

Rev. G. H. Pond was born in Connecticut, in 1810. He came to the land of the Dakotas, with his elder brother Samuel W. Pond, in 1834, and located at Lake Calhoun, where they built a log cabin on the margin of the lake and commenced farming among the Indians. The Indian agent, Major Taliaferro, resident at Fort Snelling, had already made some effort toward civilizing the red men. Forty-three years afterwards, on the occasion of the completion of a hotel at the lake, on the same site of the log cabin, Mr. Pond told the story of his settlement, presenting a graphic picture of the pioneer days in that locality. He says : "The old structure

"was of oak logs, carefully peeled.   The peeling was a mistake.
"Twelve feet by sixteen, and eight feet high, were the dimen-
"sions of the edifice.   Straight poles from the tamarack grove
"west of the lake formed the timbers of the roof, and the
"roof itself was of the bark of trees which grew on the bank
"of what is now called 'Bassett's creek', fastened with strings
"of the inner bark of the bass-wood.   A partition of small
"logs divided the house into two rooms, and split logs fur-
"nished material for the floor.   The ceiling was of slabs from
"the old government sawmill, through the kindness of Major
"Bliss, who was in command of Fort Snelling.   The door
"was made of boards split from a log with an axe, having
"wooden hinges and fastenings, and was locked by pulling in
"the latch-string.   The single window was the gift of the
•"kind-hearted Major Lawrence Taliaferro, United States
"Indian agent.   The cash cost of the building was one shil-
"ling, New York currency, for nails used in and about the
"door.   The 'formal opening' exercises consisted in reading
"a section from the old book by the name of Bible, and prayer
"to Him who was its acknowledged author.   The 'banquet'
"consisted of mussels from the lake, flour and water.   The
"ground was selected by the Indian chief of the Lake Calhoun
"band of Dakotas, Man-of-the-sky, by which he showed good
"taste.   The reason he gave for the selection was that 'from
"that point the loons would be visible on the lake'.   The old
"chief and his pagan people had their homes on the surface
"of that ground in the bosom of which now sleep the bodies
"of deceased Christians from the city of Minneapolis, the
"Lakewood cemetery, over which these old eyes have witnessed,
"dangling in the night breeze, many a Chippeway scalp, in
"the midst of horrid chants, yells, and wails, widely contrast-
"ing with the present stillness of that quiet home of those
"'who sleep the years away'.   That hut was the home of the
"first citizen settlers of Hennepin county, perhaps of Minne-
"sota, the first school-room, the first house for divine worship,
"and the first mission station among the Dakota Indians."

Mr. Pond was an ardent student of Indian character, and
probably came the nearest of any of the missionaries to talking like a Dakota, and knowing how an Indian felt.   His
desire to experience the life of an Indian led him, in 1838, to

join a half dozen Indian families from Lac-qui-parle for a
hunt on the upper Chippewa river. The occasion of their
departure was when the ducks began to fly northward. On
the way they experienced a cold rain and a flood. The windows of heaven were opened for the rain to descend as,
seemingly, they had never been opened before since the deluge.
The ducks disappeared and there was a famine in camp.
The half dozen tepees divided. One division was visited by
the Ojibway chief, Hole-in-the-Day with ten of his treacher-
ous braves. They smoked the pipe of peace, and the visitors
were royally entertained and feasted on two of the dogs
belonging to their hosts, though the entertainers themselves
were starving. The Chippeways arose in the night and cowardly and treacherously killed their Dakota hosts (three men
and ten women and children). Only one woman and one boy
escaped. Mr. Pond did not happen to be with the entertain-
ing party. He helped bury the eleven mangled bodies,
breakfasted on muskrat, and started alone, on foot, in haste,
for the mission at Lac-qui-parle. At night he slept without
fire or supper. Enriched by two weeks' experience in Indian
savage life, he was rejoiced to be at home with his scalp and
his family. In other words—those of one of his brother
missionaries—" Mr. Pond, as God would have it, was not then
with those three tents, and so he escaped."

Mr. Pond was over six feet in hight, was twice married,
and was the father of thirteen children. He was for twenty
years pastor of the church at Bloomington, in Hennepin
county. He died in 1878, and was buried in his own parish,
where he had so long, faithfully and acceptably labored.

MISSIONARY SAMUEL W. POND.

Among the missionaries who visited the St. Peter agency
at Fort Snelling in 1849, there was no one who attracted more
attention, and was more respected, than the pioneer in
the good work, Rev. Samuel W. Pond. He is a native of
Connecticut. He was twenty-three years of age, and his
brother Gideon twenty-one, when they joined the Congregational church of their native town, and became impressed with
the idea that their lives should be devoted to the good of

their fellow-men. How nobly the venerable Samuel W. Pond, whose age is away along among the eighties, has carried out those early intentions ! Every effort of his long life has been in the interest of mankind. It made no difference whether those who required his aid were white, black, or red men ; all had souls and the same Creator. He determined to go forth and labor where his services would most benefit the world. He thought his labors would be crowned with greater success outside of New England where there were fewer laborers in the field. The far west was selected as a field for work.

Mr. Pond left home in the spring of 1832, and after a tedious journey arrived at Galena, Illinois, suffering from sickness. He made a tour through Illinois, on horseback, with Rev. Aratus Kent, then pastor of the Presbyterian church in Galena. During this journey he saw many Winnebagoes, which first turned his attention to the Indians. While he was engaged in missionary work in Galena, he made the acquaintance of a man who had resided in the extreme northwest, and who gave him an account of the Dakotas. He determined to labor for the good of this people, and accordingly communicated with his brother, who accepted his invitation to join him, in the spring of 1834, when they would visit the Minnesota Indians.

While at Galena Mr. Pond was fortunate in his intimacy with Mr. Kent, who was also a native of Connecticut. Mr. Kent arrived at Galena in 1829, and from that time to his death in 1869 was an earnest and faithful minister of the gospel. His labors in an early day extended to Minnesota, and he had many friends among the pioneers of this state. Mr. Gideon H. Pond joined his brother at Galena, and the two left that place, on a steamboat, for the land of the Dakotas, landing at Fort Snelling on the 6th of May, 1834. At Prairie du Chien they called on Rev. David Lowry, the ancient and devoted missionary among the Winnebagoes, and at one time a resident of Minnesota. Mr. Lowry, like Mr. Kent and almost every one else, thought the mission of the Messrs. Pond would be a failure. Even the zealous and hopeful junior brother was led to exclaim, " We are engaging in a serious enterprise."

Mr. S. H. Pond, gives an account of his commencement to learn the Dakota language. From a white man who knew a little of the language he found out how to ask in Dakota, "What do you call this?" He wrote this down, and then approaching a Dakota who was standing by a pile of iron, he asked its name. He promptly replied. "I have always had a relish for studying languages," says Mr. Pond, and "in "times of leisure it has been my recreation, and I have often "rejoiced at the discovery of some important grammatical "rule, or the signification of some obscure word or sentence, "but no other acquisition of that kind ever afforded me so "much pleasure as it did then to be able to say in Dakota, "'What do you call this?' I had a key now to the Dakota "names of visible objects, and it did not rust in my hands for "want of use. I began the study of the language there on "the bank of the Mississippi, without an interpreter, and "my brother and I made the first collection of words for the "future dictionary."

At Prairie du Chien, Rev. Mr. Lowry did not hesitate to say to the brothers that they "were engaged in a very foolish and hopeless undertaking". They said little to him in reply, not being in the habit of arguing the case with those who were trying to discourage them. From Rev. W. T. Boutwell, who was stationed among the Pillagers (properly so named by the traders) at Leech Lake, they received the first words of encouragement. Mr. Boutwell made a heroic effort to hold that dangerous outpost, but was finally compelled to abandon it.

At Fort Snelling Mr. Pond was informed that the Kaposia band, just below St. Paul, wanted plowing done, and had a plow and oxen, but could not use them, so he volunteered to go down and help them. The Indians took down the plow in a canoe and he drove down the oxen. Mr. Pond says : "At "Kaposia the chief was Big Thunder, the father of Taoyate-"duta (called by the whites, but erroneously, Little Crow), "and the chief soldier was Big Iron. These two held the "plow alternately while I drove the oxen. I suppose they "were the first Dakotas who ever held a plow. The dogs or "Indians stole my provisions the first night I was there, and "I did not fare sumptuously every day, for food was scarce "and not very palateable."

Returning to Fort Snelling, and encouraged by Major
Bliss, then in command, and Indian agent Talliaferro, the
brothers located at Lake Calhoun, where they plowed for the
Indians and erected a log house, meanwhile occupying a temporary shelter in the woods, where they were surrounded
by a cloud of mosquitoes. Mr. S. W. Pond says : "From the
"time of our arrival we considered the acquisition of the
"Dakota language of paramount importance. We were ever
"on the alert to catch some new word or phrase from the
"mouths of the Indians. We contrived the alphabet the
"first summer we were here, and our house was completed
"and the language reduced to writing about the same time ;
"but the house was to stand but five years, while the alpha-
"bet will be used so long as the Dakota language is written.
"We had not been in our new home long before a young man
"inquired whether Dakotas could learn to read, and expressed
"a desire to learn. We taught him the letters, and how to
"use them in the formation of words, and he learned in a few
"weeks to write letters that we could understand, and was,
"doubtless, the first Dakota who learned to read and write."
    The brothers learned the grammatical structure of the lan-
guage as children learn their mother tongue. Interpreters
could not help them. One of the latter when asked about the
verb replied, "If you can find a verb in Dakota you are a
smart man !" Another when questioned as to how the
Dakotas formed the future tense said, " The Dakotas have no
future tense !" The future tense, and many rules of gram-
mar, were learned without their help. "It is one thing to
learn a word or rule in print or in writing, and quite another
thing to catch it from the mouth of an Indian."
    Mr. Pond hunted with the Indians a month, but the lan-
guage was the game he was hunting for, and he "was as eager
in the pursuit of that as the Indians were of deer". Not
one of the fifty men who accompanied him is alive to-day.
    Mr. Pond says that before the treaty with the Indians they
would assist in plowing, but afterwards not one of them
would touch a plow. Their seeming prosperity was ruinous.
When the brothers came here they found the Indians, as a
general rule, " an industrious, energetic people." Under the

treaty the older Indians gradually lost their former habits of
industry, and a new generation grew up of insolent, reckless
fellows, who spent their lives in idleness and dissipation.
As they "never regretted coming among the Dakotas" when
they did, so they "never regretted leaving them" when they
did. For nearly twenty years they devoted their lives to the
Dakotas, "and it was not without the greatest reluctance and
a feeling of bitter disappointment" that they "came to the
conclusion" that they "must leave them".

For over half a century —nearly three-score years—one of
those earliest missionaries has lived in Minnesota, and is yet
here, erect in stature, standing over six feet, and his mental
faculties are vigorous. He resides in almost the primitive
simplicity of the early days, from choice, in his own house, on
the banks of the Minnesota river. His voice is clear,
his eyes are bright, and his limbs are vigorous. The
lumber of his house he brought with oxen, on the ice of the
Mississippi river, from Point Douglas to Fort Snelling, at
which last-named place it was framed, and thence transported
by barge on the Minnesota river to its present location. The
footsteps of time have brought to this generation few more interesting personages than Samuel W. Pond, who is one of the
first missionaries to the Dakotas, who made the first collection of words for the Dakota dictionary, who first taught a
Dakota to read and write, wrote the first school-lessons in their
language for the Dakota children, and translated portions of
the Bible into Dakota. He first taught the Dakotas to plow.
The alphabet he arranged for them, and his translations for
their use, no college graduate is able to improve, for there
is reliable testimony that the Indians understand them better
than any others.

MISSIONARY STEPHEN R. RIGGS.

Dr. Riggs was not a frequent visitor at the St. Peter agency
during 1849, but his presence was always desired. At that
period, and for many years before and after, his labor with
the Indians was at Lac-qui-parle, the home of the classic
Martin McLeod. Dr. Riggs was a native of Ohio. He came
to Minnesota in 1837, and from that date to the breaking out

of the Indian war, August 1862, he was one of the most
active, zealous, and prominent missionaries in the country.
He was not only active in the field but, with the aid of S. W.
and G. H. Pond and Dr. Williamson, rendered to the Dakotas
services which were indispensable in editing, compiling, com-
posing, and publishing books in their language which were
the foundation of success in the propagation of the gospel
among them, and the key to their civilization and Christianization. He was respected by the Indians, and there is no
doubt but that he accomplished a good work in their behalf ;
though for that matter all the missionaries did—but the mass
of the Dakotas would never acknowledge it.

Dr. Riggs' mission was made less difficult in the beginning
in consequence of the primitive missionaries—the two Ponds
and Dr. Williamson—having prepared the way for him and
those who followed in the missionary field. He wielded an
able, useful, instructive, classic pen. His taste was literary.
He was a prolific publisher. His wife was an able woman—
perhaps not more so than the wives of the other missionaries—
but her advantages for an education in early life, in her New
England home, had been of a superior character. A large
family of interesting children gathered around the hearth-
stone of the mission house, some of whom, since reaching
maturity, have followed the holy calling of their parents, and
are now missionaries in different parts of the world.

When we consider the privations, hardships, difficulties,
and sufferings encountered and surmounted, by these primitive men and their families, in their earnest labors for the
thankless Sioux, we are led to conclude that had those things
occurred in Africa, or Asia, their deeds would have been
sounded throughout the republic. But as their work was on
American soil it escaped the attention of the people and was
considered a local matter of little moment. It is curious to
peruse the record of the great privations and sufferings of
those early missionaries—from cold, and hunger, and well-
grounded fear of the Indians—interspersed with rejoic-
ings "at the manifestations of the Lord's loving kindness
and tender mercies undiminished" towards them! During the whole of Dr. Riggs' life, after reaching the mission

fields of Minnesota, his great interest in his work never ceased.

REV. A. RAVOUX.

Another welcome visitor to the agency during 1849 was the Rev. Augustin Ravoux, so long the vicar-general of St. Paul. Mr. Ravoux reached the upper country in 1841. He is a native of France, came to this country in 1838, and was for some time engaged in missionary work at Prairie du Chien. After his arrival in this territory he visited Traverse des Sioux, and commenced the study of the Indian language, in which he soon became proficient. Meantime he preached to the savages by interpreters. His labor was not confined to Traverse, but he visited La Framboise's trading post at Little Rock, and eventually proceeded up the St. Peter river as far as Lac-qui-parle, the seat of the Protestant mission under Dr. Williamson and Dr. Riggs. From Traverse he returned to Mendota and taught the catechism in the Indian language to some of the half-breed families. He established a mission at Little Prairie, now Chaska. While at the latter place he wrote several religious books in the Dakota language. In 1843 appeared a volume entitled Wakantanka ti Cancu, (Path to the House of God,) of which he was the author.

Mr. Ravoux made many converts to Christianity among the wild Indians. No man was held in higher respect by the the whole community. A devoted and faithful pastor, a kind friend to the poor, he was always engaged in some act of philanthropy. He ministered to those of all denominations and all classes alike by deeds of kindness. The private soldiers in the garrison received the same kind attention that was given to the officers in their quarters. The improvident half-breeds and there were many of them in those days—who rarely looked out for the morrow, were frequently relieved from distress by his generous efforts. He has lived an eventful and useful life. Most of those with whom he was so intimately associated forty years ago have passed away, but the seed sown by him in those early days has brought forth noble fruit. There is not an old settler in the land but has a fond recollection of this excellent missionary.

REV. DR. THOMAS WILLIAMSON.

Dr. Williamson was consulted more than any other man by

the Indian agency in 1849, if we except the Ponds. He was
born in South Carolina, in 1800. Five years later his parents
moved to Ohio, and when seventeen years old young Williamson graduated at Jefferson college, Pennsylvania. In 1827
he married Miss Mary Poage, and came to Minnesota on a
tour of observation in 1834, and with his family in May 1835.
Besides his wife and infant daughter, he was accompanied by
his wife's sister, Miss Mary Poage, afterwards Mrs. G. H.
Pond, and by Mr. Alexander G. Huggins and family. Soon
afterward they proceeded to Lac-qui-parle. In this company
were the first white women who ever ascended the Minnesota.

Having labored eleven years at Lac-qui-parle and built up
a church of forty members, he left the station in charge of
Dr. Riggs and removed to Kaposia, five miles below St. Paul,
where he remained six years, when he removed to Yellow
Medicine. The outbreak of 1862 scattered the churches, but
Dr. Williamson had the consolation of knowing that all the
Christian Indians continued, at the risk of their own lives,
steadfast friends of the whites, and that they succeeded in
saving more than their own number of white people.

Dr. Williamson had not one enemy, and those who differed
with him in his estimate of the Indian character respected
him for his integrity. His belief that no member of the
Presbyterian churches had taken part in the massacre, though
contrary to general opinion, is confirmed by the most thorough investigation.

Dr. Williamson died at his residence, in St. Peter, Minnesota, June 24, 1877, in the eightieth year of his life. He
labored for twenty-seven years among the Dakotas, and for
thirty-six years was a missionary of the American Board.

The above-named are all the missionaries I met at the St.
Peter agency in 1849, except Rev. M. N. Adams, who was
stationed at Lac-qui-parle. He is now at the Sisseton
agency in Dakota. We shall take occasion to speak of his
good work, at a later period.

CHAPTER XII.

When Philander Prescott came to the upper country, in 1819, the natives depended much on the wild product of the country for food; and to some extent it was used when I arrived in Minnesota in 1849. In most instances it was easily gathered, and I found, while among the Indians in an early day, that even a white man would soon become fond of the wild sweet-potato and one or two other varieties of the wild tubers the squaws served up to us in their tepees.

According to Mr. Prescott the most prominent varieties of wild product used by the Indians were the mendo or wild sweet-potato, tip-sui-ah or wild prairie-turnip, pang-he or artichoke, omen-e-chah or wild bean, psui-chin-chah or swamp potato, pesich-ah towahapa or wild rice.

The wild sweet potato is found throughout the valleys of the Mississippi, Minnesota, and other streams in the central part of Minnesota. It grows about the bases of bluffs, in rather moist, soft, rich ground. The plant resembles the sweet-potato, and the root is similar in growth and taste. In a letter to Hon. Thomas Ewbank, dated November 10, 1849, Mr. Prescott says, "It does not grow so large nor so long as the cultivated sweet-potato, but I should have thought it the same were it not that the wild potato is not affected by the frost." The Indians simply boiled them in water when preparing them for the table. I intended to have made experiments in the cultivation of the mendo, believing it would bear cultivation, and perhaps when perfected a new variety of

sweet-potato of great value would be added to our products.
I regret my negligence in this matter.

The wild prairie-turnip grows on the high native prairies,
in size from a small hen's egg to that of a goose egg, and of
the same form.   They have a thick black or brown bark, but
are nearly pure white inside, with very little moisture.   They
grow about six or eight inches below the surface, and the
Indian women would dig them with a sharp-pointed stick
forced into the ground and used as a lever.   They were boiled
by the Indians and used in the same manner as we use our
turnips.   They were frequently split open and dried for
winter use by the squaws.   When dried they resembled chalk.
Mr. Prescott thought that when thus dried they could be
ground into flour, and that they would make very palatable
bread.

The artichoke grows where the land is rich, near fallen or
decayed timber.   It was only used for food when the Indians
were very hungry.   The wild bean was found in all parts of
the valleys where the land was moist and rich.   In regard to
this plant Mr. Prescott says : "It is of the size of a large
bean, with a rich and very pleasant flavor.   When used in a
stew I have thought them superior to any garden vegetable
that I have ever tasted."   The Indians are very fond of them,
and pigeons get fat on them in the spring.   The plant is a
slender vine, from two to four feet in hight, with small pods
two to three inches long, containing from three to five beans.
The pod dries and opens, the beans fall to the ground, and in
the spring take root and grow again.   There is no question,
in my opinion, but what this plant could be successfully
cultivated.

The swamp-potato was found—and I suppose it is so to this
day—in water and mud about three feet deep.   The leaf is as
large as the cabbage leaf.   The stem has but one leaf, which
has, as it were, two horns or points.   The root is obtained by
the Indian women ; they wade in the water and gather the
roots.   It is of oblong shape, of a whitish yellow, with a few
black rings around it, is of a slightly pungent taste, and not
disagreeable when eaten with salt or meat.

The psui-chah I believe to be of the same family as the

last, but the tuber is not so large. The stem and leaf are similar, but it grows in deeper water. The Indians are very fond of it. Both of these tubers are found in large quantities in the muskrat lodges, stored by them for winter use. It is not saying too much to call them a luxury.

The ta-wah-pah is another tuber, or rather a root, that the Indians esteem highly as food. Like the two preceding, it is a water product. The stem, leaf, and a yellow flower, are like the pond lily. It is found in the lakes, in water and mud from four to five feet deep. The Indian women used to gather it in large quantities. The root is from one to two feet in length, and is very porous, having as many as six or eight cells running the whole length of the root. It is slightly sweet and glutinous. The Indians generally boiled it with wild fowl, but often roasted it in the absence of wild game. All these roots were preserved by the Indians for winter use by boiling them and then drying them over the fire or in the sun.

The greatest product of all was the wild rice, at least as an article of food, which the Indians themselves gathered instead of the women. They used it in all their great feasts. It was found—and I suppose it is to this day—in lakes and streams where the water and mud is from three to four feet deep up to ten or fifteen. The rice harvest was a short one, being of only a week's duration. When ripe the slightest touch shakes it off. A strong wind scatters it in the water. The Indians obtained it by paddling a canoe among the rice when, with a hooked stick, they drew the stalks over the canoe and whipped off the grains. They continued to push the canoe on and whipped off the rice until the canoe was full, then carried the cargo to the shore, unloaded, and filled again until the season was ended. The rice is dried on a scaffold covered with reed-grass, under which a slow fire is kept burning. It is of a dark color, and many of the pioneers prefer it to the Carolina rice. I never did.

I do not give the botanical names of these products, prefer-ing to let them remain in their own native Dakota, just as Mr. Prescott left them so many years ago.

CHAPTER XIII.

The winter of 1850 was a quiet one at Fort Snelling, as well as throughout the whole northwest. December set in cold, and deep snow fell in all portions of the territory. Early in the winter news came that good Major Murphy had been removed from the Sioux agency and Major N. McLean, a brother of Hon. John McLean a Justice of the Supreme Court of the United States, had been appointed in his stead. Major McLean was an editor, which profession he had followed since his advent into the territory. At that time it was no small undertaking to pack up and make a journey of several hundred miles in mid-winter on sledges (as this dismissal compelled Major Murphy to do) to Galena, the nearest available point of easy transit to other parts of the world ; and even then only Frink & Walker's or John D. Winter's stages were the vehicles of travel ; which were not so bad in the winter, but in summer sometimes passengers had to bear squatter rails on their shoulders so that sloughs could be successfully traversed.

The winter months were greatly enjoyed by the primitive people, and were something of a novelty to the new-comers. As a large number of them were of Canadian-French origin they followed in the footsteps of their ancestors and observed the beginning of winter by a continued series of dancing-parties, in which they were joined by those representing all nationalities, and by none with more zest than by those of mixed blood. Many of the latter, it was said at the time, were beautiful dancers ; and they were certainly fond of that amusement.   The winters in the early days were seasons of mirth.

A VISIT TO THE TRADING POSTS.

With Samuel J. Findley I started in January on a journey from Fort Snelling by way of the St. Croix Falls to the Lake Superior region.   The object was to visit the distant trading posts where Mr. Steele was interested in purchasing fur. Mr. Findley could speak the French and Indian languages fluently, and from his long residence in the north (he was a native of Prairie du Chien) was familiar with the country and could follow a trail or make his way through the deep forests and reach any point in the woods with as much certainty as an Indian.   With plenty of blankets, buffalo-robes and provisions, we started out in the midst of a snow-storm, with a double train, by way of St. Paul and Stillwater, for the upper country.   After a hard battle all day with the snow-drifts, we only reached the half-way house between St. Paul and Stillwater.   This house had for a landlord John Morgan, an old settler, a warm-hearted, hospitable man, who made us comfortable after the tedious day's journey.   The next morning dawned with increased violence to the storm.   It was terrific, but during a lull in the early forenoon we started out and made the seven miles to Stillwater just as darkness approached.   We put up at the Stillwater House, a small but convenient place of entertainment.   At that time Stillwater had not much need of a hotel, though during the active movement of lumber the embryo city was lively.   Then old settlers had (as they have now) a great liking for the place.

PIONEERS OF STILLWATER.

Stillwater was the first home of many of the pioneers.   The first courts were held there.   Calvin F. Leach, Elias McKean, Joseph R. Brown, Governor William Holcombe, John Mc-Kusick, Socrates Nelson, Samuel Berkleo, David B. Loomis, M. S. Wilkinson, Sylvanus Trask, John D. Ludden, Henry F. Setzer, Jesse Taylor, Elam Greeley, Albert Stimson, Wm. Willim, the Mower brothers, and many other good and true men and patriots, located there.   But our Fathers!   Where are they!   May the people of that flourishing city, for all

time to come, walk the same road traveled by these men. It
will lead them to the meadow-lands whose dews are the sweet
balsams of eternity !

The storm still raged. In these times it would be
known as a blizzard. This being my first introduction to a
storm of this character I was inclined to think that farmers
in this climate could never do any out-door work in the
winter, and that the stock would all freeze. I found these
opinions erroneous. Mr. Steele and I had a great many men
at work for us during the winter, and but few days were lost
from inclemency of the weather ; and in after years I wintered hundreds head of stock and never lost one through the
influence of the storm.

Of course there was no visible track up the river from Stillwater to St. Croix Falls, and we had to pick our way up the
frozen stream the best we could. Under the most favorable
conditions there is not much pleasure or romance in traveling
on sledges in winter in Minnesota, and less when the air is
full of such fine particles of snow that when driven by a
strong wind the sting is about equal to being pelted with
nettles.

I had about made up my mind that I had enough of the
life of a voyageur, when just as night had set in we discovered in the twilight a building near by, which proved to be
Orange Walker's mill at Marine, on the left bank of the St.
Croix. After considerable difficulty we found the road leading up the bluff, and were soon resting comfortably in a fine
hotel, for those times. We had passed the Arcola mills of
the Mower boys, some miles down the river, in the snow-
storm without knowing it.

LUMBER BUSINESS ON THE ST. CROIX.

The Marine colony, an ancient settlement, was at first composed mostly of people from Marine, Illinois. The principal
business firm is known as Judd, Walker & Co. This house
employs a great many men in the lumber trade. The men are
sent into the pineries bordering on the St. Croix and its
tributaries. They cut the logs during the winter, bank them
on the streams, and in spring they are floated down the river,

gathered into a boom at Marine, sawed into lumber, and
rafted down the St. Croix and Mississippi rivers to St. Louis
and other markets.

The next day was clear ; not a vestige of the storm was
left, except the huge snow-drifts. Off early in the morning,
we passed Osceola, a lumber precinct, and reached the east
banks of the Falls of St. Croix, now called Taylor's Falls, and
gathered up some furs, and were invited by a trader named
Samuels to attend a gathering in his bowling-alley that evening at early candle-light.

FRONTIER DANCING-PARTY.

We responded at the proper time, and found many Indian
maidens dressed in blue calico gowns, and several whites and
half-breeds, enjoying a dance. Everything was orderly, and
conducted with as much propriety as such occasions are in
the old-settled portions of the east. Samuels, whose wife
was a full-blooded squaw, managed to secure the attendance
of the Chippewa maidens who were camped in the immediate
vicinity of the falls. The men who were employed in the
lumber camps, mostly from the east, seemed to require some
form of amusement, and Samuels got up this novel method
of supplying it.

The young Chippewa girls were well-behaved, modest and
diffident, but like many of their white sisters, enjoyed dancing.
Everything was conducted on the strictest line of temperance,
the men treating the maidens respectfully. At midnight a
fine supper was served, after which the dancing was continued
until daylight, when the men quietly retired to their boarding-
places, and the girls donned their blankets and went to their
wigwams. They were accompanied to the ball by some male
or female relative. Samuels said that at first the red male
admirers of the girls rather objected to their attendance, as
did their parents in some instances, but as a general rule
the objectors were present at the supper, and being the
recipients of a bountiful supply of delicacies, free, their
objections were waived. All communication between the
couples on the floor, or at the banquet-table, was through an
interpreter, as the girls could not speak English nor the boys
Chippewa.

Many beautiful cottages had been built, even at this early day, around that portion of the Falls of St. Croix in Wisconsin, while the Minnesota side exhibited much enterprise. Hon. W. H. C. Folsom was a resident of the little hamlet. He had in 1846, with Martin Mower and Joseph Brewster, been interested in building a saw-mill at Arcola.

AN EXILE FRONTIERSMAN.

After a day or two at the falls we started northward, and for the first few miles found an excellent road, made by the teams of those engaged in the lumber trade. On a branch of one of the numerous streams—the Sunrise—was an aged man named Thomas Connor, who had a squaw for a wife. He had a few goods for sale to the Indians, and entertained the voyageurs and trappers and the few wanderers who traversed the wild country. He had long been a resident in the wilderness, seldom visiting civilization. A man of good habits and good education, above the average in point of ability, it seemed strange he should lead such a life. No one was acquainted with his previous history, further than that he had resided in the vicinity for long years, nor could any one understand why he elected to become an exile in the upper valley of the St. Croix. On expressing surprise to a missionary that a man of such intelligence should bury himself in such a manner, he replied, "Oh, the woods and the country bordering on Lake Superior are full of just such men." In some instances they had been unfortunate in business in the east. Some had lost their good name and fled into the extreme western forest to brood over their sorrow. Others had committed a crime and had sought the isolated places for safety. Few had sought the lonesome wilds from love of it. They can scarcely be called hermits, because they are prone to associate with the Indians. Many of them had squaws for wives, who generally cultivated a little garden, while in nearly every instance the men traded more or less with the Indians. It is true their outfits were small, but they were well-selected; and in those days it did not require a great stock of vermillion, ochre, and other kinds of paint, glass-beads, red and blue calico, with a few Mackinaw blankets, powder, lead, shot, tobacco and a gun or two, to make a respectable stock of goods for a kind of guerrilla traffic with the Indians. In order to be a regular trader in the Indian country a license from the Indian authorities was necessary, but frequently men with Indian wives did not observe the existing laws. Mr. Connor was a favorite with the lumbermen on the streams north of his locality, because he always had good fires to camp by in the winter, and set an excellent table, and could entertain his guests with interesting reminiscences of his sojourn in the valley of the St. Croix. He passed away many years ago, as have all his contemporaries who followed the same mode of life.

A PHENOMENAL WINTER.

From Mr. Connor's place we followed the trail to Elam Greeley's logging camp at Snake river, which was not far from the present site of Pine City. Mr. Greeley was one of the primitive lumbermen on the St. Croix. He informed me that two or three winters previously, in company with a Mr. Blake, from Winnebago county, Illinois, and another person, he was engaged in logging on the Sunrise. They never banked a log on the river during the whole winter in consequence of the total absence of snow! He had kept his crew in the woods, hoping against hope, all ready for work when the snow should come, but it did not come at any one time during the whole winter sufficient to whiten the ground, and as a consequence the firm had large outgoes with no income. This was probably the only winter of the kind known in Minnesota.

From Mr. Greeley's camp we made our way to the small trading-post of Louis Jarvis, a French Canadian, whose place of business was on the banks of Pokegema Lake. From him we secured a superior lot of furs, principally marten. Mr. Jarvis was married to an intelligent half-breed girl. In earlier years a voyageur, he had saved some money while following that hard life, which he invested in the Indian trade, married the pretty Nancy Laprairie, and settled near the mission grounds on the beautiful lake, and made an uncertain livelihood in selling paint and beads to the Indians. Poor Jarvis! The hardships he endured on plains, in the forest,

and swinging the oars in the rivers and lakes, during his
engagement with the fur company, destroyed his health, and
he lived only a few months after going into business for
himself.

THE OLD INDIAN MISSION GROUNDS.

At the time of my visit to the lake the old mission had
been removed to other parts of the wilderness. The labor of
the missionaries in the neighborhood was closed, but their
good deeds followed them, though many of the Indians once
so numerous around the lake had, in consequence of the
incessant hostility of the Dakotas, abandoned the scenes of
their early home and gone to reside with their kith and kin
northward almost to the shore of Lake Superior. There
were many brave warriors in the band, but they were liable
to be caught by Dakotas in ambush, and worsted in battle.
A few half-breeds remained, mostly of the Laprairie family
blood, who delighted in war ; but the few full-bloods who
remained adopted the habits of the whites and tilled the soil
to a considerable extent. It is seldom, however, that an
Indian is either a good economist or a good farmer, though
there are exceptions, but not many.

SNOW-SHOES.

In visiting these small trading-posts and hunters' camps I
found that snow-shoes were necessary when outside the paths
made by lumbermen. To a novice they are unpleasant and
uncomfortable, and to get on one's feet in the deep snow,
after being tripped up by a misstep, is no slight task. After
one has served an apprenticeship in wearing them he can
travel with ease and speed. I am not sure but a man well-
versed in the mysteries of traveling over the snow with snow-
shoes can make as many miles per day on them as he can
without them and with boots on a hard-beaten path. Especially is this so when there is a slight crust on the surface of
the snow. There is considerable romance in wearing snow-
shoes so long as the straps which are wound around the feet
and attached to the snow-shoes do not gall the feet.

We spent a profitable month among the Indians, traders, and lumbermen, in the upper St. Croix valley and along

the tributary streams. We there renewed our acquaintance with Hon. N. Setzer, who was connected with Mr. Greeley in lumber operations on Snake river. He was a member of the first territorial Legislature. The lumber operations were crude in those early days in the pineries of Minnesota and Wisconsin. The absence of booms and other necessary facilities to make them profitable may be set down as the reason that those early lumbermen made no money in getting out logs. This I know to my sorrow, as a winter or two after my visit to the St. Croix pineries I engaged in the enterprise on Rum river and lost $17,000 in the operation; not but that there were huge piles of logs banked, and safely in the Mississippi, but there came a flood; many of the logs went over the Falls of St. Anthony and were swept down the river, and it cost more to gather them up and raft them to southern markets than they were worth. Had there been good boom privileges such disasters would not have occurred. There was one advantage the lumbermen had, however, and that was that the timber was good, and grew right on the banks of the river, so the hauls were short and the cost of banking light to what it is now. Then again the stumpage was free. At that early period the public domain, and all that was on it, was free plunder.

All the lumber used in the houses erected at an early day in this part of the northwest, and all that was rafted down the Mississippi, was secured from the lands belonging to the government, and cost nothing to those who cut it. Early in the fifties the government claimed, and in some instances secured, a stumpage but the amount was very small. The agents sent out from Washington to collect it were unable, even with the powerful aid of the government, to secure more than a mere pittance. One of the timber-agents was a brother of the President, but Mr. Fillmore met with no better success than the others.

THE RETURN.

After gathering all our furs and sending them to the Fort by voyageurs, we started home through an unbroken wilderness past the numerous lakes in what is now Chisago county. After leaving the pine lands we came into a tract of beautiful hardwood timber, mostly sugar-maple. Those groves have long since passed away ; large, productive farms and happy firesides exist in their place, mostly occupied by intelligent, industrious, hardy Norsemen and their descendents in Chisago county.

While at Taylor's Falls I desired to meet N. C. D. Taylor, a friend of my earliest boyhood, although ten years my senior, but he was absent in the pineries. Mr. Taylor was once a clerk for his uncle Nathan Lovejoy, a merchant in New Hampshire, in the vicinity of my early home. He was a resident of Alton, Illinois, in 1832. We lived in the same hamlet at the Stake Diggings lead-mines in Wisconsin. When I left for Mexico, in 1846, Mr. Taylor came to the St. Croix valley, and was one of the original preemptors of the city of Taylor's Falls. For many years he was one of the most active business men in Minnesota. In 1854 he was a member of the territorial legislature. In 1856 he was also a member, and was elected speaker at that session. In 1866 he was elected treasurer of Chisago county, and re-elected for many years. He died in 1887. Mr. Taylor was a pure, just man, in both public and private life. No taint ever attached to his name. Among the many pleasant visitors under my humble roof during many years there never was one more welcome than Nathan Chase Daniel Taylor. He was never married. No man was more universally respected.

Mr. Taylor having a large experience in mining, was of the opinion that some day copper and other mines would be discovered around the falls of St. Croix ; in which opinion all miners of experience fully concur. The formation is green-stone, much in appearance like the copper-bearing rock of Lake Superior. This dark-green trap-rock is very different from the formation around the falls of St. Anthony.

CHAPTER XIV.

The long winter of 1850 became wearisome as the spring months approached and no steamboats came. Communication to the lower country was on the ice, though early in the winter Judge Wyman Knowlton, of Prairie du Chien, laid out an air-line road from that place to St. Paul, the distance being only 313 miles ; but people preferred the ice to the new road.

Two promising schools were opened in St. Anthony, and the library association provided for intellectual treats to the young colony. Rev. Dr. E. G. Gear, in a lecture early in January, said that on his first visit to Anthony cataract, nine years before, there was only one poor cabin there, and a body of Indians were engaged in spirit worship. Out of brush the Indians had erected a large number of booths several hundred feet long, in the center of which was a dog bedaubed with various colors, which was a prominent feature in the superstitious exercises.

Lieutenant R. W. Johnson, Hon. W. R. Marshall, and other prominent citizens, lectured before the association. A sewing-circle was formed by the ladies, which was a kind of relief to the home-sickness which they naturally felt, to some extent, the first winter after their departure from their former home. Hon. John A. Wakefield organized a temperance society in St. Paul, which extended to St. Anthony. The academy building was finished and a kind of high-school was opened in it during the latter part of the winter.

Goodhue of the Pioneer was inclined to poke fun at those around the falls. That paper of February 27th said that

probably a town on the west shore of the Falls of St. Anthony
would be laid out and vigorously commenced the ensuing
spring. He added: " We propose that it be called All Saints,
so as to head off the whole calendar of saints." After the
snow disappeared in March, the Pioneer said, " We learn that
on Sunday, April 3, a fire broke out in St. Anthony, in the
dry grass, and burnt over several squares where buildings
will be." Little did Colonel Goodhue, or any one at that
time, think that in thirty-five years not only those few squares
would be built over, but that solid blocks would extend from
them for miles.

CHANGE OF COMMAND AT FORT SNELLING.

On the 27th of February Colonel Loomis received orders
to turn over the command to Colonel Woods and proceed to
Fort Leavenworth. The noble old colonel who had done so
much for the benefit of the northwest, and for Christianity,
never returned to Fort Snelling. With his departure the
missionaries lost their best friend.

On April 3d orders came for Colonel Woods to take three
companies from Fort Snelling and proceed to Iowa and
remove the Pottawatomies, Sacs and Foxes, over the Missouri
river. This order ended Colonel Wood's command and
presence-at the fort.

. Such was the anxiety for the arrival of steamboats that
little else was talked about. On the 19th of April the Highland Mary, Captain John Atkinson, landed at the fort. Many
citizens of St. Paul, Stillwater, and other places, were that
night in much the same condition as were the friends of Johnny
when he came marching home from the war.

New life and vigor was imparted to the enterprising and
enthusiastic pioneers of the upper Mississippi by the opening
of navigation in the spring of 1850 ; but it must not be supposed that the long winter months were without excitement.

ESQUIMAUX DISPATCHES BY DOG-TRAIN.

On the first of March a dog train arrived from the Red river
of the North, containing news of moment from the Arctic
ocean. I forwarded this news to the Pioneer, and received

from editor Goodhue the following evidence of appreciation :
"I am greatly obliged to you for the Esquimaux dispatches,
"and hesitated whether to make an acknowledgment for the
"favor, in print ; but finally decided not to do it."

April 3d word was received that fourteen Chippewas
were killed at Apple'river ; and the weekly mail from Prairie
du Chien brought interesting accounts of the Parkinson murder trial in Boston. All news, even if it was old, from the
great world outside of Minnesota, was thoroughly discussed.
Newspapers were read and re-read. The people were well-
informed in regard to the current events of the day. One
could tell the names of every senator and representative in
congress, and the states they represented. Then again the
health of the people, according to the population, was superior,
if possible, to that of a later period. More food was consumed
to the average man, and enjoyed with a keener relish, than
elsewhere. Colonel Goodhue, on careful investigation, said
that it took nine 'men to pole a keel-boat up the St. Croix
river, and on an average they consumed a barrel of flour and
a barrel of pork on the trip. He claimed that men eat more
here than any place in the United states. True, the luxuries
were few, but the necessaries of life were appreciated, and
so long as the wants of the inner man were satisfied there
was no danger but that the ingenuity of the people would
find proper amusement during the long winter months.

A TRIP TO THE LOWER COUNTRY.

On the 25th of April the good steamer Nominee, Captain
Orrin Smith (whose name is a household word to the pioneers
of the upper valley of the great river), appeared at Fort
Snelling with recruits and government stores for the army.
Having an important engagement at Rockford, Illinois, I took
passage on the steamer for Galena. At St. Paul and other
landings several persons came aboard bound for the lower
country ; among them was Simon Powers, who had quite a
cargo of live-stock which he was taking to the lower markets.
Among the lot was an old white mule which I had, as agent
for Mr. Steele, sold with other stock the previous fall. This
mule Mr. Steele purchased from the quartermaster's depart-

ment in 1837.   In 1849 he was capable of doing a heavy day's
work, and no one would, from his appearance, suppose he
was over fifteen years old, though Joseph R. Brown, who was
a soldier at the time, and present on the occasion, said this
same mule helped haul the stone that was used in building
Fort Snelling, and was by no means a youngster at that time.
We were all much surprised that Mr. Powers should ship
stock for the lower markets when we required so much here
and boat-loads were being shipped to St. Paul and other
towns.   Mr. Powers explained the reason by saying that he
had purchased horses the previous year in St. Louis, and
traders there, who understood their value, had requested him
to secure the descendants of horses that had, at an early
period, been introduced into the lower Red river valley by
the Earl of Selkirk.   These, with the French-Canadian horses,
were the original breeds that were in use in pre-territorial
days.   They were capable of great endurance, and were fleet,
requiring but little grain notwithstanding the extreme cold,
and were valuable either as roadsters or for the chase.   When
Mr. Perry and his associates came from the Hudson Bay
territory and settled on the reservation near Fort Snelling, in
1827, they brought their stock with them, which included
many valuable horses, and it was this blood that Mr. Powers
was transporting.   He was undoubtedly the first man in the
territory who shipped horses to the lower country for the
purpose of selling them.

On landing at Galena I was surprised to find the season
was as forward at Fort Snelling as it was in that city, and I
found that such was the case all the way to Rockford.   I
began to be impressed that, after all, Minnesota was not such
a hyperborean region as it had been represented to be.   There
was no perceptible difference in the climate between Rockford,
Illinois, and St. Anthony Falls.

A BUSINESS OFFER FROM CAPTAIN (SINCE GENERAL) KIRKHAM.

While at Rockford, I received a letter from Captain Kirkham, quartermaster in the United States army at Fort Snelling, in which he says : "Major Woods leaves to-day for Iowa,
"directing the three companies of troops to follow him in

"about ten days. I have no doubt it is to be a summer's job,
"and will require quite a heavy disbursement. I shall send
"ten days' supplies of everything with them, and two months'
"supplies of all rations except pork, flour, and fresh beef.
"These will be purchased in market. Forage will also have
"to be bought for upwards of a hundred head of horses and
"mules. Now, can you play agent or contractor? You know
"what we agreed upon before you left. If you think it for
"your interest to go, I wish you would. I am sure you
"will not regret it. I would like, in case you decide to go, to
"have you at Muscatine by the 16th or 17th. Woods will
"meet the troops at Marengo. I will bring down funds with
"me if I go, and if I cannot leave with the troops, will send
"you a draft on the quartermaster at St. Louis for a thousand
"dollars, which will be enough to start upon. P. S.- The
"steamer Lamartine went up to St. Anthony on Saturday the
"4th. A large party of us from the garrison were along.
"We took the band and had a pleasant time. The river was
"so strong that the boat could not land on the east side, but
"we stopped opposite Tuttle's place. There is no doubt now
"about the head of navigation."

I decided to accept the position of agent of the quartermaster in the expedition to remove the Indians from Iowa
to the west side of the Missouri river, and so notified Captain
Kirkham.

THE FIRST WHITE LADY PIONEER OF ORIGINAL MINNEAPOLIS.

On the 10th of May I perfected the object of my visit to
Rockford, and Miss Frances Helen Miller, of Oneida county,
New York, became my wife; and now, after nearly forty
years since that event, I can with certainty say that man was
never blessed with a better wife. She is the first white lady
pioneer who became a permanent resident of the original
Minneapolis, and is the mother of the first white child born
in that city.

RETURN TO MINNESOTA.

A two days' journey brought us to Galena whence, on Monday, the 13th of May, we embarked with our old friend
Captain Smith and his excellent clerk Maitland, for Fort

Snelling. The steamer was full of emigrants bound for the new country. Among those who have since been prominent in Minnesota affairs, and held high positions in the state, was George W. Moore, who was for a long time connected with Major John P. Owens, manager of the good old Minnesotian, a newspaper of much moment in territorial day. I met Mr. Moore a few days before at Rockford, and advised him to visit the territory. He had been a book-printer in New York.

On the way up the river we met several agents of the government picking up Winnebago Indians who had stealthily strayed away from Long Prairie, and wandered back to their old haunts and hunting-grounds on the banks of the river in Iowa and Wisconsin. The little bands gathered from time to time were marched to the hurricane-deck of the steamer, and when the last came aboard at Wabasha prairie, now Winona, the upper deck presented the appearance of an Indian encampment. They were so thickly packed that it was difficult for the pilots to reach the pilot-house. These Indians, on their arrival at St. Paul, were marched overland to the agency at Long Prairie.

ENTHUSIASM FOR MINNESOTA.

In addition to Mr. Moore, there were several others who for the first time were on their way to look for homes in the north ; most of whom were pleased with the country, and located on claims, and have been useful citizens of the state. I had during twelve months' residence caught the enthusiasm of those who had preceded me to Minnesota, in regard to the resources and advantages of the country, and was constantly doing missionary work among the numerous passengers all the way up the river, without being aware of it. The primitive inhabitants believed in the brilliant future of the upper valley of the river. This belief was contagious. Frequently an immigrant from the east would at first be disgusted with the lay of the land but, as a general rule, the longer he remained the better he was satisfied, and after a year's residence he was, like all the others, an active missionary in behalf of his adopted country.

Landing at St. Paul on the forenoon of the 16th, we were

met by Mr. Steele, and other friends, and immediately proceeded by land to Fort Snelling, which at that time was almost
abandoned by the troops, only one company remaining for
garrison duty, the other companies having left a few days
before for the wilds of Iowa, where they were to be employed
in removing the Indians, and where I was to join them without delay. During my absence Mrs. Stevens remained in the
family of J. W. Bass in St. Paul.

Having had considerable experience in the quartermaster's
department with the army in Mexico, it was thought best by
the commanding officer, Colonel Woods, that I should perfect
the necessary arrangements for the convenience of the expedition, at his headquarters; and as the steamer Highland Mary
was on the eve of departure from Fort Snelling, I went aboard
and secured passage for Dubuque, from which city I was to
proceed overland and overtake the troops at a point known
as Patterson's trading-post, some thirty or forty miles west of
Iowa city. At that time there were scarcely any settlers west
of Marengo to the immediate vicinity of the Missouri river.
The broad, vast country with its rich soil stretched out for
hundreds of miles, which had to be traversed before the
Indians could be landed on their reservation west of the river.
As the early season of 1850 was an unusually wet one, the
prairies were almost impassable for our heavily-loaded government mule-teams.

REMOVING THE INDIANS.

Previous to my arrival at the headquarters of the command
Colonel Woods had sent out runners to the different fragment-
ary bands of Indians who were scattered in the immediate
neighborhood of Patterson's trading-post, requesting them to
come in and hold a council with him. In compliance with
this request many of them responded. Old Poweshiek, chief
of the Pottawatomies, accompanied by several individuals of
his band, as well as by some of the Sacs and Foxes who were
prowling through the country, appeared, but no satisfactory
terms could be agreed upon. Colonel Woods then commenced
gathering them in with the troops. This was a slow, expensive
process, and not always attended with success, on account of

obstructions thrown in the way by traders. For instance, several hundred would be gathered ready to start the next day for their reservation when, during the night, whiskey would be smuggled into the camp, and the result was that, when moving-time came the Indians were scattered many miles in different sections of the neighborhood, and this too, although the camp was strictly guarded by the troops. The work would then have to be commenced over again. If there is one branch of service which the army despises more than another, and justly too, it is gathering up wandering bands of Indians that range over a large extent of territory, marching them into camp, and guarding them afterwards. If the musket or bayonet could be used, it would be different. Such measures would soon be effective ; but the wily, cunning red truants were wards of the government ; their only offense was in running away from their location west of the Missouri, they said because the climate was against them, and there was no game. They wanted to be let alone and live in the land where they were born, and be buried by the graves of their fathers. They knew very well that powder and ball and cold steel could not be used in forcing them back to the land of their exile. After repeated attempts to make a clean deal— and some of them were successful—Colonel Woods closed a contract with a couple of citizens to remove them : which was successfully executed.

Every member of the command had a holy horror of the fearful, bottomless roads through the wild, rich country to the Missouri. The troops under the command of Colonel Woods engaged in the tiresome and perplexing expedition were well known to the early citizens of the territory.

Colonel Woods received orders from the War department to proceed to the Lizard Fork of the Des Moines and erect a fort, which is now the site of the flourishing city of Fort Dodge. Proceeding to Muscatine, which had been our shipping point on the Mississippi, I embarked, in company with my wife who met me there, on the steamer Anthony Wayne, Captain Dan Able, for Fort Snelling. Captain Able afterwards became famous in the transportation of troops under General Grant during the earlier stages of the war on the lower rivers. He was a favorite with the first merchants of the Falls of St. Anthony, in consequence of repeatedly running his steamer up to the Falls.

FIRST IMPORTED STOCK.

At Muscatine I purchased a drove of cows, paying for them only seven dollars per head, and shipped them to Fort Snelling, to stock my embryo farm, a portion of which is now known as Minneapolis. This was my first venture in stock in Minnesota, and was also my second venture in agricultural matters. I only mention this for the purpose of showing the low price of stock in the west at that time. I paid the steamer Dr. Franklin No. 2 four dollars per head for their transportation from Muscatine to Fort Snelling ; so the cows cost me, delivered at the fort, only eleven dollars per head. They were a fair average lot, and many of their descendents are to be found in the state to-day. This was undoubtedly the first herd of cows ever introduced on the west bank of the falls, outside of those required for the use of the troops at Fort Snelling. It is well known that for many years previous to the occupation of the military reservation from a few rods above Bassett's creek down toward the Falls of Minnehaha, the government summered and wintered all their stock, which was mostly under the care of Alpheus R. French, then a quartermaster-sergeant in the army. He occupied the old government dwelling-house, which was on the margin of a deep ravine near the Palisade mills, and his stables and yards were on the bank of the river just below the dwellinghouse.

MINNESOTA CLIMATE BANISHES CHOLERA.

When we were out a few miles from Muscatine my wife told me that she had learned from the chambermaid that cholera had broken out among the passengers on the boat after it left St. Louis ; that several persons died on the way, and several others were dangerously ill with the disease. It was mostly confined to the steerage, but a number of fatal cases had occurred in the cabin. There were several deaths after we came aboard, but the further we proceeded up the river the less the dreadful disease prevailed.

On landing at Galena we met Mr. Steele, who was on his

return home from the Atlantic cities. He was accompanied
by Mrs. Steele's mother, Mrs. W. C. Barney of Baltimore.
She was the only daughter of Judge Samuel Chase, who was
one of the signers of the Declaration of Independence, and
afterwards one of the Supreme Judges of the United States.
Her husband's father was the distinguished Commodore
Josiah Barney. Better than all, she was the mother of many
beautiful, accomplished daughters. There being no vacant
state-room in the ladies' cabin, I gave up mine to Mrs. Barney, who occupied it with Mrs. Stevens.

When cases of cholera proved fatal, the remains were
buried after dark on an island or at a landing, in rough coffins
prepared during the day by the ship-carpenter. My experience on the boat during this trip convinced me that cholera
is worse than yellow-fever or black-vomit. I had been on
shipboard between Vera Cruz and New Orleans where were
many fatal cases of the latter ; but bad as those cases were,
cholera is worse. I dislike to think of that journey up the
river.

HIGH-WATER OF 1850.

As we neared the end of our journey we noticed that the
river was full of fresh-cut logs, and soon word came that the
logs had all broken through the St. Anthony boom in consequence of high-water, and had come over the falls. This was
dreadfully unwelcome news to Mr. Steele and myself, because
the main dependence of the new village of St. Anthony was
at that time centered in pine logs ; and then again the loss
would be a serious one to Messrs. Steele and Ard Godfrey,
the owners of both the logs and the mills. It was afterwards
learned that while several million feet of logs went over the
falls there was still left a sufficient quantity to keep the mills
in successful operation until the next season's logs could be
secured ; but the loss was a heavy one.

Hon. Joseph R. Brown, who came with the troops in 1819,
said that the flood of 1850 was the greatest since the occupation of the country by the government forces.

FIRST TOWN-ELECTION IN ST. PAUL.

During my absence St. Paul held a town election. Dr.

Thomas Potts was elected president. The organization was not completed too early, for the march of improvement was almost beyond belief. It far exceeded the expectation of the most sanguine and enthusiastic of those who had predicted that a great city was to be built there in the near future. St. Anthony and Stillwater were closely following in the footsteps of St. Paul.

CHIPPEWAS SCALP DAKOTAS IN ST. PAUL.

Hole-in-the-Day, blood-thirsty chief of the Chippewas, with some of his warriors, made a raid upon the Sioux encamped in the precincts of St. Paul and scalped some of the unfortunate Dakotas, and took others prisoners. Governor Ramsey called the chiefs and head-men of each tribe to meet him in council at Fort Snelling, on the 11th of June, to determine if there was any possibility that an end could be put to the frequent butcheries between the two savage tribes. A treaty of peace was agreed upon only to be broken at the first convenient opportunity.

ST. PAUL AND ST. ANTHONY IN GENEROUS RIVALRY.

Ice-, bread-, butcher- and milk-carts appeared on the streets of St. Paul and St. Anthony for the first time this early summer. Although the two places were then in the same county, there was a generous rivalry between them. Sometimes they "made faces at one another".

CHAPTER XV.

The humble house under the hill being ready for occupation, we moved into it August 6th, 1850, soon after our return from the expedition in Iowa. The only way we could reach the house from St. Anthony was by taking a small boat, with two sets of oars, above Nicollet Island. The volume of water was so great, and the current so strong, we were fortunate if the landing was made any considerable distance above the rapids.

Captain John Tapper, with his sinewy arms, required a strong assistant, with a capacious pan for bailing purposes, to make a sure crossing above the cataract. There were big rivers in those early days in Minnesota.

Pioneer housekeeping was not new to me, for I had long kept bachelor's-hall in the lead-mines, but it was a novelty to my wife, who had been accustomed to the refining influences and conveniences of a well-regulated New York household. Sometimes for weeks we would not see a white person : our only visitors were Indians. The ferry was suspended, which cut off all travel on the west side of the river.

Mosquitoes surrounded the house in such swarms that smoke would not banish them. The windows and doors were barricaded with netting, but that did not suffice to protect us from them. The beds also required bars. With all this protection, Captain Tapper was so annoyed by their depredations that one morning, after a night's duration of suffering, just before daylight he gathered some blankets and took refuge on the brow of the hill back of the house, hoping to get a little

FIRST HOUSE IN MINNEAPOLIS—ON THE WEST BANK OF THE
FALLS OF ST. ANTHONY—1850.

sleep before breakfast. He rolled himself in his blankets and
was just entering dream-land, when the hot breath of an
animal on his face startled him, and thoroughly ended his
inclination to sleep. A large timber-wolf, with several companions near by, was in search of a breakfast in the early
twilight. With a voice that drowned the roar of the near
cataract, Captain Tapper sprang to his feet, and shaking the
blankets—his only weapons of defense at the wolves, he
made a misstep, rolled down the precipice, and with a single
bound entered the door of the house, thinking he was followed
pretty closely by the wolves. He declared he would rather
be bled by mosquitoes than devoured by wolves.

MY OLD FARM WHERE MINNEAPOLIS NOW IS.

The time had come to commence preparing the land for the
plow. August, September, and October were considered good
months for grubbing out the black jack-oak which abounded
in such numbers that it was with difficulty a man could make
his way through the thicket. The land selected to be cleared
bordered on the river, running back eighty rods from the
bank, and extending about half-way up to the creek. Captain
Tapper had charge of the work. He secured men who had
experience in grubbing. The trees were all cut off ; the roots
were then grubbed out and burned with the trees. It was
expensive in clearing the land this way, but when finished
the plow moved more easily than on the prairie. The soil
was as mellow as an ash-heap. The crops that were produced
on this land in after years were so heavy that it encouraged
immigrants who saw the fields to settle in the territory. This
ground is now mostly covered with solid blocks of buildings.
The owners have large annual returns from the investments
they have made in my old grain-fields in Minneapolis, but
they cannot feel more grateful for such favors than I did for
the bountiful crops harvested so many years ago.

NATIVE GROVES THAT WERE ON THE WEST BANK OF THE FALLS.

There being many beautiful groves of hard-wood in the
immediate neighborhood, but mostly outside the precincts of
my claim, which I was anxious to preserve for the benefit of

future generations, it was with much regret that I observed,
one bright September day, a party of men engaged in felling
trees in the midst of one of the finest of the groves near where
Fifth avenue now crosses Washington avenue. I protested
against such vandalism, when the foreman informed
me that he was there by direction of the chief of the authorities at Fort Snelling, for the purpose of making charcoal for
the use of the government blacksmiths of the post! As many
of the prettiest trees had fallen by the hands of the axmen,
it was too late for making a journey to the fort in their behalf;
and probably if a commencement had not been made, I could
not have changed the result. It would not have made much
difference any way, for in a few short years nearly all the
primitive groves within the present boundaries of the city
were destroyed.

EARLY MAIL FACILITIES.

At this time there was no postoffice in St. Anthony, and if
there had been, it would have been of little use to us, on account of the difficulty in crossing the river. There were
only three mail-routes in the territory; one from St. Paul
to Fort Snelling and back once a week; from St. Paul to the
Falls of St. Croix via Stillwater and Marine mills and back
weekly; and a weekly between St. Paul and Stillwater. Our
nearest postoffice on this side of the river was Fort Snelling;
on the other side St. Paul. There were only sixteen post-
offices in Minnesota, most of them on the banks of the river
below St. Paul. We usually received our letters and papers
once a week.

OUR NEIGHBORS.

Fortunately I had a pretty good library, and Mrs. Stevens
had a piano and other musical instruments, which had a tendency to banish from the little house most of the lonesome-
ness naturally incident to pioneer life so far from neighbors.
At that time the old government-house was unoccupied, and
remained in that condition until the 25th of the following
April, when Calvin A. Tuttle moved over from St. Anthony
and occupied it. During the last part of 1850 and the first
part of 1851 we were alone on the west bank of the falls.

Ambrose Dyer, a native of Oneida county, New York, a bachelor, was at one time during the year employed to look after the mill-property, which had been transferred in 1849 to Robert Smith, member of congress from Illinois. The different tribes of Indians were never so numerous in the neighborhood as in 1850. A constant stream of Winnebagoes were coming and going. The different bands of Sioux remained in camp several months on the high-lands just above the falls. They did not interfere with my stock, but made sad havoc with my garden. As a general rule the Indians respected the private property of the whites residing outside of their own lands, but would occasionally confiscate the property of the missionaries. For instance, Rev. M. N. Adams, then at Lac-qui-parle, in a letter to me says : "The "general aspect of things here at present is pretty much as "usual. The natives have again recently been guilty of an "outrage upon our property. On last Sabbath they slaugh-"tered one of our best cows. The mere loss is but a small "matter compared with other considerations touching moral "principles and the public good. If this was the first offense "then perhaps it might be looked upon with some degree of "allowance ; but for some fourteen years the missionaries "have suffered such outrages at the hands of this lawless and "savage people. We have not yet appealed to the civil "authorities for special interference, although legally we have "a right to do so : for we are personally here each one of us "not only with the sanction of the United States government "but with guarantees of protection and all the assistance that "is in the power of the civil authorities to render us in the "prosecution of our work among this people."

There can be no question but that the cussedness of these savages was frequently annoying to the missionaries.

POLITICAL.

I had hardly become settled in my new home before I was called upon, in common with most everyone else, to take part in the selection of a candidate for delegate to congress. Then as now there was a strong feeling against what was termed monopolies. Some persons on the St. Anthony side of the

river were prejudiced against the mill-company. There was
no special reason for this. Every man's, woman's and child's
bread and butter depended on the success of this industry,
which at that time was the only one we had ; and while there
was only an average of about twenty thousand feet of lumber
sawed each day, it was our all. We could not fall back, as
our St. Paul friends did, on the resources gathered from the
Indian payments. In that village if a bill was to be collected
the collector understood very well that he would have to wait
for his money until after the payment of the annuities by the
general government to the different Indian nations. Even at
that early day St. Paul was commercial : we were manufacturing. If the mill-company wanted a particular man to run
for delegate, there were others who wanted some one else.
Party lines were not thought of by the people. The different
factions in the Indian trade had their favorites. Several
names were mentioned to succeed Hon. H. H. Sibley as delegate. Among them were David Olmsted, Colonel A. M.
Mitchell the U. S. marshal, and Captain N. Greene Wilcox
of the land-office at Stillwater : all good men. I was appointed
chairman of a committee to correspond with those residing in
different parts of the territory for the purpose of an early
meeting in St. Paul for consultation in regard to the matter.
Among others Rev. G. H. Pond was solicited to be present on
the occasion. He replied to the letter of invitation :

LETTER FROM REV. G. H. POND.

"Oak Grove, August 6, 1850. John H. Stevens, St. Peter,
"Minnesota—Dear Sir : Your note of yesterday requesting
"me to inform yourself and others whether or not I would be
"willing to attend as a delegate, the proposed convention at
"St. Paul next Saturday, was duly received.

"My reply is, that it will not be practicable for me to go to
"St. Paul on that day.

"As regards the nomination of a delegate to represent
"Minnesota in Congress, I think party feeling ought to have
"very little to do with it. We want our territory represented,
"and not a party, nor a company, nor a society. We want a
"man of respectable abilities, a man of character, a man who

"will faithfully represent us all, and one of whom we shall
"not be ashamed.

"I should be ashamed to be represented by the nominee of
"a clique. I should have been better pleased with Mr. Sibley
"if he, as a representative of the territory, had kept himself
"entirely above party and company interests ; but notwith-
"standing what he has done, his mistakes and blunders to
"which we are all liable, I would still, on the whole, prefer
"**H. H.** Sibley to any other man who has yet been named to
"me as suitable to represent our territory in the national
"council. Perhaps we have a better man : if so I hope he
"will be found and elected ; but it should be borne in mind
"that those who are most earnest to obtain the office may not
"be best qualified to fill it.

"Let us endeavor to name a good man, and if we fail to
"elect him, we shall not be ashamed of what we attempted to
"do. Better to fail in a good cause than to succeed in a bad
"one. Truly yours. G. H. Pond."

Mr. Pond had reference to Governor Sibley during the
early summer of 1849 espousing the cause of the democracy,
when he said he "should have been better pleased if he had
kept himself entirely above party". While Governor Sibley
had previously been active in everything that could possibly
benefit the territory, his politics, to the mass of the people
previous to June 1849, were unknown ; hence the announcement that he believed in the democratic party of the day was
received with regret by several of us old whigs ; and yet we
had no reason to censure him ; only we were in hopes he was
a whig.

A conference was held by the friends of the different candidates, and when election-day came there were only two candidates in the field - Governor Sibley and Colonel Mitchell—
the former being re-elected. Whigs voted for Mr. Sibley
and democrats for Mr. Mitchell. There was no party contest
in the election. The people were well satisfied with the
result, and were glad the election was over.

A non-partisan election creates more strife and bad blood
than when strict party lines are observed. What added to
the excitement was the interest taken by the different houses
engaged in trading with the Indians. Colonel Mitchell, the

defeated candidate, was a gentleman of fine abilities, a native
of Ohio, and succeeded J. L. Taylor as U. S. marshal of the
territory—Mr. Taylor declining to retain that office after
the organization of the territory in 1849. Colonel Mitchell
commanded one of the Ohio regiments in Mexico, during the
war of the United States with that republic. The election
campaign was fortunately made in about three weeks, so there
was not time for any great demonstrations on either side,
and the bad blood engendered during the time soon passed
away, and a united people joined with heart and hand again
in earnestly laboring for the development of the agricultural,
horticultural, manufacturing, and commercial resources of the
territory.

A DISTINGUISHED VISITOR.

Minnesota was honored, during the early autumn of this
year, with a visit from Miss Fredrika Bremer, the world-wide
known Swedish authoress. In those colonial times, when
the country was mostly occupied by the red men, the Indian
summers (so called) were splendid. Miss Bremer was charmed
with the one that year. On one of those choice days she visited the site which now includes the city of Minneapolis proper,
when the foliage of the trees, in their beautiful autumnal
tints, the forests brilliant in their mantles of crimson and
gold, glowed in the autumn sunlight. She was enthusiastic in
regard to the picturesque scenery on the west bank of the
falls, declaring it was the most lovely wilderness she ever
saw. Such scenery, after the first frosts, when the leaves of
the native trees seem all ablaze with celestial flame, so new to
visitors, is a familiar, annually-recurring sight and source of
delight to every resident of this state.

Little did Miss Bremer think that in a little more than one
generation the site of that unbroken wilderness that so charmed
her would contain within its limits the sixth-greatest population of her Scandinavian people in any city in the known
world ! Miss Bremer was perhaps among the first of her
countrywomen who visited us; and it would seem that she has
been a guardian-angel to her people in the city, for they have
prospered in the new land of their adoption.

CHAPTER XVI.

The improvements made in St. Anthony during the summer and fall of 1850 were satisfactory, though not as extensive as anticipated in the spring. Anson Northrup finished in June the erection of the St. Charles hotel, and for the times it was a large house, but not too commodious for the wants of the traveling public.

ARRIVALS IN 1849.

The village had been fortunate the year previous — that of 1849 by the addition to its numbers of such men and their families as John W. North, Dr. John H. Murphy, Reuben Bean, Judge Bradley B. Meeker, Dr. Ira Kingsley, Elijah Moulton, Charles Kingsley, James McMullen, Joseph M. Marshall, John Jackins, William P. Day, Silas and Isaac Lane, Francis Huot, L. Bostwick, Owen McCarty, Moses W. Getchell, Isaac Gilpatrick, J. G. Spence, Lewis Stone, Rufus Farnham, senior, Rufus Farnham, junior, Albert Dorr, William Worthingham, Elmer Tyler, L. N. Parker (who hauled the lumber from St. Croix for Governor Marshall's store), William Richardson, Eli F. Lewis, Charles A. Brown, A. J. Foster, Charles T. Stearns, Stephen Pratt, William W. Getchell, Isaac Ives Lewis, J. Q. A. Nickerson, Ira Burroughs, Samuel Fernald, William H. Welch, F. X. Creapeau, N. Beauteau, John Bean, and Amos Bean: all far above the average in regard to merit and enterprise ; and those who settled in St. Anthony in 1850 were men of equal merit ; citizens who would be an honor to any part of the Union.

ARRIVALS IN ST. ANTHONY IN 1850.

The following is a pretty full list of persons who arrived in 1850 : Judge Isaac Atwater, Edward Murphy, John Wensinger, Allen Harmon, C. F. Harmon, John S. Mann, Charles W. Christmas, William Harmon, Stephen E. Foster, George T. Vail, A. R. Young, E. A. Harmon, Justus H. Moulton, Charles Miles, Colonel William Smith, Judge Joel B. Bassett, Rufus S. Pratt, William Finch, Chandler Harmon, Reuben B. Gibson, Simon Bean, Chris. C. Gavey, Joseph Le Duc, William Stevens, G. G. Loomis, Joseph P. Wilson, Ezra Hanscomb, A. C. Murphy, R. P. Upton, Thomas Warwick, Eben How, Stephen Cobb, Joseph Dean, Peter Poncin, Thomas Chambers, Horace Webster, Henry Chambers, Geo. W. Chowen, W. W. Wales, Warren Bristol, William L. Larned, Simon Stevens, Captain Benjamin B. Parker, Waterman Stinson, Charles Gilpatrick, Hon. Baldwin Brown, John Hinkston, Charles Mansuer, William Smiley, and G. W. Tew.

SOME OF THE FIRST PASTORS.

Rev. Enos Stephens and Rev. C. W. Newcomb of the Methodist church, and Rev. W. P. Brown of the Baptist church, administered with much acceptability to the wants of the people in a spiritual way. Mr. Newcomb was a particular favorite. He subsequently became a colonel in the army, a member of congress for several terms, and then U. S. marshal for Missouri.

Mrs. Worthingham, wife of Wm. Worthingham, introduced into her grounds beautiful ornamental shrubbery and flowers. That excellent lady, long since deceased, was the pioneer at the falls in making her home beautiful, attractive and pleasant with choice flowering plants, shade and ornamental trees and shrubbery.

EDUCATIONAL.

The public schools, first inaugurated by Miss Electa Backus, were never more prosperous than during this season. The scholars came from the four corners of the globe, nearly all nations being represented. They rapidly fell into the manners, and readily observed the rules, the art, and the ways in which western schools were conducted. Those from foreign

lands vied with the native-born from the different states of
the Union in learning that which would be useful to them
through life.

It could hardly be expected that boys and girls brought
together for the first time, whose nationalities were so varied,
would make as rapid progress in mastering their books and
studies as in an old-settled school-district where pupils had
been acquainted with each other almost from the time they
left the cradle ; but a few weeks sufficed for an acquaintance
and, strangers as they were, in a month they became happy
members of the same school : but it was laborious for the
teachers, at the commencement of the school-term, to properly
manage their pupils.

St. Anthony was fortunate in the early days in securing
such educators as Professor Merrill and his associates.

LEGISLATIVE.

There was some little excitement at the fall election for
members of the legislature, but John W. North and Edward
Patch were returned to the house of representatives. Both
members were elected as democrats, though Mr. North was
generally known as a free-soiler or anti-slavery man ; but
both gentlemen were supported by those who were known as
anti-monopolists. At the election held the year before W. R.
Marshall and William Dugas were elected to the house, and
John Rollins to the council. Captain Rollins held his seat
for two years. Citizens at the falls are greatly indebted to
Governor Marshall for his services in securing the seat of the
university in their midst. He was at that time a prominent
citizen here and, in company with his brother Joseph M.
Marshall, now of Colorado, had a general-store. For valuable
services in both an official and a private capacity St. Anthony
cannot be too grateful to Governor Marshall. He was married in 1854 to Miss Abby Langford, a daughter of a prominent citizen of Utica, New York. He has resided in St. Paul
since 1852.

GEOLOGICAL SURVEY.

Among the interesting events of the previous year was the
arrival of Dr. David Dale Owen and Dr. Norwood who,

under the auspices of the United States government, made a
very thorough geological survey of the immediate vicinity of
the falls. They camped on the west bank of the river for
more than a week. About the same time General Pope, then
lieutenant in the topographical corps of engineers, took the
latitude and longitude of the falls. The former is near 45
degrees north. All of these distinguished men were favorably
impressed with the great possibilities of the future in regard
to the water-power. They agreed that when the water was
controlled by the proper improvements, that a large industrial city would exist in the neighborhood. General Pope
acted upon this belief by purchasing, through a second party,
several lots in St. Anthony.

THE LUMBER TRADE.

Large preparations were made during the summer and early
fall for lumber operations during the winter in the Rum river
pineries. Owing to the bad-faith of Hole-in-the-day, the
Chippewa chief, logging which had been prosecuted the previous winter by Joseph R. Brown on one of the tributaries of
the upper Mississippi, was abandoned, and the cut necessary
for the consumption of the mills was confined exclusively to
the pine on the two forks of Rum river. In addition to the
logs required at the falls others were in demand for a steam-
sawmill that had been projected at St. Paul by the fur company. This encouraged the lumbermen who had mostly left
that business in Maine and emigrated to this new region, to
re-embark in the same enterprise. They observed the same
rules and habits here, in regard to that industry that were
practiced in the east. As they had served an apprenticeship
to the lumber business, their experience gave them great
advantage over western men, who in some instances attempted
to cut logs in the Rum river pineries. The former frequently
made money ; the latter seldom, if ever.

VISITORS AND IMMIGRANTS.

During the beautiful autumn weather there were numbers
of visitors to the falls. Many were from the lower country ;
others from St. Paul, Stillwater, and Fort Snelling. Among

those who spent several weeks with us was Miss Harriet E.
Bishop of St. Paul. This lady, a native of Vermont, was one
of the pioneer school-teachers in the territory. She accompanied Governor Slade, a noted philanthropist of that day,
with several other teachers from her native state, to the west,
for the purpose of teaching, and improving the moral condition of the people. Only three of those ladies reached this
territory ; the others were distributed at different places east
of us where their valuable aid was more necessary than here ;
for the reason that there were scarcely enough children in the
whole territory, in convenient school-districts, to warrant the
services of more than three teachers. The country was
sparsely settled at best, and more than half the settlers were
bachelors, or recently married persons who did not have
children old enough to attend school. This was before the
immigration of those who had large families.

MANNER OF COLONIZING.

In subsequent years, so rapidly did the country settle up,
it was not an uncommon event for settlers, with a number of
boys and girls, to occupy every quarter section of land in a
township, and three or four school-districts would be organized, and rude school-houses would be built and occupied by
teachers and pupils where, the year before, there was not a
farm opened for many miles from them.

In some instances a colony was made up in the east ; an
advance member of it was sent to examine the country and
select a favorable portion of it for the colony which would
follow on advices received from him, bringing with them not
only a teacher for their school, but their minister of the
gospel. A colony from Angelica, N. Y., came out in this
way. They arrived in June, in time to secure sufficient hay
for their stock which they brought with them. They lived
during the time in their prairie-schooners, which were covered with canvas in such manner as to protect the inmates
from the rain. After securing their hay, and starting the
prairie-plows, they all joined hands and helped one another ;
put up a good log or frame house on every claim, and then
built their school-house at some convenient point, and started

a church-building. In a few weeks they were comfortably
settled, the school was in operation, their preacher occupied
the pulpit, and a singing-school and lyceum was organized.
The young men went home with the girls after these gatherings ; everything just as stable and as permanent as if they
had lived on their farms for years, instead of only months.
This could hardly have occurred without the aid of the old
preemption law, which gave the settler a year after settlement
to pay for his land, and confined him to a quarter section.
The wise provisions of this law caused nearly every quarter
section of land to be owned by an actual occupant, and that
is the reason that the state became so thickly inhabited.

THE PIONEER SCHOOL-TEACHER.

•Miss Harriet E. Bishop accomplished a good work in Minnesota. No lady here was more widely known and respected.
Her marriage, which occurred late in life, was not a happy
one. She died in St. Paul several years since. Her memory
will ever be cherished by those who had the pleasure of her
acquaintance.

A VISITOR'S OPINION OF THE FALLS.

Dr. Ashmead, a noted physician of Philadelphia, spent
several days in making a geological survey at the falls. He
expressed a fear that, at some future day, the falls would
recede to such an extent as to seriously injure the water-
power, unless measures were taken to protect them. He said
the ingenuity of man could readily devise such protection in
a manner that would be permanent.

BUFFALO-HUNTING.

On the 14th of November two British officers of high rank
in the Queen's Guards, noblemen, arrived from an extended
buffalo-hunt on the northern plains. Their names were
Wooley and Coke. They had been successful in the chase,
and were highly delighted with the appearance of the falls.
Colonel Wooley thought the prairies west of the big woods
would rival the steppes of Russia in the production of wheat.

CHAPTER XVII.

As the time approached for the meeting of the legislature of the territory, much interest was manifested in regard to its organization. By law the session was to be opened on Wednesday, January 1st, 1851. As there was no politics in the choice of delegates, so there were scarcely any principles involved, only personal preferences, in the election of officers of the legislature. The choice of a public printer seemed the most important. After an exciting contest James M. Goodhue was elected to that office.

On the 20th of January I was surprised by a visit at my home from a committee of whig members of the council and house, requesting me to proceed at once to Washington and co-operate with Hon. H. H. Sibley, the territorial delegate in congress, in matters in which they were interested. Reluctantly I consented to make the journey. Receiving from Governor Ramsey and others letters of introduction to the President and members of the Cabinet, I made preparations for the tedious journey. There were no stages in this part of the country at that time. At Mendota I hired a French-Canadian voyageur by the name of St. Martin, who had a good horse and train, to convey me down the Mississippi on the ice as far as Prairie du Chien, where I could meet a line of stages for Galena. With plenty of blankets and robes we left Fort Snelling on the 22d, the mercury nearly forty degrees below zero.

A winter journey down the river on the ice, at that day, through an almost unbroken wilderness, was not a pleasant one. We endeavored to make each day's journey to a wood-choppers' camp, or a settlement, but in this we were not always successful, and sometimes had to camp out. The voyageur was thoroughly acquainted with the route, having for many years traveled over it for the fur company. He claimed to know where air-holes in the ice were liable to be and, in most instances, he drove around them; but twice during this trip he drove into one.

Everyone who passed over the route expected to drive into these open-places several times. All went prepared. The preparation was simple; it consisted of a rope with a noose at one end which was constantly around the horse's neck, the other end being attached to the train. When a horse fell into an air-hole the rope was drawn tightly, which would choke and inflate the animal and cause it to rise like a cork. As the air-holes were generally small, it was seldom that the train went into them. The harness was attached to the horse in such a way that it could be quickly removed.

The first night brought us to Point Douglas, where we found comfortable quarters. In passing Grey Cloud island we saw one of the primitive farms of Minnesota, that of Hazen Moore and Andrew Robertson, who had in 1839 fifty acres under cultivation. A little further down the river, where Hastings now is, Joseph R. Brown had in 1831 a field of twenty-five acres of wheat, which was the first crop of wheat raised in Minnesota.

Speaking of early farming in the territory, it may be well to state here that Joseph Haskell and J. S. Norris commenced farming back of Grey Cloud as early as 1839, and Major Brown opened a farm at Traverse, near the head of Red river, and raised a fine crop of wheat in 1836. He was also the pioneer in raising tame grasses, having introduced timothy on his farm as early as 1831.

Leaving Point Douglas at daylight the next morning, we made Red Wing a resting-place, and were entertained by John Bush, the Indian farmer for Wacouta's band. Mr.

Bush came to Fort Snelling in 1825. He has resided at St. Peter since 1864, and is the oldest white resident in the state. The ride down Lake Pepin on the smooth ice was the least disagreeable part of the journey. We remained over night at James Wells' (long an Indian trader) where we had for a room-mate my friend Good Road, chief of the Oak Grove band of Dakotas. He was visiting his relatives on the banks of the lake. Mr. Wells had long been a resident of Minnesota. His wife was the daughter of another trader, Duncan Graham. Mr. Wells represented the lower country in the territorial legislature. He was killed by the Indians in the massacre at Red Wood, in August, 1862.

The next place that offered comfortable quarters was at Bunnell's, on the bank of the river. Mr. Bunnell was an early resident, and furnished wood to the steamboats.

There were a few cabins where Winona stands to-day. At La Crosse there was a good hotel. From there to Prairie du Chien we got along very well. Here I took the stage for Galena, where I was joined by others and took the familiar stage for Chicago. Ours was a jolly party, fully determined not to complain at whatever might happen. Cold coffee, hard brown-bread, scorched bacon, scant straw on the floor of the coach, too few blankets and robes, slow progress, capsizes, cold stopping-places, uncomfortable seats at the dinner-tables, and poor horses ; such trifles were made the best of, and we were thankful to escape broken limbs, frost-marks, and serious bruises.

Upon reaching Chicago the party put aside their heavy furs, and took the Michigan Central railroad for Detroit, from there to make a long and tedious stage-ride through Canada ; thence from Niagara to New York by rail was a luxury to western men. I was just fourteen days from Fort Snelling to New York, which was considered remarkably rapid transit.

At Lovejoy's hotel in New York (which was headquarters for most western men) I met Simeon P. Folsom of St. Paul, also en route for Washington, to which place we proceeded.

Arriving after dark at the city of magnificent distances, we put up at the United States hotel, and immediately called upon Mr. Sibley who, with his wife, was living near the hotel with the family of Senator Foote of Mississippi. Mr. Sibley made an appointment with us to call the next day on the Secretary of State, Hon. Daniel Webster. At the breakfast-table next morning we had for neighbors Howell Cobb, of Georgia, who was speaker of the house of representatives, Alexander Stephens, and Robert Toombs, members of congress from the same state, David Wilmott, member of congress from Pennsylvania, and others whose names were known all over the country. Mr. Folsom and myself became somewhat acquainted with these men whose names are here mentioned, some of whom became prominent in the so-called confederate states.

Minnesota in those days was looked upon by many members of congress as a howling wilderness, which would always be the home of Indians, wild fowls, and wild beasts. Mr. Sibley, Governor Ramsey, David Cooper, Henry M. Rice, and Franklin Steele had succeeded to some extent in counteracting those false impressions, and substituting correct ideas in their place.

AN INTERVIEW WITH DANIEL WEBSTER.

At the appointed hour, 11 o'clock A. M., Mr. Sibley called at the hotel for Mr. Folsom and myself to accompany him to the office of the Secretary of State. Arriving at the ante-room, we found it full of senators and representatives awaiting an interview with the Secretary. Mr. Sibley introduced us to many of them and to the president of the senate. In the meantime he had sent his name to the Secretary. Soon a colored boy came from the private office and in a loud voice announced "Mr. Sibley, delegate in congress from Minnesota". Asking Mr. Folsom and myself to follow him, Mr. Sibley led the way, and passing through the door, we stood in the presence of the "Great Expounder of the Constitution". Mr. Webster arose from his seat behind a long table, cordially shook hands with Mr. Sibley, and turned his face upon Mr. Folsom and myself. His very looks struck us with awe. Those deep black eyes seemed to penetrate us in such a manner as to cause us to be almost speechless. Mr. Sibley immediately introduced us. "Folsom, Stevens," he said, "these are New-England names." Mr. Folsom replied that his father was born in New Hampshire. I added that my father and mother were natives of Vermont. "Oh!" he replied, "I thought so." He spoke of Captain Stevens, who had taken a prominent part in the King Philip war, and after rendering a tribute to the Pilgrim Fathers, asked Mr. Sibley if Minnesota was really to be the New England of the west. Mr. Sibley replied that the territory had all the characteristics of New England, but the soil and climate were superior to it. "Well, then," said Mr. Webster, "it is proper that it should be settled by New England people." I then handed him my letters of introduction. The one from Governor Ramsey seemed to please him most. He said he was much pleased to hear from him. He had thought that transferring his home from the fertile fields of Pennsylvania to the northwest would be distasteful to him.

By this time my embarrassment had worn away. Mr. Webster asked what he could do for us. We informed him of the object of our visit, in behalf of the whig members of the legislature of the territory. He listened attentively while I made the statement. Without a moment's hesitation he replied, "Your request shall be granted." Among the papers that I presented was one recommending Joseph W. Furber for the vacant United States marshalship for the territory. "Why," he said, "here is another New England name." I replied that Mr. Furber was a native of New Hampshire. Mr. Webster said that Mr. Furber's name would be sent to the senate the next day for confirmation. When we had finished our business with him and were about to leave, he added, "Please remember me kindly to Governor Ramsey, and convey to the gentlemen whose signatures are attached to this paper (holding up a paper I had given him) the assurance that there will not be, at least at present, any change made in the Federal appointments in your territory."

STATESMEN OF FORTY YEARS AGO.

We called upon Mr. Charles Conrad, of Louisiana, Secretary of War, in regard to the sutlership at Fort Snelling, and left with the satisfaction of knowing that there would be no change of sutler at the fort.

Having matters to lay before Mr. Thomas Corwin, Secretary

of the Treasury, Mr. Stewart, Secretary of the Interior, and
the Attorney-General, all of which business was transacted in
the most satisfactory manner, we awaited further advices from
St. Paul, remaining in Washington several weeks.

We heard Henry Clay, Stephen A. Douglas, Gen. Sam Houston and Gen. Rusk of Texas, Bell of Tennessee, Mangum of
North Carolina, Butler of South Carolina, Benton of Mo., and
other great men, speak in the Senate ; and Robt. Toombs, Alexander Stephens, Howell Cobb of Georgia, David Wilmott of
of Pennsylvania, and several other able men in the House,
including our own delegate, Mr. Sibley.

During my stay in Washington Mr. Clay's compromise
measures in relation to slavery, were under discussion in both
houses.   In matters pertaining to our mission, much aid and
encouragement were given by the venerable senator from Wisconsin, General Henry Dodge, and Hon. O. Cole, member of
congress from the same state.

Mr. Folsom and I have always considered it one of the
happiest events of our lives that we were enabled to see and
become partially acquainted with many of these great statesmen who participated in the stirring events caused by the
slavery agitation of nearly forty years ago.

By the 25th of February our business was finished and we
returned to New York, where I purchased goods for the
sutler's store at Fort Snelling, and for a store to be opened in
St. Anthony.   These goods had to be shipped by sea to New
Orleans, and thence up the Mississippi by steamboat to Fort
Snelling.   It required at least sixty days for their transportation from New York to Fort Snelling.   I do not know that
the cost of transportation was much higher then than now.

HOMEWARD.

The journey home was attended with many difficulties.   I
left New-York on the 10th of March and arrived in Minneapolis on the 4th of April, making just twenty-four days on
the road.   The lakes were blocked with ice, the roads were
almost impassable, and a flood had swept the bridges away.
Some part of the journey was made on horseback, other portions on foot, or in a lumber-wagon.

At Galena I purchased for the whigs of Minnesota an entire outfit for a printing-office, to be shipped on the first steamer from that place. The good old Minnesotian, a paper of rare merit, was afterwards printed with this material, by John P. Owens, John C. Terry, and George W. Moore.

Calculating that I could reach home in a week by land, via Judge Wyman Knowlton's new route from Prairie du Chien to St. Paul, I took the stage at Galena for the former place, arriving there in time to take the weekly one-horse turn-out that carried the mail through the woods by way of Bad-Axe, Springville, Black River Falls, Clearwater (now Eau Clare), Knapp's Mills, River Falls and Hudson, to St. Paul. This journey was attended with more difficulty than any I ever made. At Beef river, about 10 o'clock at night, we were overtaken by the severest thunder-storm I ever experienced. It rained and hailed and rained again until the whole country was flooded. There were no houses or cabins for miles. My hat was almost destroyed by the hail. We fortunately got the horses under a big pine tree, the branches of which prevented them from being killed by the dreadful hail. After shivering all night we got an early start in the morning, and just after daylight ran into a drove of some thirty or forty elk. They seemed to have been so frightened by the storm as to flee to us for protection. The guns in the party were so drenched by the rain as to be useless. The elk followed us for a time and then disappeared. They were so tame we thought they might have escaped from a park belonging to a hermit whose cabin was between the head of Beef river and Black river. The remainder of the journey was attended with more comfort, but I was much chagrined on waking up the next morning after my arrival home to learn from a passenger that a steamboat had arrived at St. Paul during the night. The boat had only left Galena three days previous, and I had been so long on the way.

CHAPTER XVIII

On my return to what is now Minneapolis, I found that during the winter great preparations had been made for building in St. Anthony. Not to be behind in the good work, Mr. Steele and myself determined to erect a small block, the lower part to consist of three stores, the second-story to be for offices, and the upper part to be for a hall. We secured the services of Joseph Dean, to superintend the work. William Worthingham and A. N. Hoyt completed the masonry, and by August the block was finished and occupied entire.

THE FIRST WHITE CHILD BORN IN WHAT IS NOW MINNEAPOLIS.

Meantime an event occurred of great moment to me and mine, and of some historical importance to others. The morning of the 30th of April, 1851, was the coldest for the time of the year ever known in the country. The wind was blowing from the north like a hurricane. The air was full of snow. The river was bank-full, and the waves were high. It was deemed almost impossible to cross the river, either in a batteau, skiff, or canoe. It was necessary that I should have communication with St. Anthony, for the services of Dr. Murphy, who resided there, were required in my family. The aid of three as good boatmen as ever swung an oar, with Captain Tapper at their head, was secured. The question was anxiously discussed, " Can any water-craft at our command withstand the fierce wind, high waves, and swift current ?" Captain Tapper thought our large batteau would weather the storm.

but we were short of hands. Fortunately Rev. C. A. Newcomb, of the Methodist church on the east side, joined us.
He had remained over night with my only neighbor, Calvin
A. Tuttle, who had moved into the old government dwelling-
house, near the present site of the Palisade mill, only two
days before. The water-craft was towed up the river in the
face of the wind to a point above Nicollet island in order to
make the landing on the east side above that island. With
much difficulty and some danger the crossing was made and
they safely returned with Dr. Murphy. About noon on that
bleak, cold, eventful day, my first child, and the first-born
white child on the west bank at the falls, a little girl-baby,
was added to my happy household. The little one was called
Mary, a favorite name in the family. She lived to bloom
into beautiful womanhood. At the age of sixteen she gently
crossed the river of life, and we tenderly laid her loved form
to rest, and it quietly sleeps in Lakewood. The sun has never
shone so brightly in our household since her departure.

FIRST BOY BORN ON THE WEST SIDE.

Another interesting event, of like character, occurred on
this side of the river, in the family of my new and only
neighbor, Mr. Tuttle, just one week after the birth of my
little daughter. A boy-baby made his appearance there.
He too, just as he reached vigorous manhood, crossed the
silent river from which there is no return. He was the second
white child born at the west bank of the falls. Up to this
time there had been two births in the two families on the west
side. There had been one death, that of an infant, in the
family of Mr. Bean who resided for a short time in the old
government mill in the spring of 1850.

Mr. Newcomb, mentioned above, went to Missouri, became
a colonel in the Union army during the civil war, represented
his adopted state in congress, and was also U. S. marshal of
Missouri.

Our mail on this side of the river came to Fort Snelling ;
that for the east side came to St. Paul. Mr. Sibley succeeded
in getting a postoffice established in St. Anthony, Ard Godfrey appointed postmaster, with Joseph McAlpine as deputy,

and a weekly mail service from St. Paul. The people were then very well satisfied with their mail facilities.

INDUSTRIES ON THE EAST SIDE.

In the spring of 1851 Alvaren Allen, from Whitewater, Wisconsin, arrived with a few horses and carriages, which he was constantly solicited to loan at good prices, and almost unconsciously he found himself in the livery-stable and stage business on the east side.

Charles T. Stearns, a native of the Berkshire hills in the old Bay state, came down from Fort Gaines, where he had been employed in the construction of that fortress, and in company with Charles Manseur, just from the lower country, started a cabinet manufactory. Immigration was pouring in, and household furniture was in demand. In the absence of seasoned lumber the material used was frequently just as it ran through the saws, full of sap and soaked in river water.

Among the industries started which were the nucleus of the present mammoth manufacturing establishments of the present day, was a carriage-factory by George F. Brott, who came from New York to introduce fancy sleighs in this part of the country. Mr. Brott was successful in business, became a politician and made free-soil speeches, a land-agent and located town-sites, built mills, was sheriff of Ramsey county, married the daughter of Charles T. Stearns, emigrated to New Orleans, became a princely merchant, and is now a resident of Washington. Mr. Brott is a rustler in everything he undertakes.

Two blacksmith-shops were established this year, and A. M. Macfarland from New Brunswick opened a shoe-store. Mr. William Spooner from Sherbrooke, Canada, opened a harness and saddle business. Being an experienced workman of industrious habits, he soon built up a good trade. Mr. Spooner became a real-estate dealer. Very few of his acquaintances in after years knew he was the first harness-maker at the Falls of St. Anthony.

There was a great fascination about the real-estate business Men of almost every trade, to which they had served an apprenticeship, abandoned their business to engage in buy-

ing and selling real-estate. The crisis of 1857 financially
ruined many of them. If they had remained in their former
business they would not probably have been seriously affected.

THE ST. ANTHONY EXPRESS.

Elmer Tyler had come to St. Anthony from Chicago and
opened a merchant-tailoring establishment. Having considerable capital, he speculated in town-lots. On the 31st of
May, 1851, he introduced to the public the St. Anthony
Express, an eight-column folio weekly newspaper, neatly
printed with new material purchased in Chicago. Isaac
Atwater, who came to St. Anthony from New York City the
previous October, was the editor. While in Chicago Mr.
Tyler engaged the services of Mr. H. Woodbury and brother,
two as good practical printers as could be found in that city,
to take charge of the mechanical department of the office.
The result was that the paper had a metropolitan appearance
from its first issue. When we consider that at that time St.
Anthony had not to exceed a population of two hundred and
fifty souls, and at least one hundred of that number were
lumbermen employed in the woods a good portion of the
year, it must be admitted that Mr. Tyler had a good deal of
moral courage to undertake such a hazardous enterprise.
Aside from this, St. Anthony belonged to Ramsey county,
and in St. Paul there were several papers already in existence.
Mr. Atwater's able pen, with the aid of that of Shelton Hollister, just from Yale, made the Express second in influence
to no paper west of Chicago. The patronage of the town
placed it on a paying basis from the start. In those days
Judge Atwater was a whig, and the Express was a whig sheet,
and a strong supporter of the Fillmore administration. The
paper continued to be issued by different proprietors, managers and editors, until the spring of 1861, when it was discontinued, and the material sold and distributed among different newspaper offices in the state.

The village now had representatives of most of the trades.
Mr. Henry Fowler, with a large family, from one of the pro-
vincial cities in England, opened a clock and watchmaker's
establishment.

At this early date the village had four good lawyers, Messrs. E. S. Hall, John W. North, Isaac Atwater, and David A. Secombe ; three doctors, John H. Murphy, Ira Kingsley, and H. Fletcher. These were all the professional men, aside from the ministers, at that time ; but they kept coming right alon:

FIRST CHURCHES.

In 1849 Father Ravoux commenced the erection of a frame church-building in the upper town. In the spring of 1851 Rev. Mr. Ledow was stationed in St. Anthony. He was the first resident Catholic missionary in the village, though Rev. Mr. Galtier and Father Ravoux had, previous to that time, held services in private houses. A Methodist church was organized at the east-side residence of C. A. Tuttle in 1849, by Rev. Enos Stephens of Wisconsin. Rev. C. A. Newcomb was the resident pastor in the spring of 1851.

Rev. E. D. Neill of St. Paul preached under the auspices of the Presbytertan missionary society occasionally during 1849 and early in 1850, and in July, 1850, Rev. William T. Wheeler, formerly a Congregational minister to Africa, commenced preaching, but was succeeded in 1851 by Rev. Charles Secombe as pastor. This was the first Congregational church organized in Minnesota. A Baptist church had been organized June 24, 1850, by Rev. J. P. Parsons, formerly of the lead mines near Galena. Rev. W. C. Brown was the first pastor, and occupied the pulpit in 1851. In June of this year Rev. C. G. Ames was sent out from New England as a missionary. He belonged to the Free-will Baptist church. A church was organized October 25th following Mr. Ames's advent. The first services under the auspices of the Episcopal church were held by Dr. Gear as early as 1849, but from July, 1850, Rev. Timothy Wilcoxson held occasional services until October 1 1852, when Rev. J. S. Chamberlain was assigned to duty. It will be seen that the different denominations of Christians had a pretty full representation at this early day.

STATE UNIVERSITY.

On the same day that the Express made its appearance, May 31, an event occurred in St. Anthony of great interest to the people of the territory. It was the organization of the board of regents of the University of Minnesota ; the beginning of the magnificent seat of learning which every Minnesotian is so proud of to-day. The charter had been granted at the previous legislature. In the distribution of the public buildings by that body St. Paul was to have the capitol, Stillwater the penitentiary, and St. Anthony the university. The university had been granted several thousand acres of land by congress. William R. Marshall has always asserted that St. Anthony got the best of the bargain. The organization of the board was as follows : Franklin Steele, president ; John W. North, treasurer ; Isaac Atwater, secretary ; and William R. Marshall, librarian. The original members of the board selected by the legislature contained such well-known men as Henry H. Sibley, Henry M. Rice, Alexander Ramsey, B. B. Meeker, Isaac Atwater, William R. Marshall, C. K. Smith, Franklin Steele, and A. Van Vorhees, with John W. North as their attorney.

STAGES, BOATS AND CARS.

A much-needed service to the traveling public was supplied early this spring by the establishment of a four-horse stage-line between St. Paul and St. Anthony, by two young men by the name of Patterson and Benson. They ran a Concord-coach between those points, going and returning once in the forenoon, and going and returning once in the afternoon. The price charged was half a dollar each way. I do not see how any one could possibly have foretold at that time that in a little more than a generation there would be four or five railroad companies running half-hourly trains between Minneapolis and St. Paul, and other railroad trains several times a day, all full of passengers, and the traveling public demanding more facilities. Such a thing as a railroad was not thought of ; but after several boats had landed in lower Minneapolis, the question whether the future head of navigation on the Mississippi would be at St. Paul or at the Falls of St. Anthony was a live issue in those days. The importance of the navigation of the river between those two places at that time was considered so essential that in discussing the matter the usually conservative pen of Judge Atwater became quite radical. The new paper declared that when it was once settled, as it soon would be, that St. Anthony Falls is the real head of navigation on the Mississippi river, St. Paul would retrograde to a modest village. A line of boats did establish the fact that they could run to the Falls, but the result was not so beneficial as every one expected. John G. Lennon erected a commodious warehouse at the lower landing on the east side. Others built another at Murphy's landing on the west side ; but both investments were unremunerative. Undoubtedly had navigation been considered a necessity, boats would long since have landed at St. Anthony as often as at St. Paul, but when E. F. Drake, in the early sixties, built for the St. Paul and Pacific a railroad between the two points, and other roads followed, navigation between the two points ceased to be necessary ; and now a great many think it would not prove beneficial.

TELEGRAPHIC.

A strong attempt was made in early summer to raise enough money by subscription to build a telegraph-line from the Falls to Galena. W. Chute of the last-named place canvassed all the towns between the two points and only succeeded in getting about $16,000 subscribed. As it would require almost as much again the enterprise was abandoned. In 1860, nine years afterwards, Mr. Winslow pushed the line to completion.

THE FIRST MANUFACTURES.

Up to this time there had, with few exceptions, been only lumber manufactured at the Falls. James McMullen, who came here in 1849, during the following winter made numerous sleds and sleighs, for which he found ready sale. He may be properly classed as the first, outside of the mill company, to engage in manufacturing at the Falls.

CHAPTER XIX.

Except in the immediate vicinity of the Falls, in early summer, the roar of the cataract fell upon a pathless prairie for everything but the Indian and the wild game he pursued, but every boat that landed at St. Paul brought those who became permanent settlers of St. Anthony and its vicinity. The Express said that it required "no very sagacious observer of the change that is taking place to predict the future of the place. The important position which St. Anthony occupies must inevitably make her the great manufacturing and commercial town of the northwest."

THE SCALPING RED-SKINS.

In our efforts to encourage immigrants who were seeking lands to settle upon for farming purposes, to locate above the Falls, we occasionally received a set-back in consequence of Indian disturbances. Late this spring a war-party of Dakotas were after Chippewa scalps on Swan river. They found one of their foes who had a keg of whisky. Bloodthirsty as they were, they cared more for the whisky than for the scalp of the Chippewa, for while they ceased hostilities long enough to take a drink, the Chippewa escaped. By the time the contents of the keg were disposed of the Dakotas were drunk. When in that condition a white man's scalp is as valuable to them as that of a Chippewa ; hence they attacked a party of teamsters on the road from St. Paul with military stores for Fort Gaines, and killed a worthy man named Andrew Swartz.

Such occurrences prevented the occupation of the really good farming lands above the Falls.

In the first settlement on Coon creek, just above St. Anthony, the Indians killed such domestic cattle as they could find belonging to the whites, which discouraged the settlers.

The first military duty in the field by Lieutenant R. W. Johnson, after his arrival at Fort Snelling in 1849, was to remove a band of pilfering Indians who were engaged in killing cattle belonging ·to settlers above the Falls. His headquarters while engaged in this duty, were at the junction of Rum river with the Mississippi—now the flourishing city of Anoka. What made· it more discouraging was that the mauraders were seldom punished. Those who murdered Swartz escaped from the military authorities at Fort Ripley and were never recaptured.

A year later some Dakota Indians met a party of German immigrants above Mendota and shot one of them, Mrs. Keener, killing her instantly. In· this instance the Indians were punished in the most thorough manner. They were compelled by the government forces to surrender the murderer, Yu-ha-zee, who was tried, convicted, and hung in St. Paul, but not until a year after his conviction by the court.

IMMIGRATION, STAGES AND NAVIGATION.

As the season advanced immigration increased. Messrs. Amherst Willoughby and Simon Powers of St. Paul had established a two-horse stage and express, which made daily trips to the different towns immediately connected with St. Paul, but the volume of travel so increased that these enterprising gentlemen stocked their route with good horses, and Concord coaches imported from the factory in New Hampshire. Messrs. Willoughby & Power's line of coaches to St. Anthony was called the red line because it was painted red, Messrs. Patterson & Benson's line was known as the yellow line because the coaches were painted yellow. The rivalry between the two lines became intense, though neither offered to reduce the rates of fare.

While St. Anthony was unable to secure navigation between St. Paul and the Falls, yet through the energy of John

Rollins the river above the Falls was made an important use of in the running of steamboats to Sauk Rapids. Captain Rollins was a native of New Sharon, Maine, and was born in 1806. Before coming to Minnesota he was engaged as lumberman, and was at one time a member of the legislature of his native state. In 1848 he visited the Falls of St. Anthony, and was so pleased with the country that he moved his family here in the spring of 1849. The same year he was elected a member of the territorial council. Having had considerable experience in the somewhat difficult navigation of the rivers in his native state, he became satisfied that navigation above the Falls could be made profitable with steamers of the same style as those used on the rivers in Maine. He determined to make the experiment, and gave orders for the building of a boat similar to those used on the Penobscot. The boiler, engine, and all iron-work, were made in Bangor, and when completed were shipped by sea to New Orleans and up the Mississippi to St. Paul. The hull and all wood work was made in the village, under the supervision of experienced ship-carpenters who came from Maine to superintend the work. It was found, when the steamer was finished, that it worked to perfection. He called it the Governor Ramsey, in honor of our first governor. The problem was solved so far as the navigation of the river above the Falls was concerned. He manned the steamer with experienced boatmen who had served an apprenticeship on similar water-craft in Maine. He sent there for them. Captain Benjamin B. Parker was the master. He soon built up a prosperous trade on the river, and from 1851 and for several years, the Governor Ramsey was well patronized by the business men of the upper river. In the meantime several other boats were built and became rivals of the Governor Ramsey.

UPPER MISSISSIPPI BOATS WITHDRAWN.

During the civil war there was a great demand for small, light-draft steamers to run on the tributaries and bayous of the lower Mississippi, to transport troops and munitions of war from the deep waters of the parent stream through the shallow streams leading into the interior of the country. All the steamers above the Falls were used for this purpose. They were moved on rollers by land around the cataract, launched in the river below it, and steamed toward the Gulf of Mexico never to return. Perhaps it was just as well, as the advent of railroads up the river about the time of the removal of the steamers down the stream would have made navigation of the upper waters unprofitable. Besides, the owners of the boats obtained a good price for their property.

A REPRESENTATIVE PIONEER.

Captain Rollins was one of our most enterprising men. I once made a long winter's journey with him, when a regent of the University of Minnesota, through the Mississippi pineries, in selecting pine lands for that institution. He was capable of enduring great fatigue, as I well know from personal observation, and was considered one of the best judges of pine lands in the state. He died universally respected and lamented, at his pleasant home in St. Anthony in 1885. There is no doubt but that the navigation of the upper Mississippi, in those early days, attracted more immigration to that locality than all other efforts. Stearns, Wright, Benton and Sherburne counties felt the influence to a very great extent. Farmers were willing to settle on lands that were in the vicinity of navigable waters.

The river was very high during the whole season of 1851. On June 26th of that year a great many of the logs in the mill-pond were swept over the dam, but fortunately enough remained to supply the mill, which was kept running to its full capacity for the whole year, and at the close of the season but little sawed lumber was left for the winter market. Much of the building material required for immediate use was kiln-dried, but more of it had to be used entirely green. The shrinkage, when made into buildings, was considerable, and created wide openings in the ceilings that admitted the cold. Otherwise the houses were good. Some of them are occupied to-day by the descendants of those who built them.

FIRST MERCHANTS AT THE FALLS.

As the season advanced the merchants of the village decided

to compete for a portion of the Red river trade. The annual caravan was expected about the middle of July. Heretofore this trade had been confined to Fort Snelling, St. Paul, and at an early day to Mendota. The first real live merchant in St. Anthony was R. P. Russell, who came to Fort Snelling in the fall of 1839. Nine years later he commenced commercial pursuits, and October 3 the same year married Miss Marian Patch, a daughter of Luther Patch, and a lady of great merit. Mr. Patch with his family had been a resident of the place for more than a year. Mr. Russell was not only the first merchant, but set an excellent example to the others who came afterwards and were bachelors by getting married.

William R. Marshall, in the spring of 1849, established the second store. Later that year John George Lennon, of the house of P. Choteau & Co., the head of the American Fur Company, opened the third store. The fourth store was established in May 1851 by Messrs. Steele & Stevens. The same year Mr. R. P. Upton succeeded Mr. Marshall. J. P. Wilson opened a store in the upper part of the town, and E. Case and his son S. W. Case, opened a grocery store opposite the St. Charles. These merchants tried to attract the attention of the Red river traders, and prevent them from trading exclusively with the merchants they had formerly dealt with. When the hundred or more carts made their appearance en route for St. Paul, inducements were presented to the principal traders in the caravan, with the result of a moderate exchange of goods for furs, pemmican and Indian curiosities. Still the lion's share went to St. Paul. Many of the merchants with the expedition bought their goods for cash, having sold their furs far down the valley of the Red river to the agents of the Hudson Bay Company, receiving for them English coin.

OUR FIRST GRIST-MILLS.

Up to this time but little grain had been raised in the territory; and for that matter, with the exception of vegetables, but little of anything else to eat. In 1850 a few farmers sowed wheat, and harvested an abundant yield; but there being no mills in the vicinity it had to be shipped, in order to realize money on it, to Messrs. Fentons' mill at Prairie du

Chien, which was the nearest mill (if we except the small one
on Boles' creek, with only one run of stones) to the Falls.
The Express, in speaking of our wants in this particular, said
there ought to be a large mill of the first class for grinding
grain put up at once. That paper was confident there would
be sufficient grain grown in this vicinity in 1851 and 1852 to
keep such a mill in full operation the year round. It added
that it was an absurd idea to send all our grain out of the
territory three or four hundred miles distant to be manufactured into flour or meal, when we have the most splendid
water power in the world, of unlimited extent. Although this
is now the greatest milling center in the world, the people in
this neighborhood had to wait for several years after 1851,
before there was a grist-mill at the Falls.

AN INDIAN TREATY.

We were all very much interested in the result of the great
Indian treaty held in the early summer of 1851, at Traverse
des Sioux. At that period most of those who had ever held
an office in the territory, or traded with the Indians, and
everyone who could get away from his home, went to Traverse to be present on the occasion. Twenty-one millions of
acres of the choicest agricultural lands in the northwest were
owned by the Indians. The whites wanted it, and the Indians
wanted to sell it. Governor Alexander Ramsey, and Hon.
Luke Lea, Commissioner of Indian Affairs at Washington,
represented the United States. The territory included all
the lands west of the Mississippi river from the Iowa line to
the boundaries of the Chippewa reservation, and so west
beyond the boundaries of Minnesota. The bargain was commenced on July 2d, and lasted until the 22d of that month
before it was completed. The Indians received a large sum
in gold at the signing of the treaty, and a large annuity
annually in cash, goods and provisions, for twenty years
afterwards. The government also paid all the debts they
owed to the Indian traders. The Indians spent their money
freely on their return from the treaty, making for a short
time a large circulation of gold in the business-circles of the
territory. This treaty was the most important event that had

ever transpired in Minnesota. Its good effects were visible at once. St. Paul, St. Anthony, and Stillwater were not the only portions of the country to be benefitted. New towns were to spring up. The town-sites upon which were Winona, Shakopee, Red Wing, Mankato, Rochester, and those of other well-known cities and villages that exist now, were to be occupied by the whites.

JUSTICES OF THE PEACE.

At this time the village had three justices of the peace— Dr. Ira Kingsley, Charles E. Leonard, and Lardner Bostwick. Justice Leonard represented the upper part of the village. It was seldom the justices had any business. Once in a while a small lawsuit was brought before them, which in most instances was caused by claim-jumping. People had not been in the country long enough to get in debt to any great extent, and if they had, they had a year in which to pay. The monthly collection of bills was then unknown. B. Cloutier had a bowling-alley and a saloon. Once in a while a dispute would arise between his customers, but it was settled by an adjournment to the bank of the river, where the parties would fight it out, shake hands after the battle, and that was the last of it. The courts were seldom called upon to punish such law-breakers.

Almost every state and nation was represented in the list of settlers, though nine out of ten of the lumbermen were from Maine, the others from the British provinces, with a few from the middle states. All in all, it would be very difficult to find a more orderly and law-abiding people. They had come to the Falls to settle for life. They would grow up with the city, and aid in developing its resources. They were in favor of good habits and good morals in their every-day life.

MOSQUITOES.

This year mosquitoes were more numerous than ever. At sunset the air was filled with them. Everyone, unless protected, was made to suffer from their blood-thirstiness. I had been pretty well acquainted with this pest on the Spanish main, at the balize at the mouth of the Mississippi, at Vera

Cruz, at Corpus Christi, and Brazos Santiago—places noted throughout the world for being a great rendezvous of mosquitoes—but I never saw them more numerous than in the neighborhood of the Falls during the first few years after occupation by the whites. Neither smoke, smudges, or fire would banish them. Mosquito-bars in the doorways and around the beds were inefficient protection. The breaking up of the prairie, the draining of the ponds and marshes, the building of houses, and the results of civilization generally, have made the mosquito comparatively a pest of the past.

CHARACTER OF THE IMMIGRATION— FIRST SURVEYORS.

Most of the immigration this year was composed of farmers from different sections of the east. They wanted lands for farms, to live on permanently. This kept our land-surveyors busy in tracing the lines of the wild lands, so that the claimants could place the correct boundaries to their farms. Heretofore William R. Marshall had been the only surveyor, but his mercantile and other business pursuits were such that he could not attend to outside work. The year previous Charles W. Christmas arrived in St. Anthony from Wooster, Ohio. Mr. Christmas was a surveyor of experience. He had been employed by the government in surveying the public lands in Michigan. He at once had all the work he could do in running the lines of the land claimed by those seeking new homes in the territory. Mr. Christmas was the first register of the United States land-office at Sauk Rapids. On the organization of Hennepin county he was elected county surveyor, an office he held for many years. He surveyed the first lands into lots in Minneapolis proper and was the principal engineer on all the territorial roads running into or out of St. Anthony and Minneapolis. He made and occupied a claim on the Indian lands just above the boundary of the Fort Snelling military reservation in north Minneapolis. He lived to see Minneapolis grow into a large city. He died about three years since at the ripe age of eighty-three years.

FIRST MECHANICS.

St. Anthony had now nearly all the home mechanics neces-

sary to complete buildings from foundation to ridge. Wil
liam Worthingham, a master mason and a first-class workman, had emigrated from Chicago to the village, and was constantly employed on the foundations for houses, and also plas-
tering. He brought his workmen from Chicago. The
quarries so abundant on the banks of the river afforded the
very best material for foundations and walls. Edgar Folsom
established a lime-kiln, which afforded lime for the first coat,
but finishing-lime at first had to be imported from below
Prairie du Chien. Subsequently it was secured at Clearwater. Elias H. Conner, who came to the village in 1848,
Edward Patch and S. Huse about the same time, George T.
Vail and Justus H. Moulton, in 1850, and Joseph Dean, James
M. Garrett, and Stephen Fullard, in the spring of 1851, were
all superior master-carpenters. Up to this time we lacked a
professional house- and sign-painter, but A. Stone, a native
of New Hampshire, fortunately wandered out west, selected
St. Anthony for his home, and our wants in this particular
were supplied. He was soon followed by John Holland.
Previously the village had, to a great extent, depended upon
J. M Boal and other painters in St. Paul for work of this
character. From this time on we had our own citizens of
every trade, and were no longer dependent on outsiders for
aid in any enterprise we might undertake, to forward the
interests of our young village. While as a matter of fact I
was not a resident or a voter in St. Anthony at that time, all
my business was centered there, and I felt great interest in
its prosperity. My residence and home was on the western
bank of the river, in another county, known as Dahkotah. The
center of the river was the boundary-line between Ramsey
and Dahkotah counties.

No new village can expect praise from the traveling public
unless it contains a good hotel, or a house of entertainment
that is comfortable for those who are obliged to seek a temporary home there. St. Anthony was peculiarly fortunate in
having such a home. In 1849 Anson Northrup commenced
the erection of the St. Charles, a first-class hotel, sufficient
for the accommodation of seventy-five guests, and finished it
in June 1850.

And yet with all the bright prospects of the future, in con-

sequence of an unfortunate sale of a half-interest in the mills
and the landed property to Arnold W. Taylor of Boston, who
refused to sell his half of the lots to those who wanted to build
houses on them, the village did not make the growth that was
expected. In time, however, Mr. Steele purchased back the
property from Mr. Taylor, but the village lost while the property was thus tied up by Mr. Taylor's obstinacy.

FIRST FARMERS.

While the village was thus prospering, several farmers
occupied the agricultural lands adjoining it. In 1850 L. C.
Timpson and N. O. Phillips made two claims on section six.
Lewis Stone and his two sons made three claims near Timpson's. Mr. Finch, a brother-in-law of Hon. J. W. North, just
from New York, made a claim and a valuable farm near the
Messrs. Stone's claims. William Dugas and Joseph Reach
had good farms just above Bottineau's addition as early as
1847. William Smith and Joseph Libby, natives of Maine,
opened valuable farms near the road leading to St. Paul.
Judge Meeker purchased from a Canadian-Frenchman the
farm just below Mr. Cheever's. This farm had been worked
four or five years. Henry Cole opened a valuable farm out a
little northeast of the village. Gordon G. Loomis and Captain John Rollins made claims to the hay-lands adjoining on
the east of the village. Robert W. Cummings and Henry
Angell had claims and improved them north and east of
Messrs. Loomis and Rollins. William A. Cheever in laying
out St. Anthony city, reserved a portion of his land for farming purposes. Calvin A. Tuttle had a field of forty acres, a
portion of which includes the present University grounds, as
does the former farm of Mr. Cheever, on which large crops
were raised. John Balif once owned Mr. Tuttle's claim ;
he afterwards settled on Nine-mile creek. Washington
Getchell made a claim on section three, but sold it the
following year to Edward Patch. William L. Larned, who
was elected to the territorial council in the fall of 1851, made
a claim back of the hay-meadow in 1850, and plowed some
eighty acres and raised satisfactory crops on it for several
years. He resided on his farm. Joseph Potvin made a claim

and occupied it in 1848 northeast of the village. Mr. Gibbs, who had resided the previous year with Mr. Tuttle, opened his fine farm on the Como road in 1851. There were one or two other claims made into farms up to this time in the neighborhood of the village ; but the claimants became discouraged and only occupied their lands for a short time, and then sold out and removed from the country. Most of the farms mentioned above are now included in the east division of the city, and all are valuable, though with few exceptions the first occupants did not realize as much money for their labor as they should. The price of farm products ruled low in the early fifties. I believe Mr. Gibbs is about the only one of those named who occupies and owns at this time the original farm settled on so many years since.

THE FALL ELECTIONS OF 1851.

As the summer passed, the politicians commenced their canvass in regard to the approaching fall elections. Mr. Sibley held over, having been elected the previous fall a delegate for two years. A full ticket was to be elected in Ramsey county. At a Democratic county convention held in St. Paul George F. Brott of St. Anthony received the nomination for sheriff, John W. North for county attorney, and Dr. H. Fletcher for judge of probate, which was deemed a pretty liberal division of the county candidates. Ramsey county retained the nominations for register of deeds, treasurer, surveyor, and commissioner. The whigs did not nominate a ticket, but joined the people's party. At a convention of the latter Anson Northrup was nominated for sheriff, and Dr. Ira B. Kingsley for judge of probate. The other candidates were assigned to St. Paul. Mr. Brott and Dr. Kingsley were elected. R. P. Russell held over as commissioner. Thus St. Anthony contained, January 1, 1852, three citizens who held county offices in Ramsey county. At a district convention William L. Larned was nominated for the territorial council. Isaac Atwater was selected as the whig candidate. A lively canvass was made, and Mr. Larned was elected by a small majority. Sumner W. Farnham and Dr. John H. Murphy were elected to the house of representatives from St. Anthony. There were few offices to be filled, but the excitement was greater than at such elections now.

CHAPTER XX.

I was now pretty well acclimated in this new country, and was delighted with all that appertains to the climate. The winters are cold, but pleasant. Cold must be expected in a high latitude during the winter months. They are made for each other. Minnesota would not be real with a tropical winter ; neither would it be desirable. There is no shivering, sickening, milk-and-water cold, such as is frequently felt in a lower latitude, penetrating the bones and marrow with a damp chilliness, and affecting one with gloomy forebodings and despondent disagreeableness. Here we know what to depend on. In the lower country one day it is summer-heat, the next rain, may be sleet, the mercury low enough to afford the greatest discomfort to man and beast : taxing the mind, the body and the health ; while here we know just what to expect—a steady, vigorous, bracing, healthy (with all the word implies) cold ! We are prepared to meet the winter on his coming. Our houses, barns, stables, and outbuildings are made warm and comfortable.

While the spring months, or at least March and April, are too much like the winter months of the southern states, they are on the whole enjoyable. I have found May to be a particularly pleasant month. Spring days we have when the azure is flecked with fleecy clouds ; the air deliciously soft, moist, warm, and breezy ; the sunshine subdued, mellow, dreamy ; the maple in full, fresh leaf ; the native oak in tender half-foliage ; and birds are joyous in song : a spring resurrection of vegetable life from its winter desolation and death—as refreshing to the spirit as balmy air to the sense.

The summer season is all that we can ask or wish for. The autumns are delightful. The Indian-summer is one of the most charming seasons of the year. It comes late in the fall and is of long duration. A serious inconvenience attending it is the disastrous prairie-fires. In the fall of 1851 the Indians out west of the lakes set fires which, during a strong wind, came sweeping over the prairie, endangering my buildings and the lives of my stock. After such visitations the surface of the country had a bleak, desolate, dreary appearance, which remained until vegetation started the following spring.

The fine scenery, steel-blue sky, majestic rivers, clear lakes, leaping water-falls, gleeful streamlets, invigorating atmosphere, and health-giving climate of Minnesota—merit the praise of all who have experienced them during the half-century since white men came among the Indian natives of this land of the Dakotas. The dry air of its cold winters, and the cool nights of its hot summers, are a source of perennial pleasure. Because there was water everywhere, Nicollet called the country Undine. Equally may the red-man's Ho! and Ha-ha! express the pleasure and surprise of all at sight of the foaming waterfalls and sunny lakes.

Recollecting the youthful enthusiasm I shared with others in those days, as we appreciated the advantages of the soil, climate, facilities, resources, and location of this country, it seems not so great a surprise, as it otherwise would be, that this state has leaped from obscurity and savagery into a blaze of civilized glory. The enterprise of its people, and the energy of its progress, is a theme of world-wide praise. Here is an elevated plateau that may command the world!

CHAPTER XXI.

BLACK BEARS.

During the latter part of summer the country was full of bears. A band of Dakotas in the neighborhood of Rice Lake in two days killed twenty-five of them. They frequented the road-side between St. Anthony and St. Paul. Two were seen within a mile of the Democrat office in the last-named village. Mr. Charles Moseau, who resided on the southeastern bank of Lake Calhoun, came in contact with a huge bear of seven hundred pounds weight. A desperate fight took place between Mr. Moseau and bruin and the bear came out second-best. From that time to this those brutes have never made their appearance in this vicinity.

A WILD DEER ON SPIRIT ISLAND.

Mysteriously a deer was the occupant of Spirit Island, close to the precipice of the Falls, in 1851. The water was so high that year that the island could not be reached, and the animal was not interfered with, but it is supposed made its escape during the extreme cold in the beginning of winter when ice connected the island with the main shore ; but this is only a supposition, as no one seemed to know how it reached or how it escaped from the island.

PIONEER FARMING.

Having grubbed out and broken up, during the summer of 1850, some forty acres of land immediately on the bank of the river above my house, my youngest brother, Simon Stevens, . now of Clearwater in this state, and Henry Chambers (who died some two years since in California), were engaged during the spring and summer of 1851 in working the farm. Messrs.

Stevens and Chambers came to me in 1850. This farm was
the first one opened on the west bank of the river, aside from
the farms worked by the military authorities at Fort Snelling,
and aside too from the Indian, the missionaries, and the
Indian traders' farms. It was understood at that time that it
was also the first farm that was opened on the west side of the
river from the Iowa line to Sauk Rapids. I had a field for
wheat, one for corn, another for oats, and several smaller ones
for buckwheat, potatoes, and other vegetables. This land
makes at this time a thousand times more money for the
owners than it did at that time for me, but it was a great
advantage to the territory as an attraction to immigrants.
Almost every stranger who visited the territory was desirous
of seeing the Falls from the west side of the river, and in
most instances crossed the ferry. In doing so they were surprised, as they reached the western bank of the stream, to see
the fields of oats, wheat, and corn, that would be a credit to
central Illinois. Those fields of grain decided the destiny of
many an immigrant. It put an end to all doubts possibly
entertained in regard to the capability of Minnesota soil for
producing large crops of grain. It dispelled all fear from the
minds of those who were wavering as to the future production
of cereals in the territory. As immigration was then the
great staple of the country, it accomplished a good work in
that behalf.

NEW CLAIMS ON THE WEST SIDE.

Meantime we were endeavoring to secure more neighbors
on the reservation. It was evident to the commanding officer
at Fort Snelling that Congress was disposed to reduce the
large tract of land held for military purposes, and he ceased
to be as vigilant in keeping off trespassers as his predecessors
were. The reservation extended from the Minnesota river to
nearly a quarter of a mile above Bassett's creek, and from the
bank of the Mississippi back to the other side of lakes Calhoun, and Harriet, and Lake of the Woods. On the east side of
the river it went down nearly to the cave, and almost up to
Denoyer's. It was not necessary for the use of the troops.
The officer in command at the Fort at that time was Colonel

Francis Lee, of the Sixth infantry. In August he reluctantly gave John P. Miller, who came to the country with me, (and the only one of our company that organized in Rockford, Ill., who remained after our up-country expedition in May, 1849,) a permit to occupy one hundred and sixty acres, which was subsequently known as Atwater's addition to Minneapolis. Mr. Miller took possession of this land in August, 1851. He had since his return from the Rum river expedition, remained in St. Paul working at his trade, that of a carpenter. He had a partner with him in the claim, a Mr. Daniel Steele, who remained for over a year and then sold out his interest in the claim to Mr. Miller. They built a comfortable dwelling-house, barn, and stables, and broke up some eighty acres of land. For a year or two Mr. Miller was the most extensive farmer in the colony. He remained on his claim some three years, when in consequence of uncertainty of obtaining a title to the land, he sold out for a very fair price to his neighbor, Edward Murphy. The latter soon sold to Judge Atwater, who pre-empted it in April, 1855, and subsequently laid it out into lots for building purposes, and it is now covered all over with houses.

The Indian lands having been opened for settlers, Mr. Miller made a claim in the neighborhood of Minnetonka mills, from which time to the present day he has been one of the most prominent farmers and citizens of the county. Mr. Miller is a native of Pennsylvania, but had from boyhood lived at Bucyrus, Ohio, until 1848, when he moved to Rockford, Illinois, and from there in April, 1849, to Minnesota.

INDIANS ENCAMPED AT THE FALLS.

The two lake bands of Indians, so called because they formerly lived on the shores of lakes Calhoun and Harriet, but then residing at Oak Grove (now Bloomington), encamped on the high land above the Falls for several weeks in July and August. They had considerable money left that they had received at the Traverse des Sioux treaty held a few weeks previous. They had brought their own canoes down the Minnesota river, and then up the Mississippi to the foot of the rapids, at which point they constantly crossed the

river to the St. Anthony side for the purpose of trading. The
Express, for the benefit of eastern readers, thus described the

COSTUME OF THE DAKOTA SQUAWS :

"Their dress is a shirt, leggins reaching to the thigh, a large
"blanket and moccasins ; and the men wear breech-cloths,
"which is about the only difference in their dress. They are
"very fond of ornaments. Their leggins and ornaments are
"of divers colors ; some are black, others blue, some red, and
"others yellow. Some wear one leggin red and the other
"blue or black."

BEHAVIOUR OF THE INDIANS WHILE AT THE FALLS.

The Indians during their encampment were constantly on
the alert, fearing an attack from the Chippewas, but they
were so fond of trading, and the money they had left burned
in their pockets to such an extent, that they were willing to
risk their scalps at that time for the pleasure they experienced in exchanging their money for goods. They were
not molested, however, during their stay, and when their
money was gone they folded their tepees and returned to
their village. They, however, appeared again during the
fall with large quantities of cranberries, which the merchants
and the citizens of St. Anthony were eager to purchase. They
had previously given me the name of Mi-ni-sni — cold
water—and were always friendly, supplying my family, at the
proper season of the year, with game in abundance, but
expecting, and always receiving, pay therefor. The only
uncomfortable thing in regard to their presence was a fear
that the Chippewas might at any moment drop on them, and
in the excitement of a battle some of us might be injured by
the reckless use they would make of their guns on such an
occasion. It was always a relief to us when they had finished
their sojourn in the neighborhood of the Falls. To the credit
of the traders in St. Anthony, there was never a drop of strong
drink sold to the Indians, and as a consequence there was
never any of them intoxicated. Numerous as they were
around the Falls, I cannot remember of ever seeing an Indian,
whether Winnebago, Chippewa, or Dakota, under the influ-

ence of mi-ni-si-ca. The St. Anthony dealers should have
credit for this, for an Indian, with rare exceptions, will drink
whisky when he can get it.

NAMING THE TOWN.

We were agitating the subject of a name for our prospective
little town. It was insisted that Mr. Tuttle and myself should
select a name for it. The newspapers of the territory suggested several names. Goodhue, of the Pioneer, had no
patience when any other name than All Saints was talked of.
His letters to me were always thus addressed. Following is
a specimen, received in September of that year: "I with my
"wife and sister, three children and servant-girl, propose to
"dine with you to-morrow, Tuesday, at ALL SAINTS." This
was a pointer that I could not well misunderstand. Miss
Mary A. Scofield, a young lady of much literary merit, had
resided in my family for nearly a year. She favored the name
suggested by Colonel Goodhue, and dated all her letters and
articles for publication from All Saints, and it seemed that
this was to be the name. The christening was put off so long
that when other settlers came they had suggestions to make ;
but they could not agree what the name should be. Hon.
Amos Tuck, then a member of congress from New Hampshire,
made me a visit during the discussion, and said, "whatever
"else you do, give it a suggestive Indian name. It will not be
"long before the red-man will have disappeared from the
"face of the earth ; bestow a name on your place by which
"future generations will know that it originated from a people
"who once were its sole owners and occupants ; such names
"will be all that the aborigines will be remembered by."
We hesitated—and remained nameless.

CHAPTER XXII

As the autumn months approached, we made strenuous efforts to secure more neighbors on our side of the river. Dr. Hezekiah Fletcher, a native of Maine, with several friends, waited on the commanding officer at Fort Snelling, and received permission to occupy a claim far back, as it was then thought, in the country. It is now known as J. S. and Wyman Elliott's addition to Minneapolis. He immediately erected a small dwelling on it, which stood on the present site of the mansion of Daniel Elliott, on Portland avenue, between Fourteenth and Fifteenth streets. He remained some two years in peaceful possession of it, when he sold out to John L. Tenny who, in the spring of 1854, disposed of it to Dr. Jacob S. Elliott. Dr. Fletcher received twelve hundred dollars for his interest in the claim, from Mr. Tenny, and the latter obtained some two thousand dollars from Dr. Elliott. This seems a small price for land that is worth so many millions to-day, but it must be remembered that the title to it was in the government, and there was a good deal of uncertainty as to when, if ever, it could be obtained. To be sure, a year afterwards the land was pre-empted, and then, of course, it was worth as many thousands as Dr. Elliot had paid hundreds for it to Mr. Tenny.

Dr. Fletcher remained on the west side of the river, was elected a member of the territorial house of representatives in the fall of 1853 for the session of 1854, and was appointed register of the United States land-office in 1863. Upon the expiration of his office, he moved to Springfield, Missouri. In 1862 Mr. Tenny returned to his native state, Maine. Dr. Elliott is also a native of the same state. Several years since he moved to California, but still has large property interests in the city.

The boundaries of all the claims made in this vicinity up to the fall of 1854 were arbitrary, as the land had not been surveyed, but Mr. Christmas, and other surveyors, traced the lines over from the government surveys on the east side in such a manner as to afford very definite information where the lines would be when the government should see fit to order a survey. In fact the lines Mr. Christmas brought over proved perfectly correct. The government surveys were made in 1854 preparatory to bringing the land into market.

A few weeks after Dr. Fletcher obtained his permit, John Jackins, formerly of Maine, but previous to his settling in St. Anthony for some years a lumberman on the St. Croix, obtained permission to occupy the land immediately in the rear of my claim, and built a house late in the fall on what is now the syndicate block, but he did not occupy it until the following spring. Mr. Jackins pre-empted his land April, 1855.

Isaac Brown, who came from Maine in the spring of 1851, after Mr. Jackins moved on his claim, made some arrangement by which he secured several acres of land from Mr. Jackins. Mr. Brown eventually built a large dwelling-house on the corner of Sixth street and third avenue south. He was the first sheriff of Hennepin county, having been elected to that office at the first election previous to the organization of the county. The election was held October 11th, 1852. Mr. Jackins was chosen one of the county commissioners at the same election. Both Messrs. Jackins and Brown laid out their land in lots in 1855. Mr. Brown died many years since. Mr. Jackins was for many years a merchant in Minneapolis. He now resides in California.

Warren Bristol came from New York to St. Anthony in the spring of 1851, and resided with W. L. Larned. Having been admitted to the bar, he was anxious to settle in the territory and practice his profession. Although we had but a small population in the autumn of that year, the prospects were favorable for a large one in a short time.

Occasionally requiring aid in the way of advice on matters of law, I solicited the removal of Mr. Bristol to this new village. He responded, and late in the fall received permission from the military authorities to occupy one hundred and sixty acres of land adjoining and west of Dr. Fletcher's claim. During the following winter he built a house on his land. It occupied the site of the high-school edifice, Fourth avenue south, between Grant and Eleventh streets. Before the land came into market, he exchanged his claim for St. Paul property. He was the first district attorney of Hennepin county. He moved to Red Wing, Goodhue county, and was afterwards a member of the house of representatives, and senator from that county. He was appointed, by President Grant, United States supreme judge for New Mexico, an office which he held for many years. He is still a resident of that territory.

The time had now arrived when it was necessary that we should take earnest measures in regard to the formation of a new county and, if possible, have the boundaries of it fixed so as to secure the future county-seat in our neighborhood. We had been, since the fall of 1849, a part of Dakota county, the county-seat of which was at Mendota. An effort had been made a year before to secure the passage of a bill by the legislature making a new county, but it was deemed premature.

The members of the legislature representing this district at the winter session of 1851 were Hon. Martin McLeod of Lac-qui-parle, of the council ; and Alex. Faribault of Mendota, and Benjamin. H. Randall of Fort Snelling, members of the house of representative. Mr. McLeod was willing to assist us in the passage of the bill, but it was almost too much to expect that we could rely on the vote of Mr. Faribault, as the formation of a new county, with the boundaries as we wanted it, would interfere with Mendota. Mr. Randall, who had been a resident of Fort Snelling since the fall of 1849, and employed in the sutler's store, would aid Mr. McLeod, but it was deemed best to wait until the next session before making a strong movement in the matter.

As the election of a new delegation to the legislature for the session of 1852 was approaching, we determined to select such candidates as would be favorable to the organization of the new county. All were in favor of the re-election of Mar-

tin McLeod to the council. We had no difficulty in securing
the renomination of Mr. Randall as a candidate for his old seat
in the house of representatives, but failed in the nomination
of Mr. Eli Pettijohn, of Fort Snelling, who was in favor of the
movement : James Mc Boal, of Mendota, being the successful
candidate. The latter had moved from St. Paul to Mendota,
since the close of the last session of the legislature, having
occupied a seat in the council from that city during the two
previous sessions. As a nomination was equal to an election,
Messrs. Randall and Boal were the members of the house
for the session of 1852.

A strong movement was made against us, perhaps by a
majority of the people of the district, who were in favor of
changing the boundaries of Dakota county as follows : commencing at a point on the Mississippi at Oliver's grove—now
Hastings—following up the channel of the river to a point
opposite the junction of Coon creek with the river ; thence
running west a reasonable distance, thence south, crossing the
Minnesota river at Oak grove, and so continuing in a southerly line until a direct line west of Oliver's grove was reached;
thence east to the place of beginning. This would make a
large county, and fix the county-seat, for a while at least, at
Mendota. On the other hand, we wanted a distinctly new
county, with the boundaries commencing at the junction of
the Minnesota with the Mississippi, then following up the
river channel to Crow river ; thence following Crow river up
to the forks of said stream ; thence south to Little rapids ;
thence down the river to the place of beginning. This would
make a good sized county, which would contain plenty of
prairie, wood-land, oak-openings, and meadow-land, with a
pretty sure prospect of the county-seat remaining on the west
bank of the Falls of St. Anthony. It had become very evident that if we expected to secure the passage of such a bill,
it must be put through at the approaching session, or postponed for several years, as the opposition to the movement
was becoming stronger every day. We could hardly expect
the cordial support of representatives from the larger towns
in the territory, because they were fearful the embryo village
might be a rival to their interests.

The legislature met in St. Paul, for the session of 1852, on the 7th of January. The council was composed of nine members, the house of eighteen. Since the election the previous fall, we had been hard at work visiting, soliciting and importuning many of the new members, that when the proper time came they might aid us with their votes. While the council and house contained but few members in each body, their homes were scattered from Pembina to Reed's landing ; so a good deal of work had to be done after the session opened. A lively fight was made, and won. I had been required to draw up the bill just as we wanted it, and hand it to Martin McLeod, who would present it to the council for their consideration. In the bill I had called the county Snelling, in honor of the army officer who built Fort Snelling, but that name was stricken out by the council and Hennepin inserted instead. Otherwise the bill passed just as it was drawn, including the important provision that the first board of county commissioners should name the county-seat. It was a close shave, for the bill only passed the last working day of the session, and then only by a bare majority. It was my first and last experience in lobbying in a legislative body. Aside from the expense, anxiety and suspense, during the pendency of the bill, a lobbyist is liable to lose his self-respect. But the passage of the bill was everything to us, and to those who should follow us. The very idea of being obliged to cross the prairie and the Minnesota river, nine miles to Mendota, for county business, such as to get a deed recorded, and the like, was not to be thought of for a moment.

It is greatly to be regretted that the boundaries of the county could not have been suffered to remain as they were, but on February 20, 1855, a large part of Carver county was cut out of Hennepin county by legislative enactment, and Chaska was selected as the county-seat of the new county.

During the fall of 1851 our side of the river received a valuable addition in the person of Allen Harmon who, with his family came from Maine. He was a man of great worth, and we were pleased to have him for a neighbor, though not a very near one, as his claim was back some distance from the river. He continually resided on it, from a few days after the commanding officer at the Fort granted him permission to take it, until his death some five years ago. He had laid it all

out into building-lots, which have long since been occupied
by residences. The First Baptist church building, the new
Athenæum library, and many other beautiful and costly buildings, public and private, have been erected on Mr. Harmon's
old claim. This was the last claim made in 1851, on the military reservation on the west side of the river, except the one
made by Dr. A. E. Ames, and he did not move on it until the
next spring.

Dr. Ames arrived from Roscoe, Illinois, on the 11th day of
October. He was at the time one of the state senators from
Illinois. He came up on a prospecting tour, and was so well-
pleased with the country that he concluded to remain here.
On the 14th of October he made an arrangement with Colonel
Anderson D. Nelson, U. S. A., then a second-lieutenant at
Fort Snelling, to make the selection of a quarter-section of
land and occupy it. Dr. Ames selected the land which now
includes the court-house and jail. His first house was built
on the same block which the county buildings now occupy.
The land was then densely covered with prickly-pear, hazel-
brush, and other shrubbery, which made a considerable part
of it almost impassable. Dr. Ames resided in St. Anthony,
and practiced medicine with Dr. Murphy, until the arrival of
his family in the spring of 1852, when he immediately moved
on his claim.

Great preparations had been made during the summer and
fall by the lumbermen for active operations in the woods the
coming winter of 1851 and 1852. The work was mostly confined to the two branches of Rum river. In addition to the
mills at St. Anthony, steam saw-mills had been built at St.
Paul, and at several other points down the river. There was
every prospect in the fall of 1851 that there would be a large
local demand for logs in the spring of 1852. Among the
lumbermen who had teams in the woods in the winter, from
St. Anthony, were Messrs. Farnham, Stimson, Stanchfield,
Huse, Chambers, Pratt, Stevens, Lennon, Leonard Day and
sons, Edgar Folsom, and Stephen Cobb; from St. Paul,
Robert O'Neill. Large quantities of supplies for lumbermen
had been purchased in the lower country, during the fall, and
transported up the river before the close of navigation. As
the banks of the two branches of Rum river were swarming

with men, it necessarily required a large amount of provisions. Employment was given to all the teamsters in the country to haul these supplies from St. Anthony and St. Paul to the pineries. It required about a week to make the round trip. The head tote-teamster so called, was Otis C. Whitney, who had similar experience in Maine. He followed teaming for several years around the Falls, when he emigrated to Montana, early in the sixties, and is now one of the cattle-kings of that territory. These tote-teams had a hard, cold time of it during these early years of lumber operations in the territory. They were required to be on the road every day, as it was necessary that the camps should be supplied with provisions. They had, most of the way, poor accommodations, frequently being obliged to camp out in the coldest of weather. Elk river was the only place where good, warm, comfortable quarters could be obtained, Pierre Bottineau, of St. Anthony, having built a large hotel there the previous year. These teamsters were, as they should have been, paid liberal wages.

Continuing the list of those who became early residents on the military reservation opposite St. Anthony, we mention Edward Murphy, who came from Quincy, Illinois, to St. Anthony, in 1850, obtained a permit, in September, to occupy a quarter-section of land down the river adjoining John P. Miller's claim, but he did not take possession by actual residence until May, 1852. He immediately improved considerable land ; had one field especially prepared for a nursery and orchard which, in due time, at great expense, was occupied as such, but the fruit-trees and nursery-stock perished from some unaccountable reason, and after a few years he abandoned trying to raise apples and the larger fruit raised in his Illinois home. Mr. Murphy was the pioneer in the nursery business in this state, and like many others who subsequently engaged in the same enterprise, lost all the money employed in the undertaking, besides the work in caring for the trees, and the use of the land.

Anson Northrup made a claim immediately up the river, above the Smith or old-mill claim, of a fractional lot containing a few acres. He was a partial resident on it from February 10, 1851, to June, 1852 ; from that time he resided on

it constantly until he pre-empted it in 1853. This claim
includes the present depot and yards of the Milwaukee railroad. Mr. Northrup built a large house, in which the United
States courts were held. When Hennepin Lodge of Free
Masons received its dispensation its sessions were held in the
house. Mr. Northrup also erected a smaller house near the
site of the present woolen-factory storehouse. In this building the first public-school was held, commencing December
3, 1852. The teacher was Miss Mary E. Miller, now Mrs.
Marshall Robinson. In this building Rev. J. C. Whitney
was installed pastor of the first Presbyterian church, in June,
1853, by Rev. Dr. Chester of Buffalo, New York. There
were present on that memorable occasion other distinguished
divines of the Presbyterian order, such as Rev. Dr. Hopkins,
professor of Auburn Theological Seminary ; Rev. Dr. Fowler,
Utica ; Rev. Mr. Spencer, Milwaukee ; besides our home
members, Rev. Gideon H. Pond, Oak Grove ; Rev. E. D.
Neill, St. Paul ; with two elders, Governor William Holcomb
of Stillwater, and Dr. Alfred E. Ames of Minneapolis. Dr.
Ames, Daniel M. Coolbaugh, and E. N. Barber, were elected
elders.

Philip Bassett, in May, 1852, made a claim to the part of
the city known as Hoag's addition to Minneapolis. He only.
had it for a few weeks when, June 10th the same year, he sold
it for one hundred dollars to Charles Hoag. Messrs. Bassett
and Hoag were born in the same town in New Hampshire,
and were school-boys together. Mr. Bassett went to California, and Mr. Hoag opened a farm on the claim, which contained one hundred and sixty acres, now in the very heart of
the city ; the West hotel being built on it. Previous to coming to the territory, Mr. Hoag had been, for a long time,
principal in one of the Philadelphia high schools, but having
been raised on a farm, and more or less connected with farming while teaching, he made a successful farmer. Few of the
present generation are aware that this one hundred and sixty
acres of land were at one time sold for the pitiful sum of one
hundred dollars : hardly the price now for an inch on some
of the lots on Hennepin avenue. Mr. Hoag became one of
the most useful citizens of the place.

Previous to Mr. Hoag's purchase, Joel B. Bassett, a brother

of Philip, took up a quarter-section above the creek that bears his name, and immediately on the bank of the river. Having perfected his arrangements in the fall of 1851, in regard to it, at Fort Snelling, he moved on it in May, 1852, and for several years, and in fact until it became too valuable for that purpose, occupied it exclusively for farming. He was as good a farmer as he has since proved to be a lumberman and business man.

AN EARLY LAWSUIT AND JURY-TRIAL.

Soon after Mr. Bassett made his claim, David Bickford and Isaac Ives Lewis discovered a few fractional lots between the boundaries of Mr. Hoag's and Mr. Bassett's land, which they insisted were not covered by the permits of either of the above-named gentlemen, and immediately occupied the disputed territory by building a house on the present site of Thomas Lowry's office, Second street and Third avenue north, and in spite of a lawsuit, and against the command of the officers at Fort Snelling, succeeded in pre-empting it in April, 1855. At that period there was an important law in the territory for the protection of squatters on government land under a chapter entitled "forcible entry and detainer". In pursuance of the provisions of this law, a suit was brought against Mr. Bickford, after the organization of the county, before Justice Hedderly. A jury was called, and after a tedious trial of several days, the case was submitted to the jury. There being no room in-doors where the court was held, the jury was obliged to retire outside to deliberate on the merits of the case. It being in mid-winter, of course the weather was cold, and the jury suffered from the low temperature. There was not much comfort in discussing the evidence with the mercury pretty near zero, and the wind coming down from the north at the rate of about forty knots, which almost congealed the breath as each of the members of the jury endeavored to explain to the others the way in which he understood the evidence. After an ineffectual attempt to agree upon a verdict, one of the jury declared he had been out in the cold long enough ; he would not be frozen into a verdict contrary to his understanding of the matter ; and although he was alone

in his opinion as to the merits of the case, and as to the
proper verdict they should render, he would not return with
them to the justice's office, but would immediately leave them
to solve the question by themselves, and return such a verdict
as they had a mind to.   He then made a bee-line at as rapid
a pace as his half-frozen limbs would permit to his shanty-
home across the prairie, leaving the other jurors in a state of
astonishment.   They immediately reported progress and the
fact of the elopement of one of their number, to Justice Hedderly, and although Judge Atwater, the plaintiff's attorney,
demanded a writ of attachment to be issued by the court
against the delinquent juror for contempt of court, and that
it be given to Sheriff Brown for service, the justice denied
the motion, and a record of disagreement by the jury was
entered in the case.

   This was the first jury-trial in any justice court in Hennepin county, and the ending of it was so ludicrous, and so
different from what the plaintiff had been familiar with in
conducting cases in the courts in his New England home,
that he never had the courage to move for a new trial.   He
obtained a slight satisfaction in an encounter with the tres-
. passer, in a snow-drift on the disputed claim, not long after
the farce of the trial.

   Some of these lawsuits on the frontier were conducted in a
queer way, before justices of the peace ; but no one could
find fault with the first two justices, Hedderly and Fletcher.
They were honest, just, able men, and conducted all trials
brought before them in an impartial, proper manner ; but
there were no conveniences for holding courts in those days ;
and then the litigants, lawyers, and jurors, were all strangers
to each others.

   Mr. Lewis, who was interested with Mr. Bickford in the
claim, remained in St. Anthony until 1854, when he removed
to Minneapolis and built a large store and dwelling on the lots
now occupied as a market by Harlow A. Gale.   In the fall of
that year he filled his store with goods, and occupied the
dwelling with his family.

   Mr. Bassett was our first judge of probate, a member of the
legislature, Chippewa agent, and occupied other high trusts in
the gift of the people, in a most satisfactory manner.   He is

always a friend of the city and the county. Mr. Bickford sold out his interest in city property to Judge Beebe, many years since, and removed to Vineland, New Jersey.

Mr. Lewis for a long time transacted a large mercantile and general business in Minneapolis, which he closed out in 1859, and transferred his home to Watertown, in Carver county where, in company with his brother E. F. Lewis, he engaged in mercantile pursuits, and built a flour-mill, and pot and pearl ashery. At one time he was a member of the legislature from Carver county. He is now a resident of Idaho, and president of one of the national banks in one of the most prosperous cities of that territory.

There was up to this time several other valuable claims on the military reservation that had not been taken, and as the commanding officer at Fort Snelling had seemingly become indifferent to their occupation, people flocked from different parts of the territory to take them. Claim-houses dotted the prairie between the town and Lake Calhoun. A change in the commanding officer, just as the houses were completed, made a change in the management of the reservation. All who did not have permits, with one or two exceptions, were ordered to leave the reservation and remove their buildings and lumber. The order was obeyed, but it was an unjust one, and caused great injury to the squatters, though eventually a good many of them, after congress passed the bill reducing the reservation, held on to the boundaries of the land they had made previously, and obtained it from the government.

CHAPTER XXIII.

The Traverse des Sioux Treaty with the Indians having been perfected, persons seeking homes made haste to get hold of the best locations in the neighborhood of the Falls. Col. Emanuel Case arrived in the spring of 1851 and opened a store in St. Anthony, in connection with his son, Sweet W. Case. They came from Michigan. Colonel Case surveyed one hundred and sixty acres of land immediately north of Mr. Bassett's, on the river, and filed a claim on it. Peter Poncin, a pioneer merchant of Stillwater, wanted the same land. He had taken out a permit to trade with the Indians, built and opened a store, but as·the Indians had left, he had no customers. The dispute was settled at the government land-office, and Colonel Case was the winner. In March, 1852, he was greatly afflicted by the loss of his youngest son, James Gale Case, nearly twenty-one years old. The young man fell through a watering-place cut in the ice, near the bank of the river, and was drowned. This was the second death on this side of the river. Colonel Case had interested with him Alexander Moore, also from Michigan. A good part of the land was under cultivation for several years when, in 1855, it was laid out into lots and known as a part of Bassett, Case and Moore's addition to the village of Minneapolis. Moore ultimately became a merchant in Minneapolis, and transacted a large business, and contributed, as Colonel Case did, largely in building up the city, in its early days. Mr. Moore moved to Sauk Center, in Stearns county, many years since, and has represented that county in several sessions of the legislature. Colonel Case frequently held high trusts, and died, greatly regretted, in the summer of 1871.

In 1851, through an arrangement with the Indian agent, Joseph Menard occupied land near that of Colonel Case. After the treaty he came in possession of it, and the tract is now known as Menard's addition to Minneapolis. Mr. Menard is still a resident of the city.

Charles W. Christmas followed Mr. Menard on the Indian lands, securing a valuable claim in the fall of 1851, which he improved in 1852. He laid it out into lots as Christmas's addition to Minneapolis. His son-in law, Isaac I. Lewis, and nephew, Captain J. C. Reno, became interested in it with him. Mr. Christmas was the father of a large family. His wife and many of his children preceded him to the spirit-land. The three claims of Colonel Case, Menard, and Christmas, were the first made on the Indian lands in this vicinity.

A few more permits were granted in 1852 by the new commanding officer at Fort Snelling. Martin Layman came from Illinois and located on the land, a part of which is now known as Layman's cemetery. When surveyed by the government, it proved to be included in a school section. In 1858, after the admission of Minnesota as a state, our senators, Henry M. Rice and General James Shields, and our members in the lower house of congress, James M. Cavanaugh, and Wm. W. Phelps, obtained the passage of a bill by congress granting Mr. Layman the privilege of entering the land in the same way that other lands are secured to settlers. This was on the ground that Mr. Layman had settled on them previous to the survey, and that settlers were not supposed to know that the sections sixteen and thirty-six on the military reservation were to be set apart for school purposes. The state was authorized, by the bill that passed congress, to make selection of other government lands in the place of those claimed by Mr. Layman.

Waterman Stinson came from Maine to St. Anthony. Being a farmer in his native state, he was desirous of securing a good farm in Minnesota. Most of the immigrants to the Falls from Maine had been engaged in the lumber trade ; hence they followed that business here, and when a farmer from that state made his appearance, we were all anxious to

see that he was well settled. Mr. Stinson was the father of
numerous girls and boys of industrious habits, capable of
working a large farm, and not having the least knowledge of
speculation, he wanted a home in the country; so he was
placed on the bank of Bassett's creek, where there was not
the least prospect that he would ever be disturbed by the
extension of the village into his neighborhood. In addition
to his children, he had his aged parents to support. He
opened a large field for grain. His natural hay-meadows on
the creek were extensive and productive. His son-in-law,
Mr. Brennan, made a claim, at the same time, adjoining him,
which in after years became the property of Franklin Steele.
Mr. Stinson could not turn the tide of the expansion of the
city, which soon swallowed up his farm, and is now known as
Stinson's addition to Minneapolis. He died several years
since.

Judge Isaac Atwater, in June 1851, became interested in
the military reservation, only for a day, when he sold out for
ten dollars. He afterwards owned a large share of the Miller
claim.

John George Lennon obtained permission to occupy the
land adjoining Mr. Layman's, which is included in J. G.
Lennon's out-lots addition to the city. Captain Benjamin B.
Parker was fortunate in securing a quarter-section of land
east of Mr. Layman's, which is absorbed by his son's, the
Parkers' addition to Minneapolis. Sweet W. Case came in for
a quarter-section, as did Chandler Hutchins, back of Mr.
Lennon's. Mr. Case purchased the Hutchins pre-emption.
Mr. Case's original farm is Lawrence and Reeve's addition to
the city. While occupied by Mr. Case those claims were
greatly improved, most of the whole breadth of the half-
section being under cultivation. Mr. Hutchins's old claim
is included in Chicago, Lake Park, and several other additions. Edgar Folsom, through the good will of the military
authorities, came in possession of a quarter-section in the
neighborhood of Mr. Parker's, which eventually became the
home of Nathan Roberts, and is now included in Newell,
Carr and Baldwin's addition to the city.

Mrs. Judith Ann Sayer, a widow lady from New York,
occupied a claim near Mr. Case's, which is now Eustis's

addition to Minneapolis. About this time Mrs. Sayer sold her claim and married William Dickie of Lake Harriet.

Mr. Robert Blaisdell and his three sons, John T., William, and Robert, Jr., became the owners of claims, all now known, as follows: Robert Blaisdell, senior, Flour City addition to Minneapolis; John T. Blaisdell pre-emption, John T. Blaisdell's addition to the city; William Blaisdell's land, Bloomington addition to the city; and Robert Blaisdell, Jr.'s old · farm is now Lindsley and Lingerfelter's addition. John S. Mann, William Dickie, Eli Pettijohn, L. N. Parker, Henry Angell, and Henry Heap, occupied beautiful lands on the shores of and near Lakes Calhoun and Harriet, which are in the several Remington additions to the city. James A. Lennon, and Deacon Oliver, had claims near them; the latter is now Oliver's Park addition: the former is in the Remington addition. Charles Moseau's old claim, the site of the former Dakota chieftain's residence, is now the beautiful grounds of Lakewood cemetery.

Edmond Bresette occupied the east shore of Lake Calhoun, but, by a special act of congress, Rev. Dr. E. G. Gear became the proprietor, and it is now included mostly in Calhoun Park. George E. Huey had the claim east of Dr. E. G. Gear's, which is in one of the Remington additions; and David Gorham had the claim north bordering on Lake of the Isles, which he sold to R. P. Russell, who has made out of it several additions to the city; and George Park's claim east of the Isles, which is now Lake of the Isles addition, and N. E. Stoddard pre-empted the adjoining claim; then John Green made a claim, a portion of which land is called Lake View addition. Z. M. Brown and Hill made the next claims, which comprise the present Groveland addition. Dennis Peter's claim is known as Sunnyside addition.

William Worthingham's old claim became the property of John C. Oswald, and it now bears the novel name of Bryn Mawr addition. A little further out William Byrnes made a beautiful home, and was elected sheriff of Hennepin county, but died before his term of office expired. This old homestead of Sheriff Byrnes is now Maben, White and Le Bron's addition to the city; while James Byrne's land is included in the Oak Park addition.

There were several other claims made in 1852 and 1853 in what may now, perhaps, be classed as north Minneapolis ; some on the military lands ; others on the ceded Indian lands. Among them were those of Charles Farrington ; Elijah Austin's, now Sherburne and Beebe's addition ; F. X. Crepau's, now Crepau's addition ; Stephen and Rufus Pratt both laid out their claims in city lots, one Stephen Pratt's and the other Rufus Pratt's addition. The beautiful Oak Lake addition is mostly on the pre-emption of Thomas Stinson. Central Park is on the original land of Joseph S. Johnson. Asa Fletcher and his brother Timothy owned the land out on Portland and Park avenues, now Merriam and Lowry's addition, while William Goodwin owned what is now the Evergreen addition. Bristol's old claim was pre-empted by Jackson, and is now known as Jackson, Daniels and Whitney's and Snyder and Company's additions. H. H. Shepley's claim is divided among several additions, Viola included.

In the more southerly portion of the city Andrew J. Foster and Charles Gilpatrick had valuable farms, which are now included in the additions that bear their names. Deacon Sully's old claim is now on the map as Sully and Murphy's subdivision. The original Falls City farm of Henry Keith, made in 1852, is now owned by Judge Atwater and Judge C. E. Flandreau, which is a part of Falls City and Riverside Short-Line addition, and Dorwin Moulton's claim is Dorman's addition to the city. William G. Murphy's pre-emption is composed in part of Cook's Riverside addition, and Alfred Murphy's claim is included in the Fair-Ground addition. Hiram Burlingham's farm is included in Morrison and Lovejoy's addition. Simeon Odell's old home is now Palmer's addition, and E. A. Hodsdon's farm is the Southside addition to the city. Captain Arthur H. Mills's and J. Draper's claims were where the residence of Hon. D. Morrison is now. Galpin's and other additions are also portions of their old homes. Charles Brown's and Frank Rollin's claims are Rollin's Second addition, and Simon Bean's farm is Minnehaha Driving Park. John Wass's farm is a portion of Wass's addition. Ard Godfrey's old home has been transferred to the Soldiers' Home, and Amasa Craft's farm is Munroe Brother's addition. Hiram Van Nest's homestead is Van

Nest's addition. William G. Moffett's claim is now Minnehaha Park. Philander Prescott's claim is known as Annie E. Steele's out-lots addition.

Among the original settlers who occupied claims in 1851 and 1852, and whose old homes are not laid out into city lots, are those of Colonel S. Woods, William Finch, Samuel Stough, S. S. Crowell, Mark Baldwin, William Hanson, J. J. Dinsmore, Willis G. Moffett, Chris Garvey, H. S. Atwood, Thomas Pierce, and Titus Pettijohn. I think Messrs. Pierce, William G. Moffett, the Blaisdell Brothers, and Christopher C. Garvey are about the only ones who now own any considerable portion of those original pre-emptions. The entries made by A. K. Hartwell and Calvin Church, in the near vicinity of the Falls, are included in the original town-plat of Minneapolis. Among those who were residents on the west side of the river in the fall of 1850, were Simon Stevens, Henry and Thomas Chambers, and Horace Webster. They made claims elsewhere. Levi Smith, Edward Smith, Major A. M. Fridley, R. P. Russell, and George E. Huey, became interested with Robert Smith in the government mill-property early in 1851. Levi Smith was a brother-in-law of Judge A. G. Chatfield. He never resided here. He was the first register of the U. S. land-office at Winona. His brother Edward Smith only remained a year here. He married a sister of Governor Burns, of Wisconsin, and moved to the Pacific coast.

While the foregoing may not be a full list of the original owners of the soil in this neighborhood, I think it as correct as possible to get it at this time. George A. Camp was a resident during the exciting claim-making on the west side of the river, but he never made a claim. He was a member of his uncle Anson Northrup's household. William Goodnow, a carpenter, who built Mr. Northrup's house, also resided here, but made no claim. He committed suicide in the beginning of the winter of 1852, by jumping into the river just above the Falls. Goodnow was a young man, an excellent workman, but addicted to strong-drink, and at the time of his death was suffering from delirium-tremens. This was the first case of suicide in what is now Minneapolis, and the first victim here suffering from that terrible disease. Gordon and

William Jackins were members of their brother John Jackin's
family. They were interested in a forty-acre tract of land
joining Mrs. Sayer's claim. The younger brother William
died while occupying the claim. William Hubbard, a lawyer
from Tennessee, occupied a claim for a year or two, but
sold it and removed from the territory before the land came
into market. John Berry lived on and preempted a farm
near the Lake of the Isles, which is now within the city limits.

FIRST MASONIC LODGE AT ST. ANTHONY FALLS.

Dr. A. E. Ames, soon after his arrival in St. Anthony, in
1851, found a few Freemasons, and called a meeting of such
of them as were residents, at the parlors of Mr. Godfrey, with
a view of establishing a lodge. A petition for a dispensation
was sent to the grand lodge of Illinois. The petition was
granted, and on the 14th of February, at the same parlors,
Cataract Lodge, U. D., was organized. A. E. Ames was Worshipful Master; William Smith, senior warden; Isaac Brown,
junior warden; Ard Godfrey, treasurer; John H. Stevens,
secretary; D. M. Coolbaugh, senior deacon; H. S. Atwood,
junior deacon; and William Bramer, Tyler. Colonel E. Case
of St. Anthony, and Captain J. W. T. Gardiner of Fort Snelling, were members.

As this was the first charitable order organized in this
vicinity, where so many now exist, it will be observed that
Cataract Lodge is the parent of all similar organizations north
of St. Paul. Dr. Ames, the master, had been a member of
the Grand Lodge of Illinois, and had also been master of the
lodge at Roscoe, and Belvidere, in the same state. On the
organization of the Grand Lodge of Minnesota, he was chosen
Most Worshipful Grand Master, and in later years held high
places of trusts in the different organizations of Freemasonry
in this state.

Colonel William Smith, the senior warden, was a native of
Maine, had been a prominent citizen of that state, and master
of his lodge. Isaac Brown, the junior warden, was also a
native of Maine, and was a past-master. He was the first
sheriff of Hennepin county. Ard Godfrey, the treasurer,
also a native of Maine, had held a similar office in a lodge on
on the banks of the Penobscot.

John H. Stevens, the secretary, was initiated, passed and raised, in a military, traveling lodge, U. D., from the Grand Lodge of Tennessee, during the winter of 1848, at the National Bridge, in Mexico. The dispensation gave the officers of the lodge permission to meet on high hills, or low vales.

The senior deacon, D. M. Coolbaugh, was made a Mason in a Pennsylvania lodge. On the organization of Hennepin lodge, U. D., two years after the organization of Cataract lodge, he was selected as its first Master. The junior deacon, H. S. Atwood, was initiated, passed and raised, in a lodge in New Brunswick. His wife was a sister of Calvin A. Tuttle. The Tyler, William Bremer, I think, was made a Mason in Pennsylvania. He had a farm near the city.

Colonel E. Case, a native of New York, was made a Mason in a lodge near Rochester in that state. During a long residence in Michigan he held high positions in the Order in that state, and was for a long time treasurer of Blue Lodges in Hennepin county, and the first Grand Treasurer of the Grand Lodge of Minnesota. Captain J. W. T. Gardiner was a native of Hallowell, Maine, a graduate of West Point, and stationed, at the organization of Cataract Lodge, at Fort Snelling, commanding Company D, First regiment U. S. Dragoons. He was made a Mason at one of the western army forts.

The first who presented petitions for membership of Cataract Lodge were Isaac Atwater, John George Lennon, Anson Northrup, John C. Gairns, John H. Murphy, and Robert W. Cummings. These gentlemen were the first to become Masons at the Falls of St. Anthony.

The Grand Master of Iilinois, to whom the petition was sent, and who granted the dispensation to Cataract Lodge, was Judge E. B. Ames, long since a resident of Minneapolis.

CHAPTER XXIV

SOME OF THE ORIGINAL OWNERS OF THE SOIL AT THE FALLS.

A large majority of the original claimants and owners of
the soil on the military reservation and Indian lands in the
vicinity of the west bank of the Falls of St. Anthony, have
crossed the invisible, silent river, and preceded us to the
unknown land.

Sheriff Isaac Brown died many years since. Eli Pettijohn,
once so prominent in our midst, resides in California, and is
said to be a hale, hearty old man. Deacon Allen Harmon
lived a life of usefulness, and was called to a better world
some seven years ago. His children are among our most
respected citizens. Mr. Harmon's good deeds in this life will
ever be cherished by his old friends. Anson Northrup occupies a prominent place in the history of Minnesota. Warm-
hearted, generous, a good neighbor and firm friend, he has
reached a green old age, meriting the esteem of not only the
pioneers, but of the new citizens of the commonwealth. Geo.
W. Tew went further west at an early day, and died a few
years since.

Edward Murphy was for many years a prominent citizen on
the west side of the river. No one was more public-spirited.
He firmly believed in the future greatness of Minneapolis,
and freely expended money to develop its resources. He was
at the head in securing the running of boats up the river to
Minneapolis. His death was greatly regretted. His widow,
and his two children, Ira Murphy of this city, and Mrs. B.
Armstrong of St. Paul, survive him.

Sweet W. Case has long occupied a prominent position in

the community. For many years he has been city assessor.
He was our first clerk in the district court. He still resides
in Minneapolis. Peter Poncin emigrated to the Pacific coast
and died there a few years since. Martin Layman, one of
our most cherished pioneers, lived to see the city expand all
around him. A portion of his claim was laid out into a cemetery. He died three years ago.

Isaac Atwater is one of the most prominent men in the
state. For many years he occupied a seat on the supreme
bench of Minnesota. A graduate of old Yale, he is a classic
writer and ready speaker. As a lawyer he ranks among the
foremost. As a member and secretary of the old board of
regents of the University of Minnesota, he labored long and
earnestly in the interest of that great seat of learning. Judge
Atwater has occupied many high positions with credit to
himself and satisfaction to the community. At the birth of
the city he fortunately consented to serve as one of its aldermen. His wise course in the council tended largely to shape
the course of those aldermen who followed him in the adoption of wholesome ordinances for the city government. For
many years he was a member of the board of education. He
was one of the founders of our fine system of graded schools.
His good works are all around us, and he is still vigorous and
useful.

John George Lennon, a pioneer merchant, a man who was
always alive to the interests of the city, died in October, 1886,
at the age of seventy-one years. In the earlier years of the
occupation of this section of the state by the whites, Mr.
Lennon was at the front in all enterprises for the good of the
country, and was especially efficient at the Falls of St. Anthony
in securing immigration. As the representative of the American Fur Company in this neighborhood, he was influential
in the community, and he always used that influence for the
benefit of the people. He was a son-in-law of Major Nathaniel McLeau, at one time United States agent at Fort Snelling
for the Dakotas. His widow and an only son have their
home in Minneapolis.

Captain Parker, the old master of the steamboat Governor
Ramsey, after he moved on his claim adjoining Mr. Layman's,
became county commissioner, in 1872, and continued in office

until 1875. He died shortly after the expiration of his term
of office. Chandler Hutchins several years since moved into
the upper portion of this state, where he still resides. Capt.
John C. Reno went to Ohio in 1858, but returned to this city
in 1887, and is now an efficient business man. George Parks
sold his claim and returned to Maine where, if alive, he still
resides. He was our first supervisor of roads. N. E. Stoddard came from Ohio. He was a scientific agriculturist and
horticulturist, and was the first to improve, by a system of
hybridizing, the earliness of Ohio dent-corn. He also introduced the Stoddard seedling-potato, of much merit. He died
in the prime of manhood while a resident on his farm.

Z. M. Brown was a pioneer hardware dealer in St. Anthony.
He removed to this side of the river, and was engaged in
active business. After entering his land he sold it and
removed to Monticello in this state. He died some ten years
ago. Mr. Hill, his ancient neighbor, was the father of Hon.
Henry Hill, an early lawyer in Minneapolis. He died many
years ago at the residence of a son who resides in Brooklyn in
this county. Dennis Peters was an early settler. He was a
hard-working, honest man. I think he still resides in Minnesota. William Worthingham, the pioneer mechanic of St.
Anthony, lived to a great age, and died three years ago at his
home on Western avenue in this city.

Charles Farrington, after entering his land, sold it to Mr.
Jewett, and removed to Plymouth, in this county. He died
in 1887. Elijah Austin, a prominent farmer, died at his
home in this city, some ten years since, leaving a widow and
a son. F. X. Crepau, a pioneer of St. Anthony, resides on
his original preemption. He is a market-gardener, and has
secured a competency. Stephen Pratt, a member of the
ancient lumber-firm of Stevens, Pratt, and Chambers, lived
an eventful life on his farm. He was a member of Captain
E. M. Wilson's company of Mounted Rangers. He lived to
see the city limits include his farm. He died four years ago.
His brother Rufus H., who owned a place near him, is still a
resident of the city. A part of his homestead has been laid
out in city lots. Thomas Stinson, the preemptor of the
beautiful Oak Grove addition, was an old man when he first
arrived in Minnesota. He died soon after entering his land

Joseph S. Johnson still resides in Minneapolis. He has lived to see it grow from a small hamlet to an estimated population of over two hundred thousand. Asa Fletcher sold his farm on Portland avenue and removed to Farmington, in Dakota county, which is his present home. He is a brother of Dr. H. Fletcher. Another brother, Timothy, who owned an adjoining farm, died some fifteen years since. The Fletcher brothers were earnest, good men. William Goodwin, a son-in-law of Timothy Fletcher, who formerly owned the Evergreen addition to Minneapolis, resides in Brooklyn, in this county. Mr. Jackson, I think, soon after perfecting the title to his land, removed from the State.

H. H. Shepley came to Minnesota as an invalid. The climate was a great benefit to him. He was a respected influential citizen, and died many years since. His daughter is the wife of Abner Godfrey. Several of his sons are residents of this state. Andrew J. Foster has been efficient in building up the city. Charles Gilpatrick is one of our best farmers. As the city expanded he laid out his old home in city-lots and purchased another farm in the northern part of the county, but kept a city residence.

Deacon James Sully's name was for a long time a household word with the citizens of this county. Whenever county matters became entangled, Deacon Sully was called upon to straighten them out. For several years he served the county as one of its commissioners. When he died the state lost one of its best citizens. Children and grandchildren survive him. Henry C. Keith was for many years a prominent citizen. After he disposed of his land, he followed the business of a contractor. He delighted in church work, and was called upon to forward every work to make his follow-citizens better men. He died in 1888, leaving a widow and three children. Joseph H. Canney was a brother-in-law of Mr. Keith, his sister being Mr. Keith's wife ; and he was also a brother-in-law of J. B. Bassett. Mr. Canney preempted a small fraction of land at the junction of Bassett's creek with the Mississippi. Several years since he moved to the south, and died there.

Dorwin E. Moulton, who preempted Dorman's addition to Minneapolis, lives at Belvidere, Boone county, Illinois. During his long residence in Minnesota he was in active business life. He was a nephew of Ezra Dorman, one of the pioneers of St. Anthony. His wife was a sister of the wife of Major L. C. Walker, and a daughter of Cephas Gardner, who at one time represented St. Anthony in the territorial house of representatives.

Alfred C. Murphy was a brother of Edward Murphy. He was engaged in the saddle and harness business. A correct, just man, he was much respected by his neighbors. He died in 1887, leaving a widow and several children. William G. Murphy, also a brother of Edward Murphy, was many years engaged in business in this city. He died in early life. He was never married.

Hiram Burlingham raised a large family of children, and a few years since moved to California. His wife was a daughter of Reuben Bean who temporarily resided in the old government house, on this side of the river, as early as 1849. Mr. Burlingham's object in emigrating to California was to secure land upon which to settle his children around him. He was a hard-working man while a resident of this state.

Simeon Odell, a young, single man who kept bachelor's hall for many years on the road to the Fort, had received a good education, and was fond of books, and made as good a farmer as could be expected of a man without a wife. He sold his farm many years since, and removed to the southern part of the state, where he resides.

E. A. Hodson came to this state as a Universalist minister. In early years he led a sea-faring life. He resides near the city. He is a fluent speaker, a warm friend of the pioneers, and a man of generous impulses.

Edgar Folsom, one of the earliest pioneers of St. Anthony, resides in the city. He is a man of industrious habits. Mrs. Sayer, the only female preemptor on the military reservation, became the wife of William Dickie. She died many years ago. Mr. Dickie was a man of talent, and always popular. He removed to Virginia several years since, where he now resides.

Robert Blaisdell, a native of northern Vermont, spent many years in Maine, from which state he removed with his family to Minnesota. Industrious, a kind husband and father, an obliging neighbor, his death, in the spring of 1887, was much lamented. He was over four-score years of age at the time of his departure from this world of sorrow. His eldest son, John T. Blaisdell, resides on the land he preempted so many years ago. He is a man of strict integrity, of good business habits, and enjoys the entire confidence of the community. William Blaisdell, another son of Robert Blaisdell, also resides on his primitive claim. A great portion of the time since his residence here he has been engaged in the lumber business. He is alive to everything that benefits the city and state, and is a good man. While he has decided opinions of his own, he is willing others should enjoy the same privilege.

Deacon John S. Mann came west from Vermont when a boy. After selling his claim he removed further west, and is now a resident of Mandan, Dakota. He was the first deacon in the first Congregational church at the Falls of St. Anthony. He was also the first treasurer of Hennepin county. His first wife was a daughter of the venerable pioneer, Joshua Draper. Deacon Mann was a useful citizen, and his removal from the county is greatly regretted.

Lucien N. Parker is a resident of Minneapolis. For many years he has followed the practice of veterinary surgeon in this city, with much success. Henry Angell sold his claim and removed to California. He is remembered as a quiet, good man. Henry Heap resides in Minneapolis. He has led a just, honest life, and is respected by every one.

James A. Lennon, a brother of John George Lennon, was for many years an active business man. He dealt largely in real-estate. His death occurred in 1876. Mr. Lennon was a man of much more than average ability. He was never married.

Deacon Oliver was for many years one of the best-known men in Minneapolis, and one of the most honored of all its citizens. He was one of the founders of the Westminster church in this city. He never had any children, but his aged widow survives him. That excellent lady has recently contributed a very large sum of money for the benefit of Mc-Allister college.

Charles Moseau, after selling his farm on Lake Calhoun, moved into the city and followed the business of carpentering. He died several years since, leaving several children. He was a quiet, unassuming man, honest and faithful in every walk of life.

George E. Huy is now a resident of Great Falls, Montana, filling the office of city judge. He was the second register of deeds of Hennepin county, and also held several other offices in the city and county. He contributed much in building up the city. None of the old settlers are held in higher esteem than Mr. Huy

David Gorham, after selling his farm to R. P. Russell, moved to the neighborhood of Medicine Lake, and for most of the time has lived there. He was the first coroner of Hennepin county. Mr. Gorham has always commanded the respect of the citizens of the county.

Arthur H. Mills, for many years, was actively engaged in business in this vicinity. He was a quartermaster in the army, with the rank of captain, during the late civil war. His wife, one of the most beautiful ladies that ever resided here, died while he was in the army, leaving an only son. After the war, Captain Mills was engaged in the lumber business. He died greatly lamented by a large circle of friends.

Josiah Draper, Captain Mills nearest neighbor on the old reservation, sold his interest in his preemption and moved to Sauk Center in this state, but lived only a few years after his removal. Mr. Draper was a deacon in the Baptist church, and was a man of great worth.

Charles Brown, after the disposal of his farm, removed up the river from Minneapolis, where he resides. Mr. Brown was a good farmer and a good neighbor.

Frank Rollins lived on his farm for many years after he preempted it. He subsequently moved to Hutchinson, Mc-Leod county, in this state, where he died two years ago. Mr. Rollins was a man of great merit. Simeon Bean, a nephew of Captain John Rollins, has been engaged more or less in the lumber business. He is a resident of the state, and is a capable, honest man.

John Wass is a resident of this city, though since preempting his land he has frequently been absent from the state. He has always led an honest life.

Ard Godfrey's life has been full of interesting events. For

many years he has been extensively engaged in the milling industries of this state. He is a resident of this city. No man among the pioneers has been more efficient in accomplishing good results for the state than Mr. Godfrey. His friends are numerous ; his enemies (if any) are few. For the many favors he bestowed upon the pioneers, in territorial days, too much credit cannot be given.

Amasa Crafts lives in our midst. Since his preemption he has been engaged in different business pursuits. He is a man of sterling worth, and held in the highest esteem by the entire community.

Hiram Van Nest has, by a life of industry and integrity, accumulated a competency. He divides his time between this city and California. His wife was a daughter of the late Robert Blaisdell.

John Berry, after he sold his farm, moved into the city and resided here during the remainder of his life. He was considered one of the best farmers in the state. He left an interesting family, some of whom are residents of this city. Mr. Berry was an industrious, honest man.

Mark T. Berry, only son of John Berry, is a resident of Los Angeles, California, and is extensively engaged in fruit-raising.

Robert Blaisdell, jr., has been largely engaged with his brother William in the lumber trade. He has also extensive farming interests. His residence has always been in Minneapolis. Mr. Blaisdell is a good citizen.

Willis G. Moffett lived to a good old age, surrounded by a large family of children who had all reached maturity before his death. He was one of the most valued of the pioneers. His son, William G. Moffett, is a resident of a portion of the land he preempted. He has led a farmer's life, honored by the people of this portion of the state.

Colonel S. Woods, U. S. A., who owned the land bordering on the north bank of Minnehaha Falls, is now a resident of Oakland, California.

William Finch moved to California in 1878, and is now a resident of that state. He is a nephew of Hon. John W. North. Mr. Finch was deservedly popular.

Samuel Stough had reached middle life upon his advent

into the territory. He has been dead many years, but his memory is still green in the hearts of those who had the pleasure of his acquaintance. His aged widow, and several children, survive him. Among the latter is Mrs. Captain Mahlon Black of this city.

S. S. Crowell was one of the original members of the Plymouth Congregational church in this city. He died several years ago, greatly respected.

Mark Baldwin, after the sale of his farm, lived for a time at Litchfield, in this state, from which place he moved to California.

Thomas W. Pierce has always been a valued citizen. He is still a resident on the land he obtained from the government.

Few men were better or more favorably known than Calvin Church. He was a pure specimen of manhood. His widow, now Mrs. Captain John Noble, lives in this city.

A. K. Hartwell for many years was a merchant on Washington avenue. He now resides in California.

William Hanson lived to be over eighty years of age. He led an honest life, and died greatly regretted. His son, Hon. D. M. Hanson, was, in his day, one of our most prominent citizens. He died in the spring of 1856, while a member of the territorial council.

Daniel M. Coolbaugh, who made an arrangement with Dr. A. E. Ames to enter a portion of his original claim, was for many years one of our most active citizens. A portion of the land Mr. Coolbaugh preempted is now known as Mattison's first and second additions to Minneapolis. Mr. Coolbaugh had a large circle of friends. His widow resides in the city. Three children survive him—Rev. Frank Coolbaugh, an Episcopal clergyman of great promise, Mrs. W. E. Jones, and Mrs. L. Hael.

Gordon Jackins, who was interested in a claim in this county, with his brother William, lived and died in Hassan, in this county and state.

Rev. Abner C. Godfrey, a brother of Ard Godfrey, who preempted a fraction of land on the bank of the river below the Falls, returned east in 1856, and is pastor of a Methodist church in the interior of Massachusetts.

Edwin Hedderly, whose home joined Mr. Godfrey's, was for more than twenty years one of the most active business men in Minneapolis. His death occurred in this city.

There were one or two others who preempted land on the military reservation and the ceded Indian lands, in the immediate vicinity of the west bank of the Falls of St. Anthony, but their present residence (if they are alive) is unknown to me. There are others, not mentioned in this chapter, whose names will be recorded in the following pages.

BUT FEW ANSWER AT ROLL-CALL.

Only a few of those whose names are mentioned in the foregoing survive the years that have passed since they first occupied their lands. It is a duty I owe to their memory to record their names; to bear a willing tribute to their many virtues; to cheerfully hand down to this and future generations my testimony as to the honesty of the first occupants of the soil. The fields, which they cultivated with so much pride, are now part of a large city, teeming with a multitude of people, who have but little knowledge of those who preceded them as the owners of the land upon which their homes are made. The earnest faces, manly forms, free speech, frank manners and youthful appearance of the pioneers of those early days of trust and trial, tribulation and triumph, are so distinct in my memory that the foreground of the present, bright as it is, seems a background that brings more conspicuously into view those glowing forms of the past.

CHAPTER XXV.

The regents of the University held several sessions during 1851. At the first meeting Regent Marshall moved that immediate steps be taken for the erection of a building suitable for a preparatory department. Governor Ramsey, Sibley, Marshall, and Rice, were appointed a committee to secure a library. Advertisements were ordered published in the newspapers, soliciting the donation of a site for the University from land-owners. In response, Messrs. Franklin Steele, H. H. Sibley, W. A. Cheever, Joseph McAlpin, S. W. Farnham, C. T. Stinson, R. W. Cummings, and Henry Angell, offered lands for that purpose. After a thorough examination of the sites offered, that of Franklin Steele was accepted. This location was on the grounds and adjoining the lands of the Exposition building, and it consisted of less than five acres.

At the June meeting of the regents the secretary was directed to advertise for proposals for the immediate building of the preparatory department. Subscriptions were solicited from the citizens towards defraying the expenses of the building. Two thousand five hundred dollars were raised by the citizens for that purpose.

The standing committee, of the board on lands, for 1851, was composed of Regents Ramsey, Sibley and Van Vorhes. Regents C. H. Smith, Marshall, and Van Vorhes, were appointed a committee to devise a proper seal for the University.

The teachers in the public-school district No. 5, Ramsey county, during the summer, were Miss Mary A. Scofield and Miss Mary Murphy.

ST. ANTHONY'S FIRST CELEBRATION OF INDEPENDENCE DAY.

The seventy-fifth anniversary of our National Independence was celebrated on Hennepin Island. It being the first celebration of Independence day by the citizens of St. Anthony, it was determined that it should be one that would be a credit to old St. Anthony of Padua himself. On St. John's day the following officers were selected to act on the occasion : President, Hon. Charles T. Stearns ; Marshal, Dr. John H. Murphy, with Roswell P. Russell and G. Corvin, assistants ; William H. Larned, reader of Declaration ; Isaac Atwater, orator ; Rev. C. W. Brown, chaplain ; John H. Stevens, master of toasts ; John W. North, W. A. Cheever, and Edward Patch, committee on toasts ; Chessman Gould, Leonard Gould, and Elias H. Conner, committee on music ; S. W. Farnham, Chas. Kingsley, Sylvanus Tourtlotte, committee on salutes. The entire programme was carried out, and a more interesting and patriotic celebration probably has not since taken place in the vicinity of the Falls. The oration pronounced by Judge Atwater was worthy of the occasion. Among the distinguished visitors present was Dr. Malony, long a member of congress from Illinois, whose eloquent speech in response to a complimentary toast was greatly enjoyed. The original settlers on the reserve were mainly indebted to Dr. Malony, in after years, for the passage of the bill by congress giving them their homes for a dollar and a quarter an acre.

A DISTINGUISHED WEDDING.

Early in July, St. Anthony was visited by Miss Sarah Coates, a noted lecturer on physiology. Miss Coates was a native of Chester county, Pennsylvania. Her lectures here, as well as elsewhere, were well attended. On the 15th of the following month, at the St. Charles hotel, this lady became the wife of Captain Daniel Smith Harris, one of the pioneer steamboatmen of the upper Mississippi. At the time this was considered the most distinguished wedding that had ever taken place in the little village.

FIRST DOWNWARD MOVEMENT OF REAL-ESTATE.

On the morning of Tuesday, the 14th of July the whole vicinity was startled by what was supposed to be an earthquake. The earth trembled, and there was a crash louder than heavy thunder. It was caused by a land-slide of the west bank of the Mississippi from the high precipice into the river. An acre or two of earth, near where the gas-works now are, went down-stream, carrying trees and rock.

On the 20th of July Messrs. Church and Getchell started a meat-market in the village. Heretofore fresh meats had to be bought mostly in St. Paul, sometimes at Fort Snelling. There being no swine in the territory, there was, as a matter of course, no fresh-pork, but there was plenty of salt-pork. Veal was unknown at this time. There was fresh-beef after the middle of the summer. In some instances it could be procured in May and June, but it was of oxen from the pineries, and not desirable. Wild game was abundant at all seasons.

The people of the young village greatly lamented the death of two married ladies. Mrs. Perrin Getchell died on the 26th of July, and Mrs. Ramsdell, wife of Edward Ramsdell, and daughter of Washington Getchell, died on the 15th of August at the age of eighteen years.

Preparations having been made, and the money raised by subscription having been paid into the treasury of the University, work was commenced August 9th on the preparatory building of the University of Minnesota, and prosecuted with vigor, the building being completed in eight weeks, and on the 11th of October was ready for the reception of students. The services of Prof. E. W. Merrill were secured as principal. He was one of the best educators of the day, and the regents were fortunate in their choice.

The first singing-school in St. Anthony was organized on the 23d of August by Prof. Bennett, of Ohio. Its patronage was large for several terms.

The Express of August 23 made sport of the pretensions of All Saints. The few of us on the west bank of the river laughed with those on the other bank, but were determined that All Saints (now Minneapolis proper) should be a rival to the east side that we would not be ashamed of. It came sooner than we expected; we swallowed the Express, its editor, St. Anthony, Cheever-town and all.

August 30th D. E. Moulton, a former prominent citizen of the lead-mines of southern Wisconsin, purchased and took possession of the St. Charles hotel.

On the first of September a change was made in the command and the officers at Fort Snelling. Captain S. B. Buckner was ordered to take command at Fort Atchison, which was at the Santa Fe crossing, in Arkansas; and Captain R. W. Kirkham was sent to Jefferson barracks, Missouri. Both of these officers were greatly interested at that time in real-estate in this neighborhood.

On Monday, the 15th of September, the first temperance society was organized in St. Anthony, with Washington Getchell, president ; Isaac Brown, vice-president ; George F. Brott, secretary ; John W. North, Rufus Farnham, Isaac V. Draper, and Allen Harmon, committee.

On the 22d the entire Express outfit was purchased by Judge Atwater ; Messrs. Elmer Tyler, H. and J. P. Woodbury, retiring.

On December 13th the mercury fell to twenty degrees below zero, which proved to be about the coldest day in the winter. The ice below the Falls became gorged and spread over the low grounds at Miller's and Cheever's landings, now the Bohemian Flats, so-called. The like was never known before by the primitive settlers, and has never occurred since. Mr. Lennon's warehouse received serious injury from the ice.

The Congregational church building was finished on the 15th. It was one of the best edifices of the kind in the territory.

The winter lectures before the Library association were commenced December 16th, when the new Chief-Justice, M. M. Fuller, delivered the first lecture.

The school-census was finished December 27th, and the result showed that the village contained one hundred and eighty-five school children, a large majority of them, with their parents, only residents since the opening of navigation the previous spring : the population having more than doubled during eight months.

ST. ANTHONY PIONEERS OF 1851.

The following are among the valuable citizens who came to the village in 1851, though a few of the names should have been included in the lists of previous years : Colonel Emanuel Case, Ira Murphy, George E. Case, J. H. Brown, Sweet W. Case, James Gale Case, Mark T. Berry, A. H. Mills, S. Jenkins, A. H. Young, Dr. A. E. Ames, Norman Jenkins, J.

C. Lawrence, Thomas Self, Samuel Ross, Edward Lippincott,
Hon. Samuel Thatcher, George A. Camp, John T. Blaisdell,
Hiram Van Nest, Philip Fraker, S. B. Sutton, Joseph Le
Duc, A. G. McKenzie, Dr. V. Fell, James M. Jarrett, Lucius
C. Walker, G. B. Dutton, Christopher Greeley, William
Blaisdell, William W. Wales, Robert Blaisdell, Robert Blais-
dell, jr., William G. Moffett, John C. Gairns, Joel B. Bassett,
Fleet F. Strother, Isaac Brown, Charles Case, P. Strother,
Joseph Menard, Rev. A. C. Godfrey, Waterman Stinson,
David Bickford, Leonard Gould, G. Corvin, A. N. Hoyt, Otis
T. Whitney, Chessman Gould, Sylvanus Tourtelotte, Isaac V.
Draper, Prof. E. W. Merrill, H. H. Given, David A. Secombe,
E. L. Hall, Timothy Fletcher, William Spooner, William Mc
Farland, Henry Fowler, L. Cummings, J. C. Tufts, Z. E. B.
Nash, Edgar Nash, Z. M. Brown, Benjamin Soule, Benjamin
Brown, George Davis, William H. Hubbard, William A.
Rowell, Thomas Stinson, Rev. Mr. Jones, John Wass, Charles
Fish, Asa Fletcher, William Goodwin, Ezra Foster, Munson
Brothers, Nathaniel Tibbetts and brothers, B. F. Hildreth,
Leonard Day and sons, S. E. Foster, A. J. Foster, E. P.
Mills, James H. Mills, and William Laschell.

LAST OF THE VISITS OF THE RED-MEN.

The Indian chieftain, Man-of-the-Clouds, with several of
his tribe, came down from Oak Grove, on Christmas, seeking
presents and alms from R. P. Russell, and other acquaintances at the Falls. He said he could not expect to meet his
white friends in this neighborhood in the future, as his band
would soon move for the winter into the hunting-grounds of
the big-woods, and when spring came he should follow the
Dakotas to their reservation on the upper Minnesota river.
He was desirous of accepting such farewell gifts with the
compliments of the season as his friends, Mr. Russell and
others, should see proper to give him, which he should
cherish as tokens of friendship in his new home. As the
wily chieftain mostly solicited perishable gifts (in their
hands) such as bread, meat, sugar, coffee, and the like, it
was evident that the immediate wants of the stomach were
the tokens by which his former friends were to be remembered.

We made the old Man-of-the-Clouds and his wives and

children happy. If I remember correctly, the old man was right in saying that he was visiting the Falls for the last time. Not so, however, with Good Road, chief of the other band of the lake Dakotas. He remembered us with visits after the removal to the Redwood country ; but the close of the year 1851 in a mersure ended the protracted visits of the Dakotas to the Falls. It is true they would occasionally swarm down on us by the hundreds, but in after years their sojourn was of short duration.

Both Man-of-the-Clouds and Good Road were born on the banks of Lake Calhoun. They had great faith in the healing virtues of the water of a spring at Owen Keegan's claim, which they would come all the way from Redwood and Yellow Medicine to bathe in, and drink of. Then again they would leave the Agency in the fall for the purpose of gathering the cranberries that grew on the marshes in the neighborhood of Minneapolis. These they would sell to the traders ; though as a matter of history it is well known that after their removal to the new reservation they would, on any occasion possible, visit their old haunts on the bank of the Mississippi on the east, and to the Iowa line on the south. This was not confined to the Medewakantonwans, but to the Wahpekutas, Wahpetonwans, and other bands.

Before the outbreak in 1862, they were often the source of much annoyance to the white settlers on the meadow lands, from their wandering habits, but the end of the Indian war of 1862 and 1863 mostly ended their visitations to their former hunting-grounds, the sites of their old villages, and the graves of their fathers.

CHAPTER XXVI.

There was from the beginning a strong temperance element in St. Anthony, which included a large majority of the citizens. This element observed New Year's day by a mass convention, determined to blot out by legislative enactment the selling of all intoxicating drinks, not only in the village of St. Anthony, but throughout the territory. As the annual meeting of the legislature was near, the convention was held with a view of influencing public opinion in favor of the movement, and of strengthening the backbone of such members as were in favor of the measure.

It was decided that a territorial temperance society should be immediately organized. A committee was appointed, consisting of Dr. V. Fell, G. G. Loomis, Edward Murphy, S. E. Foster, John McDonald, Isaac Brown, Dr. A. E. Ames, E. P. Mills, W. Getchell, E. B. Stanley, Isaac V. Draper, Rufus Farnham, Dr. H. Fletcher, James McMullen, and Henderson Rogers. This committee was to carry out the views of the convention.

As a matter of history, it can be stated that they were entirely successful in their movement ; the legislature passed a moderate prohibitory law ; but at a term of the United States court held in St. Paul subsequent to the adjournment of the legislature the law was declared unconstitutional.

LYCEUM LECTURES—DELAYED MAIL.

The course of the New Year's lectures before the St. Anthony

OF MINNESOTA AND ITS PEOPLE.

Library Association commenced with a great degree of success. The attendance was large at every lecture. Dr. A. E. Ames gave the first lecture, on physiology. He was followed, during the winter, by Chief Justice Fuller ; Rev. Mr. Merrick, of the Episcopal church, St. Paul ; Judge B. B. Meeker, Isaac Atwater, W. R. Marshall, W. G. Le Duc, and Prof. Merrill. None of us expected to get our mail on time immediately after the close of navigation, but when weeks passed, and still no news from the great world outside of Minnesota, we became impatient. On the 2d of January the delayed mail arrived, containing the President's annual message delivered at the opening of Congress on the first Monday in December. The cause of the delay was the difficulty in crossing Black river, on Wyman Knowlton's road. While we were annoyed by the repeated failures of the mail, we were so pleased to hear from our friends in our early and their eastern homes, when the mail came, that we soon forgot the failures.

BY DOG-TRAIN FROM PEMBINA.

The delegates from Pembina to the legislature, Messrs. Norman W. Kittson, Joseph Rolette, and Antoine Gingras, passed through the village, on their way to St. Paul, on the evening of the 2d day of January, 1852. They were sixteen days making the journey. They came in a dog-train. In those days it was considered a remarkably rapid transit. True, the same journey is made now, by rail, in as many hours as it then required days. Three large Esquimaux dogs in single file were attached to a long, narrow, light sled, and were capable of making about forty miles a day, though it was necessary that frequent stops should be made for the dogs to rest, about one day in three. The animals were noble specimens of their species. Their heads were like those of the wolf ; they had powerful fore-shoulders ; were fleet of foot, and capable of great endurance ; and when well-trained were handled without difficulty. They readily followed a trail. Their food was mostly pemican, which is dried meat and tallow of the buffalo. These dogs were a great curiosity in St. Paul.

The third legislative assembly convened its session on the 7th of January. Governor Ramsey's message congratulated the people in regard to the treaty with the Indians. The session was a mild one. Among the laws of interest passed was one creating the county of Hennepin.

A PUBLIC DINNER TO FRANKLIN STEELE.

On January 8th, 1852, an event occurred at St. Anthony, of the greatest importance to its future prosperity. Mr. Steele, who had, in 1849, sold a half-interest in the mill and other real property in the village to A. W. Taylor of Boston, purchased it back from him, thus insuring prosperity to the place. Heretofore Mr. Taylor had refused to sell lots to those who wanted to settle on and improve them. Mr. Steele and his partner Ard Godfrey had adopted a liberal policy in relation to the disposal of property, but were, as to actual settlers, thwarted by Mr. Taylor. The sale that Mr. Taylor made to Mr. Steele was considered of so much moment to the people that it was determined by the citizens to tender Mr. Steele a public dinner at the St. Charles on the 16th of January. Messrs Charles T. Stearns, George F. Brott, Dr. J. H. Murphy, Samuel Thatcher, jr., and Pierre Bottineau, were appointed a committee to make the tender to Mr. Steele. That gentleman's reply to the invitation was as follows : "Fort Snelling, January 16th, 1852. Gentlemen : I have received your kind invitation to dinner for Friday evening. Nothing can afford me more pleasure than to meet my St. Anthony friends on that occasion."

The dinner came off according to the programme. In response to the complimentary toast, "Our distinguished and esteemed guest : may he live to see a hundred anniversaries of this joyous occasion," Mr. Steele made an eloquent speech ; returning profound thanks for the confidence his fellow-citizens had in him ; said he had been a resident of this neighborhood for fourteen years, during the last two of which the wilderness had given way to fruitful fields ; that his friends had caused the hitherto lonely country to rejoice in enlightened occupation, and the wild lands to smile with harvests. Interesting remarks were made by Hon. M. E. Ames, Judge Atwater, Major J. J. Noah, and Dr. C. W. Borup of St. Paul, Hon. Norman W. Kittson of Pembina, Hon.

Martin McLeod of Oak Grove, Hon. C. T. Stearns, Dr. J. H. Murphy, J. G. Lennon, C. A. Tuttle, and other prominent gentlemen of St. Anthony.

A PIONEER OF THE LAST CENTURY.

Among the distinguished gentlemen present on that memorable occasion was the venerable Jean Baptiste Faribault, who visited the Falls as early as 1798, fifty-four years before. He was the pioneer of pioneers in Minnesota, trading with the Indians on the banks of the Mississippi two years previous to the beginning of the present century. He had a store at Little Rapids (now San Francisco) in Carver county, in 1802. In 1805 he settled on Pike island, at the mouth of the Minnesota river. This island had been given to his wife by a vote of her Dakota friends in a grand council. She was a Miss Pelagie, daughter of a French merchant, whose wife was a native Dakota. Mr. and Mrs. Faribault had four sons, Alexander, Oliver, David, and Frederick. He had also several daughters, one of whom was the wife of an army officer of high rank. Another married Hon. A. Bailey, first territorial representative in the legislature from this district. Mr. Faribault was one of the best judges in the northwest on the quality of fur. He was small of stature, and gentlemanly in his bearing. He sent his children east to be educated. He was born in Canada, in 1774, and died at the residence of his son, in Faribault, August 20, 1860. He received a liberal education in early life, and was a pure, honest man, whose memory is cherished by all who had the pleasure of his acquaintance.

NOTABLE DEATH   EXTREME COLD —FIRST FIRE.

All classes of people were greatly surprised and grieved to learn that Hon. Henry L. Tilden, formerly U. S. Marshal, and secretary of the council, died at his home in St. Paul on on the 17th of January.

Considerable suffering was occasioned on the 20th in consequence of the extreme cold weather, the mercury falling to forty degrees below zero ; probably considerably lower, but no one had a spirit thermometer to indicate the temperature.

The Express made light of the low temperature ; said it was
true the weather was coolish, even chilly ; but no one suffered
any inconvenience, and the cold made business more lively.

On the 18th the first fire occurred in the village. Geo. F.
Brott's carriage-factory was totally consumed, at a loss of
several thousand dollars. Mr. F. B. Bachelor's paint-shop
was in the upper-story of the factory. His loss was also
heavy. The property was not insured, as the fire occurred
before the days of insurance companies in the country ; though
in consequence of the fire one of the Hartford fire insurance-
companies appointed an agent in St. Anthony.

VISIT TO THE PINERIES AND MILLE LAC.

In making an extended trip through the extreme northwest,
leaving St. Anthony on the 20th, in company with John Geo.
Lennon, I visited the pineries on Rum river, following that
stream to its source, Mille Lac, where we found several
Indian traders on the banks of the lake. The Mille Lac
Indians, so called, were of the Chippewa nation. Of the many
beautiful lakes in Minnesota, there are none superior to this.
At a subsequent visit to this lake the same winter, with my
ancient neighbor, Calvin A. Tuttle, he said the probabilities
were that some day, when there would be a great city at the
Falls of St. Anthony, the people of that city would depend
upon this lake for their daily supply of water. A person
cannot see across the lake. The distance from shore to shore
is said to be forty miles. The surface of the lake contained
numerous tents on the ice, which were used by the Indians
for fishing. A hole was cut through the ice, a small tent
placed over it, and an Indian would catch a large number of
fish from the place during the winter. The Indians had a
way of preserving the fish by drying them over a small fire,
and afterwards smoking them. It was said that fish preserved
in this way would be palateable for a long time.

Good old Father Hennepin was a prisoner on an island in
this lake two centuries ago. At that time the Dakotas had
possession of it. Large groves of hard-wood maple are found
on the borders of the lake, from which the Indians made
sugar every spring. The sap flowed into small buckets ingen-
iously made of white birch bark.

MILLE LAC AS A PROBABLE WATER-SUPPLY FOR MINNEAPOLIS.

It is not improbable that Mr. Tuttle's prediction may prove true in regard to the use of water from Mille Lac for the city at the Falls. There are no difficulties in the way that engineering cannot easily overcome in conveying the water to this point. The problem of an unlimited supply of pure water for the rapidly-increasing population of our wonderfully fine city must soon be solved, and the sooner the better.

CANADIAN STOVES   WINTER IMPROVEMENTS   SUSPENSION BRIDGE

We were (as on previous winters in traveling through the northwest) surprised to find at every trading outpost that the stoves in use were made at St. Maurce, a suburb of Three Rivers, a little city between Montreal and Quebec, in Canada. These stoves, in the early days, were in universal use in the northwest. The quarters at Fort Snelling had them. The Fur Company used them. They were brought from Canada by way of the great lakes.

Returning on the 7th of February, I was pleased to notice that several new buildings had been commenced in St. Anthony during my absence. Cold as that season was, there were some who were so impatient to make improvements they would not wait until spring but commenced operations in mid-winter. At this time St. Anthony had nine stores, one cabinet-shop, four blacksmith shops, two carriage factories, and other industries. On the 21st of February the legislature passed a bill authorizing the building of a bridge over the Mississippi from Nicollet Island to the western shore of the river. The incorporators were Franklin Steele, Henry H. Sibley, Henry M. Rice, Calvin A. Tuttle, Isaac Atwater, John H. Stevens, John George Lennon, John Rollins, A. E. Ames, and D. E. Moulton, all of Minnesota ; and Robert Smith of Alton, and Buel G. Wheeler, of Rockford, Illinois.

HIGH PRICES THE RULE IN 1852.

Perhaps because tired of living on salt meats, salt fish, venison, and other game, during the winter, when fresh pork from Iowa was placed in the market it readily sold for twelve and a half cents per pound. On the 22d of February a saloon-keeper, wishing to purchase a few eggs to make "tom-and-jerry", so that Washington's birthday could be, as he said, properly celebrated, had to pay forty cents a dozen for them.

Everything ruled high at the Falls during the winter of 1852. Even hay became scarce. The meadows back of, the city in the fall had contained a large amount of hay, which had been properly stacked, but a large portion of it had mysteriously disappeared during the early-winter, and when the owners went for it in February it was not to be found, and they never discovered what became of it.

A SOCIETY WEDDING AND CHURCH FESTIVITIES.

Our high-sheriff, Geo. F. Brott, had become convinced that it was not good for man to live alone. Consequently, on the 19th of February he married Miss Mary G. Stearns, the accomplished daughter of Hon. C. T. Stearns. Rev. Chas. Secombe, of the Congregational church, officiated on the occasion. A marriage in the village, during the early days, was an uncommon event, and it was properly observed by what would now be called the society people. Though few were given in marriage, the social season at the Falls continued all through the long winter. There were balls, parties, lectures, lyceums, and gatherings of old and young at private residences, all to close for the season, on the second of March, with a grand donation visit to Rev. C. G. Ames and his excellent wife, at the home of Deacon Allen Harmon. The committee to manage the gathering represented every church in the village. For instance, John W. North, E. P. Mills, Thomas Chambers, and H. Jenkins, were from the Congregational church ; Prof. Merrill, Mrs. Merrill, and Miss Mary Murphy, from the Methodist church ; Wm. H. Townsend, Geo. W. Prescott, Mrs. Prescott, and Miss Nason, the Baptist church ; Dr. V. Fell, Mrs. Fell, and Miss Lucy Harmon, the Free-Will Baptist church ; while Henry Fowler, Mrs. Fowler, George Burrows, H. Rogers, E. R. Ramsdell, Miss North, Mrs. C. D. and Mrs. A. H. Dorr, Miss Dorr, and Miss Adeline Jefferson, represented different churches. As the first donation visit ever held at the Falls of St. Anthony, it was a great success. Every one contributed to the worthy pastor and his wife, and every one was happy.

OTHER EVENTS OF THE WINTER.

Two days after the happy event above described, March 4, the store of Daniel Stanchfield was consumed by fire. This was the second serious fire in St. Anthony. Mr. Stanchfield had a heavy stock of goods, and all was consumed.

On the 13th Isaac Atwater was appointed reporter for the supreme court.

On the 20th the mails were only twenty-one days behind time. This fact indicated that spring was near, and that the mail-carrier could not get across the rivers between Prairie du Chien and St. Paul, in consequence of the ice breaking. The uncertainties of the mail were of more anxiety to us than our money, or anything else. On the 22d new ice must have been made, as the thermometer showed ten degrees below zero. Spring not so near as we expected.

OUR OLD COUNTY BOUNDARY.

After the adjournment of the legislature, the few of us on the west side of the river determined to celebrate, in a quiet way, the passage of the bill for a new county. We found on examination of the records that our new boundaries had at different times been included in the county of Des Moines, county of Dubuque, county of Clayton, and county of Alamakee, all of the territory and state of Iowa; and the county of Dakota, Minnesota. We were inclined to believe that, could the proper records have been hunted up, we were once included in some of the counties of Missouri.

DISCUSSING A NAME FOR OUR TOWN.

The St. Anthony Express of the 27th of March, just prior to our meeting, strongly advised selecting some other name than All Saints for our embryo village. This matter was considered, but while all rejoiced at the passage of the bill giving us a new county, when the suggestion of the Express was considered we discovered there were "many men of different minds", and a permanent name could not be agreed upon. The Express wanted to know how the name of Hennepin would suit our fancy. That paper thought it would be highly proper to name the prospective village after the first white man who witnessed the dancing waters of St. Anthony, and said the "day was not far distant when the west side of the Falls would be the second city in Minnesota, always remembering that St. Anthony will be the first". While we were pleased with the complimentary remarks in regard to our future prospects, the name of Hennepin did not strike us favorably, because it was the name of our county. Had that been called Snelling, as we wanted it, our choice would have been unanimous for adopting the suggestion, and no doubt future letters from the west side would have been dated Hennepin, Snelling county, Minnesota, instead of Minneapolis, Hennepin county, Minnesota.

INCIDENTS OF THE SPRING OF 1852.

During the last week in March, most all the teams, with the crews engaged in the lumber business in the pineries, arrived in St. Anthony. Those that were in good working order were fattened for a few weeks, and sent to the shambles. Pinery beef was the subject of funny editorials in the Pioneer.

The steamer Governor Ramsey had been completely overhauled and put in excellent condition for the navigation of the upper Mississippi for the approaching season. In the early spring Captain Rollins sold the steamer to Captain Parker, Benj. Soule, A. H. and C. D. Dorr, and Dr. C. W. Borup. In the change of the ownership of the boat the same popular officers and crew were retained. The river was free from ice on the second of April, and the steamer resumed its regular trips for the year. Captain Tapper's ferry was put in good order at the same time.

After a slight fall of snow during the first days of April, Hobart Whitson, who resided above the Falls, came upon the tracks of a strange animal. Following them for a few miles, he came near an Indian encampment. He turned over the trail to the Indians, who followed it for over ten miles, when the animal took refuge up a tree, and was killed. It was said that the strange beast was three feet high, and seven feet eleven inches long from the tip of the nose to the end of the tail. It was thought to be the first animal of the kind ever seen in Minnesota. It was probably a panther. Another animal of the same kind was seen a few days afterwards, but escaped from the Indians who were hunting it. About the same time an eagle of tremendous size soared around Cheever's hill, now the site of the University. This particular king of birds was strong enough to carry off a sheep. He was caught in a trap through the ingenuity of one of the pioneers, without being much injured. For a while this bird was the winged favorite of the village.

On the 14th of April Calvin A. Tuttle and Simon Stevens returned from an exploring expedition immediately south and west of the Falls. They reported the discovery of what is now Lake Minnetonka. The Express said the discovery created a good deal of excitement. Messrs. Tuttle and Stevens gave the lake the name of "Peninsula," from the fact it contained so many arms extending out and in all around its boundaries ; but during the following month Gov. Ramsey and a party visited the new wonder, and the governor christened it Minnetonka, a name it retains to this day. While the existence of so large a body of water was unknown to the new immigrants of 1849 and two subsequent years, the old settlers were well acquainted with its waters ; but the great beauty of the lake had never been described to the new-comers. In fact the lake had been visited by Joseph R. Brown, and a son of Colonel Snelling, as early as 1822. In after years Franklin Steele and Martin McLeod also made a pilgrimage to Minnetonka, and probably many other old residents also visited it.

A sad event occurred in the family of Mr. Fowler. His daughter was accidentally shot by her brother. It was the repetition of so many accidents ever since the introduction of firearms. The youngster did not know the gun was loaded. This was the first accident of the kind that occurred at the Falls. It is to be regretted it was not the last.

The able pen of Rev. T. Rowell, a Presbyterian clergyman of much talent, contributed articles to the Express which, with those of the editor-in-chief, Isaac Atwater, gave the paper an excellent reputation over the whole Union. Mr. Rowell had been a resident of the village since the previous year. Mr. Atwater's increasing professional business rendered it necessary that he should, in a measure, retire from the more active duties of writing editor. In May, Geo. D. Bowman, from Pennsylvania, visited the Falls on a prospecting tour. He came highly recommended as a newspaper man. Mr. Atwater made an arrangement with Mr. Bowman by which he was relieved from the arduous duties of the paper. Mr. Bowman continued on the Express for many years, and became one of the leading men of the territory and state. Like most every one else, he dealt in real-estate ; for a time successfully ; in the end, disastrously. He received an important Federal appointment in New Mexico, which he held for a long period, and it is believed he is still a resident of that territory. With the exception of Charles Hoag, who invented it, we are more indebted to Mr. Bowman than any person for the name our proud city bears.

On April 30th Rev. Lyman Palmer made his home in St. Anthony, and became one of the most useful and respected citizens of the village. For years he occupied the pulpit of the Baptist church, which greatly prospered under his long pastorate. After retiring from active labor in St. Anthony, he preached in different sections in the vicinity of the Falls. He is greatly esteemed by all denominations of Christians, as well as by the public generally.

THE UNIVERSITY OF MINNESOTA.

The so-called preparatory department of the University of Minnesota, at that time, under the auspices of Prof. Merrill, closed its first term the last week in April. All were proud of the perparatory department. We were extravagant in our expectations ; we dreamed of a mammoth educational institution at the Falls when the plans of the regents should be perfected. The officers were earnest in their work, but had scarcely any money at their command to prepare the way for anything but the preparatory school. They had secured the services of an excellent principal ; the beginning was a success ; but none of us had the least conception that in a generation this small nucleus of 1852 would expand into one of the most successful seats of learning on the continent, with more professors and teachers than there were students at the first term of the preparatory department, and with more students within its stately halls than there were inhabitants in St. Anthony, All Saints, and all the immediate country around the Falls. Since that humble beginning, the University of Minnesota has been blessed with able men in the presidential chair, talented professors of a justly world-wide reputation, and teachers who have few equals, yet none of all these were superior as educators to the first principal of the University of Minnesota, Professor E. A. Merrill, A. M.

The tide of immigration for 1852 was in a great measure centered on the banks of the Mississippi, St. Anthony receiving its full share. In early spring Ezra Dorman came up from Hazel Green, Wisconsin, and purchased property, and immediately commenced the erection of a large brick building, which was the first structure in the village made of brick. Mr. Dorman's interesting family, his son, and his son-in-law, N. H. Hemiup, with their families, followed.

Dr. C. L. Anderson arrived in May, and commenced a successful practice. He is a native of Virginia, but came to Minnesota from Indiana. Aside from his practice, he was a geologist, entomologist, and florist, of rare industry and attainments. He loved Nature in all her beautiful and wonderful works. He contributed many able articles to the press of that day. He married an excellent young lady during his stay here. His literary attainments were of a high order. Early in the sixties he removed to the Pacific slope. Tarrying a few years in Nevada, he made a very complete catalogue of the Flora of that strangely interesting region. For some twenty years he has been a resident of Santa Cruz, California, where his skill as a physician, and his attainments as a scientist, are widely appreciated. His two daughters, born in Minneapolis, are talented in a literary and artistic way.

Mr. J. Peddington also arrived in May, 1852.

A jubilee was held on the 31st of May on the occasion of the landing of the steamer Dr. Franklin No. 2, Captain Smith Harris. The Franklin steamed up almost to the foot of Hennepin Island.

Up to this period there had been only a weekly mail. Frequently, however, several weeks would elapse without mail service. Especially this was so in the fall after navigation had closed, and in the spring before navigation was resumed. On the 24th of May our delegate in congress, Mr. Sibley, obtained an order from the general postoffice department at Washington for three mails per week. The news of increased mail facilities was received by the citizens with great satisfaction. Of course the route was a short one, only from St. Paul, but it added greatly in the delivery of early mail matter at the Falls.

Very many valuable improvements were commenced in the spring of this year. Aside from Mr. Dorman's brick structure, Elmer Tyler commenced building a block on lower main street, which was the headquarters of so many merchants for so many years.

It was considered that if an ox, cow, or other animal, jumped overboard from Captain Tapper's ferry-boat, while in transit, from one shore to the other, the beast would be carried over the Falls and killed; and this had always been the case; but on June 4th, Warren Bristol had a fine yoke of oxen, which Captain Tapper was ferrying over the river. They became restless, and backed off the boat. Strange as it may seem, they came out on the shore without receiving the slightest injury.

A public meeting was held on the 6th for the purpose of adopting measures for a public cemetery. S. Thatcher occupied the chair, and Dr. J. H. Murphy was the Secretary. R. W. Cumming's beautiful grounds east of the village were selected and secured for the site. It is in use to this day for that purpose.

On the 11th of June news was received that Franklin Pierce, of New Hampshire, had received the democratic nomination for President of the United States. A few days later the proceedings of the Whig national convention that nominated General Winfield Scott for President were received. The members of both parties endeavored to get up ratification meetings, but voters were too busy with other matters, and no meetings of a national political character were held.

June 20th a rousing gathering of the people occurred in relation to securing the landing of steamboats at the Falls. Messrs. Stearns, Bristol, Tapper, Cheever, and E. L. Hall, were appointed a committee to forward the interests of the navigation of the river up to the Falls. A large sum of money was raised for the purpose of removing the boulders said to interfere with the safety of the boats, from Meeker's island up to the landing. The contract for blasting them out was let to Captain John Rollins.

Many citizens were determined to test the new temperance law. On the 22d of June papers were issued from the office of Isaac I. Lewis, then a justice of the peace, for the purpose of bringing Mr. Cloutier before the court to answer for an alleged violation of the law. John W. North appeared for the territory, and E. L. Hall for the defendant. Judgment was rendered against Mr. Cloutier, but an appeal was taken to the United States Court, and the judgment reversed on the ground that the law in question was unconstitutional.

Independence day was not observed in St. Anthony; not but what the people were patriotic, but they preferred to celebrate that memorable day by visiting the lakes in a quiet manner. Many of the citizens, headed by Al. Stone, attended a ball at the St. Louis house, near the cold-springs, below Minnehaha Falls.

On the 9th of July news was received of the death of Henry Clay, which occurred at his home in Kentucky on the 20th of the previous month. The Express appeared in deep mourning in consequence, as a token of sorrow.

July 12th the marriage of William H. Townsend and Emily J. Nason occurred. Mr. Townsend represented St. Anthony in the lower house of the first state legislature.

On the 26th of July Dr. J. H. Murphy and wife sustained a great loss in the death of their only child, Litteor Ella, a bright, promising little girl.

August 6th, Simon Stevens and Company commenced the erection of their mill at Minnetonka. At this time Captain Rollins had finished his contract for removing all the boulders, and other obstacles from the river, that interfered with the running of steamboats between Fort Snelling and the landings at the Falls.

On the 6th an exciting election came off in St. Anthony. Lardner Bostwick was elected city-justice by a majority of sixty over all opposition. This was the stepping-stone by which Judge Bostwick subsequently acceptably held for almost a quarter of a century so many different offices.

On the 13th the distinguished American authoress, Mrs. E. F. Ellet, arrived. She was accompanied by Miss Clark, who has since become so widely known as a writer. Mrs. Ellet visited the wilds of the upper country at the instance of M. Y. Beach, editor-in-chief of the New York Sun, a man of great prominence in the literary world in his day. He was a contemporary of Horace Greeley, the elder Bennett, a friend of N. P. Willis, the two Clarks, Willis Gaylord and his distinguished brother. Mr. Beach, in company with his wife, had visited us the year before, and was delighted with the new country. In the early fifties his paper had great influence throughout the Union, and had the largest circulation of any political paper on this continent. Mrs. Ellet was a lively little lady, who stood among the foremost female writers in America of that day. She and Miss Clark visited Lake Minnetonka, and were among the first to describe to the world its great extent and beautiful scenery. They camped out several nights on the borders of the lake so, as she said, she might "know just how it was to be a pioneer in earnest". Simon Stevens and a crew of mechanics were at that time the only residents in the neighborhood of Minnetonka. Stevens and some of the men who were at work with him accompanied the ladies in his boat around every nook and corner of the lake, making them comfortable and separate camps for the night, and taking them by day to the different points of interest around the lake. They were the first white ladies that ever visited Minnetonka.

The result of Mrs. Ellet's visit to this territory was the publication of two of her most delightful volumes, one of them on the women of the west, and the other on her western travels. She spent several days under my humble roof. She was greatly interested in the future of this side of the river. For many years she would write to me from her home in New York asking about the progress of Minneapolis.

A social event occurred on the 8th of August, of some moment, especially when we consider that there were only two or three bachelors on this side of the river, and only about the same number of girls; so when John Tapper married Miss Matilda Stinson we all took a holiday. Rev. Mr. Rowell, from St. Anthony, officiated at the marriage ceremony.

Our new and valued physician, Dr. A. E. Ames, was appointed surgeon at Fort Snelling, but after a service of a few weeks he resigned the office.

On the 27th of August the sad news was received that Col. James M. Goodhue, of St. Paul, editor of the Pioneer, was dead. He was only forty-two years old. Unquestionably he was the ablest editor in the valley of the Mississippi.

On the 10th of September, under the auspices of Governor Ramsey, superintendent of Indian affairs, all the trouble with the Dakotas in relation to the different interpretations of the Traverse des Sioux treaty was settled to the satisfaction of both the whites and the red men who were the chief participants in the treaty.

Tallmage Elwell came over from Wisconsin and established an art gallery in the early fall. Since that period Mr. Elwell has constantly resided in Minnesota, and he is one of our best citizens. He was the first realdaguerreian artist that settled in this neighborhood

Considerable sickness prevailed among the children during the month of September. Several fatal cases occurred, among them Charles Frederic, a son of John and Mary Orth, who died September 17th ; and Lillie, a daughter of Lardner and Eliza Bostwick, who died September 20th.

A change in the pastor of the Methodist church took place on the 25th. Rev. C. A. Newcomb was transferred to Adams, Wisconsin, and Rev. Mr. Jones, from southern Wisconsin, was appointed in his place.

Governor Ramsey appointed Isaac Brown collector and assessor of Hennepin county. This was the first appointment of any office whatever in the county. His commission was dated August 27th, 1852. A month later it would not have been necessary for the appointment to have been made, as congress, in the meantime, passed the law reducing the reservation of Fort Snelling.

The organic act passed by the legislature establishing Hennepin county contained the important proviso that upon the reduction of the reserve by congress the citizens of the county should, at the next annual election after the passage of such law, hold an election for all the county officers, and immediately after the election and qualification of such officers, they should, in due form of law, proceed to organize the county—which was faithfully complied with.

CHAPTER XXVII.

Unfortunately the law passed by congress reducing the Fort Snelling reservation contained no provision for the relief of settlers on the land, thus causing us great anxiety in regard to the future titles to our homes. A claim association was instantly organized. Stringent rules were adopted against claim-jumpers, and others who might wish to interfere with our claims. The severe measures taken by the association were of such a character that no one would be sure of his life who should attempt to jump a claim. When there was a claim in dispute in regard to the ownership, the board of arbitration appointed by the association would hear all the evidence in relation to the matter, and decide the dispute according to the facts. The decision was final, and the successful claimant had the powerful protection of every member of the association, which, as it afterwards proved, was sufficient for the entry of his land. In all instances the first one who made a claim to a quarter section of land, with suitable improvements, was recognized by the association as the proper owner of it. A book was opened by the association, and we were all obliged to enter in it the number of acres we claimed, as well as the date of the settlement, and the value of our betterments, and the number of acres cultivated. The officers of the association were Dr. A. E. Ames, president; Charles Hoag, secretary; Edwin Hedderly, treasurer; executive committee, Colonel E. Case, Calvin A. Tuttle, William Dickie, Philander Prescott, and Edward Murphy; board of arbitration, Major Nathaniel McLean, U. S. Indian agent, Anson

Northrup, and John Reidhead. Sessions were held every Saturday, at the residence of John H. Stevens. Only in one instance was the association called upon to resort to severe measures. In that instance a cat-o'-nine-tails well laid on the bare back of the trespasser on a claim down toward Minnehaha, had the desired effect. No one else attemped to interfere with or jump a claim. The offender in this instance immediately left the territory and has never been heard from since. It is true, however, that a good many compromises were made, and in some instances persons who had disputed claims were obliged to pay considerable sums of money to opposing parties in order to get peaceful possession of them.

The distinguished Syrian philanthropist, Gregory M. Wortabet, delivered several lectures in St. Anthony during the early fall. He was a native of Beyroot. His lectures attracted a good deal of attention.

Sandford I. Huse, of the firm of Farnham and Huse, and a son of Sherburne and Elvira Huse, died of consumption in Detroit, Michigan, aged twenty-five years. He was on his way home from an extended journey taken for the benefit of his health.

On the 29th the news of the death of Daniel Webster was received at St. Anthony.

L. M. Ford, who afterwards became so extensively known throughout the country as a florist, pomologist, and horticulturist, at Groveland, was engaged to teach a singing-school in the village for the ensuing autumn.

In the appointment of officers for the new United States land-office at Sauk Rapids, the President selected Charles W. Christmas for register. Aside from that of postmaster, this was the first Federal appointment bestowed upon a citizen of St. Anthony.

Lewis Stone's farm-house was destroyed by fire on the first of November.

The handsome Baptist church edifice was completed early in November. Upon its completion the members of the Methodist Episcopal church met and decided that they, too, would immediately erect a church building, a determination they strictly adhered to and in good time accomplished.

The members of the Episcopal church, as well as all classes

of citizens, were greatly pleased with the advent of Rev. Mr. Chamberlain to preside over the destinies of that church.

That popular pastor, Rev. C. G. Ames, of the Free Baptist church and his congregation occupied the school building for a meeting-house.

In October the Catholic church edifice was finished. The lots on which it was built were given to the church by Pierre Bottineau. That denomination of Christians had not only the occasional wise teaching of Rev. A. Ravoux, but other excellent members of the priesthood.

Early in November there were no less than three singing-schools under way, all well patronized. One was taught by B. E. Messer, afterwards sheriff of Hennepin county.

With the preparatory department of the University and two common schools and a lyceum, and lectures under the auspices of the library association, the prospects were favorable for a winter of profitable enjoyment. Tallmadge Elwell on November 27th delivered the first lecture of the season. His subject was Man of the Nineteenth century.

J. H. Stevens and Co. sold out their store to N. D. Shaw and Co. On November 12th the first heavy fall of snow came. From that day to March there was good sleighing in the vicinity of St. Anthony.

There was considerable sickness in the village during the late fall and early winter. Typhoid and other fevers prevailed. On the 3d of November Albert H. Dorr, one of the most active and respected young business men of the village, died. On the 4th Mrs. Cordelia, wife of Hon. J. L. Wilson, died. On the 8th Mrs. Maria H., wife of the merchant Rufus P. Upton, died, aged twenty-two years. A little later Mrs. Abbey, wife of Andrew Foster, died. There was considerable speculation in regard to what caused the dreaded typhoid fever. Some attributed it to stagnant water in the mill-pond; others thought it was the swampy lands immediately in the rear of the village. The physicians expressed no opinion as to its cause. The fever has never appeared on the east bank of the Falls in an epidemic form since.

I find it quite impossible to give a correct list of the names of those who settled in St. Anthony during the year 1852. There were several honored new settlers of the village and its immediate vicinity during that year. All made good citizens and were most cordially welcomed by those who had preceded them. At the close of the year the citizens had reason to be thankful for the great prosperity that had attended them.

THE FORT SNELLING MILITARY RESERVATION REDUCED.

The news of the passage of the bill by congress reducing the military reservation of Fort Snelling, was received by the proper authorities of Ramsey county (to which county Hennepin had been attached for judicial and other purposes) in time to give the proper notice to participate in the approaching annual election which was to take place on the 11th of October. The board of county commissioners of Ramsey county directed us to elect a full set of county officers, and designated the whole county of Hennepin as one election precinct, with the polling-place at my house.

FIRST AND ONLY UNANIMOUS ELECTION IN HENNEPIN COUNTY.

The citizens met the Saturday previous to the election and unanimously nominated the following ticket : For Representatives, Benjamin H. Randall, of Fort Snelling, and Dr. A. E. Ames, of All Saints ; County Commissioners, John Jackins, and Alex Moore, of All Saints, and Joseph Dean, of Oak Grove, now Bloomington ; Sheriff, Isaac Brown ; Judge of Probate, Joel B. Bassett ; Register of Deeds and Clerk of the board of county commissioners, John H. Stevens ; Coroner, David Gorham ; Surveyor, Chas. W. Christmas ; Assessors, Eli Pettijohn, Edwin Hedderly, and William Chambers ; Treasurer, Deacon John S. Mann ; Justices of the Peace, Eli Pettijohn, of Fort Snelling, and Edwin Hedderly of All Saints ; Constables, E. Stanley, and C. C. Jenks ; Supervisor of Roads, George Parks.

The election came off in pursuance of law ; the parties named above received every vote that was cast ; each had seventy-one votes. The election returns were sent to St. Paul, and were canvassed by the board of commissioners of Ramsey county. That body directed M. S. Wilkinson, then their clerk, to issue to each of the newly-elected officers of the new county certificates of their election, with directions to Messrs. Jackins, Moore, and Dean, and Stevens, to meet on the 21st of the same month to qualify, and to complete the organization of the county in due form according to law.

All the persons elected met at my house on that day and took the oath of office, gave bonds, and assumed the several duties they had been called upon to perform.

SELECTION OF THE COUNTY SEAT OF HENNEPIN COUNTY.

The first business transacted by the board of county commissioners, after the filing and approval of the bonds of the newly-elected officers, was the selection of the county-seat of the new county. Commissioner Jackins moved that the county seat of Hennepin county be established on the west bank of the Falls of St. Anthony. This motion was carried unanimously.

THE COMMISSIONERS SELECT A NAME FOR THE NEW COUNTY SEAT.

Then the question came up as to what name should be given to the place selected for the county-seat. Commissioner Moore thought that Albion would be a proper name. Another commissioner said that, in view of the extensive water-power, the name of Lowell would be suggestive, as the power, when improved, would make this place the Lowell of the west. A vote being taken, the name of Albion was selected, and the clerk was directed to so record it. He was further instructed to date all the records of the county under the head of Albion, Hennepin county, Minnesota. After the transaction of other unimportant business, the commissioners adjourned.

During the adjournment considerable feeling was exhibited by the residents of the county, and the almost unanimous sentiment was against the name selected by the commissioners for the new county-seat. Meantime all the necessary blanks for the use of the county had been obtained with the name of Albion, as per instructions of the commissioners, printed therein.

Also during the adjournment of the commissioners, Charles Hoag, a classical scholar, and Geo. D. Bowman, editor of the St. Anthony Express, were determined to invent a new name for the embryo city. On the 5th of November an article appeared in the Express, written by Mr. Hoag, advocating the blotting out of the name of Albion (as the commissioners had that of All Saints) and substituting that of Minnehapolis. This was the first time that the name of the future city ever appeared in print. In fact Mr. Hoag had only invented it the

previous night while in bed. In the morning he hurried over
to St. Anthony and secured its publication in the issue of the
paper of that date. The forms of the Express had been
locked up when Mr. Hoag arrived at the office with his communication, but Mr. Bowman had them unlocked, and the
article was put in type and inserted. Mr. Hoag had no time
to consult any one, except Mr. Bowman, in regard to the
name proposed, previous to its appearance in the paper ; but
when it did appear most every one was in favor of it.

In the next issue of the paper, November 12th, Mr. Bowman, in a leading editorial, said : " When the communication
"proposing this name (Minnehapolis) for the promising town
"growing on the other side of the river, was last week handed
"us, we were so much engaged as to have no time to com-
"ment on it. The name is an excellent one, and deserves
"much favor by our citizens. The h being silent, as our
"correspondent recommends, and as custom would soon
"make it, it is practical and euphonious. The nice adjust-
"ment of the Indian minne with the Greek polis, becomes a
"beautiful compound, and finally it is, as all names should be
"when it is possible, admirably descriptive of the locality.
"By all means, we would say, adopt this beautiful and
"exceedingly appropriate title, and do not longer suffer abroad
"from connection with the meaningless and outlandish name
"of All Saints."

It will be seen by the above that the editor totally ignored,
as most every one else did, the selection of the name by the
county commissioners. In short, from the appearance of
Mr. Hoag's article of November 5, the Anglo-Saxon Albion
was doomed, and All Saints would fall with it. It was evident that Messrs. Hoag and Bowman had won the victory.
It was finally settled at an accidental meeting of most all the
citizens at my house, in December, 1852. It was decided to
withdraw the silent h, and call the place Minneapolis. It is
derived from minne, a portion of the Dakota name of the falls,
and polis, the Greek for city, and was allowed by all the old
settlers to be a beautiful combination of the Dakota and
classic Greek. This settled forever one of the most trouble-
some matters the original settlers in this neighborhood had to
contend with. It was about the only thing they could not

at first unite on. For some time they agreed to disagree on
any name. It was happily settled to the entire satisfaction of
all; though when the commissioners found the sentiment was
against·Albion, they endorsed the name of Winona, but that
did not strike the fancy of the people ; hence in common
with every one else they accepted the inevitable, and fell in
line with the others.

SETTLEMENTS IN THE COUNTY.

During the year 1852, Joseph Dean, S. A. Goodrich, O.
Ames, A. L. Goodrich, H. and M. S. Whalon, E. Ames, Wm.
Chambers, and Reuben B. Gibson, took up and occupied
claims in what is now Bloomington. Rev. G. H. Pond, Hon.
Martin McLeod, Peter Quinn, Moses Starr Titus, and Victor
Chatel, all connected with the Indian department, had resided
there for years. They called the place the Oak Grove
Mission.

The old upper prairie, now known as Eden prairie, this
year received its first settlers in the persons of John and
Samuel Mitchell, their families, and their father and mother,
Hiram Abbott, and David Livingston, while Messrs. C. C.
Garvey, Samuel Stough, Mark Baldwin, William Finch,
Gilbert Hanson, J. V. Draper, and Mrs. Gordon, selected
claims on and near Brown's creek, now known as the Minne-
haha stream, which is in the present town of Richfield.

Simon Stevens, Horace Webster, O. E. Garrison, A. B.
Robinson, John McGalpin, George and Lewis Bourgeois,
James Shaver, jr., and James Mountain, took up and occupied
claims in the lower Minnetonka district.

The Messrs. Fuller brothers, and Colonel Thomas H. Hunt
claimed the present town-site of Chaska, then in Hennepin
but now in Carver county, during the late summer of this
year. Chaska had long been a trading-post belonging to the
Fur company, under the direction of one of the Faribault
brothers. It had also been the seat of an excellent Catholic
mission-school, under Rev. A. Ravoux.

In the spring of this year, Washington Getchell, Winslow
Getchell, Amos Berry, and Jacob Longfellow, made claims on
what was then called Getchell's prairie, which is now included
in the town of Brooklyn. In July of the same year, Joseph
Potvin, Pierre Bottineau, Peter Raiche, and Peter Garvais,

made claims on Bottineau prairie, which is also included in the same town. Ezra Hanscom, N. S. Grover, and John W. Brown, made claims the same year in what is now Brooklyn.

The first claim made in what is now Crystal Lake was during this year. The claimants were Rev. John Ware Dow, N. P. Warren, Josiah Dutton, Wyman McCumber, L. Wagoner, and John Garty. This was the largest settlement made in one locality in Hennepin county, during the year, outside of Minneapolis. Rev. L. Palmer also made a claim in the town, which I think was for his brother.

Charles Miles was the only one who made a claim in what is now Champlin, in 1852, while Louis P. Garvais, and Wm. M. Ewing, were the only ones who took up claims in what is now Maple Grove, the same year.

Francis Morrison, one of the most enterprising of all the old settlers, moved with his family from Vermont, late in the summer, and selected and occupied a claim above Mr. Christmas's place, on the bank of the river. He still resides on a portion of it. Cyrus C. Jenks this year occupied the claim of J. Draper. Mr. Jenks resides in Grand Forks county, Dakota.

As far as I can ascertain or remember at this time, the foregoing are the names of all the men who settled in the county, that year, outside of Minneapolis. Many of these persons had been former residents of St. Anthony. A few were from Minneapolis. They went out into the wilderness to secure new homes and open up farms. Minneapolis proper received but very few new-comers this year. The claims had all been previously occupied. There were no lots laid out for any one to buy or build upon, and there was no business that would pay to follow ; hence no immigration ; but the surrounding country in the near vicinity of the town was satisfactorily occupied by an excellent class of immigrants.

There was not to exceed, at the close of the year, twelve dwelling-houses upon the original town-site, and none conveniently near each other, as they were built on the claims taken by the owners, and could not be very close neighbors, though in a few cases the parties owning the claims would build near the boundaries of their line, instead of near the center, so they could be near neighbors. We had learned from experience that we could not expect any more improve-

ments in our immediate vicinity until the title to our land
had been secured from the government, and it was laid out
into lots ; so we were not disappointed that there was no
increase in the number of buildings, and only a very limited
number of persons added to our population, until the spring
of 1855, when we entered our land, and received a good, solid
title to our homes, at the United States land-office ; but in the
meantime, while we remained in a stationary condition, the
country around us prospered beyond our utmost expectations.
For once in our history the rural districts went far ahead of
the villages in improvements, which was perhaps all the better
for us ; because when we were in a condition to start our
town, we had a solid foundation to build upon, and had a
prosperous country to back us ; which proves that it is desirable to have the country go ahead of the village, rather than
that the village should go ahead of the country.

The whole taxable property in the county, according to the
returns of the assessors, was $43,605. The commissioners
laid a tax levy of thirteen mills on a dollar, which would
return a revenue of $566 87. When the collector (Sheriff
Brown) returned the tax-book, in February, containing the
assessments, he turned over to the county treasurer (Deacon
Mann) $566 86—all but one cent having been collected.

The first petition presented to the board of county commissioners was from A. E. Ames and others praying for the
establishment of a county-road from Little Falls creek to
Crystal lake. The petition was granted, and Colonel E. Case
and William Dickie, with the county surveyor, were appointed
commissioners to locate the road. The second petition which
was presented at the same session, November 29th, was from
Cyrus C. Jenks and others praying for the organization of a
school-district on the west bank of the Falls. The petition
was granted, and the whole county was organized into school-
district number one. The first school in district number one
was opened in a little building belonging to Anson Northrup,
which was near the corner of Third avenue south and Second
street, in December. The teacher was Miss Mary E. Miller.
Some twenty pupils were in constant attendance during the
winter. The school-trustees were Edward Murphy, A. E.
Ames and John H. Stevens. Allen Harmon, clerk of district.

CHAPTER XXVIII.

During the year eighteen hundred and fifty-three, the most hopeful indication of the future rapidly-increasing prosperity of the embryo city, new-born town, and recently-christened infant Minneapolis, was the nuptial ceremonies that occurred during that year of romantic courtship and wedded bliss ; the like of which, considering the small number of inhabitants, is a marvel. Many who came here were in the prime of early, vigorous manhood ; or fresh, beautiful womanhood ; and were unmarried. They were in a new country. Their surroundings were novel, and long life seemed before them. It was a land . of wonder, with a lovely landscape and virgin soil. There was exhilaration in the air that caused youthful blood to course more rapidly, bringing strength to limb, glow to cheek, sparkle to eye, sprightliness to step, natural grace to every movement, and an overflow of love in every heart. In the light of possibilities open to them, each was a hero, or heroine. The invigorating air, blooming prairies, fresh forests, smiling lakes and laughing waterfalls, made it an Eden to lovers, where the wild roar of the cataract was an inspiring accompaniment to their wooing. Those fair united couples gave an early boom to our prosperity that has exceeded their wildest imaginings. The frosts of thirty-six winters have powdered the locks, and care for loved ones has wrinkled the brow, of each Adam and Eve of that paradise ; but duplicates of their fresh faces and lithe forms, to the third generation, ornament our streets ; and descendants are now, as ancestors were then, keeping their loved home at St. Anthony Falls in the front rank of enlightened progress.

Mr. Edgar Folsom and Mrs. Mary Stowell took the initiative for a honeymoon, followed in quick succession by Shelton Hollister and Annie Lewis, J. C. Lawrence and Hannah Stimson, William D. Garland and Sarah E. Dorr, John M. Durman and Louisa M. Reidhead, Simon B. Bean and Margaret B. Munson, A. K. Hartwell and Maria N. Smith, George D. Bowman and Miss J. P. Derby, Z. E. B. Nash and Octavia M. Mills, W. H. Kean and Mrs. Florentine Kean, E. L. Hall and Urania Lawrence, Edw'd P. Shaw and Sarah C. Torrey, Richard Lowell and Sophronia M. Smith, Isaac Gilpatrick and Sarah Sinclair, Casper Kopp and Delena Eisennacker, Andrew J. Foster and Mary W. Averill, Robert J. Irwin and Jerusha Ann Berry, Amos P. Bean and Eveline E. Huse, J. C. Shipley and May F. Barrows, L. A. Foster and Jane Richardson, Geo. E. Huy and Mary Ticknor, D. L. Paine and Sarah Berry. In the light of the above showing for the young village, can we wonder at the extraordinary increase of the population at an early day around the Falls ? It is certain we can date back to that period the commencement of our prosperity.

INDUSTRIAL, SOCIAL AND POLITICAL EVENTS OF 1853.

Charles King, a former merchant of New York, arrived from that city with his family and invested largely in real-estate, purchasing the interest of Elmer Tyler. The latter, after accomplishing a good work in lending a helping hand at an early day in developing the resources of St. Anthony, returned to Chicago and died in that city several years since. His name will always be remembered in the history of the old village of St. Anthony from the fact that he purchased and introduced the first complete newspaper outfit from which the Express made its appearance. Mr. King resided several years in the village. He then disposed of his property and moved to Washington, D. C., and became a prominent pension agent.

The fourth territorial legislature met in St. Paul, January 5th. Hon. Martin McLeod, of Hennepin county, was elected president of the council. This excellent selection gave much satisfaction to the people of the new county, as they were proud of their talented member. To Mr. McLeod, who was chairman of the committee on schools in the council, at the first session of the territorial legislature, and to Rev. E. D. Neill, the first superintendent of common schools in the territory, the children of the early settlers are greatly indebted for the efforts that were made in their behalf; and the people of the state to-day are under deep obligations to those early and able advocates of the common-school system of Minnesota. If for no other services rendered the state, for these alone they should ever be held in grateful remembrance by the people of the state.

Dr. David Day, then a resident of Long Prairie, Todd county, after a contest of two weeks, was elected speaker of the House. The initiatory steps of the organization of the house were taken in Minneapolis the day before the election of Dr. Day to the speakership. Dr. Day was at the time the resident physician of the Indian department at Long Prairie, which was then the headquarters of the Winnebagoes. The members of the legislature at that session from St. Anthony were Wm. H. Larned of the council; and R. P. Russell and G. B. Dutton of the house. Hennepin county was represented by Martin McLeod in the council, and A. E. Ames and B. H. Randall in the house. With such excellent delegations it is not necessary to say that the interests of the people were in safe hands, at least as far as their wants in necessary legislation were concerned.

For some unaccountable reason, out of the fourteen officers elected in both houses, such as secretary, clerk of the house, sergeant-at-arms, door-keeper, and the like, none were bestowed on the residents of either bank of the Falls of St. Anthony.

On the 15th of January, Miss Eliza, eldest daughter of John P. Miller, died at the residence of her parents in what is now south Minneapolis, aged fifteen years. She was a young lady of much promise.

The citizens of St. Anthony were much pleased with the addition to their numbers of S. M. Tracy, who subsequently for many years was one of the most active citizens of that village.

The long winter months passed without excitement; the citizens generally on each side of the river pursued their usual occupations. Good reports came from the pineries in regard to the favorable condition of the lumber operations. The schools were well patronized, and the numerous lectures were well attended. The Central Hall recently built was convenient for public gatherings. Messrs. E. P. Mills and Z. E. B. Nash occupied the lower part of the building for their stores. This was the first public hall erected in St. Anthony.

• The first district court held in Minneapolis, after the organization of Hennepin county, convened Monday morning, April 4th, Judge B. B. Meeker, presiding. The county commissioners secured the parlor in Anson Northrup's house for the main court-room, and two bed-rooms in the same house, for the jury-rooms. There were in attendance on that memorable occasion, Hon. Henry L. Moss, U. S. district-attorney ; Warren Bristol, county-attorney ; Joseph Warren Furber, U. S. marshal ; Isaac Brown, sheriff ; Joseph H. Canney, deputy sheriff ; Sweet W. Case, clerk of the court ; with the following grand-jury :

Dr. A. E. Ames, foreman ; Joseph Dean, Eli Pettijohn, Moses Starr Titus, Edwin Hedderly, H. Fletcher, Wm. G. Jones, John Jackins, John S. Wales, Allen Harmon, John Bedue, John C. Bohannan, Lorenzo B. Warren, John S. Mann, Waterman Stimson, William Hamilton, A. L. Cummings, Augustus P. Thompson, and R. B. Gibson.

Pettit-jury : Geo. N. Wales, William Dwinels, David H. Smith, Elijah Austin, Norman Jenkins, Simeon Odell, John Smithyman; J. M. Snow, John P. Miller, Charles Hoag, Solomon K. Shultz, John Wass, Hiram Prescott, Hiram Burlingham, Francis Knott, Joseph C. Hutchins, Willis G. Moffett, John Gairty, Wm. G. Tuttle, Calvin Church, James Brown, Silas Pease, John Mitchell, Allen L. Goodrich, Edward Stanley, David Bickford, William Chambers, William Jones, James Mountain, Charles Moseau, and Wm. W. Getchell.

The court was in session for one week, awaiting the action of the grand jury, who were mostly engaged in ferreting out many supposed violations of the liquor-license law. There were no civil cases of moment tried before the court, and only three criminal matters ; one an indictment the grand-jury brought against Hiram Armstrong for wilfully and maliciously

injuring the personal property of a neighbor ; and two
indictments against Edmund Bresette, one for selling whisky
to the Indians, and the other for introducing whisky into the
Indian country. Isaac Atwater, who was the lawyer for both
the alleged criminals, cleared them on trial before the court.
These were the first indictments ever found by the grand jury
in Hennepin county ; and so far as civil cases were concerned
it was too early for litigation. The citizens of the county had
not sufficient business relations with each other, previous to
holding the court, for the incubation of disputes ; and besides,
they were not generally disposed to lawsuits. In the absence
of courts they had followed the precepts of those who had
preceded them into the territory ; and if credit had been
obtained, it was considered a debt of honor. As a general
rule, the first settlers of the new county were not abundantly
supplied with this world's goods, and they felt too poor to
resort to lawsuits, even if a sufficient cause existed for such a
course. In those early days people could not afford to be
dishonest with each other in their dealings. If a person pur-
posely committed a mean act in his relations with his neighbor,
public opinion and public scorn were so strongly expressed
against him that the punishment administered in this manner
was worse than if he had been tried and convicted in a court
and imprisoned.

The lawyers in attendance at the first court were John W.
North, Isaac Atwater, D. A. Secombe, E. L. Hall, Abraham
R. Dodge, Geo. W. Prescott, Jas. H. Fridley, and A. D. Shaw,
all of St. Anthony. Hennepin county had at that time only
a solitary resident lawyer, Warren Bristol, who represented
the county as its attorney.

Immediately on the adjournment of court, a fearful and
unprecedented snow-storm raged with great violence.

On the 10th of April Orrin W. Rice, then a merchant in
St. Anthony, was appointed postmaster in the place of Ard
Godfrey. Mr. Rice was a brother of Hon. H. M. and E.
Rice, of St. Paul. His wife was a daughter of J. H. Brown,
of St. Anthony. Mr. Rice was unusually esteemed by the
people of that village. His death in early life from that
dread disease, consumption, was greatly regretted by his
numerous acquaintances.

Immigration was very heavy this spring. The recently ceded Indian land in Hennepin county received its full share. As usual, the class of immigrants were of a very superior order.

A singular accident occurred at Captain Tapper's ferry on April 20th. Joseph N. Barber, one of the new settlers in Minneapolis, had purchased a choice yoke of oxen. In crossing the ferry they backed out of the boat and were carried over the precipice. No part or parcel of the oxen were ever found. A log chain was fastened in the staple of the yoke on the oxen. It is supposed the hook of the chain became attached to a rock down in the deep water, at the immediate foot of the precipice, and held the poor brutes some forty feet below the surface of the water. In most instances, when animals were carried over the Falls, their bodies would be seen immediately after the occurrence in the rapids towards Spirit island.

A MAN GOES OVER THE FALLS.

So far as known only one man was ever carried over the Falls who came out alive. In this instance not a hair of his head was injured. Even a bottle of whisky he had in his pocket at the time was not broken. The name of the man was Michael Hickey. He was engaged in working for Anson Northrup, on Boom island. Hickey used to cross Captain Tapper's ferry every morning on his way to Boom island, and recross every evening on his way to Mr. Northrup's residence. He was occasionally given to his cups, and would once in a while punish a glass of whisky, perhaps half a dozen of them with great rapidity. One Saturday evening, while on his way home, in passing a saloon in St. Anthony, he suddenly became imbued with the idea of securing a bottle of whisky to take to his home in Minneapolis for Sunday use. The more he considered the matter the more determined he became to do so. He visited the saloon for the purpose of ratifying his conclusions. The whisky was purchased, paid for, and deposited in his pocket. The saloon-keeper treated Mike for calling on him. Then Mike treated the saloon-keeper and drank, himself, on the occasion. Others came in just at that time. Mike treated them and they treated Mike. By midnight Mike was full and en route for his home over the river. On arriving at the ferry, he found that Captain Tapper had retired for the night. He knew of no reason why he should not take one of the captain's small boats and ferry himself over the river. He launched the boat, but instead of making the west-side landing, he was carried over the Falls. Early next morning a band of Winnebago Indians in making the portage of the Falls, discovered a white man, or his ghost, on Spirit island. They immediately informed Mr. Northrup and myself of their discovery. Captain Tapper had just informed me that some one had stolen one of his boats during the night. We sent for the captain, and all three proceeded down to the Falls. There stood Mike on the bank of Spirit island, without a blemish. Sending for ropes, we safely landed one on the island. Mike made it fast to himself, and we hauled him safely ashore. After he was landed, he thought of his bottle of whisky, which was in his pocket. He had not, during his imprisonment on the island, remembered that such a luxury was on his person. Taking the bottle from his pocket, and drawing the cork for the first time, he said : "Wasn't it lucky the cratur (meaning the whisky) received no harm in making the bloody trip !" evidently thinking that his escape from injury was second in consideration to that of the whisky. Poor Mike ! He was an honest, faithful servant. He has been dead for more than a score of years.

On the 6th of May Mr. Richard Rogers completed his mill for grinding wheat. It was small, but perfect. Mr. Rogers, being a millwright, superintended the building of it in person. This was the first flour mill erected at the Falls, if we except the old government mill on the west side of the river. From this small effort of Mr. Rogers in 1853, what a vast expansion in the flour industry around the Falls ! From that small beginning the milling interest of the Falls to-day excels that of any portion of the known globe.

Another dreadful snowstorm visited us on the 18th of May, fortunately without serious injury to the growing crops.

The spring of this year was a very paradise to those who had money to loan. Real-estate doubled in value so rapidly that the interest of money ruled high. For instance, the Express of May 20th says : "Money is growing scarce. It

can be obtained on undoubted real-estate security at five per
cent per month. Good paper endorsed with responsible
names at sixty and ninety days, discounts at ten per cent per
month." It was claimed that money could be made by paying such excessive rates of interest; but never having had
any personal experience in borrowing or loaning money in
those days, I cannot speak definitely in regard to the results,
further than that those who loaned the money almost invari-
ably at the proper time received the interest and principal
from those who had borrowed. Even if a loss should occasionally occur, the money loaned had received such high rates
of interest they could afford to lose.

The new postmaster had hardly warmed his seat in the
office before the all-absorbing topic of the failure of the
arrival of the mails commenced being discussed. On the 18th
of May a public meeting convened in Central hall, with Jonathan Estes in the chair, and Dr. C. L. Anderson, secretary,
for the purpose of devising plans to secure the mails from St.
Paul when due. Of course the postmaster was not to blame
for the failures. He entered a protest to the department, as
his predecessor had done, at the failure of the contractors to
supply the office with mail matter. On an investigation it
appeared there were rival stage companies between St. Paul
and St. Anthony, and the one that had the contract to carry
the mail was afraid, if they stopped at the St. Paul office to
get it, the other company would secure the passengers. This
game was shortly effectually blocked, and the complaints in
relation to the failure of the mails ceased, and with few
exceptions, thereafter so long as St. Anthony had a postoffice,
the mails were delivered promptly.

The new crop of logs commenced coming into the St.
Anthony mill-boom as early as the 18th of May, which was
several days ahead of the usual time. There was a good
stage of water in both branches of Rum river, as well as in
the Mississippi, for driving logs this season, and rapid work
was made in landing them in the boom. What is unusual, a
clean drive was made.

The Express of May 27th announced the arrival of a full-
blooded Devon bull and a cow of the same breed, imported
from the east into Hennepin county. These animals were

the property of Messrs. J. H. Stevens and John P. Miller. They paid two thousand dollars for them. This was the first importation of pure blooded stock into Hennepin county. The beneficial results expected in improving the breed of cattle in the county, in this instance at least, failed to materialize. From that day I have never believed that the Devon was a good breed of stock to propagate in Minnesota. Such, however, was not the opinion of Hon. Joseph Haskell, one of the pioneer farmers of Washington county. He imported choice Devon stock previous to the importation into Hennepin county, and met with a good deal of encouragement in breeding them. While the Devon is the most ancient of all pureblooded stock, as a general rule there are other breeds that seem to do better in this climate.

On June 3d S. M. Tracy of St. Anthony was appointed judge of probate of Ramsey county in place of Judge Wm. H. Welch who had received from President Pierce the important judicial appointment of chief justice of Minnesota. Judge Welch had resided in St. Anthony for over a year at the time of his elevation to the supreme bench of the territory. He came to Minnesota from Michigan. His appointment was received with much satisfaction by his fellow-citizens in St. Anthony. He was an able jurist, and a pure, impartial judge. He was the father of Major Abraham E. Welch, one of the most promising young officers in the volunteer service, who commanded the Third Minnesota regiment at the battle of Wood lake, September 23, 1862, in which engagement he received a serious wound. Both the father and his brave son died many years since.

President Pierce, soon after his accession to the Presidency, March 4th, made the following Federal appointments for Minnesota : Governor, Willis A. Gorman, of Indiana ; Secretary, J. Travis Rosser, of Virginia ; Chief Justice, Wm. H. Welch, of St. Anthony, Minnesota ; Associate Justices, Moses Sherburne, of Maine, and Andrew J. Chatfield, of Wisconsin. In the assignment of the different judicial districts of the territory to the new judges, Hennepin county was made a part of the Third judicial district, and Judge Chatfield was selected to preside over it. Judge Chatfield proved to be a very popular judge. For many sessions, when holding court

in Minneapolis, he was a welcome guest in my house, and was
considered by my family almost as one of their most favored
members.   Chief Justice Welch was assigned to the Fourth
judicial district, which necessitated his removal with his
family to Red Wing.   Judge Sherburne was assigned to the
Second judicial district, with headquarters at St. Paul.   He
also proved to be an able, impartial judge.   He was father-in-
law of Hon. Geo. W. Prescott, one of St. Anthony's most
respected citizens, who subsequently became editor-in-chief
of the Northwestern Democrat, the second newspaper that
made its appearance in St. Anthony, July 13th, 1853.   Mr.
Prescott became clerk of the United States court on the
admission of the state into the Union, which office he held
for many years.

•   To Hon. Wm. W. Wales, one of the most cherished of St.
Anthony's earliest citizens, were the people indebted for the
introduction of early vegetables in the vicinity of the Falls.
As early as 1852 he proved, by experimenting in his garden,
that there was no necessity for the importation by the steamboats from the lower country, in the late spring and early
summer, of such vegetables as asparagus, lettuce, radishes,
and other varieties, so welcome on our tables after the long
winter.   Mr. Wales, aside from being an accomplished horticulturist, has proved by his long and useful life at the Falls,
to be a philanthropist, and a Christian gentleman, who com-
mands the entire respect of his fellow-citizens.   For many
years he was postmaster in St. Anthony.   He was also one of
the most cherished members of the territorial legislature,
having been elected to the council in 1856.   He is always
engaged in working for the benefit of his fellow-men.

In the Express of June 17th appeared the following : " Im-
"portant changes have taken place in the Falls of St. Anthony
"during the past two years.   An immense mass of rock,
"about the center, was broken off last winter and fell, making
"a sort of rapids, rather than actual Falls, in that part of the
"cataract.   The theory, that in course of time the Falls of
"St. Anthony will so wear away as to become only rapids,
"seems highly probable from what is now taking place from
"day to day."   It was supposed at the time mentioned that
the large number of logs running over the Falls was one

cause of the breaking off of the rock. They would jam up on the precipice, almost damming the current, and when removed by the pressure of high water a portion of the rock on which the millions of feet of logs were lodged would go with them ; making an explosion not unlike an earthquake.

Several fearful thunder-storms, with heavy wind, passed over the twin villages at the Falls in the early summer of this year. On the 14th of June Rev. Mr. Chamberlain, rector of the Episcopal church, was struck by lightning, in his house, which came near terminating fatally. During the same day the dwelling-house of Geo. W. Prescott was badly damaged by the electric storm. This was the first time that any of the citizens of St. Anthony, or any of their houses, had received serious injury from the storms that were so frequent in the territory at an early day.

On the 18th of May the colony, under the auspices of Geo. M. Bertram, of Grand street, New York, arrived at Excelsior, on Lake Minnetonka. On the 14th of June the members held their first meeting in the embryo village, with their president, Mr. Bertram, in the chair. He congratulated the members on their safe arrival at their new home. A committee consisting of Messrs. Lemuel Griffiths, James Phillips, C. B. McGrath, H. Birmingham, S. C. Staples, and H. Blake, was appointed on resolutions. In making their report the committee referred to the great beauty of the location, and the extreme fertility of the soil, expressing a hope that in the near future the banks of Minnetonka lake would be settled by an industrious people.

A rapid journey from St. Paul to Chicago is recorded on the 6th of July. It was made in scant three days. The editor who copied the item recording the incident, from the Chicago journal, added the incredulous words, "That will do!" While the journey is now made with ease in palace sleeping cars in less than twelve hours, or in about one-sixth of the extraordinary time then recorded, the usual time from St. Paul to Chicago, in those days by river to Galena, and stage to Chicago, was about four days, though frequently the journey would be extended to five days. During the portion of the year when there was no navigation on the river it of course required a longer time to make the journey.

On the 9th of July, Judge A. G. Chatfield, the newly-appointed judge, held a special term of court in the little parlor of my house. The only business transacted was the discharge of two soldiers from the army stationed at Fort Snelling. They enlisted in the service before they were of suitable age, at an eastern recruiting-office. They belonged to families in the highest walk of life, and joined the army under peculiar circumstances. Their names were H. O. Billings and Wyman Williams. Their parents followed them out west and secured their discharge through the agency of the United States court. While the commanding officer at Fort Snelling, Colonel Francis Lee, was convinced that Judge Chatfield's decision was correct according to law, he and the other officers stationed there at that time were greatly disturbed at the frequent discharge, by the court, of soldiers at the Fort. Heretofore these discharges had occurred in Ramsey county. These were the first that took place in Hennepin county, and it was, too, the first occasion of Judge Chatfield appearing in a judicial capacity in the county.

The county of Hennepin, during the second week in July, through the agency of the New York Excelsior colony, received several permanent settlers of great merit. Among them were Rev. Mr. Nutting, and his brother Gen. Levi Nutting, now of Faribault, Rev. H. M. Nichols, Hon. Arba Cleveland, Geo. M. Powers, H. M. Lyman, and Joshua Moore, all from Massachusetts; and Burritt S. and Wm. S. Judd, from Ohio; and Rev. Chas. Galpin, and his brother Rev. Geo. Galpin, natives of Connecticut; and Peter M. Gideon, who has since become so widely known as a pomologist, and several other men of moment, who have occupied high positions in the country's history. Mr. Bertram, the leader of the colony, was a native of Scotland, but for many years previous to his coming to Minnesota, had been an enterprising business man in New York. He certainly accomplished a good work for Minnesota by introducing so many good men into the territory.

The Winnebagoes were particularly restless during this early summer. They could not be confined to their reservation at Long Prairie. From their long association with the whites in the lower country many of them could speak English. They would complain of their hard lot to every settler

they met. In some instances they resorted to violence in
their ill-will to the whites. On June 14th they attempted to
kill Mr. Berry, a resident up the river a few miles above St.
Anthony, with an ax, and they came pretty near carrying
their design into execution, as Mr. Berry was only rescued
by the timely arrival of neighbors. He received severe
wounds from their hands. This lawless tribe of Indians,
previous to the unprovoked attack on Mr. Berry, had discharged a gun at Mrs. Leonard, the wife of Chas. E. Leonard,
the village justice of the peace, in north St. Anthony. That
excellent lady fortunately escaped injury, but the Indians
shot a choice cow belonging to Mr. Leonard when they found
they had failed in the attempt to kill his wife. This was a
most unprovoked attack upon the life of Mrs. Leonard, as the
Indians had frequently received many favors from her husband who, with his family, were among the most respected
persons in the territory ; Mr. Leonard having frequently
received the unanimous suffrages of the voters for different
offices in their gift, which he always filled to their entire satisfaction. Similar outrages committed by this tribe of Indians
on the white settlers occurred during the summer.

The commencement for the building of the first bridge that
ever spanned the Mississippi was heralded in the several newspapers of the territory in the following historical announcement, dated St. Anthony, June 17th, 1853 :

"Notice is hereby given, that books will be opened at the
"office of Isaac Atwater, St. Anthony ; and at St. Paul, at the
" office of Rice, Hollingshead & Becker, on the third Monday
"of July next, for the purpose of receiving subscriptions to
"the capital stock of the Mississippi river bridge company,
" incorporated March 4th, 1852." Signed Isaac Atwater, D. E.
Moulton, John H. Stevens, John Rollins, Calvin A. Tuttle,
Incorporators. The first day that the books were opened,
sufficient subscriptions were made to the capital stock to
insure the success of the enterprise, and from that date to its
completion the work was prosecuted with vigor.

While we could not expect to make rapid progress in building in Minneapolis, situated as we were, not being able to sell
lots, or even to give a warrantee deed if we should sell them,
still every week some forward steps were taken.

CHAPTER XXIX.

The first bell in Minneapolis was the generous gift of eastern friends to the first Presbyterian church. The society
held meetings in the public hall over the store, near the ferry,
a block or two distant from my house. Rev. J. C. Whitney,
the pastor, and elders A. E. Ames, D. M. Coolbaugh, and J. N.
Barber, consented to have the bell placed on a tower outside
the building. The few of us on this side of the great river
remember well the first tolling of that pioneer bell, on the
west bank at the Falls of St. Anthony, on that quiet Sabbath
morning, late in the summer, announcing the hour of religious
services. The undulating sound of that bell seems to come
down to me through thirty-six years of space, mellowed by
time, as soft and sweet and pure in tone as the cradle-song of
a young mother to her first-born. As I am nearing another
ferry, to cross another river, its tender throbbings vibrate
with the well-remembered pulsations of the familiar church-
going bells of my early youth in a far-away eastern home.
From that day church-bells have heralded, above the roar of
the cataract, the hours of public worship to all around the
Falls of St. Anthony, and proclaimed the highest type of civilization. That primitive bell is in Minneapolis to-day, where
there is a population now nearly a thousand times greater
than then. That pastor, too, is with us, deservedly now a man
of material wealth, as well as of moral worth and influence
for good in the community. He continues a member of the
same church.

The hall in which religious meetings were held was also used for sessions of the United States and district courts, and for public gatherings generally. On the ground-floor was a room suitable for a store.

Hennepin Lodge, U. D., was organized and worked under the first dispensation granted by the grand lodge of Minnesota. The officers were D. M. Coolbaugh, master; J. N. Barber, senior warden; E. A. Hodson, junior warden; S. W. Case, secretary; E. Case, treasurer; Edward Murphy, senior deacon; Anson Northrup, junior deacon; Chesman Gould, tyler. The meetings were held at the house of Anson Northrup.

Another benevolent society, the Odd Fellows, was organized in July, with Charles Hoag at its head.

August 1st we had a flourishing church society, a district school, a county court, and a claim association, with an agricultural society soon to be organized.

The saw- and grist-mill on the west bank at the Falls, erected by Hon. Robert Smith and his partners, under the superintendency of Calvin A. Tuttle, were finished the first week in August. Both mills were small, but answered every purpose for the trade of that day. The boom privileges for holding logs on this side of the river were inefficient, hence the saw-mill was run under great disadvantages; but we were proud of the little mills.

The only store in the county at this time was a small one just started at Minnetonka by David Paschal Spafford. Those of us in this vicinity, as well as the settlers up the river, were obliged to patronize either the stores in St. Anthony or the sutler's store at Fort Snelling.

On the 13th of August Mr. Northrup's boarding-house on Hennepin island was burned. It was occupied by his nephew, Geo. A. Camp.

On August 20th Governor Gorman appointed Prof. E. W. Merrill, principal of the university, superintendent of common schools of the territory.

Georgiana, the first-born child of John George Lennon, died at the family residence in St. Anthony. There were in the neighborhood numerous believers that the village was unhealthy for children.

The trustees of the district-school in Minneapolis were fortunate in securing the services of Miss Mary A. Scofield as teacher for the summer term. Miss Scofield had been employed, at her home, near Rochester, New York, by Governor Slade, of Vermont, at that time at the head of an eastern organization for the purpose of supplying the west with teachers. She first taught with Miss Bishop in St. Paul, as early as 1848. She was a lady of rare merit. She became the wife of Prof. A. S. Kissell, for many years state superintendent of schools in Iowa. Her literary attainments were of a very high order.

Two new ferries were established over the Mississippi river, this summer ; one up the river a few miles above Minneapolis, by William Dugas ; the other by Edward Murphy, at the foot of the rapids, the seat of the steamboat-landing on what is now known as the Bohemian Flats.

At a Whig convention held in St. Anthony, September 1st, Dr. J. H. Murphy was nominated for the council, Messrs. Reuben Ball and Chas. F. Stearns for the house of representatives, Ira B. Kingsley for justice, and R. H. Jefferson for constable. The first Whig convention ever held in Hennepin county was convened at the new hall in Minneapolis, September 8th. The nominations were Isaac Atwater for district-attorney, Z. M. Brown for county treasurer, C. W. Christmas for county surveyor, D. M. Coolbaugh, S. A. Goodrich and S. K. Shultz for assessors ; A. N. Hoyt for county commissioner, and C. W. Farrington for road supervisor. John H. Stevens, Joel B. Bassett, A. N. Hoyt, John L. Tenny and Washington Getchell were appointed delegates to the legislative district convention to be held at Shakopee. Central committees were appointed as follows : Minnetonka precinct, Simon Stevens, Horace Webster and James Mountain; Upper precinct, Jacob Longfellow, Amos Longfellow and Geo. W. Getchell ; Minneapolis precinct, A. N. Hoyt, A. L. Cummings and C. C. Jenks ; St. Peters precinct (now Bloomington), William Chambers, Joseph Dean and S. A. Goodrich.

The Democratic convention was held in St. Anthony, September 12. Chas. F. Stimpson was nominated for the council, Daniel Stanchfield and William Dugas for the house of representatives, W. F. Brawley and James H. Brown for justices of the peace ; and J. A. West and John Beam for constables.

The second regular term of the District court was convened on the 5th of September, Judge Chatfield presiding. The same officers attended the court that appeared at the first term, except A. F. Whitney, U. S. deputy marshal, and Isaac Atwater, district attorney. The grand jury was composed of E. Case, foreman, Washington Getchell, J. N. Barber, George Parks, Chas. W. Christmas, H. S. Atwood, L. P. Warren, William Chambers, H. Fletcher, Simon Stevens, John C. Bohannan, Norman Jenkins, R. B. Gibson, John W. Dorr, Joel B. Bassett, Isaac V. Draper, Alex. Moore, Norman Abbott and Wm. W. Getchell.

Petit jury : Jesse Richardson, Edmond Borden, Wm. G. Moffett, H. Burlingham, D. H. Smith, C. W. Farrington, Ezra Foster, Thos. W. Pierce, Chas. H. Brown, Jas. Smithyman, Cyrus Hutchins, Robert Blaisdell, David Bickford, Titus Pettijohn, Simeon O'Dell, Elijah Austin, Ezra Hanscomb, J. P. Miller, Henry Whalen, John Mitchell, Wm. H. Tuttle, James Brown and Orvil Ames.

The grand jury returned several indictments, none of which, except one against Peter Poncin, for rape, were of a serious character. They presented Governor Gorman and General Fletcher, the Winnebago agent, for aiding the Winnebagoes in leaving their reservation and committing depredations on the whites. On the arrest and trial of the persons indicted, some half-dozen of them, mostly for violating the liquor law, all were cleared by the petit jury. There were no civil cases on the calendar.

At a meeting of the citizens residing in township 28 of range 24, held the first of the month, it was unanimously voted to call the town Richland, and it has been known as such since, and will probably continue to bear that name.

A meeting of the Democrats of this legislative district was held at Shakopee, on the 3d of September. They nominated Joseph R. Brown, who was then living at Mendota, for the council, and Dr. H. Fletcher, of Minneapolis, and Wm. H. Nobles, of Scott county, for the house. The same party made the following nominations for Hennepin county : For county commissioner, J. A. Dunsmore ; county attorney, D. M. Hanson ; assessors, B. E. Messer and T. W. Pierce ; constables A. Harmon and Titus Pettijohn.

The new Methodist church was dedicated on the 4th. It was one of the finest church edifices in the territory. Rev. M. Sorin conducted the services on the occasion.

Since the nominations by the Democrats in St. Anthony the nominees of the Whig convention became satisfied that a new deal should be made in the selection of the candidates ; consequently, at a meeting held before the election, Dr. Murphy withdrew as a candidate for the council, and moved that Chas. T. Stearns be the candidate in his stead. The motion was adopted. The candidates for the house also withdrew, and Henry S. Plummer was selected to run. It was decided to make no nomination for the second candidate. In consequence of the disaffection in the Democratic party in regard to their nominees, it was decided that the Whigs would support for that office the nominee of the disaffected democrats. The latter selected Cephas Gardner. This ticket was elected.

During the summer and fall of 1853 a treaty had been made with the Winnebago Indians, the ratification of which would have seriously injured this section of the state. That nation agreed to surrender all their rights in the Long Prairie country for the territory herein described : Beginning at the mouth of Crow river, thence running up the Mississippi to the mouth of Clearwater river, thence running up said river to its source, thence on a line running due west until it intersects the north fork of Crow river, thence to the place of beginning. A reservation was made for the right of way for the Pacific railroad, also of seventy-two sections for the use of the Stockbridge Indians, provided they wished to locate near the mouth of Crow river. This treaty, as it should have been, was strenuously opposed by the citizens of both Minneapolis and St. Anthony. It required hard work on our part to defeat it, but we succeeded in doing so ; and after so long a time since the event, we can not be too thankful that our efforts were successful ; had they not been, a large part of what is now Wright county would have been the very light and life of the Winnebago nation. There would have been no Dayton, Monticello, Clearwater, Otsego, Watertown, Delano, Rockford, or Buffalo, and it is doubtful if Minneapolis or St. Paul would have been nearly as large to-day in population, had that treaty been ratified by the whites.

The improvements made in St. Anthony this season were satisfactory. Mr. Cloutier erected a large house near the Catholic church. A large addition to the St. Charles was completed by the then landlord of that hotel, Captain J. B. Gilbert. Mr. Ball built a fine block above Dorman's. Wilson's improvements, corner of Main and Rollins streets, were an ornament to the village. Ed Lippincott finished his blacksmith shop opposite the mill ; Stearns, Manseur & Dickey built a large furniture manufacturing establishment ; King finished his block for stores and offices ; Geo. A. Brott completed his dwelling on the cliff, which was the finest one in the territory ; and Cheever commenced his observatory which attracted so much attention in the early days. Innumerable improvements were made on the back streets.

During the year considerable sickness prevailed in the village. It was mostly confined to young children. Among the fatal cases were the only child of Rev. Charles Secombe, a lovely little boy of some six months ; and on the 19th of March Judge and Mrs. Atwater's pleasant home was made a house of mourning by the loss of their only child Caroline, a beautiful little girl of fifteen months. The child of Isaac I. Lewis, little Henry Jay, died on the 9th of September. Dec. 4 Col. Alvaren Allen's fireside was called to greatly lament the death of their only little daughter, Ella Ophelia, at the age of twenty-three months. Those two little girls were the first-born in each family. Several other families were afflicted in like manner, including those of Dr. Murphy, J. G. Lennon and Mr. Orth.

On the 18th of September the Hennepin county Bible society was organized through an agent of the American Bible society. The officers elected for the year were Dr. A. E. Ames, president ; Rev. Mr. Harris, vice-president ; treasurer, Dr. H. Fletcher ; secretary, Miss Mary A. Scofield : executive committee, A. Harmon, D. M. Hanson and J. N. Barber ; local agents, Philander Prescott, William Finch, Rev. G. H. Pond, Rev. Charles Galpin, Rev. A. C. Godfrey, Deacon Mann, B. E. Messer, Rev. J. W. Dow, A. Harmon, Mrs. Joseph Dean, Miss Mary E. Miller, Miss Marian H. Coolbaugh, Miss Stough and Miss Moffett. This was the first organization of a kindred character in Hennepin county.

In pursuance of previous notice the first meeting of the Hennepin county Agricultural society, incorporated by an act of the legislature, approved February 28th, 1853, was held in the court house, September 7th. Dr. Ames called the meeting to order. He was elected president, and Joseph H. Canney was chosen secretary. The meeting was addressed by E. L. Hall, John W. North, Isaac Atwater, Judge Chatfield, Captain Dodge, and others. Isaac Atwater, John H. Stevens, J. N. Barber, and R. B. Gibson, were appointed a committee to draft a constitution and by-laws. On the adoption of the constitution and by-laws, as reported by the committee, the following officers were elected for the ensuing year : President, Rev. J. W. Dorr ; treasurer, E. Case ; secretary, J. H. Canney ; executive committee, J. H. Stevens, N. C. Stoddard, William Chambers, W. W. Getchell and Stephen Hall. It was decided to hold an agricultural fair in Minneapolis on the third Tuesday in October, 1853, and that the ladies be requested to send specimens of their industrial products. The following gentlemen were appointed a committee on analysis of the soil : Dr. A. E. Ames, J. H. Stevens and Charles Hoag.

THE BEGINNING OF THE MINNESOTA AGRICULTURAL SOCIETY

At the meeting above mentioned, N. E. Stoddard offered the following resolution, which was unanimously adopted : Resolved, That this society deems it expedient that there should be a convention held at St. Paul on the first Wednesday of January next, to form a territorial agricultural society, and that delegates be now appointed to attend said convention ; and that other agricultural societies in the territory are respectfully requested to send delegates to said convention. Messrs. Stoddard, A. N. Hoyt and William Chambers were appointed said delegates.

Up to this time there had been no work laid out on the Minnetonka road. For that matter, there was no road, aside from a path through the brush-lands, which was almost impassable. The citizens of both sides of the river were called upon, and they subscribed sufficient money to make a good road to the lake. O. E. Garrison was called upon to superintend the work.

At a meeting of the stockholders of the Mississippi Bridge

company, on the 24th, the following gentlemen were appointed officers for the ensuing year : Hon. John Rollins, president ; S. M. Tracy, secretary and treasurer ; Charles King, J. W. North, Shelton Hollister, R. P. Russell, Francis Morrison and S. K. Shultz, directors.

In consequence of the great influx of children into St. Anthony during the summer, when the fall and winter schools were opened it was found that there was not sufficient school-room for them. A number of private schools were opened. The Sisters made use of a large room in the upper town for school purposes. Rev. Mr. Chamberlain and his wife, who was a daughter of Bishop Chase, opened a seminary for young ladies, and Mrs. Z. E. B. Nash commenced a select-school, which became very popular. With these select-schools in addition to the preparatory department of the state university and the two district-schools, the majority of the children were accommodated. The services of Charles Hoag were secured for the principal school building in St. Anthony, while those of Mr. Clarke, an experienced teacher from Ohio, were secured for the Minneapolis school. Mr. Clarke was the first male teacher in the Minneapolis schools.

The Northampton farmers, so-called, belonging to the Excelsior colony, were wonderfully pleased with the product-iveness of the soil. Arba Cleveland planted two potatoes, from which he raised a bushel and a half of good merchant-able potatoes. The members of the colony seemed thoroughly impressed with the fertility of the section of country they had selected for their homes. The average to the acre of spring wheat was thirty bushels. These were the days that farmers made money ; more so than since that time ; probably more so than they will in the future.

A German colony arrived from the old country and settled on a lake some three miles west of Mr. Cleveland's place. Sheriff Brown named the lake Bavaria. The colony was headed by Joseph Kessler.

Ard Godfrey finished his mill at the mouth of Little Falls creek, the building of which received his constant attention for a year. He commenced sawing on the first of October. He decided to build a flour-mill.

The citizens of Minneapolis decided, early in October, to

engage B. E. Messer to teach a singing-school during the
winter. The following is a list of subscriptions to pay the
teacher : John H. Stevens five dollars, Thomas Chambers five
dollars, A. N. Hoyt five dollars, E. S. Smith five dollars, John
S. Cooper five dollars, Edwin Hedderly three dollars, William
Dickie three dollars, Calvin A. Tuttle three dollars, Geo. E.
Huy three dollars, George Park two dollars and a half, S. S.
Crowell two dollars, William Goodwin two dollars, Daniel
Scott two dollars, George Davis two dollars, Gilbert Hanson
two dollars, W. G. Murphy one dollar and a half, Chas. W.
Monson one dollar and a half. Simeon K. Odell and several
others signed all the way from fifty cents to a dollar, making
in all a sufficient amount for a continuance of the school all
winter. This was the first singing-school in Hennepin county.
Minneapolis had now not only a good teacher in the district-
school, but a good one in the singing-school. The only
school ever held out of Minneapolis proper, up to
this time, in the county, except a garrison school at Fort
Snelling, was an Indian school at the Lake Harriet mission
as early as 1836, taught by Rev. S. W. Pond.

In consequence of the increasing practice in his profession,
Dr. Murphy found that he could not well accept the nomination of the Whigs of St. Anthony for the council. A new convention was held, when Hon. C. F. Stearns was nominated in
his stead. Henry S. Plummer was nominated for the house
in Mr. Stearns' place. This ticket was elected, with Cephas
Gardner as Mr. Plummer's colleague in the house. Dr.
Kingsley and Lardner Bostwick were elected city justices.
Maj. A. M. Fridley, of St. Anthony, was elected sheriff of
Ramsey county. In the sixth council district, to which Hennepin county was attached, the candidates for the council
were Joseph R. Brown, democrat, and S. F. Cook, whig, both
of Dakota county ; for the house, Wm. H. Nobles, of Scott
county, and Dr. H. Fletcher of Hennepin county, democrats ;
and John H. Stevens, whig. The democrats were elected, as
were the candidates on the democratic ticket for the county
offices in Hennepin county, with the exception of Washington
Getchell for county commissioner.

The survey for the bridge over the river was completed,
and the estimate made to the stockholders. Mr. Newton, the

first engineer of the bridge, came near being drowned while engaged in the survey, and lost a valuable level and tripod which sank to the bottom of the river.

Thomas Chambers and Edwin Hedderly formed a copartnership and opened a first-class store in the lower room of the court-house, near the ferry. A few weeks afterward, on November 25th, Joseph LeDuc and A. King started another first-class store, near the lower ferry, on the Minneapolis side of the river. At last the citizens on the west side at the Falls could buy their tea and coffee and other necessary goods, at home.

There was a great scarcity of working oxen for the pineries this fall. They frequently sold for one hundred and thirty up to one hundred and forty dollars per yoke, which was almost double the price they had been worth previous years. There were no horses used to haul logs in the pineries.

The Winnebagoes were secretly leaving their reservation at Long Prairie to spend the winter down among the graves of their fathers in Iowa and Wisconsin; and while making the portage around the Falls committed numerous depredations on the stock of the settlers in this vicinity. Mr. Hedderly and A. N. Hoyt were the principal sufferers. Every effort was made to punish the Indians for the depredations they committed, but they escaped in their boats and were never punished.

The Rev. F. Nutting, of the Northampton colony, died on the 17th of December. This was the first death among those who came west under the Excelsior auspices. He was a man of great worth. He left his eastern home in consequence of lung difficulties. After a residence of over a year in the territory he had seemingly fully recovered his health. He had some business in the east which made it necessary to return there. Immediately on his arrival he contracted a severe cold, which settled on his lungs. He at once returned to Minnesota, but only lived a few days after reaching his home in St. Anthony. His physician said that if he had not made a visit to the east his life would probably have been prolonged many years in this climate.

CHAPTER XXX.

On the 8th of April, 1853, Major Isaac I. Stevens, of the United States army, was assigned by the war department to the duty of exploring a route for the Pacific railroad from St. Paul via St. Anthony to the Pacific coast. He had previously been appointed governor of the territory of Washington. He arrived at St. Paul on the 27th of May, but the officers and soldiers of the command that was to accompany him had arrived several days previously, and had encamped on the banks of Lake Amelia, near this village. The encampment extended to Diamond Lake. At this point all the plans were completed for the survey of the route for the proposed railroad. All the government mules, the horses belonging to the dragoons, and to the officers, were thoroughly tested with regard to the probability of their capacity for making the long journey. The numerous wagons were thoroughly over-hauled and examined. Some of these wagons had seen service in the Mexican and Florida war. The country was thoroughly canvassed for teamsters, wagon-masters, and men to serve in various capacities. Governor Stevens offered such high wages that there was danger of a large majority of our young men around the Falls, including those engaged in the pineries, going with him to the Pacific. Among those who accompanied him were W. W. Bixby, Henry Berry, and several others. Pierre Bottineau went with him as a guide. He also hired Henry Belland as a guide for Lieut. Cuvier Grover, who was to explore a more northerly route than that which Governor

Stevens was to traverse. Many of the persons in civil life whose services had been secured by Governor Stevens to accompany him subsequently became known throughout the Union. Among them were Messrs. Lander, Tinkham, Osgood, Kendall, and Stanley. Governor Stevens broke camp on Monday, the 6th of June. Captain Tapper had two busy days in ferrying them over the river. What seems a little strange at this late day is, that none of those persons from the Falls, who went with Governor Stevens on that memorable journey, ever returned to live here.

Edward Patch, G. B. Dutton, Z. M. Brown, E. B. Randall and Robert W. Cummings were appointed trustees of the John G. Potts Lodge No. 3 of the Independent Order of Odd Fellows of the town of St. Anthony Falls, in pursuance of an act of incorporation passed by the legislature, approved February 27th, 1852. This was the first Lodge of Odd Fellows ever organized at the Falls of St. Anthony.

The Library Association of St. Anthony commenced early in the Fall to secure proper persons to lecture during the winter of 1853 and '54. This Association, in the early days of St. Anthony, was a source of great benefit to the citizens of that village, morally and intellectually. In looking back to that period, at this time, the good results that flowed from that institution seem to have been the commencement of the real tendency of the citizens, which has ever distinguished them, to a high order of mental development. The Association was incorporated as early as November 1st, 1849, by an act of the territorial legislature. The incorporators were J. J. Carleton, R. P. Russell, Ira Barrows, Eli F. Lewis and Sumner W. Farnham.

It was intended by the farmers of Hennepin county to hold an agricultural fair in Minneapolis this fall, but the executive committee considered it better to postpone that event until the fall of 1854. The agricultural society was incorporated by an act of the legislature, approved February 20, 1853. The persons named in the act of incorporation were E. Case, Joel B. Bassett, Alexander Moore, Warren Bristol, H. Fletcher, A. E. Ames, John H. Stevens, P. Prescott, Joseph Dean and John S. Mann. It was determined by the executive committee, in pursuance of the resolution by Mr. Stoddard, passed at the first meeting of the society in September, to take immediate steps to organize a territorial agricultural society. After a correspondence with leading agriculturists in the state, the following notice appeared in the several newspapers published in the territory, under date of December 17th :

TERRITORIAL AGRICULTURAL SOCIETY.

• "Conference having been had among the friends of agri-
"cultural improvement in different parts of the territory, and
"a general desire having been expressed for the formation of
"a territorial society, the undersigned, delegates from the
"agricultural societies of Hennepin, Ramsey, and Benton
"counties, have deemed it expedient to call a convention for
"that purpose, to be held in St. Paul, on Monday, the 4th
"of January next, at 2 o'clock p. m., at the capital. The dif-
"ferent counties interested in this measure are respectfully
"and earnestly solicited to send delegates to the convention,
"that the whole territory may be represented in this desirable
"object. In addition to the business of the formation of the
"society, an address before the convention may be expected,
"of which due notice may be given. Signed : John H.
"Stevens, chairman executive committee of the Hennepin
"county agricultural society ; A. E. Ames, A. N. Hoyt, N. E.
"Stoddard, of the Hennepin county agricultural society ; W.
"W. Wales, Ramsey county agricultural society ; O. H.
"Kelly, Benton county agricultural society."

MINNESOTA AGRICULTURAL SOCIETY ORGANIZED.

For the purpose of completing the history of the organization of the Minnesota state agricultural society, of which there has been so much controversy in the state, and so many inaccurate statements, from time to time, this article is extended into a record of events in relation thereto that occurred in the early part of 1854.

At the territorial convention held in the hall of the house of representatives, at St. Paul, January 4th, 1854, Hon. A. E. Ames, of Hennepin, called the meeting to order, and stated the object of the convention. On motion of Hon. R. M. Richardson, of Benton, Captain William Holcombe, of Washington, was called to the chair, and John H. Stevens of Hennepin, and W. H. Moore, of Washington, were appointed secretaries of the convention. The following delegates from the agricultural counties of Ramsey, Benton, and Hennepin took their seats as members of the convention : Ramsey, J. W. Selby, C. L. Willis, A. Bennett, John R. Irvine, George Richard, Charles Symonds, James H. Brown, Geo. A. Camp, Truman M. Smith, George Hezley, C. H. Parker, and Wm. L. Ames ; Benton county, S. B. Olmstead, C. C. Crane, R. M. Richardson, and Wm. H. Kelly ; Hennepin county, A. N. Hoyt, N. E. Stoddard, A. E. Ames, Edward Murphy, John H. Stevens, E. Case William Chambers, and Isaac Brown. On motion of Dr. Ames, the following gentlemen from counties outside the call were admitted as delegates to the convention : Washington county, A. Stevens, Geo. W. Campbell, W. H. Morse, A. Van Vorhes, William Holcombe, W. R. Brown, R. Watson, John A. Ford, and John E. Mower. Dakota county, A. G. Chatfield, S. W. Cook, Thomas Foster, and A. R. French. Nicollet county, Benjamin Thompson, and Geo. H. McLeod. Scott county, Wm. H. Nobles, and Daniel Apgar, Pembina, Norman W. Kittson. Chisago county, N. C. D. Taylor. On motion of E. Murphy, of Hennepin, a committee of three was appointed to draft a constitution and by-laws for the government of the society. E. Murphy, A. E. Ames, and W. R. Brown were appointed said committee. After the committee had reported a constitution and by-laws for the government of the society, the following officers were elected for the year 1854 : President, Governor W. A. Gorman ; vice-presidents, J. W. Selby, Ramsey county ; R. M. Richardson, Benton county ; S. M. Cook, Dakota county ; John H. Stevens, Hennepin county ; Robert Watson, Washington county ; and Wm. H. Nobles, Scott county ; secretary, Dr. A. E. Ames, Hennepin county ; treasurer, C. A. Parker, Ramsey county ; executive committee, B. F. Hoyt of Ramsey, W. R. Brown of Washington, N. E. Stoddard of Hennepin, Captain J. B. S. Todd of Cass, and Wm. S. Allison of Dakota.

The new society was addressed by Governor Gorman, Judge A. G. Chatfield, A. Stevens, G. W. Campbell, J. W. Selby, Rev. B. F. Hoyt, Dr. A. E. Ames, S. M. Cook, Dr. Thomas Foster, Wm. L. Ames, and Wm! H. Nobles. The executive committee was directed to take steps, if practicable, to hold a territorial fair at some convenient place the ensuing

fall.   From that little beginning the present proud and
wealthy Minnesota state agricultural society had its birth.
Of the original members of the first society, organized so long
ago, belonging to the present state society, John H. Stevens,
of Hennepin, alone answered to the roll-call at the January
meeting in 1889.   •

The demand for brick had become so great in both St.
Anthony and Minneapolis, it was determined that steps should
be taken to manufacture them at the falls early in the spring
of 1854.   A company consisting of Messrs. R. P. Russell,
Isaac I. Lewis, David Bickford, and John H. Stevens, was
organized for the purpose on the 15th of December.   Mr.
Lewis was appointed agent, and was directed to purchase one
hundred cords of wood for burning the brick.

Charles N. Harris, a. boy who resided with his uncle John
W. North, in St. Anthony, was riding a horse, when the
animal became frightened, reared, and fell backward upon the
boy, nearly crushing him to death.   One leg was broken
above the knee, and he received other serious injury, but
recovered.   That boy became a brave soldier in the First
Minnesota regiment, and was shot through the breast at the
battle of Bull Run, and left by his comrades upon the battle-
field, supposed to be dead, and so reported.   His funeral
sermon was preached by Rev. Dr. Crary, in the presence of a
large audience, at Richfield, in Hennepin county, where his
parents and sisters resided.   After lying upon the ground for
many hours in the heat and until his wound was alive with
worms, he was taken by the confederates to the famed tobacco-
warehouse prison at Richmond, whence he was, after many
days, sent north in exchange of prisoners.   After the war
Mr. Harris was for eight years a district judge in Nevada.
Like his uncle North, he is a talented speaker and writer.
I think he now resides in California, as does also Mr. North
and Dr. Crary.

St. Anthony, as usual, received a valuable immigration during the season of 1853.   Hon. Henry T. Welles, Dr. A. E.
Johnson, the Baldwins, father and two sons, and several
others, who have since become prominent in the history of
the state, made the village their home.   It was estimated that
the town increased a third or more in population.   At the

close of the year every one seemed satisfied with the progress made in everything that was beneficial to the place.

A THANKSGIVING SERMON AS PROPHETIC AS IT IS DEVOUT.

Rev. C. Secombe, pastor of the Congregational church, in a sermon in anticipation of the coming thanksgiving, the last of December, said that " the calls for thanksgiving at the presen "time, are neither few nor small. We inhabit a charming "country. The 'green pastures' and 'still waters' of the sweet "singer of Israel, here find a remarkable exemplification. For "so high a latitude, we seem to make as near an approach to "Italian scenery the charming inspirer of the rustic muse— "as the length of our season will admit of. Minnesota, with its "carnelian lakes and laughing water falls, verdant prairies and " groves of oak, the magnificent bluffs and occasional grottoes, "can scarcely fail of becoming the birth-place of the poet, " whose soul-inspiring theme shall breathe the fragrance of "classic purity, and a christian devotion upon the latest gen- "eration. With its productive soil, and genial seasons, it is " destined to minister a wealth not to be despised even in so "great a nation. With the bracing clime and healthy atmos- "phere, it is destined to produce a race of men who will make 'the world feel their influence. With its central position, it " will command at once the advantages of the north, the south, "the east, and the west ; already but a few days ride from the "Atlantic, its geographical distance is but little more to the "Pacific, while its communication with the Gulf of Mexico is "the most easy and direct that the country affords. Such are "the circumstances in which a kind Providence has cast our " lot. Is there not occasion here for the most devout gratitude? "As we celebrate this annual Thanksgiving festival of our "fathers—as we remember their noble deeds who now slumber "in the dust as we remember that God is now calling us, "their sons, to give a character to this lovely portion of our "great inheritance how should our hearts swell with emotions "of gratitude ! How should our bosoms heave with a country's "love ! How should our souls burn with the noble purpose, "that nought of the high responsibility which has thus been "laid upon our shoulders, shall ever fall to the ground !"

CHAPTER XXXI.

The citizens of Hennepin county outside of Minneapolis, at the close of the season, had great reason to be thankful for the progress made during the year. The farmers had harvested a bountiful crop, and had a large breadth of land prepared for the reception of seed the next spring. Some five hundred farmers had made claims to land since the opening of navigation. Mills for the convenience of the farmers had been erected and finished in Minneapolis, St. Anthony, Minnetonka, at the mouth of Minnehaha stream and on that water-course in Richfield. The latter had been built in the most substantial manner by Philander Prescott, his son-in-law Eli Pettijohn, and Willis G. Moffett, and was capable of manufacturing large quantities of flour of the choicest quality.

The tendency of the immigration was west and south of Minneapolis. The Excelsior colony had located many farmers on the borders of Lake Minnetonka. Others also settled on the lake who did not belong to the colony. James Shaver, jr., Wm. B. Harrington, John P. Miller, D. P. Spafford, A. N. Gray, Samuel Bartow, R. E. McKinney, C. E. Dow, Stephen Hull, William Linlithgow, R. C. Willey, Peter M. Gideon, A. P. Biernan, and R. H. McGrath, were among the prominent farmers, each of whom made claims of a quarter-section of land. All the members of the colony, including the president, Geo. M. Bertram, and the pastor, Rev. Chas. Galpin, also claimed a quarter-section. All these claims were made in the vicinity of Minnetonka. In Richfield, James Draper, Wm. J. Duggan, Chas. Haeg, Merriman McCabe, J. A. Dunsmoor, C. W. Harris, Henry George, and Robert Townsend, John McCabe, and several other prominent men, made claims.

Bloomington, too, received many permanent farmers, among whom were J. D. Scofield, James Anderson, William Bryant, and M. O. Reily.

Minnetrista for the first time was occupied by Joseph and John Merz. Most of the vacant land in Crystal Lake was taken by enterprising farmers, including such well-known men as Rufus Farnham, jr., D. C. Crandall, Peter Schuller, Z. Gillespie, David Morgan, E. McCausland, H. R. Stillman, J. S. Malbon, and Josiah Dutton.

In Brooklyn, John M. Durnman, John W. Goodale, Asa Howe, C. R. Howe, Sylvanus Jenkins, N. H. Jenkins, Jacob Longfellow, W. W. Wales, Jr., and Thomas Warwick.

In Champlin, Joseph Holt, Augustus Holt, John Pike, B. E. Messer, Rev. Lewis Atkinson, R. H. Miller, F. Thorndyke, John Shumway, and Colby Emery.

In Dayton the immigration was tardy in reaching that beautiful township, though Paul Godine settled in the precincts of the town as early as 1851. In 1853 John Veine made a claim where the village of Dayton now stands. Other claims were taken up this year by Marcelles Boulee, Benjamin Leveillier, Daniel Lavallee, Anthony Gelinas, Louis Bibeault, Moses Desjarlois, and Edward Greenwood.

Plymouth received its first settler this year in the person of Antoine Le Count, who made a claim on the east side of Medicine Lake, late in October. Thomas Hughes, with a large family of boys, made a claim in the town about the same time. There were several other farmers settled in different parts of the county this year, whose names I am unable to mention at this time.

The father of Antoine Le Count, who was known to the early settlers as a man by the name of Le Gros, was a guide to many of the expeditions which were so common in the northwest in the territorial days. Some of these expeditions were of a scientific nature ; others for trading with the aborigines. Le Gros resided for a short time in this neighborhood at a very early day, and was employed by Franklin Steele to reside on Nicollet island. His home proper was on the banks of the Red river of the north, near, but this side of, the Canadian

line.   Pierre Bottineau served an apprenticeship to him as a
guide when he had scarcely reached his teens. LeGros met
with a violent death on the 14th day of June, 1840, on the
plains. He was shot by the distinguished explorer, Thomas
Simpson. The latter discovered in the Arctic country the
region known as Victoria Land. He had employed Le Gros
to pilot him from Fort Garry, in the British possessions, to
Fort Snelling. It is supposed that Simpson became deranged,
shot Le Gros, and another member of the expedition by the
name of Bird, and then killed himself. Antoine Le Count,
the first settler in Plymouth township, was a member of the
expedition and witnessed the sad occurrence.

D. M. HANSON.

Among the early citizens of Minneapolis, there was perhaps
no one more prominent in all that related to the public welfare
than Domiticus M. Hanson. He was a son of William Hanson, one of the earliest and most respected of the settlers, who
had also several other boys. The family had for several years
great influence in the village and county. D. M. Hanson was
a lawyer, and a politician. A fine speaker, with pleasing
address, and an ardent democrat, he had pretty much his own
way in voicing the sentiment of his party. He excelled as a
stump-speaker, and while the county was undoubtedly strong
in its whig tendencies, Mr. Hanson was this year elected
district-attorney on the democratic ticket. The next year,
in 1854, he was a candidate on the democratic ticket with H.
H. Sibley, for the house of representatives, for the winter
session of 1855, and was triumphantly elected. · In the fall of
1855 he was the candidate on the democratic ticket for the
council, and elected. At the close of the session of the legislature, on March 1, 1856, Mr. Hanson returned to his Minneapolis home. He only lived a few days after the close of the
session. At the time of his death he was only twenty-eight
years old. With his talent, ambition, and industry, had his
life been extended to this period, he would undoubtedly have
occupied the highest offices in the gift of the people of this
state. He left a widow, but no children. At one time he,
with his father and brothers, owned a large tract of land in
this city below Tenth avenue south. He had a large practice
as a lawyer, but in consequence of his political work, when

Judge Cornell came to this city, in the spring of 1854, he
formed a partnership with him, and turned over the most of
his law practice to the judge. At one time Mr. Hanson's name
was a household word, not only in Minneapolis, St. Anthony,
and Hennepin county, but throughout the territory ; now there
is not one citizen in one hundred in Minneapolis who ever
heard of it. Out of his father's large family, there is only
one a resident of the state. Gilbert Hanson resides in Otter-
tail county. Another brother, Randall, was several years ago
chief of police in this city, when Geo. A. Brackett was mayor.
He now resides on the Pacific slope. The father and mother
of this once large and influential family, with all their children
except the two mentioned, are in the spirit-land.

Among the citizens of Hennepin county who selected farms
within its precincts, is J. D. Scofield, who took a claim in
Bloomington, and resides on it to this day. Mr. Scofield has
been prominent in organizations beneficial to the farmers.
Samuel Bartow also this year settled on the banks of Lake
Minnetonka. He continues to reside on the old farm. Mr.
Bartow has held many prominent offices, including that of
county commissioner. Another settler on the shores of the
lake this year was Wm. B. Harrington. He was a descendant of the Puritan Governor Bradford, of the Plymouth colony.
Mr. Harrington's father, Hon. John Harrington, was a native
of Vermont. Both of his grandfathers were soldiers in the
revolutionary army. Mr. Harrington was a man of great
worth. He died several years ago at Hutchinson, in McLeod
county. His eldest son, Rev. Wm. H. Harrington, resides at
Excelsior. He is a popular clergyman of the Universalist
church. He also edits a newspaper.

PETER M. GIDEON.

Perhaps Minnesota was never more fortunate in the reception of a new-comer than she was this year in the person of
Peter M. Gideon, who also made a home on the borders of
Minnetonka. Since his residence on his farm, he has become
a distinguished pomologist, and has made a world-wide reputation in introducing new varieties of fruit, shade and ornamental trees. He has accomplished a great work in the
northwest in regard to raising hardy sorts of apple-trees,
which survive our rigorous climate. Mr. Gideon still resides

on a portion of the land he first claimed so many years ago. He is a native of Champaign county, Ohio, where he was born in 1820. He commenced fruit-growing in Minnesota the year after his first arrival in the territory. His labor in his experiments with fruit, flowers, shade and ornamental trees, has been very successful. For many years he has been the superintendent of the state experimental fruit-farm founded in 1878. Among the varieties of apples of great merit, he has originated the Wealthy, Peter, and Grace. He has also some forty new varieties of seedlings which promise to be of value to the fruit-growers of the west, but they are not yet fully developed.

Rev. Stephen Hull, who was the first actual settler on the upper Minnetonka Lake, was a man of much more than ordinary ability. In his earlier years he had occupied the pulpit of a prominent eastern Universalist church. He resigned the pastorate and came west. He selected a beautiful site on the narrows of the lake and erected what was at that time a good substantial dwelling, and cleared off quite a farm, which he worked for several years. The narrows, so-called, between the upper and lower lake, bear his name to this day. His old home is now the site of the Lake Park grounds. Mr. Hull made his claim in February of this year. He was a just, honest man, and when in after years he sold his farm and went to Missouri, his friends and neighbors greatly regretted his removal.

In April William Linlithgow, a young man of much promise, arrived in the territory from near Boston and selected a claim joining Mr. Hull's. Mr. Linlithgow was of Scotch descent, and what was uncommon in those days, with most of those seeking homes in the west, he was wealthy. After graduating from one of the most prominent eastern colleges, he had traveled extensively in both the old and new world. To this day it is a mystery why he selected the banks of Minnetonka for his home. A refined, polished man, with more money than he had immediate use for, he quietly settled down with a single male servant, in a romantic spot on the lake, declaring that it should be his home for life : and it was. Late in the summer of 1854, while going from his residence to Minnetonka mills, in a beautiful yacht, which he had constructed he was overtaken by a storm, and perished in the lake. Quite recently, at the same place, Mayor Rand, and others, lost their lives. Mr. Linlithgow's body was found several days after his death, washed ashore, but his yacht remains at the bottom of the lake. Early settlers in the county mourned his death. A relative from the east came and settled his estate, but the principal events of his life, previous to his coming to Minnesota, remain unknown to his western friends. One of the latter so greatly lamented his death that it was more than twenty years after that sad event, before he would take passage on any water-craft whatever on that lake.

SCHOOLS IN THE COUNTY—THANKSGIVING.

At the expiration of the year 1853 there was only one school outside of Minneapolis, with the exception of the school at Fort Snelling, which had for years been taught by the post chaplain for the education of the children of the soldiers in the garrison. At Oak Grove mission Rev. G. H. Pond had, since 1843, been instrumental in maintaining a school for the Indian children. In Crystal Lake township a school-district was organized according to law. The district included the whole north half of the county. A school, and a good one, was taught by a Miss Smith, in a claim-shanty that was on the land that subsequently became the property of J. Gillespie. This was the first regular district-school taught in any portion of Hennepin county proper, outside the village of Minneapolis.

Our new governor, W. A. Gorman, named Thursday, the 22d day of December, this year, for thanksgiving. All the different religious denominations in Minneapolis joined, and attended Rev. J. C. Whitney's church, when Mr. Whitney gave us one of the best and most practical sermons delivered before or since in this city. At that time there were several different denominations of Christians in the village, but only one resident pastor, Mr. Whitney. It is true we occasionally had preaching. Rev. G. H. Pond had the use of my parlors for holding meetings ; so had other preachers the same privilege ; but at the close of the year there was only one resident clergyman in Minneapolis.

There were six deaths in Hennepin county in 1853 : Mrs. Colonel Case in the spring, another lady of consumption, and four infants.

CHAPTER XXXII.

At the beginning of the year 1854 St. Anthony contained the following mercantile establishments : D. Baldwin & Son, James A. Lennon, S. Stanchfield, R. Ball, Richard Fewer, Moulton, Walker & Gardner, N. Hendry, N. Hohler, D. E. E. P. Mills, Holmes & Toser, J. G. Lennon, A. King, R. P. Upton, James C. Tuffts, Henry Reynolds, Dr. H. W. Whitemore, John Holland & Joseph McAlpin, Z. E. B. Nash & Edgar Nash. There were two cabinet manufactories, Stearns & Manseur, and J. B. Luchsinger ; one plow manufacturer, A. Leaming ; two carriage-makers, Bassett & Lehman, and Francis Sampson. There were two fancy and ornamental establishments, those of Alvin Stone, and B. E. Messer ; three sash and door factories, by Orin Rogers & Co., Duman & Vail, and Elias H. Connor. These gentlemen carried on an extensive contracting and building business. There were two blacksmiths, S. E. Foster, and E. Lippencott ; one harness-maker, William Spooner ; one watch-maker and jeweller, J. C. McCain ; three milliners, Miss Henderson, Mrs. Ray, and Mrs. S. McCain ; four boot and shoe establishments, those of John Wensinger, J. R. McFarland, S. C. Clark, and J. J. Kennedy ; two tailors, J. Piddington, located in 1851, and A. Bacon ; one civil engineer and surveyor, C. B. Chapman ; one meat-shop, by Samuel Ross ; two dauguerreotypists, T. Elwell, and J. R. McFarland ; eleven lawyers, Isaac Atwater, A. R. Dodge, John W. North, C. Gardner, E. L. Hall, W. Richardson, D. A. Secombe, A. D. Shaw, J C. Shepley, J. H. Trader, and S. M. Tracy ; five physicians'

Dr. Murphy, Dr. Anderson, Dr. Johnson, Dr. Ira Kingsley, and Dr. C. Jodon ; two newspapers, the Express, and the Northwestern Democrat ; one brewery, by John Orth, located in 1850 ; one baker, Geo. Wezel ; three hotels, St. Charles by M. W. Keith, St. Anthony hotel by Col. West, and the Temperance house by Samuel Ross ; two saloons, by B. Cloutier, and Brown & Smiley ; two livery-stables, by Allen & Co., and Geo. F. Brott ; one brick-yard, by Vanderpool & Walds ; two storage and commission houses, by John G. Lennon, and J. P. Wilson ; one grist-mill, by J. Shepherd, lessee ; postoffice, by O. W. Rice ; churches, Congregational, Rev. C. Secombe ; Episcopal, Rev. Mr. Chamberlain ; Baptist, Rev. Lyman Palmer ; Free-Will Baptist, Rev. C. G. Ames ; Catholic, Rev. Mr. Ledon ; Methodist, Rev. Mr. Collins ; Universalist, Rev. E. A. Hodson ; one Masonic lodge, Hon. C. F. Stearns, W. Master ; one Odd-Fellows John G. Potts lodge No. 3, installed May 29, 1851, O. Foote, N. G., E. Patch, V. G., G. B. Dutton, secretary, and E. B. Ramsdell, treasurer. In addition to the above, the extensive saw-mills employed much capital, and a great many hands, in its operations. Under all the happy circumstances surrounding the village the citizens had reason to believe that the year 1854 would prove a prosperous one for them.

The first postoffice established in Hennepin county, outside of Fort Snelling, was at Bloomington, the 1st of January, 1854. Joseph Dean was appointed postmaster. The youthful Minneapolis was scarcely behind Bloomington, for a day or two later a postoffice was given us, with Dr. H. Fletcher, postmaster. There was no mail delivered here ; it was distributed in the St. Anthony office, and usually was gathered by Dr. A. E. Ames, who had, with Dr. Murphy, an office in St. Anthony, and on his return home at noon, he would carry the few letters in the crown of his hat.

At a meeting of the board of county commissioners, on the first Monday in January, a settlement with the treasurer and collector was effected. The whole county debt at this time was two hundred and twenty-five dollars, and county orders were worth one hundred cents on the dollar. The greatest call made upon the county treasury was for money to build roads and bridges. The pioneers had, in a measure, previously

taken money out of their pockets and built many of the necessary roads and bridges, so the drain from the treasury was not
so great as it would have been had not these roads and bridges
been previously built. They had to act in the same way, that
schools and churches might be built and maintained. There
are so many ways that the pioneer is obliged to contribute to
develop the resources of a new country it is pretty safe to say
that his purse is always a lean one.

The territorial legislature convened at St. Paul on the 4th.
Joshua Draper of Minneapolis, through the influence of Dr.
H. Fletcher, the Hennepin county member of the house,
received the appointment of fireman, and Geo. W. Prescott,
through Messrs. Gardner and Plummer, was appointed clerk
of the house. This appointment of Mr. Draper was the first
one given by the legislature to a citizen of Hennepin county.

On Thursday the 19th day of January; 1854, Rev. J. C.
Whitney was installed pastor of the Presbyterian church in
Minneapolis. Rev. G. H. Pond presided. Rev. Mr. Rogers,
of the Baptist church, St. Anthony, offered prayer. Rev. C.
Secombe preached the sermon. Rev. H. M. Nichols gave
the charge to the pastor ; Rev. E. D. Neill, the charge to the
people. The interesting exercises closed with the benediction
by the pastor. This was the first installation of a minister of
the gospel of any denomination in Minneapolis.

THE WINNEBAGO TREATY.

Aside from the historical fact, perhaps in justice to those
who have passed away, mention should be made of a public
meeting held in Minneapolis, January 21st, 1854, in opposition
to the treaty with the Winnebagoes pending in the United
States senate, the confirmation of which would make the
Indians of that nation near neighbors of the citizens of Hennepin county. Charles Hoag was called to the chair, and
John H. Stevens was appointed secretary. The object of the
meeting being stated, Dr. H. Fletcher, our member of the
legislature, addressed the meeting. He had secured the
cooperation of Hon. Joseph R. Brown, Hon. Wm. H. Nobles,
the other two members of the sixth council district in the
legislature, against the measure. Messrs. C. F. Stearns, H.
S. Plummer, and Cephas Gardner, members from St. Anthony
representing the third council district, had also heartily co-

operated with them in opposition to the treaty. Messrs. S. Baldwin Olmstead, president of the council, with Messrs. William Noot, Wm. A. Davis, and Louis Bartlett, of the second council district, St. Paul, had aided in opposition to the treaty. Further remarks were made by Messrs. Hoag, Harmon, D. M. Hanson, and Hoyt, when a series of resolutions was presented to the meeting by John H. Stevens, seconded by D. M. Hanson, and were unanimously adopted. Suffice to say, that owing to the efforts made by the pioneers of Minneapolis, the treaty failed.

Considerable uneasiness developed among the settlers on the late military reservation, early in January, at the non-action of congress in relation to a bill which had, early in the session, been introduced by Hon. R. C. Malony, of Illinois, securing to them the right of preemption to these lands. Messrs. Franklin Steele, Dr. A. E. Ames, and Edward Murphy, proceeded to Washington to render such aid as they could to our delegate in Congress, and other friends in that body, to secure the early passage of the bill. These gentlemen remained in Washington all winter, at their own expense, and labored faithfully in the interest of the settlers. They secured the ordering of an immediate survey of the land by the government. Up to the early summer of 1854, when the survey did take place, all the lines between the settlers were arbitrary. These lines had been brought from over the Mississippi river, by the early local land-surveyors, Messrs. W. R. Marshall, C. W. Christmas, and C. B. Chapman, which proved, when the government had completed the regular survey, to be unusually accurate. I cannot remember, at this time, of it being necessary to alter a single boundary line between the settlers.

Dr. Fletcher secured the passage of a bill, in January, through the territorial legislature, confirming the action of the county commissioners for the Hennepin court-house, and other county buildings. This site was on the high hill that then existed immediately in the rear of the present Nicollet house. It embraced about five acres of land, and overtopped the whole country. The surface was covered with beautiful oak trees, known in the early days as oak-openings. The land was owned jointly by John Jackins and John H. Stevens, the two entering into heavy bonds with the county commissioners to give a warrantee deed of the land as soon as they had secured a good title to it from the government, free of charge. This land is worth to-day several millions of dollars, but in consequence of the rivalry between what was then called upper and lower Minneapolis, in 1856 the site was changed to one in the brush on Dr. Ames' land, thus releasing Messrs. Jackins and Stevens from their obligations to the county; but they never made anything out of the land, and the county was greatly the loser in the change. There was, however, two good results from the removal of the site for the court-house, one of which does not concern the public; the other was the annexation of the fractional township in which St. Anthony was situated, to Hennepin county. In order that the measure might be carried through the legislature, members of that body demanded in return for their votes for the removal of the site of the court-house, the annexation of St. Anthony to Hennepin county.

Another and more important site-question occurred on the other side of the river. It was demonstrated that if St. Anthony retained the site for the University, more land must be secured for that purpose. The regents had no money to help forward any beneficial movement for the University. When it was necessary that funds should be raised, they were obliged to put their hands in their pockets and donate it in such sums as the exigency of the case demanded. Mr. Steele, president of the Board, contributed thousands of dollars for the good work, for which he never expected, wished, or received, reimbursement. Judge Atwater, Judge Meeker, and other regents residing in the neighborhood of the Falls, also paid large sums for the same purpose. The original site was exchanged for the present beautiful one. Calvin A. Tuttle and others aided much. The land that Mr. Tuttle gave for this object is to-day worth a large sum of money, and probably there are few of the present citizens around the Falls who have any conception of the sacrifices these earnest men made, so long ago, in order that the University of Minnesota should not be removed from their midst. It is true that they never received any credit for what they did; their noble efforts have long since been forgotten by the older people of the state ; the more recent population never knew it ; while thousands who are now so much benefitted by the university have never found it out. In order to check the strong sentiment prevailing in the territory, that the university should be removed to some point considerably south of the Minnesota river, the regents were obliged to force measures in the commencement of the buildings, so that St. Anthony would have a charter-right to hold it for all time to come. When the distribution of the sites for the three great public institutions, the capitol, the state university, and the state penitentiary, took place, southern Minnesota belonged to the Indians, as did the whole of the territory west of the Mississippi. After the Indian lands were opened to settlers, they were occupied so rapidly it was evident that in the near future those lands would contain a large majority of voters ; that they could control a majority in the legislature, and being left out in the cold when the three principal plums were distributed, it was but natural they should wish to have a new deal, so that the recently-ceded territory should be the recipient of one or more of these public favors. The regents were continually importuned by those residing in the neighborhood of the Falls, who were really fearful that the university would be removed from St. Anthony to a more central place further south, to commence the buildings as soon as possible, and to take immediate steps in every possible way to silence home complaints at what was called non-action of the board of regents in making the necessary preparations for the erection of permanent buildings. Up to this time the bountiful grant of land by congress in the interest of the university had not been selected by the regents from the different sections of the state, principally for the reason that the public lands had not been surveyed by the government, so that selections could be made in a proper manner. The time had now come for action on the part of the regents. They had by law the right to select any unclaimed land, timber or prairie, for the benefit of the university. As a member of the board I was appointed, at the January meeting, to proceed at once to Rum river and select some ten thousand acres of pine land for the university. I was further directed to secure such assistance as would be necessary for this purpose. The services of Captain John Rollins, and his nephew Simon B. Bean, were obtained, and mainly to the superior knowledge of these two gentlemen, in relation to the best timber on pine land, was the university indebted for the choicest tract that bounded the banks of Rum river and its tributaries. It was not the most pleasant season of the year to make the selection, but mid-winter was more favorable than spring, and as the land had been surveyed, and would soon be in market, if we obtained the best and most convenient lands to the river, the selections had to be made before other parties laid claim to it. We devoted two months of the winter of 1854 to securing these lands, paying all attendant expenses, without a thought of charging the board of regents, or the state, for such work.

The first Congregational church was dedicated in St. Anthony on the 15th of February. Rev. S. Hall was master of the ceremonies. Messrs. Galpin of Excelsior, Twitchell of Rum river (now Anoka), Rice, and Secombe, all Congregational ministers, and Rev. J. C. Whitney, the Presbyterian pastor of Minneapolis, were present. This was the first Congregational church dedicated in what is now Minnesota.

The ice in the river was thin this winter. Several accidents of a serious, but not fatal, character occurred. Among the victims was John Chambers, who lived on and preempted a portion of the present Brownsdale farm. In crossing the river he fell through the ice, and was barely rescued alive. It is said he received injuries from which he never recovered.

The ferry over the river commenced running March 25.

St. Anthony's early friend, Wm. R. Marshall, was married in Utica, New York, on the 22d of March, to Miss Abby B., daughter of George Langford, Esq.

The third term of the district court of Hennepin county commenced April 3, Judge Chatfield presiding. R. P. Russell, who had recently moved over from the St. Anthony side, was foreman of the grand jury. The jury list contained the names of prominent farmers in what would now be three counties, viz.: Hennepin, Carver, and Sibley. The court was in session for three weeks, principally engaged in trying criminal cases. The first civil suit tried in Hennepin county, the only civil case of moment, was against Edward Murphy by Hiram

Burlingham, to test the fence question, which in the early days of the territory was the source of frequent litigation among the farmers. As this was the first civil suit tried in the county, and a somewhat novel one, I will give the points in the case. Mr. Burlingham had a field of some forty acres of corn. Mr. Murphy had a large herd of cattle, which he had purchased in Illinois. This stock frequently visited Mr. Burlingham's corn-field, and damaged the growing grain to such an extent that it was not worth harvesting. Mr. Burlingham sued Mr. Murphy, the owner of the stock that had destroyed his crop, for its value. Mr. Murphy contended that, as Mr. Burlingham's corn-field was not fenced, he could not be held responsible for the damage his stock had inflicted on it. The judge decided that Mr. Murphy must pay for the loss of the corn ; that in the absence of statute law, in regard to fences, a person could plant corn or other grain, without fencing it, and if it was destroyed by a neighbor's stock the owner of the stock would have to pay the damage.

The first conviction in the district court was against P. Gorman, of Eden Prairie, who was found guilty of an assault on the person of Samuel Mitchell, a farmer of that township. If I remember correctly, because of its being the first conviction, and not a very serious offense, the sentence against Mr. Gorman was suspended.

During the session the new court-house, which I had built the previous year, was destroyed by fire, which was the first store destroyed by fire in Minneapolis.

A HASTY BUT HAPPY MARRIAGE IN THE EARLY DAYS.

Some of the jurymen, from remote parts of the county, who attended the session of the court, were desirous of obtaining wives before their return home. One of them, John Mann, who had a valuable claim on the banks of the Minnesota river, just below Chaska, had been a soldier at Fort Snelling. He was a thrifty man, and was born in Germany. He went to St. Paul, one Sunday, to find out if there were any German girls coming into the country. He fortunately happened on the levee during the landing of a down-river boat that contained many German families who were seeking new homes in the territory. In watching them land, John espied a comely, healthy-looking girl in a group of women. "There,"

he said to an acquaintance who accompanied him to see the
approaching steamer land, "is my wife." He immediately
introduced himself to the parents of the girl, and to the girl.
He was thirty years old, had a good farm, and a comfortable
house ; had cows and oxen, and a reasonable amount of money.
He had in fact everything to make him comfortable except a
wife. He wanted the girl before him for that. He prosecuted
his suit with much earnestness. Fortunately a member of a
prominent German family, who had resided in St. Paul for
several years, made his appearance on the landing in the nick
of time, who knew the parents of the girl in the fatherland,
and knew John in this country equally well, and he assured
the surprised immigrants that John was all that he represented
himself to be, and that the parents who secured him for a
son-in-law would never regret it. The result was, that early
on Monday morning John appeared in court with his new
wife. He was readily excused from further service on the
jury. He immediately proceeded to his farm, and from that
eventful morning that he saw his wife land in St. Paul to this
day, he never regretted his hasty marriage. He and his wife
are among the most respected pioneers of Carver county.
They have prospered, and John believes in short courtships.

Congress passed, during the last days of March, a bill providing for a United States land-office in Minneapolis. Upon
its approval by the President, that personage appointed R. P.
Russell receiver, and M. L. Olds register. Both appointments
were popular. Mr. Olds was a son of Dr. Olds, so long a
member of congress from Ohio. His son was a lawyer of
much promise. On retiring from the land-office he became a
divinity student, and at the time of his death, a few years
since, he held a high trust in the Episcopal church. Like
most of the early clergymen of that church in the territory,
Rev. Dr. Olds was a great worker.

Messrs. Geo. E. Huy and R. P. Russell had erected a large
frame building at the corner of Eight avenue south and
Washington avenue for the accommodation of the new land-
office. This was the most commodious and expensive building
that had been erected in Minneapolis up to that time. In
addition to numerous offices, it contained large halls.

CHAPTER XXXIII.

When I think it was only thirty-five years ago that I decided to survey a portion of my ferry-farm at the Falls of St. Anthony into village building-lots, the transformations I have witnessed seem like a fairy tale, a magic vision. From the virgin prairie to a solid city of two hundred thousand persons, teeming with life, full of energy, ambition and hope, this marvelous western development bids fair to rival oriental splendor.

Finding it impossible to withstand the constant importunities for building-lots on the ferry-farm, and to prevent the lower portions of the town from taking the lead in various enterprises that were near at hand, I determined to survey a portion of the farm into building-lots ; consequently I secured the services of Chas. W. Christmas to survey and plat over one hundred acres into village lots. I determined at first to make the streets eighty feet wide, the avenues one hundred feet wide, the lots to contain as near as might be a quarter of an acre of land each, the blocks to consist of ten lots each, making two and a half acres to each block. As no one expected at that time that much of the land back of the first plateau would ever be used for any other than agricultural purposes, after consulting with all the claimants up and down the river immediately adjoining my land, we concluded there should be one avenue laid out running parallel with the river, which should be the basis for laying out the town ; that the name of this avenue should be Washington. This decision with regard to laying out the principal avenue in such a manner as to run parallel with the river as the foundation for laying out all the

other land into streets, avenues, lots and blocks, was a great
error, an error that, had my foresight been as good as my
present sight, would never have occurred. What I should have
done, was to have paid no attention to the windings of the
river, but ran the streets directly east and west, and the
avenues directly north and south. As all the land subsequently laid out and platted in Minneapolis had for a starting-
point my first survey, it made me responsible for all time for
this unfortunate early mistake. Pretty as the city is, it
would have presented a far better appearance had the points
of compass been followed rather than the windings of the
river. The only city I had lived in, previous to coming to
Minnesota, was New Orleans, and I admired the English part
so much more than the old French portion of it, that I decided
to follow, as far as practicable, the former in laying out and
platting Minneapolis proper. Most, if not all the cities on
the banks of the Mississippi and its tributaries, at this time,
had the principal part of the business confined to pretty near
the steamboat landings. The idea was general that the stores
and shops would be close to the banks of the river ; and so
they were at first ; none could be prevailed upon to invest
very far back from the river. No one ever supposed at that
time that Minneapolis would expand into a city of more than
fifty or sixty thousand inhabitants, and many looked upon
my platting the streets and avenues so wide as a great waste
of land ; and on some accounts I am rather inclined to think
it would have been preferable to have reduced the width of
the avenues and streets about twenty feet ; especially when
we take into account the great cost of paving, and other necessary expense in keeping them in repair.

NAMING THE STREETS AND AVENUES.

In naming the avenues I commenced with Hennepin, calling
it after the discoverer of the Falls ; then Nicollet, after the
French explorer ; then Minnetonka, from the lake by that
name. All the other avenues, except Second avenue south,
were named after the territories, Oregon, Utah, California,
Kansas, Nebraska, and so on. Second avenue south I named
after my wife, calling it Helen, in honor of the first woman
who permanently resided on the west bank of the Falls. The
streets were numbered the same as they are to-day. The city

council changed the names of the avenues, thus blotting out
my many old land-marks ; but probably it is much more convenient to say " First avenue south," instead of Minnetonka
avenue, the old name I had given to it. I directed Mr.
Christmas to survey an alley through each block. The survey was completed May 1st, 1854. Several lots were immediately disposed of—I should say rather given away, provided
the recipient would build a house thereon not to cost less
than three hundred dollars. As no deeds would be lawful,
none were given ; neither were memoranda or articles of
agreement signed. I trusted them, and they trusted me, and
when the proper time came, they received deeds for their
land. So it was with all others who had obtained and settled
on lots belonging to preemptors, before the land was entered.

The first lot selected on the ferry-farm claim, after it was
laid out and platted, was by Isaac I. Lewis. It was the present
site of Harlow W. Gale's market-house, corner of Hennepin
avenue and First street. Mr. Lewis erected a large dwelling
and store on it, and in company with Mr. Bickford opened the
largest stock of goods, outside of Fort Snelling, in Hennepin
county. E. H. Davie and John Califf followed Mr. Lewis.
They also selected a lot on Hennepin avenue, built on it, and
opened a hardware- and stove-store, which was the first one in
the county. Levi Brown, from Maine, established a blacksmith shop on the site of the present Northwestern bank
building. This was the first blacksmith shop in Minneapolis,
but not in Hennepin county ; there was one at the Minnetonka
mills a year before ; and Victor Chatel had for years been the
Indian blacksmith at Oak Grove mission, now Bloomington.

James F. Bradley, from New England, opened a large
carriage factory at Murphy's ferry in the lower town. This
was the first carriage factory in Hennepin county. Hoyt and
Van Nest brought into Minneapolis an extensive livery and
established stables on Third street near Third avenue south.
This was the first livery-stable in Hennepin county.

Geo. E. Huy, from the Minneapolis mill company, opened
a large lumber-yard between the river and Washington avenue
on Eighth avenue south. This was the first lumber-yard in
Minneapolis. Geo. M. Bertram, president of the Excelsior
colony, moved into Minneapolis and opened an extensive

merchant-tailoring establishment over Mr. Lewis' store.   This
was the first tailor-shop in Minneapolis.   Z. M. Brown moved
over from St. Anthony and, at the lower ferry, started the
first tin-shop in Minneapolis.   Mrs. A. Morrison accompanied
her husband, Adam Morrison, out from New York, and
opened the first millinery shop in Minneapolis.   She selected
Cataract, now Sixth avenue south, as her place of business.
A few weeks later, Miss Bertram, from New York city, established a ladies' dress-making house at Mr. Hoag's.   •

A. K. Hartwell came over from St. Anthony and opened an
insurance office, the first of the kind in the county.   John M.
Anderson, so long in the express business in this city, came
out from New York and brought with him a choice assortment
of books and stationery, which he offered for sale in the
Craft's building, the first store of the kind in the county.

John Morrison, also from New York, came out with Mr.
Anderson, and opened the first gun- and locksmith-shop in the
county, on Cataract street.   Wm. G. Murphy opened the first
harness- and saddle-shop in the city, on Hennepin avenue.

Messrs. Geo. N. Propper and Carlos Wilcox opened, in the
government land-office building, a loan and land agency, the
first in the city.

Our postoffice at this time (spring of 1854) was in a store
that the postmaster, Dr. H. Fletcher, had built near the bank
of the river, on what is now High street.

In addition to the improvements already mentioned, but
later in the season, W. D. Babbitt moved up from Illinois and
opened a large stock of goods for sale in a portion of the
Craft's building.   Samuel Hidden, a merchant from New-
Hampshire, established a business on Nicollet-avenue, near
First street, which was for years known as the Boston store.
About the same time Warren Sampson, from Michigan,
secured a lot on Hennepin avenue joining Messrs. Davie and
Califf, and opened a dry-goods store.   In the meantime Messrs.
John Jackins, and his brother-in-law, E. B. Wright, built on
the corner of Nicollet avenue and First street south, a large
brick block, the first brick store erected in Minneapolis, and
the second brick building, the first being the Bushnell house,
erected by Anson Northrup.   Both buildings were put up
under the supervision of D. M. Coolbaugh, a master-builder.

Another livery-stable was opened by Isaac W. De Kay, on Third street, and another blacksmith shop in the rear of Isaac I. Lewis' store, by Erastus Jordan. This shop was built on the site of the stables and barnyard of the ferry-farm. Here the first wheat, aside from that on the government and Indian farms, raised in the county, was stacked and threshed with the old-fashioned flail, under the direction of Eben Howe. This was before the days of threshing-machines in the territory, and for that matter, there was not wheat enough raised to pay for the importation of threshing-machines. Mr. Howe's winter's work was concentrated on those wheat stacks.

On the 25th of April, Arthur, eldest son of my neighbor Calvin A Tuttle, died at the early age of six years. He was a child of unusual promise.

The season was very forward, and the weather warm ; on the 20th the mercury reached ninety-two in the shade.

Dr. A. E. Ames and the Minneapolis delegation, who spent the winter at the national capital, in the interest of the settlers on the reservation, returned April 22d. They brought encouraging reports in regard to the preemption law being extended to the settlers on those lands.

Mr. Godfrey commenced important improvements on his mills this spring. A good levee was made at the junction of the Minnehaha stream with the Mississippi, so that steamers on their way from Fort Snelling to St. Anthony Falls could land with the greatest convenience. The steamboat men very properly called this landing, or harbor, Godfreyport.

On May 1st there appeared in St. Paul the first daily papers ever printed in Minnesota. They were twins, but the product of two distinct offices : the Pioneer by Earl S. Goodrich, and the Democrat by David Olmstead.

The opening of spring gave an impetus to trade in St. Anthony such as had not been felt at any former period. The many large buildings erected the previous year were all occupied, and new ones in every part of the village were being built. New business men moved into the village. O. W. Stoughton opened a new store. W. F. Cahill and S. L. Vawter each had a large drug store.

L. C. Walker was appointed postmaster, early in May, in

place of O. W. Rice, resigned. On the 2d of May Miss Lydia Libby died at the home of her father in St. Anthony, aged twenty years.

T. M. Griffith, engineer of the suspension bridge, arrived on May 5th and immediately assumed the duties of his office. A goodly number of men were now employed on that structure. The anchorage for the cables were of a superior kind, and secure from the possibility of moving, the earth being removed from the surface of the ledge, and excavations made under it from the river bank.

On the 10th of May Mrs. Stevens, myself and three little daughters left our home in Minneapolis for an extended eastern journey. The foliage on the trees was full grown when we left home, but traveling through Michigan, Ohio, and New York, the leaves had hardly made their appearance, and while making passage down the St. Lawrence to Montreal, and from the latter place to northern Vermont, the trees were as bare of foliage as in mid-winter. This satisfied us that Minnesota was blessed with earlier vegetation than many of the eastern states that were south of us.

The first dray made its appearance in St. Anthony May 24. John F. Hannum was the proprietor.

Rev. Mr. Ledon, of the upper town in St. Anthony, and other friends of the enterprise, built a large structure for a female academy. It was the first structure of the kind in the village. When finished it was to be under the superintendence of the Sisters.

On the 17th of June a party of government surveyors discovered in the marsh where the freight-depot of the Milwaukee road now stands, a large mud-turtle with the figures 1769 cut plainly on its back. It was supposed by these government employee that these figures were the handiwork of some of the early French voyagers who frequented this vicinity during the close of the last century.

Citizens of the Falls were honored, on the 8th of June, by a visit from ex-president Fillmore and a large party of distinguished citizens from different parts of the Union. Among them were Governor Mattison of Illinois, Attorney-General Bates of Missouri, General John A. Dix of New York, Francis P. Blair of Virginia, George Bancroft the historian, Prof. B.

silliman of Yale, and a host of others, consisting of members of congress, editors, professors, and literary people. There were many noted ladies in the excursion, with Miss Catherine M. Sedgwick, the authoress, at the head.

IMPROVEMENTS DURING THE SUMMER.

I returned from my eastern journey July 3, leaving Mrs. Stevens and the little girls at the home of Mrs. Stevens' parents in Westmoreland, New York, to spend the summer at her early home. I found that during my absence great improvements had been made on both sides of the river. The citizens had established a free ferry in the lower town, which was a great convenience to many of our citizens.

An anti-slavery convention was held in the Congregational church in St. Anthony. This convention may be said to have been almost the birth of the Republican party in Minnesota.

A daily mail had been established between St. Paul and St. Anthony.

Messrs. Rollins, Eastman, and Upton, had broken ground for a large grist-mill, to contain six run of stone, on Hennepin Island.

The Free-Will Baptist church of St. Anthony, with their pastor, Rev. C. G. Ames, transferred its meetings and its organization to Minneapolis.

The Minneapolis brick company had been very successful in making brick.

Tallmadge Elwell, the daguerrean of St. Anthony, was married July 3 to Miss Margretto Miller, at Cottage Grove.

Messrs. O. and H. Rogers started in early July a planing-machine, the first at the Falls.

W. W. Wales gave up his experiments in his garden, and succeeded Joseph Le Duc in the bookstore.

An order was received from the land department at Washington bringing into market all the land belonging to the old military reservation of Fort Snelling on the east side of the river. It was to be sold to the highest bidder, at the land-office in Stillwater. An organization of the settlers on those lands was had. Wm. R. Marshall was appointed their agent to bid the lands in, paying therefor one dollar and a quarter an acre. It was decided to surround the land-office during the sale and permit no one to bid against Mr. Marshall. The

programme, at the proper time, when the sale took place, was
carried out, and every man obtained his home.

Rev. C. Secombe was installed pastor of the Congregational
church July 30th. Sermon by Rev. H. M. Nichols of Stillwater, Prayer by Rev. Richard Hall of Point Douglas. Charge
by the pastor, Rev. J. C. Whitney, of Minneapolis. Charge to
the people by Rev. Charles Galpin of Excelsior.

M. C. Baker of Minneapolis was appointed, by the Governor
superintendent of common schools for Minnesota. Mr. Baker
was a native of New Hampshire, and had large interests in
Minneapolis real estate.

On the 26th of July Mrs. Louisa B. Cochrane, recently
from Lowell, Massachusetts, died. With her husband, Mr
Justin Cochrane, she intended to make Minneapolis her home.
She was sick only a few hours.

The First Baptist church of Minneapolis was organized,
and Rev. A. A. Russell, of Illinois, was selected as its pastor.
That organization held its meetings in Fletcher's hall.

The Congregational association of Minnesota was organized
at Excelsior July 27th, Rev. Charles Galpin, moderator, and
Rev. H. M. Nichols, of Stillwater, scribe.

FIRST NEWSPAPER PUBLISHED IN MINNEAPOLIS.

On September 2d the Northwestern Democrat, W. A.
Hotchkiss, editor and proprietor, was issued from the Minneapolis side of the river. Mr. Hotchkiss purchased the paper
early in August from the proprietors, Messrs. Prescott and
Jones. The first two issues after the purchase were from the
St. Anthony office. September 2d, 1354, therefore, dates the
first publication of a newspaper in Minneapolis, and the first
paper published on the west side of the river north of Iowa.

Captain A. R. Dodge, a prominent lawyer of St. Anthony,
died of cholera, at Syracuse, New York, on the 24th of
August.

On the 7th of *September the democrats in convention   .
of Hennepin county, made the following nominations for
county offices : H. Townsend, of Richfield, for county commissioner ; B. E. Messer, of Minneapolis, sheriff ; Geo. E.
Huy, of Minneapolis, register of deeds ; Charles Hong, treasurer ; Dr. A. E. Ames, judge of probate ; Titus, Pettijohn,
coroner ; Ebenezer Wardswell, surveyor ; Messrs. Scofield of

OF MINNESOTA AND ITS PEOPLE. 241

Bloomington, Charles Miles of Elm Creek, and William Dickie of Minneapolis, assessors.

On the 14th of September a meeting was held in Fletcher's hall to take into consideration the propriety of organizing a cemetery association. It was attended by nearly every citizen in the village. It was decided to purchase forty acres of the claim of Mr. J. S. Johnson, on the bluff directly back of Johnson's lake, for a cemetery. Messrs. Isaac Atwater, Edward Murphy, Rev. J. C. Whitney, Geo. E. Huy, and B. E. Messer, were appointed a committee to negotiate with Mr. Johnson for the land. Several subsequent meetings were held ; but the committee failed in the negotiation with Mr. Johnson. Heretofore the only place used for the burial of the dead, on this side of the river, was on the hill in the grove immediately in the rear of Hoag's lake. The land being claimed, the owner objected to it being used for a cemetery. In the meantime Martin Layman set apart a portion of his land for a cemetery, which seemed to give general satisfaction to the citizens, and no further efforts were made for the selection of a cemetery by the early settlers of Minneapolis. In later years the beautiful grounds of the Lakewood cemetery were selected.

At a convention of the whigs of Hennepin county, held September 16th, the following nominations were made for county officers : Joseph H. Canney, for commissioner ; A. N. Hoyt, for sheriff ; Isaac I. Lewis, for register of deeds ; Isaac Atwater, for district-attorney ; Isaac Brown, for judge of probate ; C. W. Christmas, for surveyor ; H. S. Atwood, for coroner ; Messrs. John Cathcart, John P. Plummer, and Wm. G. Murphy, for assessors. Messrs. John H. Stevens, Edward Murphy, H. S. Plummer, J. H. Canney, and A. N. Hoyt, were appointed the central whig committee for the ensuing year.

At a district convention of the democracy held in Shakopee Hon. H. H. Sibley and D. M. Hanson were nominated for the house of representatives ; and the following day the whigs held a convention at the same place, and nominated Joel B. Bassett and Wm. H. Nobles candidates for the house.

The Minnesota Republican, Rev. C. G. Ames, editor, an eight-column newspaper, made its appearance October 1st in St. Anthony.

At the annual election October 19th most of the candidates on the democratic ticket were elected.

FIRST AGRICULTURAL AND HORTICULTURAL FAIR IN MINNESOTA.

The annual meeting of the Hennepin county agricultural society was held October 6. John H. Stevens was elected president for one year ; Col. E. Case, treasurer ; Joseph H. Canney, secretary. It was voted to hold the first annual fair on the 20th of October, in Minneapolis. It came off at the appointed time, and it was the first fair of an agricultural and horticultural character that was ever held in Minnesota. It was a success in every department. Speeches were made on the occasion, by Governor Gorman, ex-governor Ramsey, and Judge B. B. Meeker. Among the exhibitors were Sylvanus Jenkins, Henry C. Keith, Allen Harmon, W. G. Murphy, Charles Hoag, David Bickford, Arba Cleveland, Peter Poncin, John Wass, Titus Pettijohn, Dr. A. E. Ames, D. M. Coolbaugh, John Jackins, S. Bigelow, J. H. Stevens, William Hanson, Alex. Farribault, J. W. Cormack, Isaac Wales, Norman Jenkins, W. D. Babbitt, James F. Bradley, B. E. Messer, Edward Murphy, John Chambers, Anson Northrup, Captain John Tapper, J. W. Dow, Clark Varner, W. H. Lauderdale, Mrs. J. H. Canney, Mrs. Sweet W. Case. Mrs. Charles Hoag, Mrs. D. Bickford, Mrs. D. Elliott, Mrs. W. A. Hotchkiss, Mrs. S. Hidden, Mrs. J. Boorbar, Mrs. S. Bigelow, and Mrs. Pauline Clarke ; Amasa Crafts, Davie & Calef, Geo. A. Brown, E. Jordan, T. Elwell, L. A. Smith, John M. Anderson, and Prescott, Pettijohn & Moffett. The grain, roots, vegetables, stock, swine, poultry, dairy exhibits, the mechanical and domestic department, fine arts, ladies' department and miscellaneous articles exhibited, were all of such excellence they would have done credit to one of the oldest and richest agricultural counties in New York. The premium list amounted to several hundred dollars, and they were all paid. Fortunately there were several strangers present representing several of the eastern, middle, and western states, and the extraordinary character of the grain, vegetables and stock on exhibition impressed them so favorably with the farm products of Minnesota that most of them became, in after years, permanent residents in Minnesota.

A sad and fatal accident occurred near the Lake of the

Woodt on the 30th of October.   Viennas, a lad of some sixteen years of age, a son of M. C. Gregory, was killed by the accidental discharge of a gun he was handling.   This was the first death in Richfield township.

A lyceum was organized in Minneapolis on the 7th of November.   The officers elected were John H. Stevens, president; Geo. W. Bertram and J. F. Bradley, vice-presidents ; S. Bigelow, secretary and treasurer ; M. C. Baker, Reuben Robinson and W. D. Babbitt, executive committee.   The first discussion was on the question, "Is the moral condition of the world improving ?"   T. C. Jones and W. D. Babbitt in the affirmative, J. Brown and J. F. Bradley in the negative. This was the first association of a literary character ever organized in Minneapolis.

Winter set in early this year.   On the 18th of November sufficient snow fell to make good sleighing.

On the 11th of November William Hanson's dwelling in the lower town was destroyed by fire.   Loss two thousand dollars and no insurance.   This was the first dwelling and the second building destroyed by fire in Minneapolis.

The annual meeting of the citizens of the Minneapolis school district No. 1 was held on the 11th of November. Messrs. William Hanson, J. N. Barber and J. H. Stevens were elected trustees for the year.   Allen Harmon was re-elected clerk.   The services of Charles Hoag were secured for teacher during the winter term

There were polled three hundred and one votes in Hennepin county at the annual fall election of 1854, of which Minneapolis had one hundred and thirty-two, Bloomington eighteen, Minnetonka twenty-one, Brooklyn forty, Chanhassen forty-two, and Richfield forty-eight.   Messrs. John N. Barber and Simeon K. Odell were elected justices of the peace in Minneapolis, James Shaver, jr., justice in the Minnetonka precinct, J. B. Holt in the Brooklyn precinct, and J. A. Dunsmore and R. L. Bartholomew in the Richfield district.

The Garland, an adjunct of the lyceum, a literary paper of rare merit, made its appearance in December.   Several monthly numbers appeared during the winter.   It was under the management of Mrs. S. Bigelow, Miss Mary E. Miller, Mrs. Mary Messer, and Miss Boyington.   There were more pupils in attendance at the district school than the rooms could contain, and it was decided that a select school should be opened in Fletcher's hall, with Miss Martha Boyington as teacher. By the 15th of December there were one hundred and twenty-five pupils in attendance at the schools.

W. D. Morris, who lived on his claim at Lake Harriet, succeeded, during the prior year, in maturing a few acres of broom-corn on his farm. He converted it into domestic utility by manufacturing several hundred dozens of brooms, and good ones they were. This was the first broom-corn raised in Minnesota, as well as the first manufactory of brooms in the territory.

There were filed in the Minneapolis land-office during October, November and December, four hundred declaratory statements, which meant that number of farmers, and all in Hennepin county.

Dr. A. E. Ames left for Washington on December 20th, to spend the winter in that city, in the interest of the settlers on the reservation. Franklin Steele of Fort Snelling, and Henry T. Welles also spent the winter at the national capital for the same purpose.

Several school-districts were organized in the county this year, as follows : one in Richfield in December, and a school taught by Miss Mary Townsend ; General R. L. Bartoholmew, C. Gregory, Geo. Gilmore, C. Couillard, and William Finch, built the school-house. This was the first school taught in Richfield. Another district was organized near the Richfield mills early in 1855, and a second school opened under the auspices of Miss Clarke as teacher. A school-district was organized in Eden Prairie during the early part of the year ; a very good school-house was built, and a school opened in May, taught by Miss Sarah Clarke. A school-district was also organized in Minnetonka this year, and a school-house built and a school opened with Miss Mary Carman as teacher. Another school-district was organized in Excelsior this year, a log school-house built ; a summer school was taught in it by Mrs. Jane Wolcott. Brooklyn also organized two school-districts this year ; in one a school was taught during the summer by Miss Augusta McLaughlin ; the house was built on what was known as long prairie ; the center of the other was on Getchell prairie ; the teacher was Miss Mary Huff. These schools at that time were all in a flourishing condition. They were a greater recommendation to the country than anything that could be said about it. Where there are good schools there are always good people and, consequently, good society and a prosperous community.

BOATS ON THE UPPER MISSISSIPPI.

The trade on the upper Mississippi had attained such a magnitude, during the season of navigation this year that it became evident the steamer Governor Ramsey would not be of sufficient capacity for the transportation of more than half the freight another year from St. Anthony to Sauk Rapids It was true St. Cloud had not yet been brought into existence, but John L. Wilson and Geo. F. Brott had each an eye on the west bank of the river from Sauk Rapids, and Anoka had become the center of considerable commercial importance, while Itaska, Elk River, Monticello, and Clearwater, were rapidly becoming villages of some importance, and the country around them was rapidly filling up with immigrants. As a consequence the carrying-trade had doubled. At a meeting held in St. Anthony, Major A. M. Fridley, R. Cutler, and S. M. Tracy, of St. Anthony, A. P. Lane of Anoka, and Geo. W. Sweet of Sauk Rapids, were appointed a committee to arrange for adding another boat to the trade. The movement was entirely successful. Not only one boat, but two or three were, in after years engaged in the passenger and freight trade above St. Anthony. One of the boats, the Henry M. Rice, was a craft that would have been a credit to the boats on the lower Mississippi.

CHAPTER XXXIV.

Hennepin county, as well as Minneapolis, was greatly benefitted during the year by the superior class of immigrants. Among those who selected Minneapolis for their home, was Francis R. E. Cornell who, in after years, became a member of the legislature for several terms, was also attorney-general of the state for many years, and was elevated to a seat on the supreme bench, which high office he held at the time of his death. Immediately on his arrival in Minneapolis he formed a partnership with D. M. Hanson, and at once entered into a large practice. On the death of Mr. Hanson he associated with him Judge C. E. Vanderburgh, now of the supreme court, but then a young lawyer from the interior of New York. At the time of his arrival in Minneapolis he was only thirty-four years of age, but he had previously been elected a member of the New York senate from Steuben county, and had also held other high offices in that state. From the time of his arrival here to his death he lent a helping hand in every possible way that could benefit the place. He was much interested in the schools of Minneapolis, and consented at an early day to serve as one of the trustees of the district-school. When the city required his wise counsels in her municipal affairs, he willingly served, greatly to his inconvenience, as an alderman. Thoroughly unselfish, he delighted in bestowing aid upon those who required it. An accomplished orator, an impartial and able judge, a warm friend, his death was much regretted by the whole community. Judge Cornell left an interesting family consisting of his widow, a son and daughter, who are residents of Minneapolis.

George W. Chowen came to Minneapolis in 1851, but resided mostly in other portions of the territory until 1854. Though but partially connected with Minneapolis since 1852, and may be considered a citizen of the city from that date. On the organization of the county he was selected as deputy register of deeds, and deputy clerk of the board of county commissioners, and as such recorded the first deed and the first instrument in writing that was necessary to be recorded in Hennepin county. Mr. Chowen was one of the most useful men that ever honored the city with a residence. For many years he was the register of deeds of the county. For some years previous to his death he was the head of an abstract office, which he had established at great expense. He was greatly esteemed by all classes of citizens, and his memory is greatly revered. He was one of the founders of the city.

Isaac Brooks Edwards, a native of North Carolina, but long a merchant of Gosport, Indiana, came to Minneapolis in 1854, purchased a lot on Nicollet avenue, built a house on it, and moved into it this year. He became a partner of Isaac I. Lewis in the store. After a residence of several years in Minneapolis, Mr. Edwards moved to Watertown, in Carver county, of which he was one of the original founders, and died there several years since. Mr. Edwards contributed in many ways to help Minneapolis in an early day.

Subscription papers were frequently passed around soliciting support for ministers of the gospel, and to aid in building school-houses, churches, town-halls, bridges, and laying out roads and streets, as well as for the support of teachers. Mr. Edwards always responded liberally on these occasions. He had a large family, some of the members of which are citizens of this state.

Thomas H. Perkins came from Orleans county, New York, during the year, and purchased real estate near Murphy's ferry. He still resides in the county. Mr. Perkins invested considerable money soon after his arrival in the milling industry, and aided greatly in developing that industry in this neighborhood. He has two sons, E. R. Perkins, a physician at Excelsior, and Frank Perkins, who is also a physician.

S. Bigelow came from Ohio and secured a lot and built on it, now occupied by Temple Court block. He also made a claim on Crow river. Mr. Bigelow was a prominent citizen in Minneapolis for several years. He returned to Ohio.

Many valuable mechanics made their homes in the village this year, such as Reuben Robinson, John H. Atty, Josiah Orthoudt, and Wm. H. Varner, who became prominent citizens. C. C. Berkman erected a building, and established a first-class bakery, during the summer, adjoining Mr. Lewis' store. This was the first bakery in Minneapolis. Dr. Berkman resided here many years, and then moved to St. Paul. He still resides in that city.

W. H. Lauderdale came from Ohio and took a claim near Lake Calhoun, on which he resided for several years. He was the first to introduce fancy poultry into the county. He has been a resident of the city for many years. His father-in-law, John Sloane, accompanied him to this territory. Mr. Sloane assisted C. W. Christmas in making the first survey of town lots in Minneapolis. Mr. Sloane's father was for a long term of years a member of congress from Ohio. He was also treasurer of the United States during several administrations.

J. B. Mills, a brother of E. P. Mills of St. Anthony, became a citizen of Hennepin county, late in the fall, and opened a large store in the postoffice building. Mr. Mills resided here for several years. He went to McLeod county and preempted a farm. Afterwards he became a government contractor.

Dr. J. S. Elliott came from Maine and settled in Minneapolis in 1854. He was accompanied by his family. Dr. Elliott became interested in the water-power company and made, for those early days, heavy investments in the improvements at the Falls. Wyman Elliott, his eldest son, became a resident of the village at the same time, though for a year or two he lived on a claim in Wright county. Dr. A. F. Elliott, J. R. Elliott, and Frank Elliott, also sons of Dr. Elliott, became residents of the village in 1854, as did a nephew, Dan. Elliott. Members of the Elliott family have all become prominent in the business and social circles of Minneapolis.

W. Augustus Hotchkiss came to Minneapolis in August of

this year. He immediately purchased the Northwestern Democrat, a St. Anthony plant, and moved it on this side of the river, and continued its publication for several years. Mr. Hotchkiss was one of our best citizens; perhaps no one contributed more to the early development of the resources of Minneapolis and Hennepin county. He was an earnest worker, a conscientious man, a Christian gentleman, and a firm believer in the future greatness of the embryo city. He was also a firm believer in Democracy; his paper was partisan, but more devoted to local matters, and to building up the new village and county, than to politics. When the attempt was made to dissolve the Union, he entered the service and commanded Hotchkiss' battery during the war, which became noted throughout the United States for its efficiency. Major Hotchkiss was peculiarly adapted to the artillery service, for he had in early life served an apprenticeship to that mode of warfare. The citizens of Minneapolis will, for all time to come, owe much to Major Hotchkiss for his great efforts in attracting immigration and capital here in the early days of the village. He is still engaged in the newspaper business, editing and publishing the National Republican at Preston, in this state. His family resides in this city, which is his home proper.

CLERGYMEN OF THE EARLY DAYS.

Rev. Charles Gordon Ames became a resident of Minneapolis this year. He secured a lot on Fourth street, and built a house. Mr. Ames was the second pastor of a church organization in Minneapolis, that of the Free-Will Baptist. A young man of great perseverance, well educated, a natural orator, an abolitionist, a prohibitionist, he made it interesting to the people in this neighborhood, and undoubtedly accomplished a good work among the pioneers. Thoroughly honest, he had the confidence of the whole community, whether or not it believed in his peculiar doctrines. Mr. Ames became an editor, and was elected register of deeds. He afterwards went to California. From the golden state he was called to Philadelphia, and is now pastor of one of the most flourishing Unitarian churches on the continent. When he had attained the years of maturity he became satisfied that the orthodox teachings of his early years contained many errors, and under this conviction he united with the Unitarian church, and is now one of the most popular pulpit orators of the day.

Rev. A. A. Russell, upon the organization of the Baptist church in Minneapolis this year, was selected as its pastor. He arrived from Illinois in the early summer, and immediately assumed the duties of his sacred calling. This was the third church organization, and Mr. Russell was the third pastor of a church in Minneapolis. He was a man of great worth, and his good works are visible in this city to this day. He ministered here for some five years. He was popular with all denominations.

Carlos Wilcox, a native of Vermont, selected his home in Minneapolis this year. He entered at once into active business life. In less than a year after his arrival here, he was appointed postmaster in the place of Dr. H. Fletcher. Mr. Wilcox was the second postmaster in Minneapolis. He married Miss Burgess, a sister of Mrs. F. R. E. Cornell. He is still a resident of the city.

John M. Anderson, so long a citizen of Minneapolis, dates his residence from this year. In addition to being the first book-merchant in the city, he was also the first to engage in the book-bindery business in Minneapolis.

The first building to be used exclusively for a meeting-house in Minneapolis was commenced and finished this year. This church was built on the corner of Cataract street and Fourth street south. It was owned by the Presbyterians. While it was not a very large church edifice, it was a convenient one, and we were all proud of it. Mr. Whitney filled the pulpit in this church for many years.

The different precincts outside of Minneapolis were greatly prospered during the season of 1854. The crops were good, and much of the vacant land in the county was occupied by actual settlers from different parts of the world. Among the new immigrants this year was John S. Harrington, who took a claim just above Wayzata, on the shore of Lake Minnetonka, where he now resides. Mr. Harrington has been a valuable citizen in many ways, but particularly in developing the horticultural products of Minnesota. General R. S. Bartholomew, of the Western Reserve, Ohio, made and occupied a claim on the banks of the Lake of the Woods. General Bartholomew has always been a public-spirited citizen. He was a member of the constitutional convention of Minnesota, and also represented Hennepin county in the state senate. He lives on the land he preempted so long ago.

Cornelius Couillard also selected and moved on his claim this year, near General Bartholomew's, in Richfield, and like his neighbor, is a valuable citizen.

James Hawkes was another excellent citizen who settled in Richfield in 1854. He was killed by being thrown from his wagon in Minneapolis in the fall of 1880. He served through the war in the First Minnesota infantry, and First mounted Battalion.

Bloomington was favored with many additions to her population. Messrs. T. T. Bazley had selected a claim the previous year, as had Thomas Oxborough. Both of these men made valuable farms, and assisted greatly in developing the agricultural industries of this state. Mr. Oxborough had brothers who settled near him who were good farmers and excellent citizens.

Among others who opened farms on Eden prairie this year was Robert Anderson. He followed his brother James, who had made a claim at that place the previous year, as had Wm. V. Bryant. Jonas Staring purchased a claim and moved on it this year. Joseph H. Chowen dates his residence at Minnetonka from this year. His brother, Hon. Wm. S. Chowen, who has been of so much moment to the public, had taken a claim the previous year, and opened the way for several of his old neighbors in Pennsylvania to follow him. Both of these gentlemen were brothers of Geo. W. Chowen, the pioneer of the Wyoming, Pennsylvania, colony, in Minnesota. Mr. W. S. Chowen has represented Hennepin county in the state house of representatives; occupied for years the mastership of the state grange, and has been one of the commissioners of Hennepin county several terms. W. S. and J. H. Chowen are progressive farmers. Their sister, Mrs. James Shaver, jr., was the first white woman who resided at Minnetonka, having made her home there with her husband in the fall of 1852. Another sister is the wife of A. N. Gray, also a pioneer, and the millwright of the old Minnetonka mill company. Mrs. Shaver was the mother of the first two children

born on the borders of Minnetonka—twins— Bayard T. and
Bernard G. Shaver, born August 12, 1852. These young men
have reached a vigorous manhood, and are prominent citizens.
It could hardly be otherwise when we consider the good
mother they were blessed with.

The vacant land around the lake was mostly occupied by
actual residents this year. Aside from those who settled in
the neighborhood of Excelsior, such men as A. P. Beeman, J. H.
Clark, and others, we find that Wm. H. Ferguson, a native of
Scotland, occupied the long point of land extending into the
lake on the south shore below Excelsior. Mr. Ferguson was
a man of much more than ordinary ability. He was drowned
in the lake late in the fall of 1857.

William Harvey, also a native of Scotland, made a claim in
the fractional township of Excelsior this year. L. P. Sampson also settled in Excelsior this year. Mr. Sampson was for
many years the postmaster in that village. Silas A. Seamans
took up a vacant quarter-section of excellent land a little west
of Excelsior, this summer, and soon had, not only an excellent
home, but a good farm. Z. D. Spaulding also settled on a
farm this year near Excelsior and, like his neighbors of that
period, endured many hardships.

Minnetrista had, previous to this year, only two settlers,
the Merz brothers. During the season Messrs. M. S. Cook,
N. H. Sanders, and J. W. Buck, made claims and occupied
them. John Carman made a claim on what is known as
Carman's Point. He was the father of Mrs. Cook, and of
Miss Mary, the first school-teacher at Minnetonka. His son
Frank is still a resident of Minnetrista. Cook's bay, on the
upper lake, took its name from M. S. Cook. Independence
for the first time was settled late this year by Job Moffett,
closely followed by Messrs. E. Hoisington, John B. Perkins,
Irvin Shrewsbury, and John H. McGary. The first settlers of
this town were men of a good deal of enterprise. Medina,
too, for the first time received settlers, Messrs. Stephen Bean
from Maine, and A. F. French of Ohio, making claims. Two
brothers from Germany, by the name of Kassula, also opened
farms, this year, in this township ; and most of the vacant land
in Brooklyn was taken this year. Among those who settled
in the town in 1854, were Otis H. Brown, N. Crooker, C. H.

Ward, and John P. Plummer. Osseo village was occupied this year by Warren Sampson, Isaac Labosiniere, Clark Ellsworth, S. Brown, and D. B. Thayer, though the immediate country had been settled before, by Messrs. Bottineau, Potvin, Raiche, and Garvais.

Champlin this year added many settlers to her population; the most prominent of whom were Rev. W. Hayden, Samuel Colburn, and John G. Howell. Dayton was honored in 1854 with an unusually enterprising immigration, consisting of such men as E. H. Robinson, John Baxter, James Haselton, and George Mosier. In the neighboring town of Hassan Patrick A. Ryan, Alexander Borthwick, Harvey Hicks, Dennis Ford, Alpheus Mascrey, and Joseph Green, made claims; which was a very good commencement when we consider that there were no roads to reach the town, and that it was in the heart of the big woods.

The first settlement was also made in Greenwood township this year, by Mathias Harff. The only way Mr. Harff had to reach his claim was by an Indian trail. He found it more desirable and cheaper to transport his supplies by the river in a batteau; that is to say, by following up the Mississippi to Crow river, thence up that river to his claim, which was on its banks. Louis P. Garvais and Wm. M. Ewing were the sole occupants of Maple Grove up to this year, when they were joined by Harvey Abel, A. O. Angell, Wm. E. Evans, Patrick Devery, and O. R. Champlin. Mr. Evans was from Vermont, and was in search of a country where he could plant a colony from his native state. He thoroughly explored the then wild west, and wisely selected the beautiful, fertile wilderness in Maple Grove, where he, and those who came after him, have made the place blossom like the rose. Mr. Evans has been frequently called upon by the citizens of Hennepin county to occupy various offices in their gift. David Marchant, a carpenter, had previously opened a farm in this township, which was probably as much his home as any place, as he was a single man, and had only a temporary residence elsewhere, while working at his trade.

Plymouth township this year made rapid progress in the reception of settlers. Francois Huot, G. D. Brawley, David Gorham, James Hughes, Edward Burke, Jonas H. Howe,

C. W. Farington, and several others, including the three
brothers, the Parkers. A more enterprising and better class
of citizens could not be added to any new county than that of
the immigration to Plymouth in 1884 ; but the same may be
said in relation to the immigration of the whole county.
Many of them had large families, such as Mr. Hughes of
Plymouth, and John P. Plummer of Brooklyn. The last-
named gentleman was frequently honored by the citizens of
Hennepin county with high offices, which he filled with great
fidelity to the interests of the people. He was the father of
several boys, four of which he sent to the Union army, some
of whom attained high rank.

NAVIGATION OF THE MISSISSIPPI TO ST. ANTHONY FALLS.

The citizens of St. Anthony and Minneapolis determined
to secure one or more boats to run from the lower ports to
the Falls of St. Anthony. At a meeting at the St. Charles,
with John W. North in the chair, and Edward Murphy secretary, the sum of fifteen thousand dollars was subscribed by
the citizens of the two towns. The capital stock of the St.
Anthony steamboat company was placed at thirty thousand
dollars. The money in due time was all raised. At this
meeting it was determined to call the first boat that should
be built or purchased for the trade the "Falls City". It was
further determined that it should leave Pittsburg for the
Falls about the first of April, 1855. A board of directors
consisting of A. M. Fridley, J. B. Gilbert, Z. E. B. Nash, and
R. Cutler, of St. Anthony, and Edward Murphy, of Minneapolis, was selected to carry out the wishes of those who had
so liberally subscribed to the enterprise. These gentlemen
were instructed to send a competent agent at once to the Ohio
river for the purpose of either purchasing or building a boat
suitable for the trade. Suffice to say, in due time the instructions were pretty well carried out by the committee. In
subsequent years a steamer called the "Falls City", was in
the trade. Regular trips were made from the Falls of St.
Anthony to the ports on the lower Mississippi, commanded
at different times by Captain Edward Murphy, Captain J. B.
Gilbert, and Captain John Martin, all stockholders. Captain
John C. Reno was also master of boats that ran regularly
between St. Anthony Falls and ports down the river.

The first execution in Minnesota, according to the law of the territory took place in St. Paul, on the 27th of December when the Dakota Indian Yuhazee was hung for the murder of a German woman above Shakopee, in November, 1852.

There were a good many territorial roads laid out this year from St. Anthony and Minneapolis to different parts of the territory ; the most important of which was one from the Falls to the St. Croix, and from Minneapolis to the western boundary of Sibley county. These roads were established by special acts of the legislature. In some instances there was considerable money expended on them. The money was raised by subscription in St. Anthony and Minneapolis.

The suspension bridge spanning the main channel of the Mississippi had, on the 5th of December, received its last floor beam. On that day Mr. Griffith, the engineer, invited the gentlemen of the press at the Falls, and their ladies, to cross the structure upon the first span that ever united the opposite banks of the Mississippi river. Of course the bridge was far from being completed ; it would require months of hard work before it could be used for teams, and for that matter, for foot-passengers. The length of the span was six hundred and twenty feet ; vertical deflection of cables forty-seven feet, which were four in number, and each comprised of five hundred strands of No. 10 charcoal iron wire.

On December 4th the first fire company was organized in St. Anthony. G. B. Hubbard was appointed foreman, R. W. Cummings first-assistant, S. M. Rickers second-assistant, D. S. Moore secretary, and Dr. John H. Murphy treasurer.

Among the prominent professional men who became citizens of St. Anthony were the well-known lawyers, N. H. Hemiup, Geo. A. Nourse, Wm. J. Parsons, and Edwin Smith Jones. In subsequent years Mr. Nourse became much interested in politics. He moved to the Pacific slope, and was elected attorney-general of Nevada. He is now a prominent member of the San Francisco, California, bar. A daughter of General Nourse is the wife of a son of Hon. John W. North, the pioneer lawyer of St. Anthony. They also reside in California. Mr. Hemiup has also made St. Anthony, now east Minneapolis, his home. He was for many years judge of probate of Hennepin county. Mr. Jones moved from St.

Anthony to Minneapolis in the spring of 1855. He was a partner of Judge Atwater, at that time. He also became judge of probate of Hennepin county, and during the war was a commissary with the rank of captain. He has retired from the practice of law, and is now president of the Hennepin country savings bank. Judge Jones was the first person admitted to the bar in Hennepin county, which was on motion of Isaac Atwater, at the April term of the district court Judge Chatfield presiding, in 1855. Mr. Parsons remained in St. Anthony for over a year, when he also removed to Minneapolis, where he continued the practice of the law Subsequently he moved to St. Cloud, and from that place to St. Paul, where he died a few years since.

Chas. L. Chase, a native of Connecticut, settled in St. Anthony this year. He was a brother-in-law of Captain J. B. Gilbert. Mr. Chase established a bank and real-estate office, and was for several years an active business man in that city. He was appointed secretary of the territory by President Buchanan, and after the retiring of Governor Medary, early in 1858, he was, by virtue of his office, Governor of Minnesota, which position he held until May 24th.

Another gentleman who has become prominent in this part of the state who came to St. Anthony this year is W. W. Eastman. In company with Captain Rollins and R. P. Upton he immediately commenced the erection of a large flour mill on Hennepin island. He was also a pioneer in the milling business on the west bank of the Falls. He became the owner of Nicollet Island, and other valuable property in this neighborhood. Mr. Eastman is an enterprising citizen, helpful to this city, in which he still resides.

Early in the season the name of D. Morrison, Bangor, Maine, appeared on the register of the St. Charles hotel in St. Anthony. A gentleman of exceedingly keen perception, it only required a glance at the almost undeveloped water-power, and other advantages in the neighborhood, to convince him that here was a rare opportunity for investment. Not only Minneapolis and St. Anthony, but the whole state, has been greatly benefitted by Mr. Morrison's removal to Minnesota in 1855.

Citizens on both sides of the river were pleased with the outlook at the close of the year 1854.

CHAPTER XXXV.

The territorial legislature convened in St. Paul on Monday the third day of January. Joseph R. Brown represented the west side of the river in the council, and Messrs. H. H. Sibley and D. M. Hanson in the house of representatives. The delegation from St. Anthony was Hon. Chas. T. Stearns in the council, and Major A. M. Fridley and Daniel Stanchfield in the house. M. C. Baker of Minneapolis was elected one of the clerks in the council, and the editor and proprietor of the only newspaper published in Hennepin county, W. Augustus Hotchkiss, was elected one of the territorial printers. This was the first honor of the kind ever paid to a Minneapolis editor. It was worthily bestowed, and when we considered that the paper had been published in the county less than six months, while there was the Pioneer, the Democrat, and the Minnesotian, in St. Paul (the two former dailies), we felt that the county was coming to the front in influence.

The annual meeting of the territorial agricultural society was held in the hall of the house of representatives on the 10th of January, Governor Gorman, the president, in the chair. The annual address was by Hon. H. H. Sibley. Of the many addresses before the state agricultural society none have been more eloquent and impressive. The following gentlemen were elected officers of the society : John H. Stevens of Hennepin county, president ; J. W. Selby of Ramsey, Capt. Wm. Holcombe of Washington, Hon. H. H. Sibley of Dakota, Hon. S. Baldwin Olmstead of Benton, Sweet W. Case of Hennepin, B. W. Dodd of Nicollet, and Hon. Joseph R.

Brown of Sibley, vice-presidents ; Edward Murphy of Hen.
nepin, secretary ; C. H. Parker of Ramsey, treasurer. On
motion of W. A. Hotchkiss of Hennepin, Major P. B. Furber
of Ramsey, A. Larpenteur of Ramsey, Jas. S. Norris of Washington, N. E. Stoddard of Hennepin, and Joseph Haskell of
Washington, were appointed the executive committee for the
year.

An interesting discussion followed which was participated
in by several members who wished to impress upon the
public the fact that Minnesota was not only a grain-producing
territory, but afforded superior advantages for stock of every
description. Rev. B. F..Hoyt of St. Paul thought the society
should declare the self-evident fact that the territory was
decidedly a sheep-raising or wool-growing country. In order
to show the opinion that was entertained by the society at
that early day in regard to the probability of Minnesota
becoming a wheat-producing region, I copy the following
resolution, which was adopted by the society. It was introduced by Mr. Hotchkiss :

"Resolved, That it is the opinion of this society that the
"climate and soil of Minnesota are particularly adapted to the
"successful growth of wheat."

Here is another introduced by Governor Holcombe of
Washington :

"Resolved, That in the opinion of this society Minnesota
"is a good stock-growing country, on account of its grasses
"being more nutritious, and its climate more healthful, than in
"other regions south of it."

It must be admitted that the members of the Minnesota
agricultural society had a pretty correct knowledge in regard
to the capability of the soil. Since that time the state has
become known all over the world for its great productiveness
in wheat, stock and wool.

For the first time the citizens of St. Anthony and Minneapolis, through the enterprise of the butchers in the former
place, observed New Years with turkey on their tables. The
price of the turkey, in those days, was twenty-five cents per
pound. The importation was overland in sleighs from Central Iowa.

The Carson League, a temperance organization, was started

in Minneapolis, with Rev. J. C. Whitney, president, and A. K. Hartwell, secretary. Nearly every man and woman in the village became members of the organization.

At the annual meeting of Hennepin Lodge No. 4, held in Masonic hall, on St. John's day, the following officers of the lodge were elected for the year 1855 : E. A. Hodsdon, W. M.; J. N. Barber, S. W.; John H. Stevens, J. W.; E. Case, treasurer ; Charles Hoag, secretary ; S. J. Mason, S. D.; R. Robinson, J. D., Calvin Church, Tyler.

The first stage line from Minneapolis and St. Anthony by way of St. Paul and Taylor's Falls to Lake Superior, was established early in January of this year. The proprietor was William Nettleton, now of St. Paul, but then a resident of what is now Duluth.

A brass band, the first organized at the Falls, under the superintendence of Mr. Lawrence, became prominent not only in musical circles, but in festivals and social gatherings, this winter. One can hardly imagine how much enjoyment there was in the presence of this new organization.

Franklin Steele and Isaac Atwater were elected members of the Board of Regents by the legislature in joint convention early in January. Major A. M. Fridley of St. Anthony and M. Black of Stillwater were elected at the same time. making all the members of the Board in January, 1855, as follows : Franklin Steele, Isaac Atwater, A. M. Fridley, H. M. Rice, S. Nelson, Rev. J. G. Rheildaffer, J. H. Stevens, H. H. Sibley, Alex. Ramsey, B. B. Meeker, A. Van Vorhes, Geo. W. Farrington, and M. Black. Messrs. Steele, Atwater, Fridley, Meeker, and Stevens, were residents or owners of property at the Falls. The other members of the board were all friendly to the University, and aided in every possible way to push it forward to completion.

In the early part of January Mr. J. J. Kennedy of St. Anthony moved over to Minneapolis and opened a boot and shoe store. This was the first establishment of the kind in Minneapolis.

SUSPENSION BRIDGE OPENED FOR TRAVEL.

Up to this time, during the suspension of navigation, the citizens of the territory had only weekly mail service from the lower country. Through the energy of Hon. H. M. Rice, our delegate in congress, a tri-weekly mail from Dubuque to St. Paul was established, commencing January 15th.

The completion for travel of the suspension bridge was observed by a grand celebration of the citizens at the St. Charles hotel in St. Anthony, on the 23d of January. Nearly all the citizens on each side of the river participated in the event. While the bridge was not entirely finished, yet it was thrown home to the traveling public. The toll-house was completed, and the directors selected Captain John Tapper to occupy it and receive toll. The order of exercises in celebration of the event was as follows : First, citizens and the mechanics of the work with the invited guests convened at the St. Charles hotel at 1 o'clock, when a procession of over a mile in length was formed and moved from the hotel headed by a band of music, all under the direction of Dr. J. H. Murphy, Marshal of the Day, and Z. E. B. Nash, assistant, and Captain John Martin, standard-bearer, and passed down Main street and crossed over to Nicollet island, where a cannon was stationed to boom forth the peculiar joy of the occasion. From the island the procession crossed over the bridge into Minneapolis, passed down Washington avenue, up Second street to the bridge, recrossed, passed down Main street, St. Anthony, and up Second street to St. Charles, where six long tables were spread with a dinner for the company. The officers of the day were Wm. J. Parsons, president; John G. Lennon, John H. Stevens, R. P. Russell, and J. B. Gilbert, vice-presidents. After dinner toasts were drank, and responses made by L. M. Olds, Captain J. H. Simpson of the corps of U. S. topographical engineers ; T. M. Griffiths, engineer of the bridge ; J. H. Trader, Wm. P. Murray, St. Paul ; Oscar F. Perkins, now of Northfield, Minnesota ; H. H. Sibley; Geo. D. Bowman, editor of the St. Anthony Express ; Geo. F. Brott, John Mc M. Holland of Shakopee, and Captain John Tapper. Probably this was one of the most interesting meetings that had been held in the village.

On the 22d of January a large meeting was held in Minneapolis, by the citizens, protesting against a bill that had been introduced and was likely to pass through congress, granting a large amount of land to the Minnesota and Northwestern railroad company. This was a Minnesota company, the

charter of which had previously been granted by the territorial legislature. Messrs. Joel B. Bassett, E. Hedderly, Dr.
H. Fletcher, Isaac Brown, and B. E. Messer, made speeches
against the passage of the bill. This was the first measure
taken by congress which ended in subsequent sessions of
that body granting to this state several millions of acres of
the public domain to aid in building railroads.

On the 27th of January Frederick, youngest son of D. M.
Coolbaugh, died aged six years.

The Winnebago chief Winneshiek, and six of the principal
men of his tribe, arrived in St. Anthony on the 25th. They
were on their way to Washington for the purpose of a treaty
with the United States government with reference to their
lands. Winneshiek declared that his people could not and
would not remain at Long Prairie. Neither the government
nor he could prevent them from leaving their reservation,
which they hated so thoroughly, and until a new and better
home should be selected for his nation the whites above the
Falls of St. Anthony must expect to be more or less visited
by members of his tribe.

Two men by the name of John Burke and John Banvil,
working in the pineries for Leonard Day of St. Anthony,
were killed by the Indians on Rum river.

Two of the pastors of the churches at the Falls, Rev. J. C.
Whitney of Minneapolis, and Rev. J. B. Mills of St. Anthony,
and presiding elder Rev. David Brooks who resided in St.
Anthony, each received presents of valuable sleighs this
winter.

On the 15th of February the gratifying news was received
of the extending of the preemption acts by congress to settlers
on the recent Fort Snelling reservation. This secured to
each settler his home.

The claim association, which had accomplished such a great
benefit to the settlers, was immediately dissolved on the news
of the passage of the preemption law, which was received
with great satisfaction by the settlers. Public meetings were
held and many thanks bestowed upon Henry M. Rice, Franklin Steele, Dr. A. E. Ames and others who were instrumental
in pushing the bill through congress. The members of the
national house of representatives from Illinois, E. B. Wash-

burne, Wm. A. Richardson, and Col. Thos. H. Benton of
Missouri, took part in the debate and warmly advocated the
interests of the settlers. Mr. Rice made several speeches in
their favor. In the senate Mr. Stuart of Michigan, Stephen
A. Douglas and Gen. Jas. Shields of Illinois, and Cooper of
Pennsylvania, advocated the passage of the bill, while Salmon
P. Chase of Ohio, and Senator Walker of Wisconsin, favored
an amendment that would have been fatal to the bill.

About the same time of the news of the passage of the
bill through congress bringing relief to the settlers in Hennepin county, word was received that the delegation that had
been sent to the Ohio river for a steamboat, had been successful, and the Falls City, Captain J. B. Gilbert, would arrive at
the Falls on the opening of navigation. This important
announcement was as follows :

"For St. Anthony, M. T., direct, and all landings on the
"upper Mississippi. The new and substantial steamer Falls
"City, now being built and finished at Wellsville, Ohio, J. B.
"Gilbert, master, will leave Pittsburgh for the above and all
"intermediate landings, on the opening of navigation of the
"upper Mississippi. For freight or passage apply on board,
"or to John Flack, Pittsburgh, R. Cutler or P. F. Geisse, Wells-
"ville, Ohio, W. Eberhart, Rock Island, Illinois, Geo. R.
"West & Co., Dubuque, Iowa, R. P. Upton, Z. E. B. Nash,
"D. E. Moulton, St. Anthony Falls ; E. Murphy, John
"Jackins, Minneapolis ; Burbank & Co., St. Paul. The Falls
"City is an entirely new and speedy boat ; powerful
"machinery, built by Geisse, of very light draught, excellent
"accommodations, will be splendidly furnished and finished,
"built expressly for the St. Anthony steamboat company,
"under the immediate supervision of R. Cutler, engineer ;
"and will run as a regular packet from Rock Island or
"Dubuque to the Falls of St. Anthony, through the season,
"and be manned by careful and reliable officers and men."

At last the fond hopes of the people at the head of navigation were about to be realized.

Dr. Ames arrived home from Washington March 1, having
been entirely successful in his mission to Washington. A
bill had been introduced in the legislature which, had it
become a law, would have changed the relations of St. Anthony

to us on the west bank of the river for many years, if not for all time to come. The provisions of this bill were to make a new county out of Benton and Ramsey. The southern line was at Denoyer's; the northern a mile south of Itaska; the eastern the Mississippi river; the western at the junction of the two branches of Rum river; with the county-seat at St. Anthony. Probably with a little stronger effort on the part of the citizens of St. Anthony, the bill would have passed the legislature. With two county-seats at the Falls the prosperity would have been increased, but it is doubtful if there would have been a matrimonial alliance between the two cities.

There were fifty-one teams in the pineries from St. Anthony during the winter. A mill was commenced at the junction of Crow river with the Mississippi, by E. H. Robinson and John Baxter.

ST. ANTHONY BECOMES A CITY.

On the 4th of March Dr. Ames arrived from Washington. St. Anthony was no longer a village; the legislature had granted a city charter to the place. At the first city election Henry T. Welles was elected mayor over John Rollins by a small majority. Both candidates were very popular. The other officers were Lardner Bostwick, city justice; John Orth and Benjamin Spencer, aldermen from the first ward; Daniel Stanchfield and Edward Lippencott, from the second ward; Robert W. Cummings and Caleb D. Dorr, from the third ward. The city council at its first session selected W. F. Brawley for city clerk, Dr. Ira Kingsley for treasurer, S. W. Farnham for assessor, B. J. Brown for marshal, E. L. Hall for city attorney, Z. E. B. Nash for collector, Isaac Gilpatrick for street supervisor, and Geo. D. Bowman for city printer.

A terrific wind-storm on Sunday, March 21st, swept over Minneapolis. The roadway of the new suspension-bridge was forced from the cables, the castings to which the suspension wires were fastened giving way about midway between the towns on either bank of the river. This was the most severe storm that has ever passed over Minneapolis since its settlement.

On the 27th of March the Republican party in Minnesota was organized in Central hall in St. Anthony. Wm. R. Marshall occupied the chair.

A Farmers' Club, the first in Minnesota, was established in Minneapolis with Dr. Ames president, N. E. Stoddard, Chas. Hoag, and S. W. Case, vice-presidents ; Allen Harmon, treasurer, and Edward Murphy secretary. This was the parent of these organizations, not only in Minnesota, but the whole northwest, and was a real benefit to the farmers.

Holy Trinity church in St. Anthony was consecrated the first Sabbath in April, by Bishop Kemper of Wisconsin.

The citizens on both banks of the river met with a great loss in the death of Shelton Hollister, one of the most promising young business men in the territory. Mr. Hollister had only been married a short time. His death occurred April 20.

The Minnetonka mills were destroyed by fire April 2d ; and about the same time the stable of Mr. John Dugan of Richfield took fire from a candle in the hands of his son while taking care of the horses, and the stable, horses, and boy were soon reduced to ashes. While endeavoring to save the boy, Mr. and Mrs. Dugan and another son were badly burned.

Hon. Martin McLeod, long an Indian trader, abandoned that business and settled on his farm at Bloomington.

The trustees of the district school in Minneapolis secured the services of Mrs. Hubbel, from Connecticut, as teacher for the spring and summer terms. Miss Boyington remained as principal in the select-school.

The two new steamers, the H. M. Rice and the North Star, with the Governor Ramsey, engaged in the trade from the Falls to Sauk Rapids. Mr. Calvin Church established a daily stage-line from Minneapolis to St. Paul, greatly to the convenience of the citizens of both places. In consequence of the destruction of the roadway on the suspension-bridge it became necessary for Captain Tapper to resume service with his ferry again. Rev. Seth Barnes, a prominent universalist clergyman, arrived in St. Anthony. He is a son-in-law of Ezra Dorman.

The proper instructions having been received from Washington, by the local officers of the land-department, the settlers on the late reservation commenced proving up their preemptions. So rapidly were their homesteads entered that by the 15th of May most of them had their duplicates.

CHAPTER XXXVI.

Now that my old ferry farm could be no longer used for agricultural purposes, I was anxious to secure another farm, and after consulting with Hon. Martin McLeod, who was somewhat acquainted with the country west of Minneapolis, it was decided to prospect in the then comparatively unexplored country west and southwest of Minneapolis. I say comparatively unexplored, because only the missionaries, the Indian traders, and the voyageurs, had passed over that region.

PROMOTERS OF THE ENTERPRISE AND MEMBERS OF THE PARTY.

During the early part of May there had arrived in Minnesota, from different parts of the Union, several gentlemen who wanted to select homes and move west with their families. Among them were Hon. Samuel Mayall, a member of congress from Maine, his brother James H. Mayall, state senator Vinton, also from Maine, Andrew J. Bell of Virginia, and several others, who desired to join me in the expedition. Their object and mine was to locate in a new country where there was rich agricultural land, and where no claims had been taken. Mr. McLeod was to be the guide of the party, the members of which were James H. Mayall, M. Vinton, Isaac B. Edwards, A. J. Bell, Hon. Martin McLeod, and John H. Stevens, with George Parks as teamster.

A JOURNEY THROUGH THE BIG WOODS.

The party left Minneapolis on the morning of the 17th of May. The first night they encamped at nine-mile-creek. On the morning of the second day they were joined by the

one who was to guide them through the wilderness to the
promised land. The county of McLeod bears his worthy
name. A man of noble form, commanding presence, cultured
intellect, he was dignified, eloquent, persuasive, charming.
The second day's journey brought us to a brook near where
the village of Carver now stands. From this point, on the
morning of the third day we commenced the difficult journey
through the big woods. Turning a due west course, on the
19th, with facilities to clear the way for teams, the way was
toilsome to those who were unaccustomed to swinging the
axe, and unused to felling trees. Before noon all hands were
blistered, and when twilight came we were only eight miles
on the way. Ethiopians never had faces of more sable hue.
We camped for the night on the shores of what is now known
as Lake Benton, since included in the Lutz farm. During
the next day's journey we came to a curious ancient building
of huge oak-logs, in the dense forest. It was two stories high,
without doors or windows, the only entrance being at the top.
Evidently it was the work of the last century, for J. S. Letford, a member of the legislature from Carver county, found
in the neighborhood of the strange structure, in the centre of
a maple tree he had cut down, and which was at least a
hundred and fifty years old, a pistol of French manufacture.
It was probably concealed in a sapling and the growth of the
tree had encircled the weapon. On the evening of the 20th
we camped by a lake, and wild animals prowled around us
all night long, in consequence of which Mr. McLeod called
the place of our discomfort Tiger Lake, a name it bears to
this day.

THE HOME OF THE BUFFALO.

Early on the morning of the 21st we found an Indian trail
and followed it through the forest to the prairie. From the
dense, shady, native woods, to the open, smooth, sunny plains,
the change was so sudden, and the contrast so great, that a
new world of wondrous beauty seemed open to our view.
For three days we had traveled in the heavy belt of timber
which extended from the cloudy waters of the Minnesota river
to the borders of the northwestern open country called by the
red men Ta-tonka-ka-ga-pi, or the home of the buffalo. From
the foliage overhead, trembling in the breeze, with glimpses

of blue sky beyond, we had come to a groundwork of living green o'ertopped with bright, delicate flowers that gracefully yielded to caresses of the gentle zephyrs that wafted their fragrance to us, as we stood with uncovered heads, enchanted by our first view of the lonely, lovely wilderness, now first visited by white men for settlement.

A few days previous to our toilsome journey through the woods a terribly destructive fire had occurred which swept across a portion of the timber land over which we traveled. It was said to have originated in a wigwam midway between the Minnesota river and the prairie. The fire left scars upon the larger trees which are visible to this day. In crossing the burnt district every step taken, and every blow of the axe, was accompanied by a shower of soot blacker than the rich soil of that region that produced such abundant harvests in after years. The deep, rich loam, when roads were laid out over the route that we traveled, when soaked by copious rains, caused the bottom of the highways to fall out.

TAKING POSSESSION OF A NATURAL LAWN AND PARK.

The lovely vision of the prairie, dotted with groves, extending far out to the western horizon, gave assurance that the time was near when this fair domain would be the happy abode of man. This pioneer party predicted that before the snows of another winter should whiten the landscape, or the rainbows of summer cease to arch the clouds with a halo of glory, this seeming fairy land would teem with an enlightened class of immigrants ; a prophecy soon fulfilled, for the first prairie team was engineered through the woods to that land of promise on the 11th of June, by a man who introduced to the present townsite of Glencoe a cradle, and was the father of the first white human flower in that region that blossomed with a smile upon its mother's bosom. That father is now a resident capitalist of California, Wm. S. Chapman, and that babe, grown to maturity, is the wife of a son of U. S. Grant.

THE TOWNSITE OF GLENCOE.

There was a diversity of opinion as to the point which we should select for the center of the colony we proposed to introduce. We were satisfied with the soil, timber, prairie and water. Some of the party wanted to establish the proposed townsite a short distance west of the crossing of

Buffalo creek ; others were favorable to the peninsula-shaped prairie that extended into the timber three or four miles up the stream from the crossing. After a thorough examination of the adjoining country it was decided to select the last-named point. This was the origin of Glencoe. Each member of the party selected a claim in the vicinity. We continued our journey to a point on the Minnesota river near Traverse des Sioux, with a view that if a more desirable location could be found we would abandon the one already made. We skirted the timber to High-Island Lake, now New Auburn, some ten miles. From the lake we went directly to the Minnesota river, where the city of St. Peter now stands, where we arrived the second day out from the lake. From this point we followed the river to Bloomington Ferry, and thence home. The entire distance traveled presented continued inducements to occupy farms, but we could not improve on the selection already made. Vigorous measures were taken to call the attention of immigrants to the advantages of the newly-explored country for agriculture. Our efforts were attended with success, and by fall settlers had located along the route we had traveled, to a surprising extent. That section is now among the most favored agricultural communities of a favored state.

CHAPTER XXXVII.

Though absent from Minneapolis only two weeks, we found more buildings in process of erection than there was in the place when we left. We found, too, that the village had, what it never contained before, a burglar, and a sneak-thief. The store of Wm. D. Babbitt was broken open, one night in May, and some two hundred dollars in money stolen ; and a sneak-thief took from a boarder at Mr. Bushnell's hotel three hundred dollars. These were the first depredations of this character in Minneapolis. A span of horses had also been stolen. It is singular that neither the sneak-thief, the burglar or the horse-thief were ever discovered in such a way that they could be punished.

Just about this time a young man committed suicide by cutting his throat, another attempted to cross the river in a canoe and was drowned, and a man died from the effects of strong drink.

Up to this time we had been proud of our record ; but Minneapolis was no longer an infant, and it could not expect to retain its innocence and purity when we could no longer select the persons we wished to have make homes with us. Again, in these early days, the prosperous cities away up north were infested, during the summer, with persons known in New Orleans as wharf-rats, who came up the Mississippi early in the spring and returned late in the fall. Heretofore St. Anthony and Minneapolis had not been of sufficient size to attract the attention of these light-fingered gentry.

The most important event that occurred here in May of

this year was the importation by Captain Rollins, from Iowa and Illinois, by steamer to the St. Anthony steamboat landing, of two thousand bushels of wheat, to be ground at the Hennepin Island flouring-mill, of which Captain Rollins was one of the proprietors. This importation of grain, on the 26th, was the subject of general comment by the business men of that day in this vicinity. The enterprise was a large one for those times.

There was not sufficient wheat raised by the home farmers to supply the first merchant mill built at the Falls, and the owners of the mill had to depend upon Illinois and Iowa to supply the demand. How different in the same locality in 1888, when there was delivered at the Falls of St. Anthony 44,552,730 bushels of wheat, all the product of the northwest, and of this large amount there was manufactured at the Falls 7,099,180 barrels of flour, one-third of which was exported to the old world to feed the hungry inhabitants of Europe. The combined daily capacity of the twenty-two flour mills at the Falls, in 1888, was 37,475 barrels ; one of them, the Pillsbury A, is the largest mill in the world, with a daily capacity of 7,200 barrels ; while the ancient mill (and it was a large one for the times) was incapable of turning out more than one hundred barrels per day, and was idle a portion of the time from inability of its owners to secure enough wheat to keep it running.

During the first half of the year several young couples in Minneapolis wisely concluded to add to their felicity wedded bliss. Among them were Nelson Pratt and Mary A. Midwood, Geo. W. Townsend and Martha E. Stough, Joseph LeDuc and Elizabeth Bertram, Eli B. Gifford and Mary F. Judd, Josiah P. Harrison and Jane E. Haycock, and Edgar Nash and Virginia V. Bartholomew.

Sheriff Messer completed the census of Hennepin county early in the summer, and his returns indicated a population of 4,171-- a large number considering that so short a time had elapsed since the occupancy of the county by the native red men. Not an acre of her lands were brought into market until the spring of 1855.

The suspension-bridge was repaired and open to travel early in the summer. The engineer of the bridge, Mr.

Griffiths, was presented with a valuable token of appreciation of his services, by Mr. Sibley and other directors, on the occasion of the completion of the bridge. There were two other bridges built over the Mississippi, a year or two afterwards ; one opposite Christmas' addition to Minneapolis, and the other opposite Calvin A. Tuttle's St. Anthony residence ; but the suspension-bridge outlived them, and had not the city council, in 1875, decided to replace it by a larger structure, it would undoubtedly have been a good bridge up to this time.

ARRIVAL OF CAPITALISTS AND PROFESSIONAL MEN.

As the summer approached, there arrived in Minneapolis Simon P. Snyder and Wm. K. McFarlane, both natives of Pennsylvania. These gentlemen immediately entered into partnership, and for several years were the most active business men in Minneapolis. Their business was confined to operations in real-estate and banking. This firm contributed very largely in developing the resources of Minneapolis, and for that matter the whole territory. They employed a large capital in their business, and having the utmost confidence in the country, they adopted measures to spread a knowledge of the advantages of the territory throughout the Union by distributing a large number of circulars in most of the states. These papers contained articles setting forth the advantages of the immediate neighborhood of the Falls of St. Anthony, as well as the whole territory ; and probably to Messrs. Snyder & McFarlane are the citizens of Minneapolis more indebted than to any others for the rapid progress in the early industries on the west side of the Falls. Nor were their good works confined to Minneapolis ; they extended all over the territory. To these men are many farmers indebted for the money with which they entered their land.

Soon after the Messrs. Snyder & McFarlane had selected Minneapolis as their business center, Hon. C. H. Pettit came and at once opened a banking-house. Mr. Pettit was one of the prominent men of the early days of Minneapolis, and worked for everything that could benefit the place.

H. B. Hancock and Uriah Thomas selected Minneapolis as their residence about the same time. Their business was dealing in real estate and loaning money. In addition, Mr.

Hancock was an accomplished lawyer. This firm was for several years very prominent in business circles of the neighborhood, and contributed, as did Messrs. Snyder & McFarlane and Pettit, very much to the prosperity of the place. These three firms introduced into Minneapolis a good deal of capital, and coming here, as they did, when the settlers required every dollar they could possibly raise to pay the government for their land, which had just come into market, their arrival was most welcome, not only to those who had to prove up their preemptions, but to the business men generally, as it afforded them an opportunity which had never existed before of obtaining money at reasonable rates of interest whenever the emergency of their business required it.

Early this summer another physician was introduced into Minneapolis, Dr. W. H. Leonard who, from the time of his arrival to this day has occupied a high position in the profession. This addition to the citizenship of Minneapolis gave us three resident physicians, viz.: Dr. A. E. Ames, Dr. J. S. Elliott, and Dr. Wm. H. Leonard.

There was a great scarcity of mechanics early in this building season, so that when L. T. Tabour and J. Doty came up from the lower country and decided to remain in Minneapolis, those who had a good deal of masonry work found no difficulty in its completion. Mr. Tabour is still an honored citizen of Minneapolis.

Hon. Lewis Harrington, of Hutchinson, came to Minneapolis at this time, and immediately occupied a prominent position in the engineering requirements of the county. It will be readily seen that the village was fortunate in the high class of immigration in the early summer of 1855.

AN ABOLITION CONVENTION CREATES A FLURRY.

For the celebration of the Fourth of July a committee, of which W. D. Babbitt was chairman, secured the loan of a cannon from the commanding officer at Fort Snelling, which was used at the opening of an abolition convention held here on that day. This circumstance created quite an excitement in the community, and angered the military authorities at Fort Snelling. The gun was, however, used previous to the meeting in welcoming the day which the members of all political parties were celebrating. This fact coming to the attention of the commanding officer, appeased his wrath at what he considered a misuse of it at the abolition meeting. There was much comment in the papers in relation to the affair. Major Sherman, and Captain Bragg of Buena Vista memory, were stationed at Fort Snelling at this time.

On the 6th of July a meeting of the settlers on the late reservation was held for the purpose of tendering a dinner to Hon. H. M. Rice for his great service in aiding the passage of the law through congress which secured them their homes. A committee of arrangements consisting of R. P. Russell, W. A. Hotchkiss, D. M. Hanson, S. Hidden, Edward Murphy, Thomas McBurney, B. F. Baker, Geo. E. Huy, John Jackins and John H. Stevens, was appointed for the occasion. Mr. Rice declined the invitation in a letter to John H. Stevens, saying that he only performed his duty, and the result was as gratifying to him as it was beneficial to them.

DISTINGUISHED VISITORS.

Hon. Charles Sumner, the distinguished member of the United States senate, visited Minneapolis on the 10th of July. He was surprised at the beauty and growth of the place. From that time, during his long service in the senate, he was a warm friend of Minneapolis, and whenever national legislation was required for the benefit of the village or city, he lent a helping hand in securing the favorable action of the senate.

Hon. Edson B. Olds, member of congress from Ohio, the father of our register of the U. S. land-office, also visited Minneapolis early in July.

There was considerable feeling in regard to the non-action of the commissioners appointed by the government for laying out and establishing the military road from the west bank of the Falls of St. Anthony to Fort Ridgely. The government had granted five thousand dollars to aid in the construction of the road after it was established by the commissioners. As one of the commissioners I had always been ready to perform the duty assigned me, but there were two others, and their presence could not be obtained to act with me. The chief of the corps of topographical engineers in the territory, Gen. J. H. Simpson, could not apply the money because there had been no legal road established. Determined that the money should not be returned to the United States treasury, steps were taken at this time to complete the survey of the road. By this action a pretty good highway was established from the Falls to the east bank of the Minnesota river, upon which Fort Ridgely was built. This was the only road from Minneapolis that ever received aid from the general government ; all the others were built by the county or by private subscriptions of the people immediately interested in them. Of course in the early days the counties had no money to expend on the public highways, and as a consequence they were mostly opened and worked by subscriptions until such times as a poll and property road-tax was authorized by the legislature. Fortunately, as a general rule, it did not require any very large sums of money to make the roads passable. The big-woods was an exception, however.

It was now evident that the stock in the suspension-bridge would pay a good dividend, for the first month's receipts amounted to fourteen hundred and eighty-two dollars.

A severe storm swept over this part of the territory on August 1st. Several houses in Minneapolis were damaged, and the pioneer merchant of the place, Thomas Chambers, suffered severely.

Dr. C. L. Anderson, of St. Anthony, commenced, August 1st, the erection of a brick residence on Third street south, and Dr. J. S. Elliott's elegant brick building was finished. The latter was by all odds the finest residence in the place.

The whigs in the neighborhood of the Falls of St. Anthony were considerably surprised that the St. Anthony Express, heretofore a strong whig paper, had become a democratic sheet. The announcement was made in the first issue of that paper in August.

FIRST USE OF GOVERNOR STEVEN'S ROUTE.

Malcom Clark, a distinguished trader among the Blackfeet Indians, on the extreme upper Missouri river, utilized Gov. Steven's route through the northwest by leaving Sauk Rapids with a train of carts loaded with merchandise, bound for his trading-post in the Rocky mountains. Mr. Clark was the first man from the Rockies to use the road surveyed by Gov. Stevens, and he found it a good one. He started in August.

Rev. Mr. Creighton, a distinguished divine, from Monticello, was engaged with resident ministers at the Falls, in delivering temperance addresses during August. Up to this period, and for more than a year afterwards, there had been no saloons in Minneapolis, and the pastors of the several churches, backed by a large majority of the citizens, were determined there should be none in the future. Mr. Creighton was a brother of Col. Wm. Creighton who, with Prof. E. W. Merrill and others, were the founders of Monticello, and were prominent in the territorial years.

Dr. Geo. H. Keith arrived in Minneapolis during the late summer and made it his permanent home. He became a leading citizen of the place; represented the county in the legislature; occupied a high military position during the war, and was postmaster of the city at the time of his death.

At a joint meeting of the executive committee of the Territorial and Hennepin county agricultural societies, held in Minneapolis September 8th, it was determined that the two societies should join for the purpose of holding a fair on Wednesday and Thursday, October 17th and 18th.

The first drug-store in Minneapolis, and a good one, was opened on Helen street, in September, by Savory & Horton.

BEGINNING OF A REPUBLICAN RULE.

In politics for the first time the issue was between the democrats and republicans. The whigs did not put a ticket in the field. After the election there appeared to have been a Know-Nothing ticket, but it received only eighteen votes in the county. A large majority of the whigs voted the republican ticket. The republicans had a majority of about twenty votes. The whole number of votes polled in the county was nineteen hundred and fifty-five. Two of the republican candidates for the house of representatives from Hennepin county, Jas. F. Bradley and Thomas Pierce, were elected, as was Arba Cleveland of Carver county. J. B. Bassett was the republican candidate for the council. He carried the county, but his competitor, Hon. D. M. Hanson, received a sufficient majority in Carver county, which belonged to the same legislative district, to overcome Mr. Bassett's majority in Hennepin. Alexander Gould was elected county commissioner. Allen Harmon was elected treasurer by ten votes over J. S. Johnson, democrat; Lewis Harrington, county surveyor : and

N. Jenkins and S. Coburn, assessors. There was a tie vote between Horace H. Shepley and J. Bohanan for the same office. From the time of the first organization of the republican party in Hennepin county in 1855 to the present, as a general rule, the county has been republican.

The second annual fair of Hennepin county was held on the 17th and 18th of October, under the patronage of the territorial society. It was a great success. Many of the counties in the territory were represented. The annual address was delivered by Hon. Martin McLeod. The occasion brought the largest concourse of people that had ever gathered in the territory. For the first time in the history of the upper Mississippi valley the dairy was represented by a good display of cheese, the product of Mrs. J. B. Bassett. The chairmen of the different department committees were Governor Ramsey of St. Paul, Mrs. J. W. Selby of St. Paul, Captain Holcombe of Washington county ; N. E. Stoddard, Col. E. Case, Charles Hoag. Franklin Steele, W. A. Hotchkiss, and Mrs. B. E. Messer, of Hennepin county. At the close of the fair the following officers of the Hennepin county agricultural society were elected for the year : John H. Stevens, president ; Isaac I. Lewis, secretary ; Dr. A. E. Ames, corresponding secretary ; Col. E. Case, treasurer ; N. E. Stoddard, Asa Keith, Allen Harmon, Martin McLeod, and Norman Jenkins, executive committee.

BUSINESS HOUSES IN MINNEAPOLIS AT THE CLOSE OF THE YEAR.

Following is a correct list of the business houses in Minneapolis in the fall of 1855 : Stores—Thomas Chambers, Lewis & Edwards, Jackins & Wright, S. Hidden, J. H. Spear & Co., Tuffts, Reynolds & Whittemore, Joseph LeDuc, J. E. Fullerton, L. C. Elfelt, A. F. McGhee, Davie & Calef, and T. L. Bibbins. Drug-stores—Savory & Horton, and S. S. Crowell. Book-store—John M. Anderson. Watches and jewelry—E. F. Crain and J. Farrant. Painters—R. A. Smith, B. E. Messer and C. Rummelsburgh. Carriage- and sleigh-makers—J. F. Bradley and James B. Hunt. Blacksmiths— I. L. Penny, E. Jordon and Brown & Co. Boots and shoes— John Wensinger, J. J. Kennedy John French and Mr. Loud. Gun- and locksmith—J. Morrison. Tailor—F. Wilkinson. Bakery—Berkman & Bickford. Harness-maker—W.

G. Murphy. Land-agents Carlos Wilcox, R. Allison, Snyder & McFarlane and W. P. Curtis. Bankers—Snyder & McFarlane and C. H. Pettit. Surveyors and civil engineers Lewis Harrington, C. W. Christmas and H. C. Smith. Lawyers—Cornell & Hanson, Atwater & Jones, W. J. Parsons and H. B. Hancock. Physicians—Drs. Ames, Anderson, Leonard, Wheelock and Rouse. Newspaper - Northwestern Democrat, W. A. Hotchkiss, editor and proprietor. Hotel Minneapolis House, C. Bushnell, proprietor. Livery-stables—DeKay & Bartholomew and J. Kingsbury. Dr. Wheelock only remained a short time. He went to Clearwater.

Up to this time there was only one saw-mill on the Minneapolis side of the river, and no grist-mill. There was, as the winter set in, five organized churches : Presbyterian, Rev. J. C. Whitney, pastor ; Baptist, Rev. A. A. Russell, pastor ; Rev. E. W. Cressey and Rev. T. B. Rogers had occasionally preached before the First Baptist society previous to the arrival of Mr. Russell ; Free Baptist, Rev. C. G. Ames ; Methodist Episcopal, Rev. Mr. Salisbury, pastor ; this gentleman was the first settled pastor over the Methodist church in Minneapolis. That denomination had no church building, but the meetings were held over T. L. Bibbin's store on Helen street (now Second avenue south). There were only two associations of a charitable character, the Masonic and Odd Fellow's organizations.

It cannot be doubted, even in these progressive times, that the above was a pretty good exhibit for a one year old village.

ST. ANTHONY IMPROVEMENTS.

The progress made on the St. Anthony side was still more remarkable. Thomas E. Davis, John F. Sanford, and Fred Gebhard of New York, had become interested with Mr. Steele in St. Anthony real estate, and Richard Chute and John S. Prince had also secured a large interest in it.

Hon. D. Morrison had now arrived in St. Anthony and had secured the contract for furnishing all the logs necessary for the mills. The mills had been leased by the proprietors to Messrs. Lovejoy & Brockway for the year. New life and new energy had been given to the city. The home demand for lumber had been so great that the mills were run to their full capacity.

David Edwards had built a large stone structure, three stories high. The lower story was for stores, the second for offices, and the third was a commodious hall. Mr. Edwards occupied the lower story with a general assortment of goods.

NEW BUSINESS MEN.

Among the new business men for 1855 were Crandall & Co., D. M. Anderson, M. M. Goodwin, Mrs. Sayre, Mrs. Robinson, Mrs. J. H. Pearl, Mrs. Widdigen, William Harmon & Co., G. F. Cross, W. E. Forster, Charles Fish, J. Piddington, Orrin Curtis, J. J. Monell, Geo. E. H. Day, B. Thompson, J. & G. H. Hawes & Co., Healy & Bohan, J. Good, S. Kohle, House & Bailey, C. Johnson & Co., E. L. Hemple & Co., Geo. Thurber, and J. H. Kelley. Dan Stimson, Moses Hayes, Geo. A. Nash, N. H. Heminp & Co., L. G. Johnson & Co., Richard Martin, Tracey & Farnham, Dr. C. W. Le Boutillier,, John Bourgeois, Bassett & Leaming, and J. W. Monell, had all got nicely under way in business at the commencement of the new year.

John S. Pillsbury selected St. Anthony for his home this year. Not only the citizens of Minneapolis, but the people of the entire state, are greatly indebted to him for services in a public and in a private capacity.

H. G. O. Morrison also settled in St. Anthony in 1855. He too was a valuable acquisition to the place.

SCHOOLS, CHURCHES AND SOCIETIES.

The greatest blessing to any community, and more especially to all new settlements— churches, schools, and benevolent societies—were unusually prosperous in St. Anthony during 1855. Rev. Mr. Nelson was the resident Methodist minister. There were no changes in the pastors of the other churches. The first officers in the Holy Trinity church, J. S. Chamberlain, rector, were Henry T. Welles and William Spooner, wardens ; and J. B. Gilbert and Geo. D. Bowman, vestrymen. Seth Barnes became the permanent pastor of the Universalist church. St. Mary's school for young ladies, under the direct superintendency of Rev. and Mrs. Chamberlain, had a large number of scholars. Miss Mary L. Knight, Miss Kennedy, and Miss Thompson, were teachers in the popular institution. There were select schools opened in St. Anthony this year— one of great popularity by Prof. D. S. B. Johnson, in the academy building where the higher branches of mathematics, natural sciences, and ancient and modern languages, were taught. Professor Johnson became one of the most prominent citizens in St. Anthony, and for years with great ability edited the Express. He has long been one of the most respected citizens of St. Paul.

Miss Lucy D. Holman taught a select school in the basement of the Congregational church, which was well patronized. The two district schools were overflowing with scholars. Hon. John B. Gilfillan, our late member of congress, was the principal of one of them. Prosperity delighted to attend upon the after life of most of the early teachers in St. Anthony. The ladies were happy in their married life. Mrs. Thomas Gardiner (then Miss Knight) is now the only resident in Minneapolis of those pioneer female teachers.

The subject of education was a matter of deep concern to the early settlers of Minneapolis, and it was taken hold of by the people in a most commendable way. And like efforts were general throughout Minnesota. The annual accessions to the population were of the most reliable, exterprising and desirable kind. Among them were men of capital and very enlightened views. The foundation of the magnificent system of union schools for which modern Minneapolis is so celebrated was really laid in 1855, at a school meeting held in the largest hall in the village, on November 28th. Nearly every resident in the village was in attendance. John H. Stevens, F. R. E. Cornell, and J. N. Barber, were elected trustees, and Charles Hoag, R. P. Russell, and Dr. H. Fletcher, were appointed a committee to confer and advise with the trustees in the selection and purchase of a site for a school-house. On motion of Mr. Cornell the legislature was petitioned to authorize the trustees to levy a tax for ten thousand dollars for the purchase of a lot, and to build a house on it. This movement eventually secured the old Washington school-house grounds, which have so recently been transferred to the county, upon which the court-house is being built.

The Royal and Select Masons of the territory received a dispensation, late in November, from the proper authorities in New York, to establish a council in St. Paul. The charter members were A. T. C. Pearson, Dr. A. E. Ames, John H. Stevens, Col. E. Case, Geo. A. Camp, Thomas Lombarde, and William Lyon. This was the first charter for a council granted in Minnesota.

The celebrated brothers, the Hutchinson family, consisting of Judson, John, and Asa, visited Minnesota for the first time this late fall. They were anxious to become interested in a new town-site. They were taken through the woods by way of Glencoe, to the Hassan river, by a party of Minneapolis friends. They were so charmed with the country that, in connection with others, they laid out and platted Hutchinson. The Hutchinsons became prominent in Central Minnesota. They are all gone now, except John, but they left a noble work which will perpetuate their memory.

FIRST MORTGAGE FORECLOSURE IN MINNEAPOLIS.

On the 29th day of December the first advertisement appeared for the first mortgage foreclosure in Hennepin county. Levi Brown was the mortgagee; C. H. Elliott, and I. C. Penney, mortgagors. The property to be foreclosed was lot ten in block forty in the original plat of the town of Minneapolis. Atwater & Jones were the attorneys. The whole lot, and all the improvements on it, was sold for two hundred dollars. It is worth to-day more than two hundred thousand, without the buildings. Property has come up some since them.

FIRST SETTLEMENT OF CORCORAN TOWNSHIP.

Every township in Hennepin county had been more or less occupied by settlers previous to 1855, except Corcoran. Up to that year it had remained an unbroken wilderness. Though one of the best agricultural towns in the county, it was the last one settled. In the spring of this year Benj. Pounder, who was prospecting for a claim on government land, ventured into the big-woods and selected a quarter-section near the town-line. He had scarcely secured the logs for the erection of his cabin before he was followed by Patrick B. Corcoran and Morris Ryan, who made claims and commenced clearing land for farms. The same season Joseph Dejardins, Isaac Bartlett, John McDonnell, Francis Morin, Fred Reinking, Fred Schuette, and one or two other farmers, occupied land ; so by the time winter set in there was quite

a colony in the town. All the towns in Hennepin county
were prosperous during 1885. Eden Prairie lost its pioneer
this year in the death of N. Abbott.

CHARACTER OF THE FIRST SETTLERS IN HENNEPIN COUNTY.

There were at the time of the completion of the census
this year, in Hennepin county, 1,128 families, which made a
population of 4,171, less than four persons to each family.
The question is often asked me, " By what class of persons
was Hennepin county settled?" I can answer that at the
time alluded to, that is, when the census was taken in 1855,
the birthplace of the head of each family was ascertained,
and there were of American birth among the pioneers 790, and
of foreign birth 338, showing 452 more heads of families that
were American than there were foreigners; but we were not
unmindful of the fact that the birthplace of a man did not
prove or disprove his merit. But it was a matter of interest
to all, and served to attract to each settlement like nationalities and kindred spirits, whether they were Irish, French,
Germans or Americans; and it is doubtful if any county
could show a more intelligent and industrious people than
the first settlers in Hennepin county.

The valuation of taxable property had increased from
$54,363 in 1853, to $157,000 in 1854, and $505,781 in 1855;
showing a wonderful increase of wealth added to the county
in a short period.

CHAPTER XXXVIII.

On Wednesday the second day or January the Minnesota State Agricultural Society held its annual meeting in St. Paul. Governor Ramsey was elected president. The vice-presidents were John H. Stevens of Hennepin, John H. Hartenbower of Olmstead, Clarke W. Thompson of Houston, Samuel Hull of Fillmore, Arba Cleveland of Carver, William Fowler of Washington, General James Shields of Rice, John Wakefield of Scott, Prof. E. W. Merrill of Wright, Lewis Stone of Benton, N. M. Thompson of Dakota, William Freeborn of Goodhue, C. F. Buck of Winona, A. F. De LaVergne of LeSueur, Chas. E. Flandreau of Nicollet, and B. F. Hoyt of Ramsey. Treasurer, J. W. Selby of St. Paul. Secretary, Dr. A. E. Ames of Minneapolis. Executive Committee, Charles Hoag, Henry H. Sibley, N. E. Larpenteur, L. M. Ford, and Wm. H. Nobles. It was voted that the first annual fair be held in Minneapolis in October, at which time the election of officers for 1857 should be had. Judge Norton H. Hemiup was appointed postmaster of St. Anthony early in January, in place of Hon. Lucius C. Walker.

BUFFALOES AT THE HEAD OF SAUK RIVER.

Two very large herds of buffaloes came down from the northwest, late in the fall, and at the beginning of January were grazing near the head of Sauk river, some fifty miles west of St. Cloud, and they remained in that vicinity for several months. This was the last appearance of these animals in the Sauk river country.

The United States land-office was opened in Minneapolis

on the 9th of October, 1854. There had been paid into the office by the settlers on the west side of the river for their homes, mostly in Hennepin county, up to January 1st, 1856, the large sum of $199,770 98. The number of acres entered was 150,071. To this should be added 10,760 acres covered with military land-warrants ; making the whole number of acres entered at the office since the establishment of the office up to January 1st, 1856, 160,831. The number of preemptions allowed was a little less than 1,000. The parties residing at the Falls who entered the largest amount of land were Carlos Wilcox, who secured about 2,000 acres ; H. G. O. Morrison and Richard Chute, jointly a little over 1,500 acres. All the rest of the land went into the hands of farmers, actual tillers of the soil ; industrious, thrifty, moral and intelligent.

January was exceedingly cold, but this did not prevent the people of St. Anthony and Minneapolis from attending lyceums, dancing-parties, and amusements generally.

ST. ANTHONY ANNEXED TO HENNEPIN COUNTY.

The legislature passed an act annexing St. Anthony to Hennepin county. The same bill contained provisions to locate the county buildings in the lower town. No measures of a public character had ever created so much excitement in this community, and it was many years before the bitterness engendered ceased.

Minneapolis received, during the winter, several citizens who became prominent, in the persons of Hon. Delano T. Smith, and Hon. David Morgan, and others, who added greatly to the industries of the city.

The sad news was received that Dr. F. W. Ripley, a young physician of unusual merit, was frozen to death in a storm while making a journey from Glencoe to Forest City. He was accompanied by Mr. John McClelland of Glencoe, whose feet were frozen so severely as to render amputation necessary above the knees. Dr. Ripley had made his home in the family of Hon. D. M. Hanson in this city. The information of Dr. Ripley's fate was received in Minneapolis on the same day that Mr. Hanson died. A citizen of Hutchinson, a Mr. Collier, perished in the same storm.

As spring approached the improvements in St. Anthony and Minneapolis were beyond all precedent. Activity and progress characterized both places. Over fifty buildings were in process of erection in Minneapolis, and as many more in St. Anthony. The prosperous season commencing so early, plainly indicated that Minneapolis at least would double in population and improvements before the close-of navigation in the fall of 1856.

The municipal election in St. Anthony resulted in the election of Alvaran Allen for Mayor. The contest was a spirited one. Mr. Allen being a thorough business man, made a good Mayor.

The average value of lots in Minneapolis, in the spring of this year, was only five dollars each. There were about two thousand of them, which added ten thousand dollars to the valuation of taxable property in the city.

Among the improvements commenced were those of Col. Cyrus Aldrich, Sidney Smith, and William Garland, each one building fine residences; while Ivory D. Woodman, and several others, erected fine business blocks.

Minnehaha Hook and Ladder Company No. 1 was organized this spring. A. F. McGhee was elected foreman, and Wm. A. Todd, secretary. This was the first fire organization in Minneapolis, and it was a good one.

Carlos Wilcox resigned the postmastership, and Dr. A. E. Ames was appointed in his stead. Two new saw-mills were added to the industries at the Falls, that of D. W. Marr on the St. Anthony side, and that of Pomeroy, Bates and Co. on the west side. Both were steam mills. J. M. Winslow commenced the erection of a large hotel in St. Anthony. The Minneapolis Water-power Improvement Company was organized May 20th, Hon. Robert Smith president, D. Morrison treasurer, Geo. E. Huy secretary, with Messrs. R. Smith, D. Morrison, G. K. Swift, Geo. E. Huy, R. P. Russell, Dr. J. S. Elliott, and J. S. Newton, directors. The capital stock was -$60,000. From this small beginning the present mighty and well-regulated system of controlling the vast water-power of the Falls has matured. Only one of the original incorporators is now connected with it, Hon. D. Morrison, and he owns much more than his original interest in the property.

At a meeting of the Board of Regents of the State University, on the 26th of May, Franklin Steele, president, in the

chair, on motion of Hon. H. H. Sibley, seconded by John H.
Stevens, it was resolved that bonds be issued for fifteen
thousand dollars in sums of not less than one thousand dollars
each, with interest not to exceed twelve per cent per annum,
to be used for the erection of buildings, and to purchase more
land adjoining the University site. The building committee
consisting of Judge Meeker, John H. Stevens, S. Nelson, A.
M. Fridley, and Isaac Atwater, were instructed to solicit
plans for the building. The Board of Regents of the University of Minnesota, in May, 1856, were Franklin Steele
president, Fort Snelling ; Ex-Governor Ramsey, Hon. H. M.
Rice, and Rev. J. G. Rheildaffer, St. Paul ; John H. Stevens
and Isaac Atwater, Minneapolis ; Judge B. B. Meeker, and
A. M. Fridley, St. Anthony ; Hon. A. Van Vorhis, Socrates
Nelson, and Mahalon Black, Stillwater, and H. H. Sibley of
Mendota. This was the commencement of the steps taken to
erect the buildings necessary for the University.

On the 29th day of May the site for the union school-
house of Minneapolis was selected by the trustees and voters.
It was the northwest half of block 77. The purchase was
made from W. D. Babbett for two thousand five hundred
dollars. In 1887 this same ground was sold to the county to
be occupied, with the other half of the block, by county
buildings, for more than one hundred thousand dollars, not
counting the school building on it. Something of an increase
in value during the thirty-one years. The trustees immediately proceeded to erect a double brick school-house which,
when completed, was the best building of the kind north of
St. Louis. It was destroyed by fire in 1864. In this old
building the celebrated Professor Stone for years presided,
and graduated as good scholars as any teacher in the west.
Many of our present best business men were instructed in
that old house, such as Clinton Morrison, Ira Murphy, the
Ames boys, the Hedderleys, and many others. Nor should
we neglect to mention that many of the daughters of the
pioneers of Minneapolis, who are now the first ladies of the
city, and proud mothers of interesting children, were educated under the humble roof of that old school-house. This
was the first union school in Minnesota and the memory of
it and its first principal, is fondly cherished by the hundreds

who were educated there, as well as by their parents and
guardians. More than a score of stately school edifices at
this time adorn Minneapolis, for the education of some eighteen thousand children, but there was more pride in the first
union school-house, humble as it was, than in any that have
been built since.

As a matter of record, I will mention that the 13th of June
1856 was the coldest day for the season of the year ever
known by the pioneers. Stoves were replaced and fires built.
Cold as was the season, there was a good crop in the territory.

MURDERS AND OUTRAGES.

Many crimes were committed in June. On the 11th a
young married woman, Mrs. Mary Jane Hathaway, wife of
John A. Hathaway, was murdered at their home on Crow
river, in what is now Hassan township. The family had
recently settled on their claim. The unfortunate lady was
shot through the head with a pistol. Her little child, about
fourteen months old, was found playing in its mother's blood.
Every effort was made to discover the murderer, but to this
day the brutal fellow seems to have escaped punishment.
Mrs. Hathaway was unusually respected by the few settlers
at that time on Crow river. On the 12th, Susan, a Dakota
girl, aged about ten years, an adopted daughter of M. S.
Whallen of Oak Grove, while her foster-mother, a neighbor,
Mrs. Ames, and three little children, one of whom was Susan,
were in the sitting-room, several Chippewa Indians entered,
threw little Susan out of the door, cut her throat, scalped her,
and fled before the men who were near by could reach the
house. This Dakota girl had been given to Dr. Williamson
by her parents at Kaposia, when she was five or six years old.
She had lost the little knowledge she once had of her native
language, and only her marked Indian features remained to
indicate her origin. Mr. Pond, of blessed memory, her neighbor and pastor, saw in her evidence of Christianity. Mrs.
Whallen, under whose care she was making good progress in
all that was desirable to prepare her for usefulness and happiness here and hereafter, loved her as a daughter. Two
other residents of Hennepin county had recently met violent
deaths, and so strong was the feeling of the citizens of the
county in regard to these brutal murders, that a mass meet-

ing of citizens was held on June 17th, in Barber's hall, to take energetic action to punish the perpetrator. Rev. A. A. Russell was called to the chair, and Dr. A. E. Ames was appointed secretary. John H. Stevens, Isaac Brown, Samuel Hidden, Dr. H. Fletcher, and J. H. Spear, were appointed a committee to express the demands of justice in these trying events which have clouded the good name of the county. John H. Stevens reported the following, which was unanimously adopted :

" This county, for the first time in its history has, during
" the past week, been visited with wilful and malicious mur-
" ders, attended by a barberous and fiendish spirit, which call
" loudly for a decided expression of the sentiment of the
" people ; that it is the duty of every law-abiding citizen and
" every lover of justice, to use his utmost endeavor to bring
" the perpetrators of these foul crimes to punishment ; that
" while we cannot restore the lost lives, or blot out the out-
" rages that have been inflicted upon individuals, or the wrongs
" to their families and citizens generally, we can and will
" take measures to punish the guilty ; that we have full con-
" fidence in the power of the civil authorities to impartially
" administer the laws, and to legally punish all crimes ; that
" we deprecate any attempt on the part of individuals to
" resort to violence, or to take the execution of the law into
" their own hands."

Other crimes, of the worst character, were committed at this time. Though thirty-three years have passed, none of the murderers have been apprehended or brought to justice, and probably they never will be. Mr. S. A. Jewett, father-in-law of Dr. Keith, and brother-in-law of our respected citizen, J. S. Johnson, paid a high tribute of respect to the memory of one of the murdered men, John P. Allen. There were no other depredations committed upon the lives of citizens of the county for many years.

THE STATE FAIR.

The executive committee of the Minnesota Agricultural Society met on the 16th of June and decided to hold a fair in the fall. Hon. H. H. Sibley, chairman of the committee, headed the movement by contributing fifty dollars to the enterprise. Other members of the society signed liberally.

Some twelve hundred dollars was raised by the citizens of
Minneapolis to pay premiums. Simon P. Snyder was chosen
treasurer in place of J. W. Selby, resigned.

On the 24th of June the Minnesota Historical Society held
a meeting to lay the corner-stone of the society's hall. The
address on the occasion was by Lieut. Maury, U. S. Navy.
Unfortunately the building was never completed.

The contract for building the court-house was let on the
25th of June to Charles Clarke, recently from Steuben county,
New York. Mr. Clarke and his accomplished family were
valuable additions to Minneapolis. The late Hon. Charles
W. Clarke, so prominent in agricultural matters, was the eldest son of Mr. Clarke.

The caravan from Red river arrived ahead of time this
year. It was exceedingly rich in furs and pemmican.

The Northwestern Democrat had, up to this time, been an
uncompromising democratic paper. The issue of July 5th
came out a strong Republican sheet. It created a good deal
of excitement. From that period Major Hotchkiss, the editor
and proprietor, never swerved from what he considered his
political duty, and for the next year or two made it lively for
his old democratic friends.

A contract was let July 3 to Messrs. Stone, Boomer & Boyington, to build a new bridge over the Mississippi, in the
lower town, for $46,000.

On the 6th of July, through some unknown agency, the
projecting rock broke from the precipice over which the
water pours on the west side of the Falls, which destroyed the
mill-race and suspended all operations of the saw-mills.

The first real, live observance of the Fourth of July by the
united twin cities took place in a grove on Nicollet Island.
Free access to the island was generously granted by the
Bridge company. George E. H. Day presided. The Divine
blessing was asked by Rev. A. A. Russell. Dr. George H.
Keith gave the address; followed by C. C. Gray and Rev.
Mr. Nelson.

Secretary J. Travis Rosser resigned his office in consequence of the ill-health of his wife.

A Mr. Dillon established a fishery near the lower ferry.
For years he supplied us with fresh fish.

Minneapolis was no longer a village. On the 12th of July, 1856, Isaac I. Lewis had a capital of forty thousand dollars employed in his trade. Messrs. Ames & Bascomb, from Hennepin, Illinois, had thirty thousand dollars invested in their dry-goods business, and Messrs. Jackins and Wright had as much more money in their store, while Samuel Hidden, L. C. Elfelt, John H. Spear & Co., J. B. Atkinson, Joseph LeDuc, Tufts, Reynolds & Whittemore, A. L. McGhee, Martin Ferrent, Bibbins & Bigelow, L. W. Henry, Savory & Horton, S. S. Crowell, and E. H. Davie, employed a large capital and enjoyed a large trade. Messrs. Snyder & McFarlane had a capital of $180,000 in their land-agency and banking outfit. Hon. C. H. Petit had a capital of $150,000 in his bank and land-agency. Hancock & Thomas, Carlos Wilcox, Dan R. Barber, and Delano T. Smith, all had many thousands of dollars at their command.

There were early in July the following contractors who had all the work they could possibly do : Chas. N. Daniels, Joseph Dean, Reuben Robinson, J. E. Patterson, A. K. Hartwell, J. B. Ferrin, D. M. Foss, John L. Tenney, Arnell & Wilson, and Kingsbury & Ward.

Of the many booms that have passed over Minneapolis since the land sales in 1855, there was none that exceeded that in the summer of 1856. Many who arrived that summer became prominent citizens. The city was favored with such men as Rev. D. B. Knickerbocker, now Bishop of Indiana, Chas. E. Vanderburgh, D. Y. Jones, S. H. Jones, Daniel R. Barber, Erastus N. Bates, Adolphus Bradford, Robert R. Bryant, Daniel Bassett, and C. A. Weidstrand.

A union board of trade was organized the first of July with the following officers ; Hon. D. Morrison, president ; Richard Chute and John Jackins, V. P.; I. I. Lewis, corresponding secretary ; N. H. Hemiup, recording secretary ; R. P. Upton, Treasurer ; Edward Murphy, R. P. Russell, S. Hidden, Samuel Stanchfield, and Daniel Edwards, directors. Committee on commerce, Richard Chute and John Jackins.

A military company was organized at the Falls of St. Anthony, called the Falls City Light Guards, on the 15th of July. The following officers were commissioned by the Governor : Captain, H. R. Putnam ; lieutenants, J. J. Clarke,

and J. Hollister. Many of the members of this company
became distinguished soldiers during the war for the Union.
Some of them attained high military appointments. This
was the first organization of a military company at St.
Anthony.

I have already alluded to the first school-house built in
Minneapolis, but as a matter of history in regard to it I copy
the following notice, which appeared in the Democrat, in
Minneapolis, August 2d, 1856 :

"Sealed proposals will be received until 6 o'clock p. m.,
"August 15th, 1856, for building a school-house in Minne-
"apolis, according to the plans and specifications to be seen
"at the office of Dr. C. L. Anderson, in Savory & Horton's
"drug-store, Helen street, Minneapolis. (Signed) John H.
"Stevens, F. R. E. Cornell, C. L. Anderson, Board of Trustees."

Andrew Jackson Morgan, an editor, and a pioneer of Minnesota, died at St. Paul August 25th. Mr. Morgan was a
native of Ohio, and was an early and good friend to Minneapolis. I had known Mr. Morgan's brother, Gen. Geo. W.
Morgan, in Mexico. His mother was a sister of one of the
secretaries of the United States Treasury, and gave my second daughter her name. Mr. Morgan was only twenty-eight
years old at the time of his death.

On the 21st of August Dr. A. E. Johnson, of St. Anthony,
discovered nearly four feet of the remains of a Dikelocephulus
Minnesotansis, immediately below the Falls, where workmen
were blasting for the mill of Rogers & Co. The specimen
was a very large and perfect one. It was taken from a piece
of rock that had occupied about the middle strata of the upper
magnesian limestone. Owens, the geologist, speaks of this
rare and imperfectly-known species of fossil as being first
found ninety or one hundred feet below the base of the lower
magnesian limestone near the margin of Lake St. Croix above
Stillwater.

A tri-weekly stage-line was established August 25th between
Minneapolis and Monticello, by Messrs. Hanson & Libbey.
It was a great convenience to the citizens residing on the line
of the route, as well as to the people of Minneapolis and Monticello.

The farm of Mr. Christmas was laid out and platted as

North Minneapolis. Isaac I. Lewis and Captain John C. Reno purchased an interest in the new town-site. Messrs. A. Wolcott & Co. purchased a block of land on the bank of the river from the proprietors of North Minneapolis, and commenced the erection of a large steam-mill.

A postoffice was established at Moffett & Pettijohn's mill, near Minneapolis, and James A. Dinsmore appointed postmaster. The name of the postoffice was Harmony. This is the same postoffice that is now called Richfield. At the time the postoffice was established the town was known as Richland. Afterwards, by a vote of the citizens, it was changed to Richfield, and then the postoffice took that name, and remains so to this day.

On the 11th of September Thomas Warwick, a pioneer, and one of the best citizens of Hennepin county, was married to Miss Mary E. Smith.

The Democrat speaks of a herd of short-horns brought from Kentucky for Messrs. Hoag and J. H. Stevens. They paid a large price for some thirty head, but the agriculture of the territory was not sufficiently developed to make it profitable to raise blooded stock. A scrub would bring as much in market, those early days, as a short-horn, unless it was for beef.

The Republican party was thoroughly organized in Hennepin county. Dr. H. Fletcher headed the party in Minneapolis, and H. G. O. Morrison in St. Anthony. The following were the original Republicans in Minneapolis : J. B. Bassett, A. K. Hartwell, T. Pettijohn, Wm. G. Moffett, John M. Styles, J. H. Spear, Joseph LeDuc, J. M. Anderson, Lyman Case, Joseph H. Canney, W. H. Rouse, Samuel Franklin, Simeon K. Odell, Allen Harmon, E. A. Hodgdon, E. S. Jenks, Zelotes Downs, S. Clarke, T. W. Pierce, Delano T. Smith, Henry C. Keith, Z. M. Brown, Asa Keith, W. A. Hotchkiss, A. Crain, F. Duhren, Josiah Orthoudt, and Alfred Murphy. Such men as Judge Cornell and others soon fell into line.

The original Republicans in St. Anthony were H. G. O. Morrison, Lardner Bostwick, Dr. J. H. Murphy, S. W. Farnham, William Spooner, Dr. C. W. Le Boutillier, G. G. Loomis, Alonzo Leaming, Richard Chute, Henry Meniger,

Geo. P. Baldwin, J. C. McCane, James M. Jarrett, E. W. Cutter, J. C. Johnson, John Glass, Casper Kopp, Geo. A. Nourse, R. P. Upton, Wm. H. Townsend, Thomas T. Newell, J. H. McHerron, John Lucksinger, Stephen Cobb, C. Kellerman, Martin Conzet, H. Webber, T. Smith, J. W. Gillam, Francis Swett, R. W. Cummings, Dan S. Balch, E. Lippincott, William Lashelle, Dr. H. W. Gould, J. B. Hix, M. W. Getchell, J. Macomber, and David A. Secombe.

This was a formidable list of prominent men in the two cities. The Whigs and Democrats were about equally divided as to those who composed the new party. Such old Whigs as Isaac Atwater, and A. M. Fridley, became Democrats. John W. North had left his home in St. Anthony and taken up his residence in the new town of Northfield. This accounts for the omission of his name in the St. Anthony list.

In Richfield the original Republicans were Gen. R. L. Bartholomew, J. H. Perkins, R. Robinson, William Finch, William and James Dinsmore, Denison Townsend, George Gillmore, C. Couilard, Job Pratt, Jesse Richardson, R. Van Valkenburg, and Samuel Stough. In Bloomington, William Chambers, R. B. Gibson, S. A. Goodrich, M. S. Whallon, and J. Harrison. In Eden Prairie, W. C. Collins, Captain Terrell, J. S. P. Ham, and A. D. Rouse. In Excelsior, Stephen Hull, O. Wilcox, P. M. Gideon, and Rev. C. Galpin. In Minnetonka, S. Bartow, James Shaver, jr., and H. S. Atwood. In Wayzata, W. B. Harrington, John S. Harrington. In Brooklyn, Rev. J. W. Dow, A. H. Benson, Captain John C. Plummer, C. D. Kingsley, J. M. Durman, A. B. Chaffee, Rufus Pratt, and Dea. Palmer. In Champlin, W. W. Cate, W. W. Woodman, W. Hayden, John Walker, and J. M. Mullholland. In Maple Grove, W. E. Evans, G. B. Brown, and Dea. R. R. Woodward. In Dayton, S. Anderson, J. B. Hinckley, N. Herrick, A. C. Kimball, and A. Clarke. In Hassan, H. S. Norton, and J. McLenlock.

It should not be supposed that the above list contains all of the original Republicans in the several towns, but those led off in the new party. The citizens in the new counties of Carver and McLeod also became deeply interested in the Republican party. The leaders in the former county were Isaac Burfield, Robert Miller, John S. Letford, George M.

Powers, Henry M. Lyman, A. W. Adams, Theo. Bost, L. H. Griffin, H. H. Williams, S. D. Hurd, and A. Keller. In the latter county James Phillips, R. A. Grimshaw, Lewis Harrington, A. J. Bell, W. W. Pendergast, William S. Chapman, Henry Elliott, B. E. Messer, C. L. Snyder, James Chesley, James Pollock, A. J. Snyder, John Hubbard, and U. Wilson.

Many in the above list have occupied high positions in both the civil and military history of the Northwest.

The second annual territorial fair came off in Minneapolis October 8, 9 and 10. Governor Alexander Ramsey, the president, gave the annual address. The fair was a success in every department. It was attended from all parts of the territory. The fair grounds were on what is now Tenth street, Minneapolis. Over two thousand dollars were paid out in premiums. At least half of this money was received at the gates ; the other half was made up by the citizens of Minneapolis, as follows : Steele & Stevens $50, Henry T. Welles $25, Parsons & Morgan $25, Snyder & McFarlane $25, L. W. Henry $25, W. G. Murphy $25, Savory & Horton $25, T. L. Bibbins & Co. $25, Lewis & Bickford $25, E. H. Davie $25, James Hoffman $25, E. Case $25, Isaac Atwater and Richard Martin $25, Hancock & Thomas $25, E. H. Crane $25, John H. Spear & Co. $25, A. E. Ames $25, Martin McLeod $25, R. Chute $25, R. P. Russell $25, Edward Murphy $20, Charles Hoag $25, M. L. Olds $30, William Hanson $15, F. R. E. Cornell $15, Charles Hepp $10, S. S. Crowell $10, Martin Ferrant $10, Allen Harmon $10, Alex Moore $10, John George Lennon $10, M. L. Cook $10, Richard Stout $10, E. S. Jones $10, W. D. Babbitt $10, Henry Chambers $10, B. F. Baker $10, A. K. Hartwell $10, Henry S. Plummer $10, Francis Morrison $10, George D. Richardson $10, M. C. Baker $10; George W. Chowen, George E. Huy, Sweet W. Case, William Dickie, Smith & Charlton, H. S. Birge, C. C. Berkman, William D. Garland, H. G. O. Morrison, C. W. Borup and C. H. Oakes ten dollars each ; Delano T. Smith $15, Carlos Wilcox $15, Alexander Ramsey $25, H. H. Sibley $50, W. A. Gorman 10, and Calvin A. Tuttle $15 ; A. L. Moore, J. B. Atkinson, C. L. Anderson, Calvin Church, J. R. Webb, N. E. Stoddard, E. Hedderley, George A. Nourse, R. P. Upton, David Edwards, J. P. Wilson, John L. Tenney, W. W. Wales,

J. J. Kennedy, Tufts & Reynolds, Albert Webster, Robert O. Neil, E. F. Parker, Norman W. Kittson, and Isaac Van Etten, five dollars each. The list is only given that the present generation may know the liberality of the pioneers of Minneapolis.

The officers elected at the annual meeting for 1857 were Henry H. Sibley of Dakota county president, and a vice-president from each county in the territory. Dr. Ames, Secretary ; S. P. Snyder, Treasurer.

A large party under the auspices of Dr. C. L. Anderson and several citizens of Minneapolis, explored the country west of Glencoe this fall. They discovered the Kandiyohi lakes, and named several bodies of water, which names are retained to this day. Lake Lillian took its name from the wife of E. Whitefield, the artist of the expedition.

The total number of votes polled in Hennepin county this year was 1,761, against 73 four years previously. This exhibits the remarkable rapidity with which the county has become populated.

A fatal explosion occurred at the large steam saw-mill of Pomeroy & Bates, at the mouth of Bassett's creek, this fall, killing Mr. Hays the engineer. This was the first accident of the kind that ever occurred in Minneapolis.

The real estate transactions were lively in both the cities at the Falls during the late fall and early winter. Judge Bassett sold his entire farm, consisting of 140 acres, to William D. Garland and A. Bradford. The price was two hundred and fifty dollars per acre. J. S. & D. M. Demmon purchased eighty acres from Francis Morrison, at good round figures. The citizens on the east side of the Falls subscribed sixty-five thousand dollars for the building of a railroad from the Falls to St. Paul.

Ivory F. Woodman & Co. established a pork-packing house in Minneapolis. This was the commencement of the pork business in Minnesota.

Hartwell & Co. opened a wood-yard in the city, the first enterprise of the kind at the falls.

E. F. Crain, proprietor of the city jewelry-store, had built in the upper story of his new block a prominent cupalo in which he placed a town clock, the first in the territory.

Minneapolis received a large addition to her population this year, men of great merit, and some of them became well known throughout the Union. Among them were Colonel Cyrus Aldrich, Judge C. E. Vanderburgh, Rev. D. B. Knickerbocker, now Bishop of Indiana, Eugene M. Wilson, William S. Heath, H. A. Partridge, John H. Hatton, Fred Chalmers, C. W. Paulding, S. P. Spear, William B. Cornell, T. M. Linton, H. L. Birge, L. M. Kiefer, R. J. Mendenhall, Thomas G. Barnes, G. H. Hamlinton, M. C. Smith, William A. Todd, Adolphus Bradford, Geo. H. Woods, H. C. Smith, David Charlton, L. W. Henry, Thomas Hale Williams, J. C. Sherburne, George D. Richardson, J. Russell Webb, Winslow T. Perkins, John H. Spear, Charles K. Sherburne, C. D. Davidson, and J. C. Reno.

W. M. Barrows arrived in St. Anthony this year. His brother, Fred C. preceded him the previous year. The brothers have accomplished much in the lumber business. Frank Beebe cast his lot with the people of Minneapolis, and became one of the leading lawyers in this state. Daniel R. Barber, long an influential citizen, came this year. Dr. A. L. Bausman, one of the pioneer dentists, was a valuable addition this year. John and his brother Nicholas Bolferding also became residents of Minneapolis, as did T. M. Bohan of St. Anthony. Other residents this year were R. R. Bryant, Josiah H. Chase, R. P. Dunnington, August Ende, Harlow A. Gale, Thomas K. Gray, Elias H. Moses, J. W. Munson, Peter Rauen, Godfrey Scheitlin, and O. T. Swett. Many of these names became prominent in the history of the neighborhood of the Falls.

There were two new church buildings erected during the year; the Episcopal, Rev. D. B. Knickerbacker, rector; and the Methodist, Rev. W. H. St. Clair, pastor. Rev. Mr. Robinson succeeded Rev. C. G. Ames as pastor of the Free-will Baptist church, and on the organization of the Congregational church Rev. Norman McLeod was chosen its first pastor. Mr. McLeod was a brother of Martin McLeod, and is a man of great ability. The trustees of the church were Charles Clarke, E. N. Bates, Samuel Hidden, B. F. Baker, L. P. Chase, W. K. McFarlane, Dr. W. H. Leonard, C. E. Vanderburgh, and Mr. Walcott.

CHAPTER XXXIX.

The year 1856 was a prosperous one, not only for the citizens of Hennepin county, but for those of the whole territory. The two lovely sister towns, St. Anthony and Minneapolis, so fair to look upon in their youth and rural beauty, had expanded into thriving cities. As I cannot in detail further follow the progress and marvelous development of the now united cities I will merely repeat that Minneapolis proper was first settled in 1849, but there were only a few families here for several years thereafter ; and I will add that the first settlers were as happy in their poverty as their descendants now are in their wealth. The pioneers were as contented in their rude cabins, with plain surroundings, coarse clothing and homely fare, as others who now live in elegant mansions, with costly furnishings, cradled in luxury, and reposing on couches of ease. It required fortitude to meet the trials incident to a new country, but the frontier life had its charms. The hardships incident thereto strengthened us for good deeds and unselfish work, that made us better citizens. All were seemingly on a level. Those were happy days of free and cordial social life and charming simplicity. There were no schools, but most of the children were babes, and they had refined and educated mothers. There were no ministers of the gospel, but we observed the sabbath. Far away from the sound of the church-going bell, we yet rested from our labors one day in seven at least. On Sunday wives were particular in having each one of the family tidy. Our clothing, though coarse, was substantial and comfortable. Compared with the more ample dress and costly vestments of recent date, our raiment would now be unfash-

ionable ; but parents of the present time, if thrown upon
their own resources and dependent upon their industry, could
not better sustain themselves and their families in respectable honest poverty ; and with the greatest respect for them,
we must say that it is to be doubted if they would as cheerfully make the effort. To the untiring industry and intelligence of the pioneer ladies of Minnesota we were all indebted
for domestic happiness, that now seems to have been bliss.

In looking back upon the events of the past forty years in
Minneapolis I seem to awake from a dream. The transform-
ation can scarcely be realized. Nearly everything has changed.
The few pioneers whose lives have graciously been prolonged
are in the sear and yellow leaf. Their beards are frosted with
age, and their locks powdered with the snows of many winters.
For many summers the genial sun has imprinted upon the
tresses of these first ladies of this new land the light of its
caresses. All these marks of time are a crown of glory for
good works.

Instead of rude cabins, elegant residences surround me.
Where the wolf sat and howled, are ten-story brown-stone
business blocks. Tall spires point toward the heavens from
fine temples of worship. A net-work of railroads is all around
me. Millions are invested in manufactures. Commerce is
unceasing. All that art and science can do for us is being
done. All these things have come to pass in a little over one
generation, many of them within the last decade. If the possibility of such changes had been suggested to me on that
October morning in 1852 when the first election was held in
Minneapolis, I should have said, " Behold ! if the Lord would
make windows in Heaven, then might these things be !"

One hundred and fifty-seven years had elapsed since the
discovery of the Falls of St. Anthony by the missionary Louis
Hennepin, before a claim was made to the soil in the neighborhood of the Falls. For more than ten years after the
latter event, no progress of moment was made in developing
the wonderful natural resources of the neighborhood.

When we consider that it is but a few years since this was
the home of the red man, and when we view the great city of
to-day, we can hardly imagine what a mighty destiny is in
waiting for those who will soon follow us.

CHAPTER XL.

On New Years Day 1857, there was a meeting of the Union Board of Trade of St. Anthony and Minneapolis. The following officers were elected for the year : Samuel Hidden president, David Edwards and John H. Spear vice-presidents, N. H. Hemiup corresponding secretary, T. L. Bibbins recording secretary, R. P. Upton treasurer, Z. E. B. Nash, D. Morrison, Richard Chute, John Jackins and Edward Murphy directors.

Early in January Edward Patch was appointed postmaster in St. Anthony.

The first restaurant in Minneapolis was established by L. F. Harris the first part of January.

The new county officers elected for 1857 and 1858 were Rev. C. G. Ames register of deeds, Edward Lippencott sheriff, G. G. Loomis county commissioner, Geo. A. Nourse district-attorney, John L. Tenney county treasurer, and Edwin Smith Jones judge of probate. For the first time the citizens of St. Anthony voted in Hennepin county. The voters on the west side of the river residing in the county were liberal in selecting many of the officers from St. Anthony.

Judge Joel B. Bassett was elected to the council from the Hennepin district in place of D. M. Hanson deceased, and W. W. Wales of the St. Anthony district was elected to the council to fill a vacancy occasioned by the resignation of John Rollins. Asa Keith of Richfield, John P. Plummer of Brooklyn, Rev. W. Hayden of Champlin, and Delano T. Smith of Minneapolis, were elected to the house of representatives,

D.M. & M. Ry.
Double Track Stone Arch Bridge
Minneapolis, Minn.

while Jonathan Chase and Henry Hechtman were elected to the same office in the St. Anthony district. The session for which they were elected, 1857, was the last one under the territorial authority.

The legislative session of 1857 was more important than any that had preceded it, from the fact that members of that body had the disposal of the vast amount of land granted to Minnesota in aid of building railroads, and took the necessary steps for the territory to become the state.

The citizens of Minneapolis met early in March for the purpose of rendering a tribute to Hon. Henry T. Welles, who had visited Washington during the session of congress, and had contributed largely in making Minneapolis a railroad center, in the passage of a bill granting railroad lands to Minnesota. It was decided that a public dinner should be given to Mr. Welles as a slight token of appreciation of his great services in behalf of the people which compliment Mr. Welles declined. Messrs. Eugene M. Wilson, S. P. Snyder, Cyrus Aldrich, Isaac Atwater, C. H. Pettit, and other prominent citizens, participated in the meeting.

The news of the appointment of Samuel Medary, a prominent editor of Ohio, as Governor of Minnesota, was received early in the spring. Charles L. Chase of St. Anthony was selected by President Buchanan as secretary of the territory.

New towns sprang up this spring all over the territory. Many of them were of course paper town-sites. To-day the location of many of those sites is unknown.

AN INDIAN REPUBLIC.

The Hazlewood republic, established on the upper Mississippi by Rev. Dr. Williamson and Rev. Dr. Riggs, among the Dakotas, promised good results this year. One great trouble the missionaries had to contend with was the difficulty in getting the red men to wear shirts, pants, vests, coats, hats, and short hair, instead of breechcloths, blankets, leggins, and long hair. Dr. Riggs in March of this year writes : "We "continue to make some progress ; occasionally we have need "for the barber to operate upon a new subject. When a man "doffs the Indian and dons the white man's dress, by far the "most important part of the ceremony is cutting off the hair. "A few weeks since Robert Chaskay was spending the evening

"at Mr. Renville's. For some time previous Chaskay had
"been promising to put on pantaloons as soon as he could
"obtain a full suit. Renville intimated to him that he doubted
"whether he had such intention. Looking up at a coat and
"pantaloons which hung against the wall, Chaskay said 'if
"you will give me those I will put them on.' No sooner said
"than done. Renville pulled down the clothes and gave them
"to Chaskay, and then had the privilege of cutting off his hair.
"As those locks cost him so much, he said he must hang them
"up as a house ornament."

Rev. A. A. Russell, one of the most faithful of ministers in
Minneapolis, resigned his charge over the Baptist church May
1st. Samuel Hidden was appointed postmaster May 1st, in
place of Dr. A. E. Ames. On the 12th of May Carlos Wilcox
was married to Miss Mary S. Burgess, a sister of Mrs. F. R.
E. Cornell ; and on the 2d of June C. H. Pettit was married
to Miss Deborah Williams, daughter of Captain Williams.

On the 3d of June Mrs. Margaret Marble, one of the captive women taken at Spirit Lake, by the Indians, in March,
was brought by Indian Agent Flandreau to St. Paul. Inkpaduta, her captor, sold her for a keg of powder to a couple of
Dr. Williamson's Lac-qui-parle Indians.

The election of delegates to attend the Constitutional con-
vention for the formation of a state government, came off on
June 1st. The delegates elected from this district were Dr.
A. E. Ames, Col. Cyrus Aldrich, David Morgan, and Erastus
N. Bates, of Minneapolis ; Rev. W. Hayden of Champlin,
Gen. R. L. Bartholomew of Richfield, W. F. Russell and Rev.
Chas. B. Sheldon of Minnetonka, Henry Eschlie, Albert W.
Combs, and T. D. Smith, of Carver county ; B. E. Messer of
Hutchinson, McLeod county. From the St. Anthony district
Judge B. B. Meeker, Wm. M. Lashelles, Calvin A. Tuttle,
Charles L. Chase, Dr. John H. Murphy, L. C. Walker, Peter
Winell, and D. A. Secombe, S. W. Putnam, and D. M. Hall.

On the 17th of June the new Governor, Samuel Medary,
removed Rev. C. G. Ames from the office of register of deeds.
An hour after Mr. Ames was decapitated, the county commissioners restored him to office.

William D. Washburn arrived in Minneapolis early this
season, and has from that time occupied a prominent place in

the history of the city and country. No one man has accomplished more for the land of his adoption than has General Washburn. He has always been at the head and front of every movement that would benefit the country.

Rev. A. Gale, from Massachusetts, was called to the pulpit of the Baptist church, in June. He was an excellent citizen and a good pastor. He was peculiarly fitted for pioneer work in the church. He accomplished much good in the city, state, and northwest. He died several years since while making a journey through the Holy Land. His memory will ever be fondly cherished by those who had the pleasure of his acquaintance.

SPIRIT LAKE CAPTIVES.

On the 3d of May Miss Gardner, the surviving captive of the Spirit Lake raid, was rescued in the wilds of Dakota. She arrived in St. Paul on the 26th of June. One of the Indians, young Inkpaduta, engaged in the massacre at Spirit Lake, was killed by members of the Hazelwood republic, not far from Payzhehootaze, late in June. The bones of the chief who led the murderers at Spirit Lake was found many years since near the present town of Ortonville. Most of the red devils engaged in that horrible affair met with violent deaths. Old Inkpaduta's band of Indians were declared outlaws. Their red brothers were as eager as the whites to exterminate them.

The members of the constitutional convention met in St. Paul on Monday the 15th of July.

Rapid progress was made in building the two new bridges over the Mississippi this early summer. They were ready for the traveling public before the winter set in.

The first appearance of grasshoppers since the organization of the territory occurred this year. They made their appearance on the Fort Snelling prairie, and rapidly spread over the portion of the country north of the Minnesota river. Their greatest injury to the crops was in Hennepin county.

GREAT DEPRECIATION IN PRICE OF PROPERTY.

As the fall approached the money market became seriously stringent. Numerous banks in the western states became insolvent. Minnesota had not sufficient currency for the transaction of ordinary business. The result was a great fall in the price of real estate. Corner lots that would readily bring three thousand dollars in Minneapolis in May, could not be sold in October for three hundred dollars. Property of all descriptions depreciated in price.

Hon. Chas. E. Flandreau, agent for the Dakota Indians, was appointed territorial judge. Hennepin county was assigned to his judicial district.

A high school was opened in Minneapolis under the care of Prof. A. A. Olcott. The immense Winslow hotel in St. Anthony was was finished and furnished in the most complete manner. Mr. Winslow let the house to M. V. and D. J. Mattison.

A distressing accident occurred on the 20th of August at the residence of Mr. John Reidhead, about four miles above Minneapolis. Two of his children were burned to death in a stable. Mr. Reidhead was highly esteemed in the county.

The two principal political parties in the neighborhood of the Falls organized in the most thorough manner early in September. James A. Lawrence of St. Anthony represented the democracy, and Colonel Cyrus Aldrich of Minneapolis, represented the republicans.

Woodbury Fisk, a prominent young business man from New Hampshire, who had made St. Anthony his home for a year or more, was married to Miss Mary A. Sinclair, an estimable young lady of St. Anthony. Mr. Fisk became one of the leading merchants and millers at the Falls. He died late in the winter of 1889.

The Constitutional convention met in St. Paul July 13th, and closed August 29th.

Messrs. W. A. Croffut and Edwin Clarke having purchased the St. Anthony Republican from Rev. C. G. Ames, those gentlemen, on the 28th of September, published the first number of the Daily News, the first daily newspaper ever printed at the Falls of St. Anthony.

On account of so many bank failures, the country was flooded with worthless bank-bills. A person who had retired at night with a pocket-book well filled with currency which was considered good, might awake the next morning to find that he could not buy a breakfast with hundreds of dollars of that currency.

The Cataract hotel was finished and opened to the public

the first of October. The Nicollet house, erected by J. M. Eustis, was also ready for guests this fall. Woodman's hall, capable of holding more people than any room in the territory, was completed this fall.

The second annual Minnesota fair was held in St. Paul, commencing October 1st. Messrs. J. W. Bass, D. C. Taylor, and Major P. P. Furber, were the committee on management. The annual address was delivered by the president, Hon. H. H. Sibley, on the third day of the fair. The officers elected for 1858 were Judge M. Sherburne president, J. W. Selby vice-president, Simon P. Snyder treasurer, John Murray jr. secretary.

Franklin Cook, so long a leading citizen and engineer, arrived in Minneapolis this year. He was at once elected county surveyor. The mill company's dam across the Mississippi, which was in process of erection, proved to be the most gigantic undertaking of any similar work on the great river. The new board of directors were Hon. D. Morrison, Hon. W. D. Washburn, Dr. Jacob S. Elliott, Geo. E. Huy, Leonard Day, and H. E. Mann. Gen. Washburn was appointed secretary and agent, and Mr. Mann treasurer. The stockholders had paid in several hundred thousands of dollars. Now the hard times made it difficult for them to raise more money to complete the work. They persevered, however, and in time the work was finished.

Many new and beautiful structures were completed this season. The finest bank building in the state was completed and occupied by Messrs. Snyder, McFarlane & Cook, on Hennepin avenue.

A lecture association was organized in St. Anthony with James R. Lawrence president, Hon. David Heaton vice-president, Edwin Clark secretary, and R. C. Graves treasurer. This was the first organization of the kind at the Falls.

There being no small change in circulation, the merchants issued fractional notes of ten, fifteen, twenty-five and fifty cents, which obtained a wide circulation. The following is a correct copy of one of them :

"Minneapolis, Min., Oct. 20th, 1857.

"25 cts. This certificate for twenty-five cents will be "redeemed with current bank notes, at our store, corner of

"Bridge and First street, when presented to the amount of
"one dollar.   Moore & Power."

Mr. Alex Moore, the senior member of the firm who signed
the above, was one of the first commissioners of Hennepin
county. The firm were the successors of I. I. Lewis & Co.,
and A. Bradford. The place of business was where Harlow
A. Gale's city market house now stands. These were times
that tried a man's character. If he was a good man, he was
proved to be such ; if he was a bad man, he appeared in his
real character.* Messrs. Snyder, McFarlane & Cook, C. H.
Pettit, and Beebe & Mendenhall, the prominent bankers of
Minneapolis, rendered all the aid to the poor that was in their
power. They loaned many thousands of dollars on securities
which were considered good, but in the end proved worthless.
As the winter months approached, instead of any relief in the
money market, it became more stringent. Such dreadfully
dark days in financial matters had not occurred since the
panic of 1837. The bottom disappeared from everything
except politics.

The following gentlemen were elected to fill the county
offices for 1858 and 1859 : Clerk of the court, H. A. Partridge ;
judge of probate, E. S. Jones ; register of deeds, C. G. Ames ;
treasurer, David Morgan ; county commissioner, F. Thorn-
dike ; county surveyor, F. Cook. Messrs. A. C. Austin, J. C.
McCarnard, and Fred Bassett were elected assessors. The
first election for members of the state senate and house of
representatives was held this fall. E. N. Bates and Delano
T. Smith were elected senators, and R. B. Gibson, Dr. Geo.
H. Keith, William S. Chowen, and J. B. Hinckley, members
of the house of representatives from Hennepin west ; and
Jonathan Chase, senator, and L. C. Walker and William H.
Townsend to the house of representatives from St. Anthony,
which election district was known as Hennepin east. Hon.
James R. Lawrence of St. Anthony was elected district-
attorney for the Fourth judicial district, which comprised
several counties. Mr. Lawrence was a son of Judge Lawrence, a distinguished jurist of New York. He had recently
made St. Anthony his home. He was one of the most eloquent speakers that ever addressed a Minnesota audience.
He died early in life. With his great talent and popularity,

had his life been spared, he would unquestionably long ere this have occupied the highest trusts in the gift of the people. He has two children residing in Minneapolis—James A. Lawrence, of the firm of Wilson & Lawrence, and Mrs. Reeve, wife of Colonel C. McReeve.

James M. Jarrett had purchased the block Mr. Steele and I had built in 1851 and changed it into a first-class hotel. He was the landlord for several years, when he sold it to J. W. Thurber, who gave it the name of the Tremont.

The first syrup made from sorghum in Minnesota was manufactured this fall at Elm creek, now Champlin, in this county, by H. W. Richardson. As syrup in large quantities is now made from the early amber and other varieties of sorghum, Mr. Richardson deserves special mention as the first one in this section who was successful in the enterprise.

The census of Minnesota was ordered by congress preparatory to the admission of the territory as a state. By the returns St. Anthony had a population October 1st, 1857, of 4,720 ; Minneapolis and the Reserve 4,120 ; the rest of the county 4,523 ; total 13,363.

October 15th a daily mail via St. Paul was established by the postoffice department from the Falls to Prairie du Chien. This was the first daily mail service over this route.

Charles E. Vanderburgh and Miss Julia N. Mygatt of New York were married this year. Arthur H. Mills, a pioneer, and Miss Abby Newell were married October 24, in New Haven, Connecticut. W. W. Eastman, who has been so prominent in the destinies of this immediate country, settled in St. Anthony this year. On the 1st of November, at Dr. Bausman's office, in Minneapolis, the Minnehaha fire company reorganized with W. A. Todd for president and foreman, Fred Chalmers, treasurer ; A. L. Bausman, F. Chalmers and W. Wringley, executive committee.

The St. Anthony Express was sold this fall to Prof. D. S. B. Johnson and Chas. H. Slocum. Prof. Johnson was editor-in-chief. Mr. Slocum had charge of the local columns. Both of these gentlemen have since become prominent in this state.

Mrs. Mary C. Smith, wife of senator-elect Delano T. Smith, died suddenly November 15th. On the 17th Walter Carpenter, a brother of Mrs. J. B. Bassett, died.

The advertisement of O. M. Laraway, dealer in groceries and provisions, corner of Second and Bridge streets, appeared in the journals of the day. Mr. Laraway, during his long residence in Minneapolis, has been honored with many high local and federal trusts, which he has worthily held.

R. J. Mendenhall, who had made the city his home the previous year, associated with him in business Mr. C. Beede, a man from New England. They extended their kind deeds to a large number of persons who were affected by the panic.

Simon Stevens, the pioneer of Minnetonka, was married by Rev. A. D. Williams to Miss Kate C. Cole, early in December, and Henry Oswald was married by the same clergyman to Miss T. Sieber.

The first state legislature met in St. Paul December 2d. The following is a complete list of the justices of the peace in Hennepin county, elected and qualified to serve for 1858 : Bloomington, E. B. Stanley, George Cook ; Corcoran, John Molan, Israel Dorman ; Dayton, A. C. Kimble, W. P. Jones ; Hopkins, H. H. Hopkins, L. Holman ; Eden Prairie, W. O. Collins, H. F. Durgin ; Excelsior, O. Wilcox, E. Day ; Greenwood, T. R. Briggs, A. S. Leusbeye : Hassan, S. Anderson ; Island City, John Carman ; Medicine Lake, D. Parker, F. Huot ; Maple Grove, William Trott, John B. Bottineau ; Minneapolis, Henry Hill ; Minnetonka, A. B. Robinson ; Maple Plain, Wm. F. Hillman, Irvin Shrewsbury ; Richfield, Geo. W. Irvin ; Lower St. Anthony, Wm. McHerron, J. C. McCain ; Upper St. Anthony, Anton Grethen, George W. Thurber ; Wayzata, J. A. Colman, Wm. A. Spafford.

The first New England Society was organized late in December, with Colonel Cyrus Aldrich, a native of Rhode Island, president ; vice-presidents, natives of New England states, D. Morrison, Maine ; Wm. M. Kimble, New Hampshire ; E. N. Bates, Massachusetts ; Thos. Hale Williams, Rhode Island ; Henry T. Welles, Connecticut ; and A. E. Ames, Vermont. Forefathers day was observed by the society with all honors. W. A. Croffut, then a young man just from the land of steady habits, contributed much that made the event interesting. Then, as now, Mr. Croffut was talented, and his presence at an assemblage of this kind could not fail of making an impression.

MEN OF MARK WHO ARRIVED IN EIGHTEEN FIFTY-SEVEN.

A large number of immigrants located in the two cities this year. Among them were Hon. R. J. Baldwin, General W. D. Washburn, Samuel C. Gale, Eugene M. Wilson, Jacob K. Sidle, Rev. J. F. Chaffee, Judge E. B. Ames, Major A. C. Morrill, Jesse Bishop, Josiah H. Chase, H. D. Beeman, David Heaton, William A. Croffut, J. C. Williams, John C. Oswald, Edwin Clarke, George A. Brackett, Dan M. Demmon, Henry Oswald, William Garcelon, Nathan Herrick, W. W. Winthrop, Paris Gibson, William Lochren, Jared S. Demmon, P. H. Kelly, D. Y. Jones, Anthony Kelly, L. M. Stewart, William P. Ankeny, Fred Chalmers, Captain Williams, Asa B. Barton, Dr. S. F. Rankin, Solon Armstrong, Thomas G. Barnard, William Buckendorf, C. G. Bugbee, H. C. Butler, W. H. Chamberlain, Gilbert Clough, D. M. Clough, Thomas Gardiner, J. G. Gluck, Anton Grethen, C. B. Heffelfinger, Michael Hoy, L. Mell Hyde, B. F. Inks, J. G. Jones, W. H. Lauderdale, James R. Lawrence, James W. Lawrence, S. B. Loye, Michael Lyons, Peter McKernan, W. W. McNair, Charles Robinson, and Fred L. Smith.

It was hoped that the financial panic which had so recently swept over the country would end before the close of the year, but it rather increased, and the people accepted the hard times with as much cheerfulness as they could command. So depressed were the citizens by the financial crisis that places of amusement were comparatively unattended, though the best musicians were appreciated, such as Ole Bull and Adelina Patti, who appeared at an early day before the people at the falls. Fortunately we had in our midst Prof. Widstrand, one of the best teachers of music in the northwest, and many ladies in this city to-day, daughters of the pioneers, are indebted to him for their musical education.

CHAPTER XL.

The year 1858 opened under gloomy circumstences. Trade was depressed, currency depreciated, business paralyzed, real estate valueless, and financial ruin to all classes seemed inevitable. The crops of 1857 were poor. The flow of immigration ceased. Since the 24th of August, when the Ohio Life Insurance and Trust Company failed, no one could borrow money, for no one had it ; and yet the people were hopeful. The fractional currency issued by the merchants and bankers was a convenience. The News and the Republican, two of the leading newspapers at the Falls, opposed the issue of these notes, which led to a warm controversy between Messrs. Snyder, McFarlane & Cook, C. H. Pettit, O. M. Laraway, Alex Moore, Jackins & Wright, Beebe & Mendenhall, A. Clarke, and other business men. Gosport, Tekoma, and Brownsville was about all the money that was in circulation, and it was claimed by many of the citizens that this currency was of doubtful character. At all events the bills issued by these banks served an excellent purpose for the occasion.

A new board of trade was organized the first of the year, for the purpose of rendering every possible relief to business men and citizens generally. The officers were Captain John C. Reno, president ; Richard Chute and William M. Kimball, vice-presidents ; T. S. Bibbins and Judge Hemiup, secretaries ; William D. Washburn, treasurer ; John S. Pillsbury, D. Morrison, W. D. Babbett, Samuel Hidden, and Edward Hedderly, directors. The efforts of this organization were attended with good results in many instances. This was the first public position held by Mr. Pillsbury, and his earnest labors in behalf of the business interests in this neighborhood at that early day plainly indicated a brilliant future was in store for him.

FORT SNELLING PROPERTY SOLD.

Franklin Steele and others purchased the Fort Snelling property, which caused an excitement of some magnitude. An investigation of the sale was ordered by congress, the result of which proved Mr. Steele to be the honorable man he was known to be by all his acquaintances. Subsequently Mr. Steele and those associated with him transferred to the government the buildings and the necessary amount of land required by the government for parade-grounds, gardens, hay-lands, and building purposes, outside of the garrison.

The early year was attended with large revivals in both cities. Joel B. Bassett and Otis Bradford were appointed county commissioners in place of Geo. W. Chowen and Mr. Thorndyke, resigned. Geo. A. Brackett, who has since become such a useful and prominent citizen, opened business in Minneapolis early this year, on the corner of Second and Minnetonka streets (now Second avenue south). This was Mr. Brackett's first business venture in Minneapolis.

The United States land-office was moved from Minneapolis to Forest City, in Meeker county.

A bill was introduced into the Legislature in February in favor of the state issuing five million dollars in bonds to be used in building the land-grant railroads. At first this bill met with serious opposition in Minneapolis by such able men as Colonel Cyrus Aldrich, M. S. Olds, F. R. E. Cornell, W. D. Washburn, Chas. E. Vanderburgh, Geo. A. Brackett, Judge E. B. Ames, C. A. Tuttle, Edwin Hedderly, Henry S. Birge, R. J. Baldwin, D. Morrison, Dr. J. S. Elliott, Geo. E. Huy, Wyman Elliott, Leonard Day, D. M. Coolbaugh, P. H. Kelly, and W. P. Ankeny. On the other hand, Senator Bates, representative Geo. H. Keith, and many others, approved of the measure.

Margaret, daughter of Joseph Tuay, was burned to death at her father's house in St. Anthony.

The legislature passed the bill establishing an agricultural college at Glencoe. Rev. J. C. Whitney, in the early spring

of this year, retired from the pastorate of the First Presbyterian church to accept a similar position at Forest City.
Orin Curtis was elected Mayor of St. Anthony. W. W.
Wales, who had so acceptably filled the mayor's chair in that
city during 1857 refused to be a candidate for re-election.

At the election April 15th in regard to the five million loan
bill, the citizens of St. Anthony and Minneapolis voted in
favor of the measure by over fifteen hundred majority.

The steamers running above St. Anthony on the Mississippi
this year were the H. M. Rice, William Harmon, owner,
Enterprise, Levi Cosset, owner, and North Star, J. M. Gil-
man, owner. The Young brothers, A. R. and J. B., were the
masters of the last two boats.

Sixty-four of the business men published a notice that they
would receive state script at par for debts or for goods.

IMPROVEMENTS AND CHURCHES.

Richard Chute purchased of L. M. Ford this spring two
thousand shade trees, with which he lined the streets of St.
Anthony. By this act alone Mr. Chute became a public ben-
efactor. The different churches in Minneapolis were repre-
sented as follows : Baptist, Rev. Amory Gale pastor ; S. A.
Jewett, James Sully, and Joshua Draper, deacons ; Geo. H.
Keith, and C. B. Goodyear, clerks ; Joseph S. Johnson,
treasurer ; J. C. Weld, collector ; James Sully, S. A. Jewett.
Geo. H. Keith, H. Fletcher, and J. P. Abrahams, trustees.
Plymouth, Rev. Norman McLeod, pastor ; Charles Clark,
Samuel Hidden, D. R. Barber, J. H. Spear, Dr. William H.
Leonard, B. F. Baker, S. P. Chase, A. Walcott, and Charles
E. Vanderburgh, trustees ; W. H. Leonard and Cyrus Snow,
deacons ; Erastus N. Bates, clerk. Free-will Baptist, Rev.
A. D. Williams, pastor ; Allen Harmon, deacon ; Henry C.
Keith, Edwin S. Jones, and Henry Hill, trustees ; Rufus
Cook, clerk ; Charles Sherburne, sexton. Gethsemane, Rev.
D. B. Knickerbacker, rector ; Henry T. Welles and Captain
John C. Reno, wardens ; Judge I. Atwater, Dr. A. E. Ames,
W. S. Phinney, W. J. Parsons, C. H. Wood and Alfred Mur-
phy, vestrymen ; M. B. Horton, clerk ; S. W. Phinney, treas-
urer. Presbyterian, Rev. F. A. Griswold officiated occasion-
ally as pastor after the removal of Rev. J. C. Whitney to
Forest city ; Joseph LeDuc, elder ; D. M. Anderson, S. S.

Crowell, J. L. Tenney, and J. T. Grimes, trustees. Methodist, Rev. T. M. Gossard, Rev. J. D. Rich, pastors ; Rev. J. W. Dow, local elder ; Solomon Weill, E. J. Scrimgeon, A. Jackson Bell, R. W. Plummer, J. Oudhoudt, J. Cyphers, and T. S. Bibbins, stewards ; Joseph Dean, S. Weill, and A. J. Bell, leaders.

W. P. Day commenced supplying the residents of Minneopolis with milk this spring. He was the city's first dairyman.

On April 17th, Emily Mygatt, the only child of Hon. R. J. Baldwin, died

THE UNION SCHOOL AND BISHOP KNICKERBACKER

The union school opened for the spring and summer under the most favorable conditions. As this was the first regular term with a full corps of teachers, their names are given : George B. Stone, superintendent and principal ; Miss S. S. Garfield, Mrs. Julia A. Titus, Miss H. E. Harris, and Miss Adeline Jefferson, teachers. Rev. D. B. Knickerbacker, now Bishop of Indiana, was secretary, and one of the directors of the union schools, and to that gentleman is the public indebted to a great extent for the success of those schools. Perhaps no one man contributed more in every possible way for the benefit of Minneapolis, and it was a great loss, not only to the city, but to the state, when he became Bishop of Indiana. His good works in the ministry for more than a generation in Minneapolis, will be lasting for all time to come.

Minneapolis had six good hotels at this time—the Nicollet, the Cataract, the Bushnell, the American, the Wilber, and the Minnesota ; while St. Anthony led off with the large Winslow, Jarrett, St. Charles, Revere, Union, and the Cheever.

Dr. Philo L. Hatch arrived in Minneapolis from Dubuque, this early summer, and from that time to this has had much influence in the city.

At the first Minneapolis election held this summer, Henry T. Welles was elected president of the corporation, and Charles Hoag, William D. Garland, Isaac I. Lewis, and E. Hedderly, trustees ; William A. Todd, clerk ; John Murray jr., treasurer ; C. C. Berkman, marshal ; and David Charlton, city engineer. These officers were elected under the new corporation act granted to the city by the first legislature. It was deemed better that the affairs of the city should be governed by a president and board of trustees, rather than a mayor and city council.

Hon. E. M. Wilson was appointed by the President United States attorney for the new state of Minnesota.

Dr. S. H. Chute was married in St. Anthony May 8th to Miss Helen E. H. Day.

The state being admitted into the Union, the new law of township organization was carried into effect. On the 13th of May the several townships elected new officers. In St. Anthony James B. Gilbert was selected for chairman, Richard Fewer and James C. Tuffts, supervisors ; Dan M. Demmon, town clerk ; James A. Lennon assessor ; James W. Ellis, collector ; and James Holmes, overseer of the poor. Minneapolis elected R. P. Russell, chairman ; Daniel Bassett, D. B. Richardson, Edward Murphy and I. I. Lewis, supervisors ; Geo. E. Huy and Henry Hill, justices of the peace.

St. Anthony and the country generally sustained a great loss in the death of Judge S. M. Tracy, on the 13th of May. Judge Tracy was one of the most prominent young men in the state.

Henry H. Sibley and the other state officers were sworn into office May 24th.

The Nicollet house was opened by a banquet on May 26th. Judge E. B. Ames presided, with Colonel Aldrich, Judge Cornell, D. Morrison, W. W. Eastman, Judge Atwater, Joel B. Bassett, Edward Murphy, Henry T. Welles, James R. Lawrence, B. F. Baker, and J. B. Gilbert, vice-presidents. Speeches were made by the above, and by Governor Sibley, E. M. Wilson, and others.

Anson Northrup purchased the steamer North Star for the navigation of the Mississippi from Fort Ripley to the falls of the Pokegema. This was the first boat ever placed in the trade above Sauk Rapids.

The first editorial convention ever held in Minnesota convened in St. Paul June 3d. Most every paper published in the boundaries of the state at that time was represented. C. Stebbins of the Hastings Independent occupied the chair, and David Blakely of the Bancroft Pioneer was chosen secretary. The executive committee consisted of Marshall Robinson of the Glencoe Register, A. J. Van Vorhis of the Stillwater Messenger, Thomas Foster of the Minnesotian, Mr. Dodge of the Free Press, Mr. Hensley of the Mankato Independent, and Mr. Brown of the Brownsville Herald.

In pursuance of adjournment the state legislature met June 2d, Governor Sibley's message being delivered that day. This was the first message delivered to the legislature by the governor after the state was admitted into the Union.

Eliza, wife of Deacon John S. Mann, died at the residence of the family June 24th. She was one of the pioneer women of Minnesota, and was greatly respected by the whole community. She was the daughter of Deacon Joshua Draper, and was thirty-seven years old.

A grand celebration was held on Nicollet Island July 4th, Colonel Aldrich presiding. This was followed by observing the anniversary of the West India emancipation on July 31st. Speeches were made on that occasion by Samuel C. Gale, Rev. C. G. Ames, Prof. G. B. Stone, Geo. A. Nourse, and others. This was the first appearance of Mr. Gale before a Minneapolis audience. A more eloquent effort had never been made in the city.

On the 16th of August news was received of the successful landing of the Atlantic cable.

A beautiful flag was presented to James M. Winslow, proprietor of the Winslow hotel, St. Anthony, by the ladies of that city. The committee who officiated on that occasion was composed of Mrs. Sumner W. Farnham, Mrs. Isaac Atwater, Mrs. R. B. Graves, and Mrs. S. H. Chute.

On the 18th of August Geo. A. Brackett was married at Excelsior, by Rev. Chas. B. Sheldon to Miss Annie M. Hoyt of Minneapolis.

W. P. Ankeny was appointed postmaster of Minneapolis early in the fall, in place of Samuel Hidden, resigned.

Several British noblemen arrived in St. Anthony, and spent several days in visiting the upper country. Among them were the Earl of Shaftsbury, Lord Cavendish, Lord Grosvenor, Sir George Simpson, and Rt. Hon. H. Ellis. They were accompanied by Dr. John Rea, the celebrated Arctic explorer.

On September 14th it was decided that it would not be desirable to hold a state fair this fall There was no response to the executive committee from the different cities and towns in behalf of the fair. The fact is there was no money in the hands of the citizens to contribute for such a purpose.

HENNEPIN COUNTY ELECTION.

At the first annual election after the organization of the state government of Minnesota, which was held in Hennepin county in October of this year, the following gentlemen were elected a county board of supervisors : Bloomington, Hon. Martin McLeod ; Brooklyn, E. T. Alling ; Corcoran, Israel Dorman ; Dayton, A. C. Kimball ; Eden Prairie, Aaron Gould ; Excelsior, R. B. McGrath ; Hassan, S. Finical ; Independence, Irvin Shrewsbury ; Maple Grove, A. C. Austin ; Minneapolis township, R. P. Russell ; Minnetonka, Fred Bassett ; Plymouth, Francois Huot ; Richfield, Joel Brewster ; St. Anthony township, Captain J. B. Gilbert ; Greenwood, N. D. Fennell ; Minnetrista, S. L. Merriman. At the same election, Messrs. Nelson S. Hoblit, G. D. Rich, Colonel Aldrich, and Daniel Bassett, were elected supervisors of Minneapolis ; Richard Strout, sheriff of Hennepin county ; Geo. W. Chowen, register of deeds ; H. O. Hamlin, auditor ; A. C. Morrill, county attorney ; and Franklin Cook, county surveyor. In St. Anthony David Heaton was elected senator, S. Lawrence, and R. S. Alden, members of the house of representatives. In Hennepin county William D. Washburn, Aaron Gould, R. B. McGrath, and A. C. Austin, were elected to the house ; the senators holding over.

On September 25th a herd of buffaloes made their appearance on the Amos James farm, near Hutchinson, in McLeod county.

On the 26th John Baxter of Dayton was married to Miss Mary E. Nettleton ; and on the 4th of October George W. Chowen was married to Miss Susan E. Hawkins.

C. H. Pettit's paper, the Journal, made its appearance late in September.

On the 19th of October Prof. S. H. Folsom, recently of Maine, opened a select school in St. Anthony. Over four hundred resident children of Minneapolis attended the union school at the fall term, ranging from four to twenty-three years of age, and not one of them was born in the city.

The population of Minneapolis this fall was a little over four thousand ; that of St. Anthony was a little larger.

On the 1st of November Rev. E. D. Neill was appointed Chancelor of the University of Minnesota. The appointment was a popular one. No one had contributed so much to the educational interests of the territory. He was an earnest friend to all that would benefit the people. He had been a constant visitor to St. Anthony, preaching to the citizens in the early days without pay. He gave the first lecture in the old town before the library association, and has always been faithful to every trust. A Christian minister, eloquent, talented, energetic, his hands are full of good work. He was one of the originators and promoters of of the early organizations that have so greatly benefitted the north star state.

The first lodge of good templars was established in St. Anthony late in the fall of this year. Geo. A. Camp, Miss Hannah C. Stanton, Rev. J. F. Chaffee, Mrs. Calista Chaffee, A. P. Connelly, Kate H. Hall, Henrietta Murphie, L. P. Foster, Miss Jane Morrison, and Miss Sarah G. Cleveland, were the first officers of the organization.

James P. Howlett of Minneapolis was married in Tecumseh, Michigan, on the 9th of November, to Miss Sarah Graves.

Hard as the times were, there were two hundred buildings erected in St. Anthony during the season of 1858, at a cost of $310,000 ; and in Minneapolis one hundred and seventy, at a cost of $275,000. No one could imagine where the money came from necessary for the erection of these buildings.

As the winter set in it was determined by the citizens of Minneapolis to organize a lecture association. Samuel Hidden was chosen president of the association ; Samuel C. Gale, secretary ; and John C. Williams, H. D. Beeman, and Dr. Geo. H. Keith, executive committee. The object of the association was intellectual improvement during the long winter evenings. Through the wise management of Mr. Gale and the other officers of the association, the citizens were favored with many choice lectures during the winter.

The practicing physicians at the Falls at the end of December this year were Dr. J. H. Murphy, Dr. A. E. Ames, Dr. M. R. Greeley, Dr. J. S. Elliott, Dr. W. H. Leonard, Dr. B. Jodon, Dr. A. Ortman, Dr. W. D. Dibb, Dr. C. W. Boutillier, Dr. C. L. Anderson, Dr. P. L. Hatch, Dr. J. B. Sabine, and Dr. Simon French Rankin.

Most of the physicians belonged to the allopathic school, though Dr. Elliott's practice was herbal, and Dr. Hatch's homeopathic. The latter was the pioneer in his practice in Minneapolis, as Dr. Elliott was in his ; though Dr. Ira Kingsbury, the primitive physician in St. Anthony, belonged to the same school. Dr. Leonard, at that time, was a member of what is termed the old school class of physicians.

Financially the year ended as it commenced, under a cloud, and yet there was much that made life enjoyable. Thomas Hale Williams, C. M. Cushman, and Charles H. Clarke, supplied the citizens with choice books and the magazines of the day. Several matrimonial alliances were effected at the close of the year. Among them were D. B. S. Johnson, editor of the Express, to Miss Hannah C. Stanton ; Mark T. Berry to Miss N. J. Rowell, and George Davis to Miss Helen M. Coulliard. Mr. Johnson assumed the editorial chair of the Express on the elevation of Isaac Atwater to the supreme . bench of the state.

Frank L. Morse, a prominent citizen of the county, arrived in St. Anthony, and S. C. Robinson made Minneapolis his home this year. So did Jacob A. Wolverton and H. D. Rockey.

The merchants and business men were constantly on the alert, devising ways and means to continue in trade under the depressing circumstances that surrounded them· H. M. Carpenter, a resident of St. Anthony since 1854, exhibited a good deal of tact in conducting a large trade throughout the hard times.

As the new year approached the weather became extremely cold, but there was plenty of fuel at cheap rates.

On the third of January a union commercial association was organized in the interest of the merchants and business men of the city. The object of the association was to aid in every possible way the business men of the two cities during the stringency in money matters that prevailed in the north-west. Colonel William M. Kimball was elected president of the union ; Mayor O. Curtis, and Edward Murphy, vice-presidents ; S. W. Farnham, treasurer ; William D. Washburn, corresponding secretary ; Henry Reynolds, recording secretary ; W. D. Washburn, John S. Pillsbury, Samuel Hidden, John C. Reno, and Colonel Cyrus Aldrich, were appointed the board of directors. This organization was the source of a good deal of benefit to all classes of citizens. Its labors were on the mutual aid principle. Through the instrumentality of W. D. Washburn the citizens on both banks of the river held a series of meetings the first part of January to devise measures to induce the building of railroads leading to and concentrating at the Falls. These meetings were largely attended. Dorillus Morrison and many other prominent men participated in the deliberations.

On the 10th of January a daily stage line from the Falls to LaCrosse was established by Colonel A. Allen, and his partner Chas. L. Chase ex-secretary of the territory. This was a much-needed movement. Subsequently it was united with J. C. Burbank's line of stages.

A lodge of good templars was established in Minneapolis at this time. The officers were Rev. A. D. Williams, Paul

Fitzgerald, Miss Nellie Elliott, A. C. Weeks, D. M. G. Merrill, James F. Bradford, Hiram Van Nest, and Miss F. A. Towne. This was the first organization of the order in Minneapolis.

The iron foundry of Messrs. Scott & Morgan, in St. Anthony, was now in full operation. This was the first iron works of moment at the Falls. Mr. Morgan, one of the proprietors, afterwards became a general in the Union army. He died from the effect of injuries received in the war.

On the 14th of February Chas. K. Sherburne of Minneapolis was married to Miss Lucy, the eldest daughter of the pioneer, Deacon Allen Harmon.

NOTABLE SOCIAL GATHERING—THE PUBLIC SCHOOLS.

The residents at the Falls, natives of the middle, western, and southern states, celebrated the first of March with a grand banquet at the Nicollet. O. Curtis, Mayor of St. Anthony, represented Iowa ; Dr. B. Jodon, Maryland ; Wm. McHerron, and Chas. E. Vanderburg, New York ; David Charlton, Indiana ; Geo. W. Wilson, Virginia ; J. E. Past, Delaware ; Deacon A. M. Oliver, Missouri ; Robert W. Brown, South Carolina ; Wm. Carathuers, Tennessee ; Levi Estes, Oregon ; L. C. Walker, Illinois ; A. B. Herman; Michigan ; W. Howell Robinson, California ; Calvin A. Tuttle, Wisconsin ; Wm. K. McFarlane, and Robert W. Cummings, Pennsylvania ; C. H. Pettit, Ohio ; Captain Gonzales, Texas ; R. J. Mendenhall, North Carolina ; H. D. Beeman, Georgia ; ex-Governor W. A. Gorman, Kentucky ; Harvey Officer, Mississippi ; and Dr. J. H. Murphy, New Jersey. Socially this was a grand meeting.

Money was so scarce that the teachers in the public schools were unpaid for their services. They all resigned. This was more than the patrons of the schools could endure. A public meeting was called the last day of February to consider the matter. Judge E. B. Ames was called to the chair, and Rev. D. B. Knickerbacker acted as secretary. After active efforts by Henry T. Welles, Dr. Fletcher, Colonel Aldrich, J. B. Bassett, Dr. Ames, Charles Hoag, D. M. Coolbaugh, Deacon James Sully, A. Bradford, H. S. Plummer, Deacon Harmon, Rev. D. B. Knickerbacker, Prof. Stone, F. R. E. Cornell, and Edward Murphy, the school was relieved of its financial difficulties. Even at this early day the union school was the pride of Minneapolis.

Lumbermen were made happy by the cheerful news, early in March, that pine logs would bring seven dollars per thousand in the lower markets. This was a considerable advance over the prices of the previous year.

A union gathering in Minneapolis was held February 14th, Hon. Martin McLeod in the chair. Most of the prominent citizens were present. Speeches were made by Messrs. Cornell, Vanderburgh, E. M. Wilson, Henry T. Welles, and others.

A novel organization was perfected in St. Anthony on the 13th of March, by the young folks. It was known as the juvenile society. The officers were L. P. Foster, Hattie Heaton, Frank O'Brien, Aggie Day, Rachel M. Chaffee, James Fall, Chas. H. Slocum, Samuel A. Lewis, and G. B. Whedden·

On the 31st of March Harlow A. Gale was appointed county auditor, in place of H. O. Hamlin, resigned. This was the commencement of Mr. Gale's public services in Minnesota. He has been true to every trust, and and all his labors have been in the interests of the city, county and state, as well as in the interest of morality. All classes are better for Mr Gale's advent into this city in 1856, from which period he. has made his home in Minneapolis.

In consequence of the hard times, the news of the gold discoveries at Pike's Peak was received this early summer with delight by many citizens at the Falls. They sent Isaac I. Stevens over to the mines to make a thorough examination of the mines and report. The result was that from sixty to one hundred persons left the Falls for the new El Dorado. Most of them, in time, returned to this state.

At the Annual municipal election in St. Anthony O. Curtis was re-elected Mayor by a small majority over D. E. Moulton. J. B. Gilbert, Richard Grover, and J. C. Foster, supervisors ; J. H. Pearl, clerk ; the other town officers elected were Dr. S. H. Chute, David Edwards, and Wm. M. Lashelle.

In Minneapolis Colonel Aldrich, A. J. Bell, and J. S. Malbon, were elected supervisors. The other officers were H. C. Keith, Collin Hamer, Cyrus Snow, G. D. Richardson, Amos Clarke, and J. C. Williams.

The dreadful state of affairs in the financial world made the people, in some instances, desperate. Suicides were frequent. Murders were committed, and murderers were lynched, in Wright and LeSueur counties. Fatal accidents frequently occurred. Executions against property for debts were numerous. Richard Strout, sheriff of Hennepin county, had placed in his hands judgments for eighty thousand dollars from the time he assumed his office on January 1st up to April 10th, against debtors. Of this amount he collected twenty thousand dollars.

Two new papers were established in Minneapolis this spring, the Atlas, by Col. Wm. King; and the Plaindealer, by H. E. Purdy. The Atlas was Republican, and the Plaindealer Democratic. Both were conducted with talent. It was a fortunate thing for this city, and for the state, when Colonel King made his home in Minneapolis.

Dr. A. E. Ames was appointed this spring associate commissioner of the court of claims for Minnesota.

The fourth session of the annual Methodist conference was convened in St. Anthony May 4th, Bishop Baker presiding. Rev. J. O. Rich was assigned to Minneapolis, and Dr. Cyrus Brooks to St. Anthony.

On the 24th of May Bayard Taylor commenced a series of lectures in the two cities.

The Minneapolis postmaster, Wm. P. Ankeny, was married May 11, in Schellsburg, Pennsylvania, to Miss E. M. Schell.

Ginseng suddenly became an important article of commerce this spring. That root was about the only commodity in Minnesota that readily brought cash. Large quantities were sold in the Minneapolis and St. Anthony markets. The big woods was full of the plant, and the gathering of it enabled the farmers to pay their taxes. It also enabled them to pay their debts to the merchants. It afforded quite a relief to the citizens during the trying times of the panic. Benj. S. Bull, a resident of Minneapolis since 1855, erected a commodious dry-house with the proper conveniences for preparing the ginseng for the Chinese market.

Misfortunes still attended some of the enterprises of the twin cities. The upper and lower bridges were destroyed by the high water on June 3d. There was only one hour's difference in their destruction; the one at 8 p. m., and the

other at 9 p. m.   Besides the loss in the bridges, the high
water in the river seriously damaged the mills and booms.
It was claimed that the river was the highest ever known at
the Falls.

Meetings were held in both cities in regard to the railroads.
Judge Meeker, Judge David Morgan, and others, participated
in them.

Dr. Chas. W. Borup, a pioneer, and a prominent business
man, died in St. Paul May 6th.

Messrs. Chase and C. C. Secombe commenced the erection
of a paper-mill in St. Anthony this season, the first in the
state.   It was completed during the year, and the enterprise
proved a successful one.

The water in the northwestern rivers was unusually high
this summer.   The steamer Anson Northrup went through
Big Stone Lake and Lake Traverse to the Red river of the
north.   The Hudsen Bay company, and J. C. Burbank of St.
Paul, purchased the boat.   This was the beginning of a large
trade by steamers on the Red river of the north.

Rev. Dr. Horace Bushnell, the distinguished New England
divine, arrived in St. Anthony in August, and remained in the
vicinity for many months.

Politics ruled supreme in Minnesota from August to
October, in consequence of it being the occasion of the second
state election.

There being no woolen mills in Minnesota, Messrs. Chas.
Hoag and John P. Plummer were obliged to send their wool
crop to Cedar Rapids, Iowa, a distance of over four hundred
miles, to be made into cloth.

A mechanics' institute was organized in St. Anthony Sept.
8, with Messrs. M. W. Getchell, H. W. Gould, Dr. J. H.
Murphy, John B. Gilfillan, and H. B. Taylor, as officers.

D. B. Dorman, a leading banker, was accidentally shot
while on a hunting expedition.   The wounds were of such a
severe character that they disabled him for life.   He died
many years since.

The state was full of imported orators.   Speeches from the
stump were of an every-day occurrence.   Among those of a
national reputation who canvassed the state were Senator John
P. Hale of New Hampshire, Speaker Grow of Pennsylvania,

Frank Blair of Missouri, Governor Willard of Indiana, and many others.

The state fair was held jointly with the Hennepin county fair, in Minneapolis, October 5, 6 and 7. Judge M. Sherburne delivered the annual address. The officers elected for 1860 were Chas. Hoag, president ; A. Jackson Bell, secretary.

Dr. C. L. Anderson, who accompanied Hon. W. H. Noble into the Rocky mountains as geologist, returned from the expedition. Dr. Anderson reported important discoveries of mineral wealth in the Rocky mountains. This was before the days of very much mining in what is now Montana and Idaho.

On the 8th of October six persons were drowned in Minnetonka, among whom were Martin B. Stone and wife and two children.

At the annual fall election this year Col. Cyrus Aldrich of Minneapolis was elected to congress, while L. Bostwick of St. Anthony was elected judge of probate of Hennepin county. The other county officers chosen were Joseph Dean, treasurer; Harlow A. Gale, auditor ; General Bartholomew of Richfield, and Jesse Bishop of Minneapolis, senators ; J. P. Abraham, H. E. Mann, A. C. Austin, and Irvin Shrewsbury, members of the house of representatives. In St. Anthony David Heaton was elected senator, and D. A. Secombe and Geo. P. Baldwin, members of the house. Chas. E. Vanderburgh was elected judge of the district court. He has been continuously on the bench, district and supreme, ever since.

November 1st W. A. Croffut sold his half of the Evening News to Uriah Thomas. He returned to New England and commenced the publication of another paper.

November 2d H. H. Hopkins started down the river from Murphy's landing with a large flat-boat loaded to the guards with Minnesota products, which he sold at good rates in the southern markets. This was the first venture of the kind from Minnesota. It proved a profitable one.

Mr. Collins Hamer, the Hennepin county official, had in November a serious adventure with a bear in Carver county.

On the 17th of the month Rev. D. B. Knickerbacker was made rector of the church of Gethsemane, by Bishop Whipple. Rev. H. M. Nichols was called to the pastorate of the Plymouth church at about the same time—Rev. Norman Mc-

Leod, the first pastor, having accepted a call in Wisconsin.
J. M. Brewer, a prominent business man, died in St.
Anthony November 30. He was a son of Dr. Luther M.
Brewer of Wilbraham, Massachusetts.

November 24th Chas. M. Cushman was married by Rev.
Mr. Nichols to Miss Em. S. Clarke.

The Minnesota Beacon, a temperance and agricultural
paper, made its appearance the 1st of December, Messrs.
Hyde & Williams, proprietors and editors. During December
there was quite a perceptible improvement in money matters.
A good crop had been raised in Minnesota. The merchants
were more prosperous in the two cities. In St. Anthony
such business men as Josiah H. Chase, H. M. Carpenter,
Thos. F. Andrews, and John S. Pillsbury, introduced large
stocks of goods, and many Minneapolis merchants, including P. H. and Anthony Kelly, so well known, followed in
the footsteps of their friends in St. Anthony. The medical
fraternity were fortunate in the latter city by the addition of
Dr. S. F. Rankin to their number. Minneapolis also received
valuable citizens in the persons of the three Harrison
brothers and their families and friends who accompanied them.
There were others who came to the Falls this year, including
Hon. O. C. Merriman, and Wm. E. Jones, who have proved
to be among the best in the land. On the whole a slight
increase in the population was observable; perhaps sufficient
to make good the decrease caused by those who emigrated
on account of the hard times the previous year.

The vote was 3,130 cast in Hennepin county at the fall
election, of which St. Anthony polled 981, Minneapolis 852,
and the county outside of the cities 1,297.

Captain Merriman and Wm. E. Jones, two of the new
arrivals, became largely interested in lumber. Both were
called to high municipal and other offices, which they filled
with satisfaction to their constituents. Captain Jonathan
Chase, who preceded Messrs. Merriman and Jones to the
county, also became an extensive lumberman, and has
repeatedly held high positions with honor and fidelity to his
trusts.

CHAPTER XLII.

A MOVEMENT TO UNITE ST. ANTHONY AND MINNEAPOLIS.

Early in the year 1860 there was a very general movement by residents on both sides of the river towards uniting the two cities under one municipal government. The question was whether a first-class city should exist at the Falls, or two rival towns. At a public meeting held in the court-house with Col. Wm. M. Kimball in the chair, and Mayor R. R. Graves of St. Anthony, secretary, Mr. Cornell offered a series of resolutions in favor of a single, simple, inexpensive town-government. Dr. Chute thought that not only the two cities should be united, but he had a plan to organize a new county to consist of only the united city ; having only one set of officers to perform all the duties of city and county. Mr. Hoag offered a resolution declaring that the name of the city when united should be Minneapolis. This, he said, would secure votes in favor of the union from those who were now opposed to it. Mr. Murphy hoped the consideration of the name would be postponed until it was decided whether it would be for the interests of the people to have a union. Mr. Hoag replying to Mr. Murphy's remarks contended that Minneapolis, under her name, had grown twice as fast as St. Anthony. It was the county-seat, and to retain the name would require no changes in the papers already recorded. In common with nine-tenths of the people he preferred the name ; first for euphony ; second, because St. Anthony has no significance ; and third, because Minneapolis is named twice throughout the world, where St. Anthony is named once. Minnesota contains more saints, in name, than any other state in the Union. Mr. Bradley told the story of Polly Jones, and thought we had better wait for the wedding before we cried about the name. Deacon Harmon had yet to learn what Minneapolis is to gain by the union. In reference to the name to be given to the united city, Mr. Cornell said that he did not like either St. Anthony or Minneapolis. They were too long for convenience. Rev. Dr. Horace Bushnell had been invited to be present at the meeting, and he said he never declined an invitation to a wedding. The first thing that struck him with surprise on coming here was the rivalry and jealousy by which these two cities were nullifying their influence. Just as a family, if John and James are always quarrelling, the family influence is gone. With the two towns made into one, there would be twenty times more influence. The present policy is a killing one. Make a park of Nicollet island after the union. If a new name is to be selected, he would suggest Minneaut, or Minneanton. If neither of these suited, try · Minneanthony. Hon. E. M. Wilson was in favor of the union of the two cities at some future time—but not now. Possibly the postoffice would have to be on Nicollet island. When the toll on the suspension-bridge was abolished, then would be the proper time to agitate the movement. Dr. Boutillier said the citizens of St. Anthony had been forced to an annexation to Hennepin county ; now they were in favor of an annexation of the two towns. After further consultation, a committee on names was selected, consisting of Charles Hoag, Dr. A. E. Ames, E. M. Wilson, R. J. Baldwin, Edward Murphy, Nath. Kellogg, R. W. Cummings, A. Blakeman, Dr. Boutillier, end Dr. H. Bushnell. A committee to draft a charter was also appointed. Messrs. F. R. E. Cornell, R. J. Baldwin, E. B. Ames, H. B. Hancock, Henry T. Welles, John Rollins, Henry Hetchman, N. H. Hemiup, and E. A. Raymond, were appointed members of it ; when the meeting adjourned for two days. During the adjournment the excitement became great ; several meetings were held, and unquestionably the movement would have been successful could an agreement have been made in regard to the name of the to be consolidated city. The citizens of St. Anthony insisted on .St. Anthony, and those on the west side of the river wanted Minneapolis ; hence after a good deal of work, excitement and bad-blood, the movement failed, simply because neither side would yield the name of its favorite city.

Edwin Clarke, one of the proprietors of the Evening News, was married New Years day to Miss Ellen F. Rowe.

It was extremely sickly at the commencement of the New Year. There were many cases of malignant typhoid fever. Rev. Mr. Hyde, Harlow A. Gale, Hon. J. P. Abraham, and many others, suffered from the disease.

A new board of regents was appointed by Governor Ramsey, consisting of John M. Berry of Rice county, Jared Benson of Anoka, E. O. Hamlin of Benton, Col. Wm. M. Kimball and Uriah Thomas of Hennepin.

Rev. A. D. Sanborn, of Dodge county, was called to the Free-Will Baptist church in Minneapolis. Business was unusually dull during the winter. Merchants, bankers, mechanics, professional as well as laboring men, were greatly discouraged. A law passed the legislature reorganizing the Minnesota agricultural society. On the fifth of March an election was held in St. Paul for the officers of the society, which resulted in the choice of the old officers, viz.: Charles Hoag for president, J. H. Baker of Blue Earth for secretary, and J. W. Selby of Ramsey for treasurer.

Early in the spring J. B. Bassett & Co. purchased the pail and tub factory from Messrs. Harmon & Eaton, in Minneapolis.

The Minneapolis Athenæum was incorporated by law April 2d. The first officers were E. S. Jones, president ; Thomas Hale Williams, librarian and secretary ; the other officers were David Morgan, Wm. F. Russell, J. S. Young, and Col. Aldrich. At that time the library contained only three hundred volumes

At the spring election in St. Anthony R. P. Graves was elected mayor, and John B. Gilfillan, city attorney ; D. Edwards, assessor ; John Babcock, treasurer ; Solon Armstrong and John Henry, trustees. This was Mr. Gilfillan's first office of moment. Through subsequent years, by his talent, honesty and faithful service, he was honored with many high trusts, and was elected to congress.

The officers elected in Minneapolis were Daniel Bassett, B. F. Baker, and M. S. Hoblitt, supervisors ; Cyrus Beede, treasurer ; Cyrus Snow, town-clerk ; Collins Hamer, assessor ;

J. C. Williams and J. F. Bradley, city justices ; the other officers were J. M. Anderson, David Morgan, Joseph LeDuc, and E. S. Jones.

April 5th the Congregational church building was burned. It was the work of an incendiary. There was much excitement in regard to its destruction. On the following day the people met in mass convention, with Dr. Levi Butler in the chair, to devise measures for the discovery and punishment of the parties who set fire to the building.

John S. Pillsbury, Dr. J. H. Murphy, O. T. Swett, C. Crawford, William Lochran, Richard Fewer, Henry Hetchman, and E. W. Cutter, were the members of the new board of aldermen in St. Anthony, though some of them had previously held seats in the board. This was the real commencement of the official life of Mr. Pillsbury. He served his apprenticeship in official duties as an alderman in the ancient town of St. Anthony, and eventually held for several terms the highest office in the gift of the people of Minnesota. It is unnecessary to say that he made a good alderman. Mr. Lochran, who has so faithfully served the people in many high trusts, also commenced his official life as an alderman in St. Anthony. He was a good member of the board. For that matter, all the other members were good ones. Ex-mayor W. W. Wales was the city clerk for that year.

The new board of regents of the University met in St. Paul April 5th and organized by the election of Gov. Alex. Ramsey as president, Col. W. M. Kimball as treasurer, and Uriah Thomas as secretary.

A. A. Clement leased the Nicollet house this spring.

Messrs. Robert W. Cummings, Dr. H. Fletcher, William Finch, Dennis Schmitz, and J. B. Hinckley, were elected county commissioners under the new law, at a special election in April, for Hennepin county.

Hon. U. S. Willey, a leading lawyer and member of the house of representatives in this state, died at Forest city. Colonel Willey had formerly resided in Minneapolis.

During the recent session of the legislature a law was enacted in relation to educational matters of the city, giving power to the board that had not been previously given to the trustees of the district-school. At the first election held in

May of this year, Orrin Curtis was elected president of the board ; C. Crawford, secretary ; and Dr. S. F. Rankin, treasurer. Great progress was made in the education of the children under this organization. Prof. Chase was elected a member of the corps of teachers of the union schools in Minneapolis this spring.

June 1st Wm. S. Chapman was appointed deputy U. S. marshal for Hennepin county, in which capacity he was to take the census of Hennepin county.

On the 10th of June the whole row of buildings from First street to Second street was destroyed by fire. This was the most extensive fire that had ever occurred in the state.. The sufferers were Martin Ferrant, W. R. Johnson, L. Ford, H. D. Wheelock, D. Y. Jones & Co., J. Miller, John I. Black, C. B. Sanborn, Amos Clarke, Dr. A. L. Bausman, C. S. Webster, Isaac B. Edwards, Hopper & Gould, Curtis H. Pettit, John Lee, L. H. Williams, J. H. Thompson, Samuel Hidden, Vrooman & Crocker, Dr. Wm. H. Leonard & Co., B. F. Baker, John E. Bell & Co., Wheeler & Nutting, Gale & King, and Thomas Hale Williams.

July 1st Geo. Galpin's new boat steamed from Excelsior to Wayzata. This was the first steamboat navigation on Lake Minnetonka.

On the 4th day of July an accident occurred at Lake Calhoun, which carried sorrow and mourning to almost the entire community at the Falls. The pastor of the Congregational church, Rev. H. M. Nichols his wife, and son aged twelve years ; his brother-in-law, Hon. Arba Cleveland, and his two children aged eleven and thirteen years, were drowned in the lake. Mr. Nichols was one of the most pleasing speakers of the day, and greatly respected by all classes.

On the 8th, Frank, only son of O. C. Merriman, died in St. Anthony.

On the 22d of July Rev. Joseph R. Manton, of Quincy, Illinois, occupied the pulpit of the First Baptist church. Afterwards Mr. Manton became pastor of the church, and has continually been a resident of Hennepin county since.

On the 24th, James R. Lawrence, the district-attorney, who resided in St. Anthony, moved to Chicago.

Political clubs of every description were organized in Hennepin county this year. There was a Lincoln club, a Douglas club, a Breckenridge club, a Bell club, in favor of the candidates for President, in almost every township. The liveliest organization at the Falls was the Wide-Awakes, which the warm winds of August incubated. Among the members were Geo. A. Brackett, John G. Williams, Harlow A. Gale, Dr. A. L. Bausman, Benj. S. Bull, F. R. E. Cornell, David C. Bell, Wm. S. King, C. H. Pettit, O. M. Laraway, J. D. Gray, Collins Hamer, John E. Bell, with Samuel C. Gale for president, and J. W. Wolverton for secretary.

Loren Fletcher came to the city this summer and purchased an interest in the dry-goods store of L. F. Allen.

On the 13th of August Mrs. Dr. Fletcher, one of the pioneer ladies of Minneapolis, died.

ABOLITION EXCITEMENT.

On the 21st great excitement was caused at the Falls, and for that matter throughout the state, in consequence of W. D. Babbitt, a Mrs. Gates, and Mrs. Gray making complaint before the district court that one Eliza O. Winston, a slave, the property of Col. R. Christmas of Issaquena, Mississippi, was restrained of her liberty by her master, at the residence of Mrs. Thornton, Lake Harriet, where the parties were temporarily residing. The writ was placed in the hands of the sheriff, Richard Strout, for service and that officer brought Eliza and Col. Christmas before Judge Vanderburgh. F. R. E. Cornell appeared for the complainants. Col. Christmas made no attempt at a defense, when the court ordered the girl to be discharged from the custody of the sheriff; after which Col. Christmas asked the girl if she would go with him, and she replied that she would. In the meantime Messrs. Babbitt; Bigelow, and others, gathered around her. Colonel Christmas asked her a second time if she would return with him to her mistress. She said she would, but not at that time, and would go out to Mrs. Thornton's the next day. She left the court-house in company with the complainants, and it is supposed made her way to Canada.

The Methodist annual conference was held this year in Red Wing. Rev. J. F. Chaffee was assigned for the year to Minneapolis, and Rev. John W. Clipper to St. Anthony.

The Wide-Awakes had done such good service in Minneapolis, that the Republicans perfected an organization in St Anthony with D. A. Secombe, president, and H. O. Hamlin, secretary.

On the 17th of September, Senator Wm. H. Seward, Chas. Francis Adams, and General Nye, visited Minneapolis.

The state fair was held at Fort Snelling September 26, 27 and 28. The annual address was delivered by Cassius M. Clay of Kentucky. The officers were Charles Hoag, president, J. H. Baker secretary, and W. F. Wheeler superintend't.

October 10th John L. Lovejoy, a prominent citizen, died in St. Anthony, greatly regretted.

At the general election held November 6th, 1860, 2,525 votes were polled in Hennepin county, against 3,130 the previous year. The officers elected were John A. Armstrong, sheriff ; Geo. W. Chowen, register of deeds ; Harlow A. Gale, auditor ; S. H. King, surveyor ; Geo. E. H. Day, coroner ; L. Bostwick, court-commissioner ; W. W. McNair, county-attorney ; and Rufus J. Baldwin was elected senator, and F. R. E. Cornell, and W. Hayden, members of the house. On the east side David Heaton was elected senator. St. Anthony being attached to Anoka and Isanti counties, the members of the house were from those counties. A new board of county commissioners was elected for 1861, consisting of Ezra Hanscombe, James Sully, A. Blakeman, J. B. Hinkley, and William Finch.

On the 20th of November Hon. Martin McLeod died at his Oak Grove residence, aged 47 years.

Navigation closed this year on the 24th day of November.

On the 27th of this month the daily Atlas made its appearance in Minneapolis, and a few days afterward the St. Anthony evening News resumed its daily, while the Plaindealer was moved from Minneapolis to La Crescent.

The vote in the county was 605 less than the previous year. There were few additions to the population by immigration. On the other hand many persons belonging to the floating population left the county. This was in consequence of the continuation of the dreadful stringency in the money market. About all the transactions in real-estate were forced sales, in which the courts had almost complete control. Mortgage foreclosures were numerous.

Alonzo H. Beal established this year a first-class photograph gallery.

The shrinkage in the value of property at the Falls since September, 1857, had been marvelous, but at the close of 1860 a reaction had taken place ; at least prices in real-estate had reached the bottom, and from that period a gradual increase in the price of real-estate was observable. Richard Martin, esq., the first banker in St. Anthony, having established his business in that city as early as 1854, loaned large sums of money, much of it secured on real-estate. In time he collected his loans. In October, 1857, Messrs. J. K. Sidle & Co. opened in Minneapolis a similar business to that of Mr. Martin in St. Anthony. This firm also loaned out large sums of money without meeting any loss in their transactions. These facts are only mentioned for the purpose of showing that the crisis from 1857 to 1860, severe as it was, did not totally destroy the business at the Falls.

As the new year approached the citizens of the two cities made the usual arrangements for lectures and lyceums for the winter months. The strictest economy was observed in all matters, to the extent of giving up many of the luxuries of life. Hard times ruled supreme.

CHAPTER XLIII.

The first day of the year was generally observed as a holiday by the people of the two cities. At the annual meeting of the board of trade Joel B. Bassett was elected president, Edward Murphy and Orrin Curtis, vice-presidents ; Owen T. Swett, O. M. Larraway, J. H. Talbot, Joseph Van Enman, and J. B. Bassett, directors. The news of the firing of the first gun on Fort Sumter, January 9th, by the South Carolina authorities, was received by telegraph on the evening of that day. The universal sentiment of all parties found expression at the Falls in " The Union must and shall be preserved !" and from that eventful evening until the close of the war, St. Anthony, Minneapolis, and Hennepin county, as well as the whole state of Minnesota, did their whole duty.

On January 17th J. Fletcher Williams, who had been city editor of the Minnesotian, presented his valedictory to the readers of that paper and transferred his pen to the Pioneer.

A military company was organized in Minneapolis with W. D. Washburn, captain ; H. A. Partridge, Fred Chalmers, and C. H. Woods, lieutenants.

The annual meeting of the state agricultural society was held • in St. Paul, February 4th. Charles Hoag was re-elected president ; L. M. Ford, secretary ; J. W. Selby, treasurer ; executive committee, Gen. Alex. Chambers, Wm. L. Ames, J. H. Baker, Jared Benson, John W. North, and John H. Stevens.

Baldwin Brown, who came to St. Anthony with his stepfather, John Hingston, in 1849, and who has been one of the most useful citizens from that day to this, commenced building a steamboat for the upper river trade. This enterprise gave employment to many workmen during the dull times of that severe winter While the people on both sides of the river were obliged to use the utmost economy, they contributed for those who were worse off than they in this world's goods. When news was received that there was great suffering in Kansas for want of food, Dr. Murphy, J. C. McCain, David Lewis, W. Bowman, John Rollins, Richard Chute, and Dr. S. H. Chute, in St. Anthony, and E. S. Jones, Daniel Bassett, H. L. Birge, and Geo. W. Chowen, in Minneapolis, were appointed a committee to raise funds for the relief of the people of Kansas. The joint committee had the pleasure of sending over one thousand dollars to that section of the Union. This would be considered but a pittance these days, but then a thousand dollars was equal to many thousands now.

On the 17th of February the publication of the daily edition of the Atlas was discontinued.

February 23 Rev. E. D. Neill resigned the office of chancelor of the University.

In view of the fact that new postmasters would be appointed in the two cities by the incoming administration, soon after the 4th of March the republicans held elections for a choice. The result in St. Anthony was : W. W. Wales 108 votes, L. H. Lennon 89 votes ; in Minneapolis, John S. Walker 283, D. Bassett 193, Cyrus Snow 12, and Captain Putnam 9. President Lincoln appointed D. Heaton in St. Anthony. David Morgan was appointed in Minneapolis. He was not a candidate before the people.

The people of the two cities were kindly remembered by the administration after the 4th of March, as John Hutchinson, a resident of Minneapolis, received the appointment of secretary of Dakota, and W. D. Washburn was made surveyor-general of Minnesota, while Lucius C. Walker of St. Anthony was appointed agent of the Chippewa Indians.

At the annual spring election in St. Anthony Hon. O. C. Merriman was elected mayor ; D. B. Bowman, treasurer ; D. Edwards, assessor ; J. H. Noble, marshal ; Chas. F. Stimson, supervisor ; Messrs. Peter Weingart, Richard Fewer, Qwen T. Swett, and J. S. Pillsbury, re-elected aldermen. Members of the board of school directors were S. H.

Chute, J. B. Gilbert, and Charles Henry. The election of town officers in Minneapolis, held April 2d, resulted in the choice of Collins Hamer, chairman ; and J. H. Thompson, and E. B. Ames, supervisors ; Geo. A. Savory, clerk ; D. R. Barber, assessor ; and J. P. Howlett, treasurer.

The large mill owned by J. B. Bassett was burned April 2. There was some 4,000 bushels of wheat belonging to C. Hamer and John E. Bell, stored in it, which was destroyed. I have often wondered if ever another western town suffered as much from fires as did Minneapolis.

On the 13th of April the daily evening News ceased to exist. Several years after this date I was associated in the publication of a daily and weekly newspaper with three of the young men who were on the News at the time of its suspension. I refer to Col Le Vinne Plummer, Fred. L. Smith, and Willard S. Whitemore.

The returns of the assessors this spring showed that the personal property in Hennepin county amounted to $560,366, of which St. Anthony had $146,325, and Minneapolis $302,411. Outside of the cities $11,630. The real estate in St. Anthony amounted to $800,992, in Minneapolis $1,054,812.

War was at hand, and military organizations were the order of the day. People at the Falls determined to be the first in their efforts to preserve the whole Union. For all time to come the community in this neighborhood should be proud of the noble record of the citizens of Hennepin county in the trying times of the spring and summer of 1861. A company was raised at once in St. Anthony, another in Minneapolis, the former under the command of Captain Geo. N. Morgan, the latter under Captain Harry R. Putnam. Captain Morgan became one of the most efficient officers in the army, and rapidly rose by merit to the rank of general, while Captain Putnam was transferred from the volunteer to the regular service. He too became an officer of high rank. Mayor O. C. Merriman of St. Anthony, and other influential citizens, on both sides of the river, were active in every possible way in aiding the volunteers. Captain Merriman may be properly be called the war-mayor of St. Anthony. He has ever since his residence on the east side of the river taken an active part in all measures that would be a benefit to to the vicinity of the

Falls, as well as the whole country. All party feelings were thrown aside during these exciting times. The raising of troops for the war absorbed every other interest.

In addition to those already mentioned, the following residents at the Falls received Federal appointments : Dana E. King, register of the U. S. land-office at Forest city ; Delano T. Smith, third auditor of the treasury department at Washington ; Geo. E. H. Day, Indian agent east of the Rocky mountains ; and Rev. C. G. Ames, Consul at Porto Rico.

Several parties from this vicinity had wintered in the south and were obliged to leave the confederacy in haste ; among them were Dr. Geo. H. Keith and John Kyrk.

J. Mason Eustis was appointed contractor at Fort Snelling. Messrs. Geo. A. Bracket and H. H. Brackett were associated with him.

Then, as now, wheat was a great staple at the Falls. Early in May William Blaisdell sold two thousand bushels to Messrs. Gibson & Eastman for seventy cents per bushel. At that time this was considered a large price. It was thought that in consequence of the war the price of wheat would advance, but instead of an upward tendency it fell the following fall to forty-eight cents per bushel.

On the 27th of May Daniel Bassett died. He was the father of Judge Joel B. Bassett, Daniel Bassett, jr., and Mrs. Joseph H. Canney.

At the municipal election held at Minneapolis in May S. H. Mattison was elected president of the board of supervisors. The other members of the board were J. H. Jones, John E. Bell, E. H. Davie, and E. Hedderly. There was a new school board elected this spring. The members were O. B. King, David Morgan, T. A. Harrison, Isaac Atwater, with Rev. D. B. Knickerbacker, secretary. Several new teachers were employed. The able corps were Prof. Geo. B. Stone, principal ; assistant principal, Miss L. M. Rogers, of New Hampshire ; Miss Boutwell, Miss Walcott, Miss Sarah L. Jones, Mrs. Pomeroy, Mrs. Rice, Miss Hoyt, Miss Clark, and Mr. D. Folsom.

The streets in Minneapolis were in bad condition this year. Complaints were made July 3 to president Mattison of the supervisors that the hill near Barber's on Helen and Fourth

streets was so badly gulled as to be impassable for carriages.
A person at this time would hardly suppose that there had
ever been a steep hill at the corner of Second avenue south
and Fourth street.

The deputy county-treasurer, John Morrison, died July 14.
Nathan Herrick sold to farmers 24 reapers up to July 14.
He was the pioneer in the farm-implement and marble business.

Loren Fletcher became associated about this time with
Chas. M. Loring. This progressive firm became prominent.

The Downs brothers, Henry, Thomas and John who had for
several years resided with their parents at Lake Calhoun, now
took honorable rank as citizens in business for themselves.

Business on the west bank of the river was increased during
the season in additions to the retail trade by John I. Black,
John E. Bell, and others, and merchant tailoring establishments by J. H. Thompson and Peter Schrappel.

Cyrus Aldrich, M. C., appointed David Cooper Bell, of the
firm of John E. Bell & Co., his private secretary. This took
Mr. Bell to Washington, where a new phase of life was opened
to him during that stormy congress. He became a prominent
citizen of Minneapolis, and his good deeds will be held in lasting remembrance. He has borne an honorable part in the
upbuilding of this great city from a frontier village. On his
father's side, he is of Scotch-Irish stock. On his mother's
side he is of New England ancestry, and his grandfather
Owen Cooper lived to complete a full century, having passed
his one hundredth birthday.

September 1st Samuel Thatcher of St. Anthony died. In
his death the pioneers in this vicinity met with a great loss.

OFFICERS ELECTED IN EIGHTEEN HUNDRED AND SIXTY-ONE.
The officers elected for the year in Hennepin county were
A. Blakeman, Henry S. Plummer, D. R. Barber, Wm. Finch,
and J. B. Hinckley, county commissioners; N. H. Hemiup,
judge of probate; H. O. Hamlin, clerk of the district court;
John S. Walker, county-treasurer; and Isaac Brown, coroner.
For the legislature, Rufus J. Baldwin, senator; F. R. E.
Cornell, and John C. Past, members of the house of repre-
sentatives. St. Anthony, David Heaton, senator; Jared
Benson and J. H. Allen, members of the house.

There were several changes in the newspapers during the

fall. J. B. King and Geo. D. Bowman were at one time editors
of the Atlas. On the 30th of October the old Express was
sold, root and branch, to John L. Macondald of Belle Plaine,
who issued the Enquirer with the old material. This was Mr.
Macdonald's first enterprise in Minnesota. He has since been
state senator, member of the state house of representatives,
judge of the district court, and member of congress.

A DOUBLE-WEDDING.

On the 4th of November there was a double-wedding in
Minneapolis. Mr. Lucius A. Babcock was married to Miss
Ellen M. Sully, and Mr. Seymour L. Fillmore was married to
Miss Annie Sully. The brides were sisters, and daughters of
Deacon James Sully of Minneapolis.

Mr. Fillmore enlisted in the volunteer service of the war
for the Union, and died of camp-fever at Nashville, Tennessee.

Mr. Babcock also entered the Union army, was wounded
at the battle of Guntown, Mississippi, and died in Andersonville prison on the second birthday of his son Charles N.
Babcock who is now an excellent lawyer in Minneapolis.
He was buried in the Andersonville cemetery. His eldest
brother was a brigadier-general of Northern troops, was
wounded while leading a charge at the battle of Winchester,
and died after having both legs amputated. The youngest
and only remaining brother, a lieutenant in the Union army,
was killed at the battle of Gettysburg. The Babcock brothers
were cousins of Judge Isaac Atwater.

Mrs. Fillmore and Mrs. Babcock reside in Minneapolis
to-day, one in and the other near their early home.

In addition to those already in the field, there were, during
the summer and autumn, a great many soldiers enlisted in the
volunteer service from St. Anthony and Minneapolis, as well
as from Hennepin county. Dr. Levi Butler raised a whole
company from the county precincts, for the Third regiment,
and there were equally as many more enlisted in the Second
regiment which was organized early in July, and a number of
men were sent during the year to the First regiment.

CHAPTER XLIV.

MR. AND MRS. M. N. ADAMS AS MISSIONARIES AND OLD-SETTLERS.

GOODWILL MISSION, SISSETON AGENCY, SOUTH DAKOTA,
May 24th, 1889.

In compliance with your most reasonable request, I would respectfully submit the following statement of facts, to wit : I was born February 14th, 1822, at Sandy Springs, Adams county, Ohio ; received my collegiate education at Ripley, and my theological training at Lane Theological Seminary, Cincinnati, Ohio, graduating in June, 1848.

Mrs. Adams, whose maiden name was Rankin, daughter of James Rankin, was born December 19th, 1827, near Knoxville, East Tennessee ; educated at Ripley, Ohio, and Mission Institute, Quincy, Illinois, where we were married July 9th, 1848 ; and having been commissioned as missionaries of the American Board of Commissioners for Foreign Missions to the Sioux or Dakota Indians, we embarked on board of a Mississippi river steamer, for Fort Snelling, Iowa Territory, as it was then known.

On arriving at Galena, Illinois, the last of the week, we rested there until after the Sabbath, according to the Fourth Commandment ; and on resuming our journey by the first boat for St. Paul, leaving Galena, we arrived at St. Paul July 24th, 1848, and Ft. Snelling at noon the same day.

St. Paul was then only a wayside-landing, with one small trading-post, with a few trinkets and Indian curiosities in store ; and there were less than half-a-dozen resident white families there.

Fort Snelling, and H. H. Sibley's trading post at Mendota,

were then regarded as the head of navigation. Our boat, on which we shipped our household goods, and supplies for one year only, reached the foot of the island opposite Mendota, from which point the freight was transferred to Fort Snelling in barges, by the steamer's crew.

During our detention, awaiting the annual meeting of the Dakota Mission, at Kaposia, Dr. T. S. Williamson's station, in the autumn of 1848, Mrs. Adams and I applied ourselves to the study of the Sioux or Dakota language, the customs and practices and character of the natives, among whom we were to live and labor as missionaries ; and for the time being were kindly and hospitably entertained at the mission home of Rev. T. S. Williamson at Kaposia, four miles below St. Paul, on the west side of the Mississippi river.

Meantime I reconnoitered the field, visited Red Rock, and held services at St. Paul and Grey Cloud Island, reaching the latter by an overland route, on horseback, guided over a trackless prairie by a pocket-compass to a point opposite the island, where I was kindly met by one Mr. John Brown, who safely transferred me across (in a small canoe) to his island home, while I swam my horse alongside of the canoe, and in like manner returned after the Sabbath.

In like manner, in filling an appointment to preach at St. Paul, I rode on horseback to a clump of grape-vines and bushes opposite St. Paul, where I tied out my horse, and was ferried over in an Indian canoe, in the morning, and after service was returned in the afternoon in like manner by an Indian's kindness. The Divine services were then held in St. Paul in the primitive log schoolhouse. On that day (to which I especially refer) we had only about twelve adult English-speaking people, and fifteen or eighteen children, at that service ; which comprised about all the English-speaking people of that small village of St. Paul, where now there is a population of upwards of two hundred thousand—a city of schoolhouses and consecrated churches.

At another time I accompanied the venerable Dr. T. S. Williamson, who held Divine service in the house of one Hosea, a Canadian Frenchman who had married a Dakota woman, a member of the Presbyterian mission church at Lacquiparle : and at that Sabbath afternoon service, in the

Dakota language, there were only about half-a-dozen adults, and a like number of native children, present.

At that time Minneapolis, on the west side, was not founded, and no improvements there, except a small saw-mill guarded by a soldier of the U. S. army detailed on that special duty. The Falls of St. Anthony and Minnehaha were then in their primitive beauty and grandeur, and the little village of St. Anthony did not then amount to much more than a mere portage-encampment for lumbermen and fur-traders of the upper Mississippi country.

Fort Snelling was then quite a military post ; a small U. S. garrison, but important, for the national flag was there displayed, signaling the fact that there was power on the part of the U. S. government ; and that was usually respected, altho' sometimes contemned by Indian braves who gloried more in an eagle-feather of a certain description, those times, than in the Flag of our Union.

At the annual meeting of our Dakota Mission, held at Kaposia in September, 1848, it was decided that myself and wife should go to Lacquiparle mission station, and unite with Rev. S. R. Riggs in mission work among the Sisseton and Wahpeton Sioux or Dakotas of that region ; in which we most heartily concurred. Accordingly on the 19th day of September, 1848, we set out from Kaposia station via Ft. Snelling, Oak Grove, Shakopee and Traverse-des-Sioux. Owing to the want of roads, bridges and ferries, those times, this was a difficult and tedious overland route. Yet it was not without occasional episodes and little diversions ; as when a rawhide tug-strap broke and let the patient ox out, and the two-wheel cart tilt back on a steep hillside grade, dumping the wives of the missionaries, with their children, baggage and all, out in a rolling attitude toward the overflowing brook below ; and amid the cries from the frightful disaster, and the joyful exclamations that after all no one was seriously hurt, all was gathered up, restored, and the journey resumed, with heartfelt thankfulness that only that had happened us.

Then again, as we journeyed in road and without roads, we encountered one of those bottomless sloughs, partly covered over with a mere tuft of grasses, when suddenly one of our oxen broke through the grass covering and went down in the marsh, or bog, up to his sides, and bellowed like a calf for fear that would be his grave ; and our women and children fearing the same fate, jumped from the mission cart and ran from tuft to tuft until they reached terra firma ; and then, on seeing how soon we roped the poor ox and the cart out of the slough, and reloaded, concluded that that was an eventful day when we went from Oak Grove mission station to Shakopee.

But we had not crossed the Rubicon. By the time we reached the Minnesota river at Shakopee it was dark, and pouring down rain. There was, just as we expected, no bridge and no ferry there. There were, however, some Indian canoes on the opposite side of the river. After a long time we succeeded in getting an Indian to bring one or two over for us ; and lashing two canoes together, side by side, we improvised ferriage for all, except our two good, patient oxen and my horse, which we compelled to ferry themselves over, after the most primitive manner, each one swimming for himself to the other shore. Hungry, tired and sleepy, we reached the mission station at Shakopee ; were kindly received and entertained by Rev. Samuel W. Pond ; and all felt satisfied with the rich and varied experiences of the day and the journey.

From Shakopee we proceeded next on our way, and camped out two nights between Shakopee and Traverse-des-Sioux, where St. Peter is now situated. The first day we were suddenly and almost without any warning compelled, by reason of a heavy rain-storm, to go into camp ; but before we could pitch our tent and get our baggage into it, we were nearly drenched with the rainfall, and we were surrounded with a flood of water, so that it was with difficulty that we kept our blankets dry and suitable for encampment for the night. This encampment was at or near where Jordan is located.

The next day we had a tedious time making our way thro' the big woods below Le Sueur. That night one of our oxen, worn down, or disgusted with the roads, or without roads, deserted us. After two or three hours search for him the next morning, all in vain, we concluded to go on without him, leaving a hired man with the cart to bring all on the journey when the truant ox should be found, which was done the evening of the same day ; and that day we arrived safely at

Traverse-des-Sioux ; and there we rested over the Sabbath in obedience to the Fourth Commandment.

On that Sabbath day, while at Traverse-des-Sioux mission station, two events occurred to make that day memorable : First, it was a communion Sabbath, when the little band of missionaries, providentially there, celebrated the Lord's Supper, in obedience to Christ, who said to his diciples, " Do this in remembrance of me." Second, in the afternoon of that same day some natives who had been down to Mendota and St. Paul, returned with a supply of whisky, and several Indians were intoxicated, and one man was killed, only a few hundred yards from the mission station ; and but for the help of two of our young men from the mission the man who was in charge of the trading-post would have been killed by them. In attempting to rescue my horse from the danger of being shot by the intoxicated furious party, one shot from a musket was discharged at my feet, and another over my head, by an Indian too drunk to aim and fire on time, at a white man.

The next week, resuming our journey across the prairie to Lacquiparle from Traverse-des-Sioux, one hundred and twenty-five miles in a northwestern direction, after camping out four nights, we reached our destination safely, blessed with good health. Lacquiparle mission was one of the oldest mission stations of the A. B. C. F. M. among the Dakotas. A Presbyterian church of seven members was organized there by Dr. T. S. Williamson early in 1836, which in 1848 had increased to upwards of fifty members. On arriving there we at once entered upon mission-work, teaching school, having from forty to fifty day scholars, and studying the Dakota language, and reciting the same, during the evenings and mornings.

Meantime, as a matter of experiment, as well as duty and privilege, we ventured to take six native children into our family to board, lodge, teach and train, and so demonstrate the possibility, not only, but also the feasibility, of educating and training Indian children, as the right arm of the mission-work, and the hope of success, in the work of civilizing and Christianizing the Sioux or Dakotas. Nor were we disappointed as to the anticipated results. To us, it was a work as interesting as it was new and arduous. Rev. S. R. Riggs, with whom we were intimately associated in missionary work at that station, seeing the manifest success and good results of the experiment, from an attitude of toleration with many doubts and misgivings as to the work, was convinced and converted, and became a warm friend and faithful advocate of the plan and work of establishing and maintaining some such manual-labor boarding-schools as the sine qua non of missionary labor among the Dakotas, and among the aboriginal tribes of the Northwest ; and hence he subsequently ventured to establish and maintain a manual-labor boarding-school at Hazlewood station near Yellow Medicine Agency, in Minnesota ; and always, up to the day of his death, he gave me the credit of inaugurating and successfully demonstrating the practicability of such manual-labor boarding-schools among the Dakotas. Others had tried it, but failed in the attempt.

But our connection with the Dakota mission was not of long continuance— only about five years when, owing to the failure of Mrs. Adam's health, we were constrained to resign and leave that field of labor, and go East in order to secure medical treatment of Mrs. Adam's case. It pleased the Lord to bless the change of the field of our labors, and the means used for the recovery of Mrs. Adam's health, and to give us work in the Home field, in Minnesota, as at St. Peter and in that vicinity for a number of years consecutively, during the early settlement of that state ; and later, to widen the field of my labor in various departments of Christian work, and especially in preaching the Gospel of Christ; and for the period of ten years it was my privilege to preach the Gospel as Chaplain of the U. S. Army, previous to our return to the Dakotas, the people of our first love and service for the Master.

We are now, by the special and wonderful grace of God, engaged once more in mission-work, among the Dakotas. Here at Goodwill mission station we have some few of the very Indians who were at Lacquiparle, Minnesota, and whom we taught there years and years ago ; and we have here many of the children of their children, in these two manual-labor schools, that of Goodwill, and that of the U. S. Government-school, in all upwards of two hundred pupils, studious, contented, interesting and hopeful, under faithful tuition, discipline and training in knowledge and the industrial pursuits and avocations of life.

We feel assured—even if we do not fully understand all
about the way that we have been led and brought to resume
missionary labor among this people, so poor and needy—that
our labors cannot be in vain, nor all our hopes be lost or
disappointed. " Hitherto the Lord has helped us ;" and now,
after more than forty years labor and personal experience, so
varied, in the remembrance of all His love and mercy and
faithfulness, and His great and precious promises to us as in
His Holy Word, we can well afford to trust Him in time to
come.

It is a matter of deep heartfelt interest, and devout thankfulness to God, that we have been permitted, in His kind
Providence, to have some humble part in the great work of
laying the foundations of learning and religion in this the
comparatively new Northwest, and that we have witnessed the
settlement, growth and prosperity of Minnesota from the very
beginning. " Behold what God hath wrought !" '

The remembrance of our association and work with the
early settlers and pioneer friends is to us here, in our mission
home, out on the coteau des prairies of Dakota, very precious
and grateful indeed ; and from this high elevation, so near
heaven above, we do most heartily congratulate you all in the
enjoyment of your Christian homes, home-comforts, and the
manifold blessings, comforts and hopes of Christian associations and work, to the honor of Christ and the ultimate glory
of God.   Yours, very truly,   M. N. ADAMS.

CHAPTER XLV.

From the private journal of Hon. Martin McLeod we quote an account of his journey, accompanied by two British officers, with Pierre Bottineau as guide, from Pembina to Ft. Snelling :

Sunday, 26th February, 1837. Left La Fourch, Red River Colony, Territory of Hudson's Bay, in the evening, and came three miles up the settlement to prepare for an early start to-morrow to St. Peters, 750 miles from this—on foot.

Monday, Feb. 2. Started at daybreak ; cold, with a sharp head-wind. About 10 p. m. a severe snow-storm commenced ; obliged to take shelter in the house of Mr. Micklejohn. Came about nine miles ; 5 p. m. cleared off ; prospects of a fine day ; preparing snow-shoes, etc., for journey.

Tuesday, 28th. Started at daybreak ; bad walking, snow deep, crossed the long traverse and waited until the dogs came up. At 3 p. m. had to encamp ; dogs too fatigued to proceed ; dogs never travel well the first day.

Wednesday, March 1. Left encampment at sunrise ; found it exceedingly cold sleeping out after having been in the house for two months. Came forty miles to-day. Arrived at a shanty where we found fourteen persons, men, women, and children, without food. They had been living for seven days on an occasional hare and pheasant. The hunter's life is ever a precarious one. We relieved them with pemmican from our stock for the journey, which will in all probability be the cause of our fasting some days before we reach Lake Traverse, the first trading-post from this, distant more than 400 miles.

Thursday, 2d. Left shanty early ; morning pleasant ; struck off into the plain at the head of Swamp river, from thence

made a long traverse to a point on Pembina river fifteen miles
from the head, where we encamped, having come more than
forty miles to-day. This is my third day on snow-shoes, and
I feel exceedingly fatigued.

Friday, 3d. Had a cold and stormy night ; unable to leave
camp before 9 o'clock ; wind ahead until 12 o'clock, when it
changed to the north and brought with it a snow-storm which
caught us on the prairie many miles from shelter ; 3 p. m.
came to a small wood on the bend of Tongue river ; one of
our party, Mr. P., not having come up, we encamped. Mr.
P. has no snow-shoes ; he persisted in not bringing any with
him, which may yet lead to unhappy consequences, as he is
unable to keep up with us on the plains, and should we be
separated by a storm he will inevitably perish ; indeed the
poor fellow this day said that he would perish in this journey.
Feel miserably fatigued, and my feet are severely blistered
with the strings of the snow-shoes ; at every step the blood
from my toes oozes through my moccasins. We came through
a beautiful prairie to-day enclosed on three sides by woods
which can be distinctly seen from the middle of the prairie ;
on the north by the wood on Pembina river, west by Pembina mountain, south by the trees bordering Tongue river ·-
forming almost a complete circle of at least 100 miles.

March 4th. Came a long distance to-day ; snow deep and
very heavy, which clogs the snow-shoes and makes them
exceedingly fatiguing to carry. Encamped on a branch of
Park river ; find Major Long's map of the country very
incorrect.

Sunday, 5th. Encamped at 3 p. m. on a bend of the second
branch of Park river, near the coteau des prairies, having
come about fifteen miles only ; snowing fast, which obliged
us to camp. All the rivers in this country are very crooked,
and the timber growing upon their banks is in every instance
that I have seen in proportion to the size of the streams.

Monday, 6th, Bad walking ; snow deep ; encamped at 2
p. m. on Saline river, one of our party being too fatigued to
proceed. Came about eighteen miles through an immense
burnt prairie. The further southward we come the more
snow we find. Banks of the Saline very high, with timber
(elm and oak) growing down their sides to the edge of the

stream which is five yards wide. Near the mouth of the
river is a salt factory which must prove profitable as salt is
worth sixteen shillings per bushel at R. R. Settlement 250
miles hence. The water here is perfectly fresh and palatable;
it is from a small lake about twenty miles from this down-
wards that the saline flows.

March 7th. Last night excessively cold ; to-day unable to
leave camp ; so stormy that it is impossible to see the distance of ten yards on the plain, and the distance to the next
wood or place of encampment is more than thirty miles,
which would endanger our lives should we attempt to cross
the plain in the storm. Such is one of the many disadvantages encountered by the traveler in this gloomy region at
this inclement season.

March 8. Wind north and piercing cold on the prairie.
Crossed the great plain and arrived at Turtle river at 3 p. m.,
where we encamped ; came thirty miles.

March 9. Excessively cold and stormy until noon ; came
long distance to-day ; encamped long after sundown on a
branch of Goose river; feel very fatigued ; my feet cut and
swollen from the continual use of the snow-shoes which,
however, I begin to like, and prefer keeping them on where
there is but little snow, and where they might be dispensed
with ; I also find (sore as my feet are) that I travel a greater
distance in a day with than without them ; such is custom.

March 11. Unable to make the "grande traverse" (fifty
miles) to Shienne river, the day being misty, and the land-
marks which guide the traveler on the plain not visible.
Came a short distance and encamped on the lower tributary
of Goose river.

March 12. Started at daybreak, route principally on immense
hills ; not a tree or shrub visible ; saw thirteen buffaloes ;
one shot at by the guide, but not killed, though severely
wounded ; Mr. P. unable to keep up with us ; afraid to lose
him, consequently we are unable to get across the plain to a
place of encampment ; obliged to take up our place of rest for
the night in a pond among a few rushes, the only shelter for
miles around in this dreary and monotonous region. During
the past months, in moments of extreme suffering, I have
seen and felt the interposition of a ruling and merciful Prov-

dence. This evening, while we were all suffering the severest torments for want of water, and without hope of getting any for many hours, the guide espied at a distance the carcases of two buffaloes. Being a hunter himself, curiosity led him to the spot when, Lo ! to his great delight and our relief, he found a few small pieces of wood, brought there by a hunter a few days previous, by which means we were enabled to melt a kettle of snow.

March 13. Passed a more comfortable night than we had expected ; morning miserable, having to creep out from under our buffalo skins, tie on our snow-shoes, and take to the plain to warm ourselves ; no fire, no water, no breakfast. I took a small piece of frozen pemmican, and ate it with a handfull of snow, at the same time walking as fast as possible to warm myself. Soon after we started a violent storm came on ; guide said we were lost and would all perish ; advised him to take a direct course, as near as possible, and for that purpose to keep before the wind. At 3 p. m., having walked since daybreak more than thirty miles, we perceived through the drift a clump of trees, where we arrived soon after, happy to escape passing a second night on the plain, where it is more than probable we should have been all frozen to death. The guide says we did not come much out of our route, and that we are on a branch of Shienne river, called the river of rushes.

March 14. Last night so cold could not get a moment's sleep ; to-day in camp ; guide unable to go on, with sore eyes.

March 15. Last night as cold as the former ; day pleasant ; in camp ; guide still unable to "see his way".

March 16. Came through two prairies and encamped on Shienne river.

A MOST DISASTROUS TURN IN THE EVENTS OF THE DAY.

Friday, March 17th, 1837. This morning, when we left the camp, the weather was very mild and pleasant ; guide discovered tracks of a deer and went in pursuit of it ; meantime Mr. H., Mr. P. and myself, directed our course across the plain towards a point of wood on Rice river ; suddenly about 11 o'clock a storm from the north came on that no pen can describe. We made toward the wood as fast as possible ; it was distant about three miles. I was foremost, the dogs following close to me, Mr. H. not far distant, Mr. P. two miles behind. In a few moments nothing was perceptible, and it was with difficulty that I could keep myself from suffocating; however, I hastened on and in a short time caught a glimpse of the wood through a drifting cloud of snow. I was then not more than three hundred yards from it, as near as I can possibly judge. At that instant I also saw Mr. H., who had come up within thirty yards of me and called out that I was going the wrong course, exclaiming, "keep more to the right". I replied, "No, no; follow me quick." I perceived him to stoop, probably to arrange the strings of his snow-shoes. In an instant afterwards an immense cloud of drifting snow hid him from my view and I SAW HIM NO MORE. I cannot describe what my feelings then were; what must they have been in a few seconds afterwards when I found myself at the bottom of a ravine more than twenty feet deep, from which I had to use the greatest exertion to save myself from being suffocated by the snow which was drifting down upon me. Upon gaining the edge of the ravine, which I effected with the greatest difficulty, having my snow-shoes still on, as my hands were too cold to untie the strings of them, which were frozen, I found the poor faithful dogs with their traineau buried in a snow-bank. Having dug them out, my next effort was to gain the wood, which I knew was on the opposite side of the ravine about twenty yards over, yet I could not distinguish a tree, so close and thick was the snow drifting. An hour's exertion with the dogs and traineau through the deep snow in the ravine brought me into the edge of the wood, which I found was composed of only a few scattered trees, which would afford but a miserable shelter. I tried to make a fire. My matches were all wet; my hands were too cold to strike a spark with the flint and steel; what can be done? "I must not perish," said I to myself. I then thought of my companions. Alas, poor fellows! there can be no hope for you, as I have all the blankets, buffalo-robes, provisions, &c., the dogs having followed me in the storm. Having dug a hole in a snow-bank, I made a sort of shelter with my cloak and a blanket, and rolled myself in a blanket and a large buffalo-robe. I was then completely wet through, for a shower of sleet had accompanied the storm; in a few moments it began to freeze ; I was then so cold that I feared much that I should perish during the night. The night came ; the storm continued unabated ; my situation was truly miserable ; companions and guide in all probability perished ; myself in great danger of freezing also ; and in a strange country some hundred miles from any settlement or trading-post. I cannot say what I felt, although my usual feelings would raise to my relief frequently, and I would say to myself, " What is passed cannot be helped ; better luck next time ; take it coolly"— which I was evidently doing with a vengeance. The greater part of the night was passed listening to the roaring of the storm, and the dismal howling of the wolves, together with the pleasant occupation of rubbing my feet to keep them from freezing.

Saturday, 18th.   Never was light more welcome to a mortal. At dawn I crept from my hole, and soon after heard cries. Fired two shots ; soon after guide came up ; he had escaped by making a fire, and being a native, and a half-blood, his knowledge of the country and its dangers saved him. Mr. P. was found with both his legs and feet frozen. All search for Mr. H. proved ineffectual. Remained all day near the scene of our disaster in the hope that some trace of Mr. H. might be found.

Sunday, 19th. Started early with poor P. on the dog traineau, having left all our luggage behind ; at 2 p. m. found dogs unable to proceed with P., and he suffering too much to bear the pain occasioned by moving about. With the help of guide made a hut to leave Mr. P. in, where he will remain for five or six days until I can send horses for him from Lake Traverse, sixty miles from this. Left with P. all our blankets and robes, except a blanket each (guide and myself) ; also plenty of wood cut, and ice near his lodge to make water of. Out of provisions ; obliged to kill one of our dogs ; dog-meat excellent eating.

Monday, March 20. Morning stormy, accompanied with snow ; unable to leave camp till 2 p. m., when guide and myself started ; came a long distance and encamped in the Bois des Sioux ; feel very weak and unwell.

March 21. Left the Bois des Sioux at sunrise and arrived at dark at the trading-house at Lake Traverse, having traveled

forty-five miles to-day, with a severe pain in my side and knee.
March 22d. At trading-house ; feel unwell.

March 23. Sent the guide with another person and two
horses and a cart for Mr. P. and my trunk, &c, with instructions to the men to search for the body of Mr. H., in order
that it may be decently interred at the trading-house.

April 1st. For the past nine days have remained at the
trading-house, where I am well treated by Mr. Brown, the
gentleman in charge for the American Fur Company. Saw
the game of la crosse played very frequently, both by the
squaws and Indians. It is a very interesting game when well
contested, and the female players are most astonishingly
expert.

April 2d. This morning the two men returned. Poor P.
is no more. They found him in his hut, dead. He had
taken off the greater part of his clothes, no doubt in the
delirium of a fever caused by the excruciating pain of his
frozen feet. In the hut was found nearly all the wood we
left him, his food, and a kettle of water partially frozen.
Everything indicated that he died the second or third day
after our departure from him. No trace of the body of Mr.
H. was found. The poor fellow has long ere this become
food for the savage animals that prowl around these boundless wilds. Thus has miserably perished a young and amiable man at the age of twenty, in the full vigor of youth, full
of high hopes and expectations.

April 3. This day poor P. was consigned to his last abode,
the silent and solitary tomb. It is a source of consolation to
me, amid my troubles, that I have been enabled to perform
this last duty to a friend with all due respect. Would that I
could say the same of Mr. Hayes. I have, however, left
directions with all the Indians near this post to search for his
bones and inter them. They are about to depart on their
spring hunts and will in all probability find his remains. I
CAN DO NO MORE.

April 5, 1837, left Lake Traverse at 10 o'clock ; came twenty
miles through a hilly prairie, and encamped at 3 p. m.

April 6, came forty miles to-day, and encamped at Pomme
de Terre river.

Friday, April 7. Cold and stormy ; had some difficulty in

getting across Pomme de Terre river ; made the horses swim ; got the baggage and the cart across on some pieces of jammed ice ; arrived at Lacquiparle at 2 p. m.; well received by Mr. Renville, who has a trading-post for the Indians here.

Saturday, April 8.   As the weather appears unsettled, prevailed upon by Mr. R. to remain with him till Monday.   To-day visited a Mr. Williamson, a missionary sent into this country two years ago by the American Board of Foreign Missions, for the conversion of the Dakota Indians of this place.   Mr. W.'s family resides with him.   He has two assistants (a young lady, his wife's sister, and a young man who tried to convert me) in his arduous undertaking   Mr. W. can now speak a good deal of the Dakota language, and I believe has made some translations from the Bible.

Sunday, April 9.   Went to hear Mr. W. preach.   He also read a chapter from the Testament in Dakota, and a young man present another in French.   A number of the Psalms of David were sung in Dakota by half-breeds and Indians.   The audience consisted of half-breeds, Indians, Canadians, and a few whites.

Monday, April 10.—Came thirty miles ; encamped at 5 p. m. at river L'eau de vie.

April 11.   Came thirty-five miles ; encamped at 6 p. m. near the St. Peters river.   Crossed to-day Custor and Petite rivers.   Saw a great number of flocks of wild geese and swans.

April 12.   Came thirty miles ; encamped at 6 p. m. in a small grove of oaks.

April 13.   Came thirty miles ; encamped at 5 p. m. at the Monte de Sioux, at the trading-house of Mr. Provencalle.

Friday, April 14.   Embarked at sunrise in a canoe with Indians and squaws who are going down to where the St. Peters joins the Mississippi at Fort Snelling.   Have for company ten Indians and squaws, in three canoes.   These people have in one of their canoes the bodies of two of their deceased relatives, which they intend carrying to a lake near the Mississippi more than one hundred miles from this.   In many instances these people bring the bodies of their friends much farther when it is the wish of the dying person to be deposited in a particular place   At 3 p. m. obliged to encamp in consequence of rain coming on.   Here I found the benefit of a good skin-lodge, which was put up by the females in a short time, and we all got under it round a snug fire, cooked our victuals, and felt exceedingly comfortable.

Saturday, April 15. Morning rainy ; did not leave encampment till 11 o'clock ; 3 p. m. passed Petite rapids, and arrived at the trading-house of Mr. Faribault, where we stopped a few moments.

Sunday, April 16. Three p. m., at long last, have arrived at Fort Snelling, St. Peters, having escaped a variety of dangers, and endured great fatigue and privations in the Sioux country.

MEMORANDUMS.

To-day, April 20, 1837, wrote to Alex'r Christie, esq., Hon. Hudson Bay Co., giving him the particulars of my unfortunate and melancholy journey from Red river. Wrote also to Mr. Logan and Mr. Millian of Red river. May 3 sent them by Mr. Bottineau, the guide. April 22, wrote to J. R. B., Lake Traverse, requesting him to inform me of the result of the Indians' search for the remains of my unfortunate friend, Mr. Hayes. Wrote to Mr. Renville, Lacquiparle. Wrote to Mr. G. H. P., a missionary assistant at Lacquiparle.

Saint Peters, May 29th, 1837.—Saw Frenier, a half-breed Sioux from Lake Traverse, who informed me that the band of Indians who hunted this spring not far from the scene of our disaster on the 17th of March, had been unsuccessful in their search for the remains of Mr. Hayes. There cannot now be any hope of his remains being ever heard of, at least by me, as I shall leave this place in a few days hence.

THIRST IN SNOW-COVERED COUNTRIES.

Travelers have not deemed the fact worth mentioning, and therefore no one who has not suffered can imagine or believe that during the winter man is exposed on the cold and snow-covered plains of North America to the most painful of privations ; that even while walking on frozen water, he is agonized by parched and burning lips ; and that by snow, eaten under such circumstances, the thirst of the traveler or hunter is proportionally increased. When out in either of these capacities the agony sustained by them from thirst is often very great ; it is truly painful while it lasts, and contrary to the sufferer's expectation, he finds that by eating snow his mouth is more and more inflamed, and his desire for drink fearfully augmented ; while a lassitude comes over him which water only can dissipate.

It is to be observed, however, that it is only on the plains that the experienced hunter or traveler is exposed to such hardships. That occurs frequently in this country where the traveler's route is for the most part through wide plains, covered with long rank grass and snow stretched out in all directions, presenting a smooth, white, unbroken surface terminating in the horizon.

Everyone going to any distance, at this season, carries as an essential article in his equipment a small kettle in which he melts snow and boils water. To allow the water to boil is a necessary part of the process ; for if the snow is merely melted the water has a smoked and bitter taste, and a drink of it if far from refreshing. On the contrary, when the water is allowed to boil, and then cooled by throwing into it plenty of the purest snow, no spring water is more delightful to the taste or more satisfying to the wants of the thirsty traveler.

BUFFALO HUNTING IN THE WEST.

The first season of the buffalo hunting commences about the 15th of June, and is continued to the 1st of August. The second season commences in September and terminates late in the fall, generally about the 1st of November, leaving time sufficient to return home before the cold weather sets in. I allude to the Brules' hunting, as the Indians who inhabit the buffalo country kill these animals at all seasons.

The Brules usually set out with five hundred to six hundred carts, drawn principally by oxen, their wives and daughters accompanying these carts for the purpose of preparing the meat, which is done by stripping it from the bones, and spreading it upon a scaffold of poles elevated three to four feet from the ground, under which they build a fire of the buffalo dung. In this manner they continue to dry the meat as fast as it is killed by the hunters. It requires the flesh of twelve of the largest animals thus prepared to load a cart drawn by one ox ; and allowing six hundred carts to the spring season, would make seven thousand two hundred of these animals killed in about a month by the Brules alone, not including any of the various Indian tribes, such as the Sioux, the Mandans, Grosventres, &c., all of whom inhabit the buffalo country and des-

troy these animals by tnousands ; and add to this, too, that in
the spring nearly all the animals killed are cows, the meat of
the male not being good after a certain season. These different causes account for the rapid decrease of the buffalo within
the last few years. I have been informed by a Brulo hunter
that at the last hunt they had to go a journey of fifteen days
to the west, six farther than they ever went before.

In the fall hunt, besides the dried meat, they make pemmican, and also bring home a great quantity of the meat in its
natural state. The pemmican is made by drying the meat, as
I before mentioned ; it is then beaten into small pieces and
placed into a sack made of the buffalo skin, into which is poured
a quantity of the melted fat of the animal ; when it cools
it is pressed into the sack, which is sewed up ; in this
manner it will keep three or four years. The sacks are various
sizes, but the common sizes are from one hundred to one
hundred and fifty pounds.

The usual number of horsemen attending these hunts are
about five hundred ; however not more than from two to three
hundred act as hunters, and are those who possess the swiftest
horses. The hunters are exceedingly expert ; notwithstanding
which many accidents occur. I have seen many of them with
broken legs, broken arms, and disabled hands ; this latter
accident frequently occurs from their manner of loading their
guns. They never use wadding. The powder is carelessly
thrown in, in more or less quantities, the ball is then tumbled
in upon it, and off goes the shot. This is done to save time,
and it is almost incredible what a number of shots one person
will discharge in riding the distance of three or four miles,
the horse at the top of his speed.

A gentleman who has lived many years in the buffalo country
says that upon the least calculation four to five hundred
thousand of these animals are killed yearly on this side of the
Missouri.

ASSINIBOIN BELIEF IN FUTUIRTY.

The Assiniboins believe that in another life to obtain enduring happiness they have to climb a very high and steep
mountain, the ascent of which is so difficult and dangerous
that it requires many attempts, perseverance, and great fortitude to gain the summit ; but once there, a delightful and

boundless plain is spread before them, covered with eternal verdure and countless herds of buffalo and the other animals which they delight to hunt ; and that they will find all their friends who left this life before them, enjoying an uninterrupted course of happiness, dwelling in beautiful skin tents which ever appear new.

Those who have done ill in this life and have been successful enough to gain the summit of the hill, are there met by the dwellers of the happy plain, and those who knew them in this life bear witness against them. They are then immediately thrown down the steep, and should their necks not be broken, never again attempt an ascent.

Those who have done good in this life are welcomed with universal joy, and immediately admitted to all the privileges of their never-ending hunting and happiness.

This is equal to the Happy Valley in Rasselas.

JOURNEY ALONG THE SOUTHERN SHORE OF LAKE SUPERIOR.

In October, 1836, Mr. McLeod made the journey from Sault St. Marie, following the lake shore by boat to the now Minnesota territory, which he crossed to the Red river of the North. Of this journey we quote from his daily record of the events :

The distance from the Sault to La Point is 450 miles as we had to come (that is, by the coast). We are yet sixty miles from La Point, consequently have been twenty-four days coming 390 miles. In this route we met with many dangers. At this season the great lake is continually in a state of agitation, and a batteau with twenty-one persons and provisions in it is a no difficult thing to swamp—a misfortune which we luckily escaped a number of times.

In making the traverse of twenty-one miles at Long Point we fortunately got a few hours of fair weather, but no sooner had we crossed than there sprang up a breeze which would have immortalized us all in a very few moments. The Indians wait a number of days for good weather to pass this dangerous traverse ; they then paddle their canoes some distance from the shore and commence singing a hymn to the Great Spirit, entreating him to give them fair weather until they have crossed over ; after which men, women, and children, take their paddles and work silently but dilligently until they have crossed. Indeed nothing can be more impressive than the simple but

sincere manner in which these primitive people worship the
Great Being. One instance of this I had the happiness to
witness in our route through the lake. Upon a very calm
night while at least three miles distant from what we all supposed an uninhabited shore we suddenly heard a number of
voices singing. Upon inquiring of our boatman what these
voices meant he immediately replied, with an air of great
carelessness, that it was nothing but some savages praying,
and that it was their custom always to solicit the Great Spirit
at the top of their voices.

The appearance of the land along the whole coast of the
lake is not at all favorable for agricultural pursuits. Indeed
I am inclined to think that it will never be settled. There are
also but very few good harbors for ships.

Of the journey from Lake Superior to the Red river settlement Mr. McLeod writes under date of December 20th, 1836 :
The whole distance we had traveled on foot from November
26th, as we came, is about 645 miles. During that time we
lived upon a pint of boiled rice each per day, and were four
days without food of any kind except two ounces each of meat
and a small partridge divided between nine persons.

THE LIFE OF MAN.

How vain our hopes ; how futile our aspirations. What is
the life of man ? 'Tis but the shadow of an existence ; yet in
that shadow of a shade how much is comprised ! How few
there are who can look back to the bright days of their youth,
the sunshine of life, and feel that their dreams of renown and
splendor, or the more virtuous desire of domestic happiness
approach realization. All life is ideal, and our very existence
is but a dream.

But a few brief years have passed since I entered the por-
tals of manhood, yet I have frequently tasted of the bitter
fruit of this transient pilgrimage. I have been tossed, like a
weed, upon the waves of doubt and uncertainty, and have seen
the friends of my youth wrecked upon the shores of disappointment. I have seen promises—the most solemn—broken ;
friendships the warmest—buried in the cold grave of oblivion
or forgetfulness ; and ties "dearer than these, than all"—
forever crushed, and have felt the misery that follows them ;
and yet I am but upon the verge of "life's journeying".

CHAPTER XLVI.

It is not within the scope of these recollections to even attempt a connected narration of the local events transpiring at the Falls of St. Anthony in the order of their occurrence and in detail to the present time. Our record is nearing completion. The most important occurrences of the year 1862 here, as elsewhere, were in relation to the raising of troops for the war of the rebellion, and for the protection of our immediate frontier from the Indians.

At the meeting of the Legislature on the first Wednesday of January the pioneer Presbyterian minister of Minneapolis, Rev. J. C. Whitney, was elected chaplain of the house of representatives.

The establishment of a pork-packing house in Minneapolis by P. H. and A. Kelly, was of great benefit to the farmers.

Reports of the gallant bearing of the Second regiment of Minnesota volunteer infantry at the battle of Mill Spring gave great satisfaction, as it indicated that all our troops would sustain the splendid reputation given to our soldiery by the First Minnesota.

Wheat was only fifty-five cents per bushel at the mills.

Early in February Dr. A. A. Ames graduated at Rush College. This was the first graduation of a Minneapolis boy at any medical college.

H. E. Purdy, the former talented editor of the Plaindealer in Minneapolis, sold out his interest in the newspaper business in Minnesota and removed to Belmont, New York, where he resumed editorial charge of the Southern Free-Trader.

Col. King was of the opinion that Mr. Purdy used porcupine quills in editorial writing.

At the annual meeting of the Minneapolis Athenæum this year David Morgan was elected president, Samuel C. Gale vice-president, David C. Bell secretary, and Thomas Hale Williams treasurer. The board of directors consisted of Dr. A. L. Bausman, Frank Beebe, and J. H. Green. There were at that time only 1,713 volumes in the library.

Godfrey Sheitlin, who had been a resident of Minneapolis for a year or two, engaged largely in the ginseng trade, paying out over $50,000 during the year for the root. He introduced borage, rape, and poppy seed on a large scale, and found those articles could be profitably grown. He also experimented in making wine from rhubard, raspberry, strawberry, currant and cranberry. In all he made some fifty barrels of wine out of the different native fruits. With others he established a large linseed-oil factory.

On March 9th this year Dr. C. L. Anderson left the Falls overland for the Pacific Coast. He had many friends, and his departure was deeply regretted.

As spring approached it was evident that the several manufacturing industries at the Falls of St. Anthony were about entering upon a career of prosperity. The large iron works of Messrs. Scott & Morgan, as well as the factories of R. C. and O. H. Rogers, and Captain John Rollins, were crowded with work, and the flour and lumber mills were prosperous.

The Hennepin county Temperance League was organized in March with Dr. Geo. H. Keith, president; Jared S. Demmon, Geo. W. Chowen, and T. L. Curtis, vice-presidents; Geo. F. Bradley, secretary; O. M. Laraway, treasurer; and H. N. Herrick, W. R. Smith, Geo. H. Rust, J. C. Williams, and A. H. Rose, directors.

At the town election held April 1st S. H. Mattison, J. H. Jones, and F. Beebe were elected township supervisors; D. R. Barber, assessor; Geo. A. Savory, clerk; R. J. Mendenhall, treasurer; J. C. Williams and John Murray, jr., justices; M. Nodaker and Hiram W. Wagner, constables; with James O. Weld, road-overseer in the first ward; S. H. Mattison, second ward; E. B. Ames, third ward; and Martin Layman, fourth ward. The city charter of Minneapolis had been

repealed by an act of the legislature. This was done by a
petition of the citizens in the interest of economy ; a township government being much cheaper ; and to show the patriotism of that period I will mention that the salary of the
officers were only one dollar per day. Even the services of
that efficient man, D. R. Barber, as assessor, were only com-
pensated for with that sum per day. With the prospect of
high taxes to support the government during the war, the
citizens at the Falls reduced the taxes for the support of their
municipal organization to the lowest possible amount. Always
patriotic, no portion of the Union contributed more liberally
to the suppression of the rebellion.

The municipal officers in St. Anthony this year were O. C.
Merriman, mayor ; W. W. Wales, city clerk ; David Edwards,
assessor ; Wm. Lashells, supervisor ; E. Lippencott, marshal.

Dr. K. Spencer became a dentist at the Falls this spring.
Captain Tapper, so long employed at the ferry and the sus-
pension-bridge, moved to his farm in Iowa. Judge William
Lochran resigned his trusts and went to the war. Dan M.
Demmon was selected as alderman in place of Wm. Lochran.
Wyman Elliott commenced a market garden on a large scale.

The ladies of the county organized a Soldiers' Aid Society
with Mrs. F. R. E. Cornell, president ; Mrs. Dorillus Morrison and Miss Nellie Elliott, vice-presidents ; Miss Littie Hob-
lett, secretary ; Mrs. Harlow A. Gale, treasurer ; and Mrs.
A. D. Foster, Mrs. Washington Pierce, Mrs. E. A. Davis,
Mrs. Town, Mrs. Bissel, Miss L. F. Hawkins, and Miss Lucy
Morgan, managers. This organization accomplished a noble
work for the soldiers. Mrs. Foster, the head of the board of
managers, was one of the early pioneers of St. Anthony, having accompanied her husband, Mr. A. D. Foster, to the Falls
in 1848. She was a worthy contemporary of those excellent
pioneer ladies, Mrs. R. P. Russell, Mrs. Ard Godfrey, Mrs.
Captain John Rollins, and Mrs. Anson Northrup. Both Mrs.
Foster and her husband have always taken an interest in all
that would benefit the community.

As the summer advanced, military matters became lively.
O. C. Merriman, Richard Strout, J. C. Whitney, and Geo. A.
Camp, raised companies of men for the war. A little later
Eugene M. Wilson was at the head of a company of mounted

rangers. W. F. Russell had secured a company of sharp-shooters. In the meantime Captain Geo. N. Morgan of St. Anthony had been promoted to the coloneley of the brave and far-famed First Minnesota, C. B. Heffelfinger of Minneapolis promoted from a sergeant to a first lieutenancy in the same regiment, William W. Woodbury to a captaincy; James P. Howlett, to quartermaster; Levi Butler, to surgeon; M. R. Greely, to assistant-surgeon; and several other promotions followed in rapid order.

P. H. Kelly of Minneapolis aided in securing men and material for the army. D. Morrison, W. D. Washburn, G. W. Chowen, G. H. Rust, R. J. Baldwin, H. G. Harrison, S. W. Farnham, D. B. Dorman, E. W. Cutter, Wm. Finch, Paris Gibson, and Richard Strout, were a committee appointed by the citizens of the county to raise money for the benefit of the families of those noble men who enlisted at this time.

Prof. Geo. B. Stone, who had accomplished so much in the public schools at Minneapolis for the benefit of the students, retired from the superintendency at the close of the September term. As and educator he had no superior.

While the citizens at the Falls were aiding in the suppression of the rebellion, news was brought through the big woods to Governor Ramsey at St. Paul, by Captain Geo. C. Whitcomb, of the first massacre of whites by the Indians in Meeker county. This news was received on the 19th, and almost simultaneously with news of murders a day later at the Redwood Indian agency. The day after this, August 20, Minneapolis and St. Anthony was filled with refugees from the frontier. It is unnecessary to say that the doors of the citizens were thrown open to those fleeing for their lives, and every possible assistance was rendered. Meantime every means was taken to check the the overwhelming disaster.

Events which occurred on the frontier were of the most painfully absorbing interest. They are recorded elsewhere.

CHAPTER XLVII.

I come now to the Sioux Massacre of 1862 ; not to write a history of its momentous events ; but to present a brief narration of some of the incidents that made such a painfully-vivid impression upon the frontier settlers of the Northwest ; presenting, as it does, an exhibition of the darkest passions, and the perpetration of crimes the most revolting that a savage nature can conceive. It was infamous in its conception, fiendish in its execution, and fearfully disastrous alike to whites and Indians. There are those who freely express their conviction that no reference to the immediate precipitation of that massacre can be complete, correct and just, that does not include, among the other numerous causes, the statement that the leaders engaged in it thought the union of the states would be destroyed, and that then was their opportunity to repossess the lands they had ceded to the government. The withdrawal of the troops from the frontier, the battles disastrous to the Union arms, the seemingly financial embarrassment that delayed the payment of their annuities, gave plausibility to those ideas. The combined result was the massacre of 1862, that was one of unparalleled mutilation, murder and rapine.

SOME OF THE CAUSES OF THE OUTBREAK —NEAR AND REMOTE.

The Dakota annuity tribes in Minnesota at the time of the outbreak were the Medawakontons, Wapatons, Sissetons, and Wapakutas, numbering in all about 6,200 persons. Their annuities aggregated about $555,000. These tribes were connected with wild bands scattered over a large extent of country, including Dakota and west of the Missouri to the Rocky mountains. The government had provided a civilization fund to be taken from their annuities and expended in improvements on the lands of such of them as should abandon their tribal relations and adopt the mode of life of the whites. The wild, blanket Indians denounced the measure as a fraud upon their rights.

Major Galbraith, Sioux Agent, writes : The radical, moving cause of the outbreak is, I am satisfied, the ingrained and fixed hostility of the savage barbarian to reform and civilization. As in all barbarous communities, in the history of the world, the same people have, for the most part, resisted the encroachments of civilization upon their ancient customs ; so it is in the case before us. Nor does it matter materially in what shape civilization makes its attack. Hostile, opposing forces meet in conflict, and a war of social elements is the result—civilization is aggressive, and barbarism stubbornly resistant. Sometimes, indeed, civilization has achieved a bloodless victory, but generally it has been otherwise."

Whatever the cause of the tragedy, the execution was the result of a conspiracy under the guise of a " Soldiers' Lodge", and matured in secret Indian councils. In all these secret movements Little Crow was the moving spirit.

THE SITUATION AT THE CRITICAL MOMENT.

Now the opportune moment seemed to have come. Only thirty soldiers were stationed at Fort Ridgely. Some thirty were all that Fort Ripley could muster, and at Fort Abercrombie one company was all the whites could depend upon to repel any attack in that quarter, The whole effective force for the defense of the entire frontier, from Pembina to the Iowa line, did not exceed two hundred men.

It is in evidence that Little Crow repeatedly stated in the secret councils that the Indians could kill all the white men in the Minnesota Valley, and get all their lands back, as well as finally receive double annuities.

THE FIRST VICTIMS OF THE SAVAGES.

The first blow fell upon the town of Acton, thirty-five miles northeast of the Lower Sioux Agency, in Meeker county, on Sunday, August 17th, 1862, at 1 o'clock p. m., where six

Indians of Shakopee's band killed Mr. and Mrs. Jones, Mr. Baker, Mr. Webster, and Miss Wilson, and then fled. This attack seems to have been unauthorized and premature, for on the same day a counsel was held, presided over by Little Crow, at Rice creek, some forty miles distant, at which it was decided that a general massacre of the whites should commence the next morning. The final decision was made about sundown, and early the next morning the entire force of warriors of the Lower tribes, painted and armed, were scattered over a region forty miles in extent, ready for the slaughter. There were some two hundred and fifty of these at the Lower Agency, who surrounded the houses and stores, before some of the inmates were awake. The blow was entirely unexpected. The traders and government employes were killed, the stores plundered, and the buildings burned. Nathan Myrick, James W. Lynd, A. J. Myrick, and G. W. Divoll were among the first victims. W. H. Forbes and G. H. Spencer, though severely wounded, escaped.

THE INDIANS SPARE NOT THEIR EARLIEST AND BEST FRIENDS.

Early on this fatal Monday morning Mr. Prescott and Rev. J. D. Hinman learned from Little Crow that the storm of savage wrath was gathering, and that their only safety was in instant flight. Mrs. Hinman was, fortunately, at Faribault. The white-haired interpreter, Philander Prescott, nearly seventy years of age, hastily left his house soon after his meeting with Little Crow, and fled toward Fort Ridgoly. The other members of his family remained behind, knowing that their relations to the tribe would save them. Mr. Prescott had gone several miles along the west bank of the Minnesota river when he was overtaken. His murderers came and talked with him. He reasoned with them, saying: "I am an old man ; I have lived with you now forty-five years, almost half a century. My wife and children are among you, of your own blood ; I have never done you any harm, and have been your true friend in all your troubles ; why should you wish to kill me ?" Their reply was : "We would save your life if we could, but the WHITE MAN MUST DIE ; we cannot spare your life ; our orders are to kill all white men ; we cannot spare you." It is said upon the authority of the Indians that he was shot while talking with them and looking calmly into their eyes.

Mr. Prescott was the true, tried, and faithful friend of the Indian, and had labored long in their interest. His benevolence to the red-men kept him ever poor. Mr. Hinman escaped to Fort Ridgely.

The number of persons who reached Fort Ridgley from the Lower Agency was forty-one. Some arrived at other places of safety. Among those who escaped were J. C. Whipple, C. B. Hewitt ; and J. C. Dickinson and family, including several girls, who kept the government boarding-house. Mr. Hunter was killed on the way, as was also Dr. P. P. Humphrey, the physician to the Lower Sioux, with his sick wife and two children. The doctor's eldest boy of about twelve years escaped.

At the Redwood river ten miles above the Agency, on the road to Yellow Medicine, resided Mr. Joseph B. Reynolds, in the employment of the government as a teacher. His house was within one mile of Shakopee's village. His family consisted of his wife and niece—Miss Mattie Williams—Mary Anderson and Mary Schwandt, hired girls. William Landmeier, a hired man, and Legrand Davis, a young man from Shakopee, was also stopping with them temporarily. Mr. Patoile, a trader from Yellow Medicine, was also there, on his way to New Ulm. On Monday morning, learning of their danger, they started out on the prairie, and when nearly opposite Fort Ridgely, Petoile and Davis were killed. Mary Schwandt was wounded, and died soon after. Mary Anderson and Miss Williams were captured unhurt.

On Sunday, the 17th, George Gleason, government storekeeper at the Lower Agency, accompanied the family of Agent Galbraith to Yellow Medicine, and on Monday afternoon, ignorant of the terrible tragedy enacted below, started to return. He had with him the wife and two children of Dr. J. S. Wakefield, physician to the Upper Sioux. On the way he was killed, and Mrs. Wakefield and two children captured.

Early on the morning of the 18th, the settlers on the north side of the Minnesota river, adjoining the reservation, were surprised to see a large number of Indians in their immediate neighborhood. They were seen soon after the people arose, simultaneously, all along the river from Birch Coolie to Beaver Creek, and beyond, on the west, apparently intent on gathering up the horses and cattle. When interrogated, they said they were after Chippewas. At about 6 or 7 o'clock they suddenly began to repair to the various houses of the settlers, and then the flight of the inhabitants and the work of death began.

In the immediate vicinity of Beaver Creek, the neighbors, to the number of about twenty-eight, men, women, and children, assembled at the house of John W. Earle and, with several teams, started for Fort Ridgely, having with them the sick wife of S. R. Henderson, her children, and the family of N. D. White, and the wife and two children of Jas. Carothers. There were also David Carothers and family, Earle and family, Henderson, and a German named Wedge, besides four sons of White and Earle ; the rest were women and children. They had gone but a short distance when they were surrounded by Indians. When asked, by some of the party who could speak their language, what they wanted, the Indians answered, "We are going to kill you." Wedge, Mrs. Henderson and children, Eugene White, and N. D. White, and Redner, son of J. W. Earle, were killed. The other men escaped, and the women and children were captured.

WHOLE GERMAN SETTLEMENTS ANNIHILATED.

Some two miles above the neighborhood of Earle and White was a settlement of German emigrants, numbering some forty persons. Early on the morning of the 18th these had assembled at the house of John Meyer. Very soon after, some fifty Indians, led by Shakopee, appeared in sight. The people all fled, except Meyer and his family, going into the grass and bushes. Peter Bjorkman ran toward his own house. Shakopee, whom he knew, saw him, and exclaimed, "There is Bjorkman ; kill him !" but keeping the building between him and the savages, he plunged into a slough and concealed himself, even removing his shirt, fearing it might reveal his whereabouts to the savages. Here he lay from early morning until the darkness of night enabled him to leave—mosquitoes swarming upon his naked person, and the hot sun scorching him to the bone. The Indians immediately attacked the house of Meyer, killing his wife and all his children. Seeing his family butchered, and having no means of defense, Meyer effected his escape, and reached Fort Ridgely. In the meantime the affrighted people had got together again at the house of a Mr. Sitzon, near Bjorkman's to the number of about thirty, men, women, and children. In the afternoon the savages returned to the house of Sitzon, killing every person there except Mrs. Eindefield and her child. From his place of concealment Mr. Bjorkman witnessed this attack and massacre of an entire neighborhood. At night he escaped. On the way he overtook a woman and two children, one an infant of six months, the wife and children of John Sateau, who had been killed. Taking one of the children in his arms, these companions in suffering hurried on together. Mrs. S. was nearly naked, and without shoes or stockings. They finally reached the Fort, where Mrs. Sateau found two sons, aged ten and twelve years, who had reached there before her.

Near 'Beaver Creek Patrick Hayden, John Hayden, Mr. Eisenrich, Mr. Eune, Edward Manger, Patrick Kelley, and David O'Connor were killed. Four miles from the Lower Sioux Agency, on the Fort road, Thomas Smith, and Mr. Sampson and two children were killed. Near Birch Coolie Peter Pereau, Andrew Bahlke, Henry Keartner, old Mr. Closen, Frederick Closen, Mr. Pignur, and Mrs. William Vitt were killed.

A flourishing German settlement had sprung up twelve miles below Yellow Medicine. They learned of their danger on the evening of the 18th, and the whole neighborhood, with the exception of one family, assembled at the house of Paul Kitzman, and struck out on the prairie toward the head of Beaver creek. They traveled all night, and in the morning changed their course toward Fort Ridgely. They continued in this direction until the sun was some two hours high, when they were met by eight Sioux Indians, who told them that the murders were committed by Chippewas, and that they had come over to protect them and punish the murderers ; and thus induced them to turn back toward their homes. One of the savages spoke English well. He was acquainted with some of the company, having often hunted with Paul Kitzman. He kissed Kitzman, telling him he was a good man ; and they shook hands with all of the party. The simple-hearted Germans believed them, gave them food, distributed money among them and, gratefully receiving their assurances of friendship and protection, turned back. When near their home they were suddenly surrounded by fourteen Indians, who instantly fired upon them. All of the eleven white men were killed. Only two of the women and a few of the children escaped death. Over forty bodies were afterwards found and buried on that field of slaughter.

BATTLE AT THE LOWER AGENCY FERRY.

On Monday morning, the 18th of August, 1862, at about 9 o'clock, a messenger arrived at Fort Ridgely, from the Lower Sioux Agency, with news that the Indians were massacring the whites at that place. Captain John S. Marsh, of Company B, Fifth Regiment Minnesota Volunteers, then in command, took a detachment of forty-six men (there were then in the Fort only seventy-five or eighty men), and accompanied by Interpreter Quinn, immediately started for the agency, distant twelve miles. They made a very rapid march. When within about four miles of the ferry, opposite the Agency, they met the ferryman, Mr. Martelle, who informed Captain Marsh that the Indians were in considerable force, and were murdering all the people, and advised him to return. He replied that he was there to protect and defend the frontier, and he should do so if it was in his power, and gave the order "Forward!" Between this point and the river they passed nine dead bodies on or near the road. Arriving near the ferry, the company halted, and Corporal Ezekiel Rose was sent forward to examine the ferry, and see if it was all right. The captain and interpreter were mounted on mules, the men were on foot, and formed in two ranks in the road, near the ferry-house, a few rods from the banks of the river. The corporal had taken a pail with him to the river, and returned, reporting the ferry all right, bringing with him water for the exhausted and thirsty men.

In the meantime an Indian had made his appearance on the opposite bank, and calling to Quinn, urged them to come across, telling him all was right on that side. The suspicions of the captain were at once aroused, and he ordered the men to remain in their places, until he could ascertain whether the Indians were in ambush in the ravines on the opposite shore. The men were in the act of drinking, when the savage on the opposite side, seeing they were not going to cross at once, fired his gun, as a signal, when instantly there arose out of the grass and brush, all around them, some four or five hundred warriors, who poured a terrific volley upon the devoted band. The aged interpreter fell from his mule, pierced by more than twenty balls. The captain's mule fell dead, but he himself sprang to the ground unharmed. Several of the men fell at this first fire. The testimony of the survivors of this sanguinary engagement is, that their brave commander was as cool and collected as if on dress parade. They retreated down the stream about a mile and a half, fighting their way inch by inch, when it was discovered that a body of Indians, taking advantage of a bend in the river, had gone across and gained the bank below them.

The heroic little band was already reduced to about half its original number. To cut their way through this large number of Indians was impossible. Their only hope now was to cross the river to the reservation, as there appeared to be no Indians on that shore, retreat down that side and recross to the fort. The river was supposed to be fordable where they were and, accordingly, Captain Marsh gave the order to cross. Taking his sword in one hand and his revolver in the other, accompanied by his men, he waded out into the stream. It was very soon ascertained that they must swim, when those who could not do so returned to the shore and hid in the grass as best they could, while those who could dropped their arms and struck out for the opposite side. Among these latter was Captain Marsh. When near the opposite shore he was struck by a ball, and immediately sank, but arose again to the surface, and grasped the shoulder of a man at his side, but the garment gave way in his grasp, and he again sank, this time to rise no more. Thirteen of the men reached the bank in safety, and returned to the fort that night. Those who were unable to cross remained in the grass and bushes until night, when they made their way to the fort or settlements.

These are only a few of the incidents of this terrible massacre near the Lower Sioux Agency. The horrible details of mutilation, and worse crimes than murder, are here unrecorded out of respect for the victims, living and dead. Turn we now to tragedies of the same day enacted elsewhere.

CHAPTER XLVIII.

During all that fatal 18th of August, the people at the Upper Agency pursued their usual avocations. As night approached, however, an unusual gathering of Indians was observed on the hill just west of the Agency, and between it and the house of John Other Day. Judge Givens and Charles Crawford, then acting as interpreters in the absence of Freniere, went out to them, and sought to learn why they were there in council, but could get no satisfactory reply. Soon after this, Other Day came to them with the news of the outbreak below, as did also Joseph Laframboise, a half-breed Sioux. The families there were soon all gathered together in the warehouse and dwelling of the agent, who resided in the same building, and with the guns they had, prepared themselves as best they could, and awaited the attack, determined to sell their lives as dearly as possible. There were gathered here sixty-two persons, men, women, and children.

Other Day, and several other Indians, who came to them, told them they would stand by them to the last. These men visited the council outside several times during the night; but when they were most needed, one only, the noble and heroic Other Day, remained faithful. All the others disappeared, one after another, during the night.

About 1 or 2 o'clock in the morning, Stewart B. Garvie, connected with the traders' store, known as Myrick's, came to the warehouse, and was admitted, badly wounded, a charge of buckshot having entered his bowels. Garvie was standing in the doorway of his store when he was fired upon. At about this time Joseph Laframboise went to the store of Daily & Pratt, and told the two men in charge there, Duncan R. Kennedy and J. D. Boardman, to flee for their lives. They had not gone ten rods when they saw in the path before them three Indians. They stepped down from the path, which ran along the edge of a rise in the ground of some feet, and crouching in the grass, the Indians passed within eight feet of them. Kennedy escaped to Fort Ridgely, and Boardman went to the warehouse.

WONDERFUL ESCAPE OF YOUNG PATOILE.

At the store of Wm. H. Forbes, Constans, book-keeper, a native of France, was killed. At the store of Patoile, Peter Patoile, a nephew of the proprietor, was shot just outside the store, the ball entering at the back and coming out near the nipple, passing through his lungs. An Indian came to him after he fell, turned him over, and saying, "He is dead," left him. The clerks in the store of Louis Roberts had effected their escape. When the Indians became absorbed in the work of plunder, Patoile crawled off into the bushes, on the banks of the Yellow Medicine, and secreted himself. Here he remained all day. After dark he ascended the bluff out of the Yellow Medicine bottom, and dragged himself a mile and a half further, to the Minnesota, at the mouth of the Yellow Medicine. Wading the Minnesota, he entered the house of Louis Labelle, on the opposite side, at the ford. It was deserted. He lay down upon a bed and slept until morning. Joseph Laframboise, Narces Freniere, and an Indian, Makacago, found him there and awoke him, telling him there were hostile Indians about, and he must hide. They gave him a blanket to disguise himself, and going with him to a ravine, concealed him in the grass and left him, promising to return as soon as it was safe to do so, to bring him food, and guide him to the prairie. He lay in this ravine until near night, when his friends, true to their promise, returned, bringing him some crackers, tripe, and onions. They went with him some distance out on the prairie, and enjoined upon him not to attempt to go to Fort Ridgely, and giving him the best directions that they could as to the course he should take, shook hands with him and left him. Their names should be inscribed upon tablets more enduring than brass.

Over an unknown region without an inhabitant, sleeping
on the prairie and in deserted houses, wounded, without food
for days after his scanty supply was exhausted, young Patoile
wandered, traveling some two hundred miles in twelve days,
when he came to some white men who had returned to the
homes they had deserted to look after their crops and cattle.
He was in the Sauk Valley, forty miles above St. Cloud. He
was taken in a wagon by these men to St. Cloud. His wounds
were dressed, his recovery was rapid, and he enlisted in the
Minnesota Mounted Rangers and served in the campaign of
1863, against the Indians.

OTHER DAY, A FULL-BLOODED INDIAN, SAVES A LARGE PARTY.

We now return to the warehouse at Yellow Medicine, which
we left to follow the strange fortunes of young Patoile. Other
Day was constantly on the watch outside, and reported the
progress of affairs to those within. Toward daylight the yells
of the savages came distinctly to their ears from the trading-
post, half a mile distant. The Indians were absorbed in the
work of plunder. The chances of escape were sadly against
the whites, yet they decided to make the attempt. Other
Day knew every foot of the country over which they must
pass, and would be their guide.

The wagons were driven to the door. A bed was placed in
one of them, and Garvie was laid upon it. The women provided a few loaves of bread, and just as day dawned, they
started on their perilous way. How their hearts did beat !
This party consisted of the family of Major Galbraith, wife
and three children ; Nelson Givens, wife, and wife's mother,
and three children ; Noah Sinks, wife, and two children ;
Henry Eschelle, wife, and five children ; John Fadden, wife,
and three children ; Mr. German and wife ; Frederick Patoile,
wife, and two children ; Mrs. Jane K. Murch, Miss Mary
Charles, Miss Lizzie Sawyer, Miss Mary Daly, Miss Mary
Hays, Mrs. Eleanor Warner, Mrs. John Other Day and one
child, Mrs. Haurahan, N. A. Miller, Edward Cramsie, Z.
Hawkins, Oscar Canfil ; Mr. Hill, an artist from St. Paul ;
J. D. Boardman, Parker Pierce, Dr. J. S. Wakefield, and
several others.

They crossed the Minnesota, and escaped by way of the
Kandiyohi lakes and Glencoe. Garvie died and was buried

on the way. Major Galbraith writes : " Led by the noble Other Day, they struck out on the naked prairie, literally placing their lives in this faithful creatures hands, and guided by him, and him alone. After intense suffering and privation, they reached Shakopee on Friday the 22d of August, Other Day never leaving them for an instant ; and this Other Day is a pure, full-blooded Indian, and was, not long since, one of the wildest and fiercest of his race."

Government gave John Other Day a farm in Minnesota. He died several years since. His wife was a pure white.

Early in the evening of Monday, two civilized Indians, Chaskada and Tankanxaceye, went to the house of Dr. Williamson, a few miles above the Agency, and warned them of their danger ; and two half-breeds, Michael and Gabriel Renville, and two Christian Indians, Paul Maxacuta Mani and Simon Anaga Mani, went to the house of Mr. Riggs, the missionary at Hazelwood, and gave them warning of their danger. There were at this place, at that time, the family of Rev. S. R. Riggs, Mr. H. D. Cunningham and family, Mr. D. W. Moore and his wife, and Jonas Pettijohn and family. Mr. Pettijohn and wife were in charge of the government school at Red Iron's village, and were now at Mr. Riggs'. These friendly Indians went with them to an island in the Minnesota, about three miles from the mission. Here they remained until Tuesday evening. In the afternoon of Tuesday, Andrew Hunter, a son-in-law of Dr. Williamson, came to him with the information that the family of himself and the Doctor were secreted below. The families at the saw-mills had been informed by the Renvilles, and were with the party of Dr. Williamson. At night they formed a junction and commenced their perilous journey. A thunder-storm effectually obliterated their tracks, so that the savages could not follow them, and they escaped. On the way they were joined by three Germans who had escaped from Yellow Medicine, who afterwards left them, with a young man named Gilligan, and were killed. All the others, reached the settlements unharmed.

The news of the murders below reached Leopold Wohler, three miles below Yellow Medicine, on Monday afternoon. Taking his wife, he crossed the Minnesota river, to the house of Major Joseph R. Brown. Major Brown's family consisted of his wife and nine children ; Angus Brown and wife, and Charles Blair, a son-in-law, his wife and two children. The Major was away from home. Including Wohler and his wife there were then at their house, on the evening of the 18th of August, eighteen persons. They started early on the morning of the 19th to make their escape, with one or two of their neighbors, Charles Holmes, a single man, being of the party. They were overtaken near Beaver Creek by Indians, and all of the Browns, Mr. Blair and family, and Mrs. Wohler, were captured, and taken at once to Little Crow's village. Messrs. Wohler and Holmes escaped. Major Brown's family were of mixed Indian blood. This fact probably accounts for their saving the life of Blair, who was a white man. Crow told him to go away, as his young men were going to kill him ; and he escaped, being out five days and nights without food. The sufferings he endured caused his death soon after.

J. H. Ingalls, a Scotchman, who resided in the neighborhood, and his wife, were killed, and their four children captured. Two of them, young girls, of twelve and fourteen years, were rescued at Camp Release. The two little boys were taken away by Little Crow, and their fate is shrouded in mystery. A Mr. Frace, residing near Brown's place, was also killed, and his wife and children captured.

At the town of Leavenworth, on the Cottonwood, in Brown county, the family of Mr. Blum were all, except a small boy, killed while endeavoring to escape. On Tuesday morning, Philetus Jackson was killed while on the way to town with his wife and son. Mrs. Jackson and the young man escaped. Mr. Henshaw and Mr. Whiton were also killed.

Early in the forenoon of Monday, August 18th, Indians appeared in large numbers at the town of Milford, adjoining New Ulm. The first house visited was that of Wilson Massipost, a widower. Mr. Massipost had two daughters, intelligent and accomplished. These the savages brutally murdered. His son, a young man of twenty, was also killed. Mr. Massipost and a son of eight years escaped. Mr. Mesmer, his wife, son, and daughter, were instantly shot. At the house of Agrenatz Hanley all the children were killed. The parents escaped. Bastian Mey, wife, and two children, were killed in their house, and three children terribly mutilated who recov-

ered. Adolph Shilling and his daughter were killed. Two
families, those of Mr. Zeller and Mr. Zettle, were completely
annihilated : not one left to tell the tale of their sudden destruction. Mr. Brown, and son, and daughter, were killed.

ONLY A GLIMPSE OF THE SITUATION.

Thirty thousand panic-stricken inhabitants at once deserted
their homes, and were destitute of the necessaries of life.
As the panic-stricken fugitives poured along the various
roads leading to the towns below, on Monday-night and
Tuesday, indescribable terror seized the inhabitants ; and the
rapidly-accumulating tide, gathering force and numbers as it
moved across the prairie, rolled an overwhelming flood into
the towns along the river. As no wisdom could direct it, no
force resist it, so no pen can describe it. It was gloomy,
chaotic, terrific. This record, incomplete, inadequate, seems
insignificant, when we consider that it covers but a small portion of the territory involved, and extends over scarcely more
than two days time, during which some eight hundred whites
were foully murdered, and a large number of the fairest
women and girls of the land, bereft of their kindred and pro-
tectors, were dragged into a loathsome captivity by savages
whose crimes would make murder by contrast a mercy.

SOME OF THE RESULTS ACHIEVED.

Of the prompt action of the authorities in taking measures
for the protection of the frontier, and the heroic conduct of
those engaged therein, I will not here write. The military
history of the Sioux war is now being written by participants.
Some of the results achieved were, the release of all the white
captives, about the first of October, 1862, to the number of
about one hundred, and half-breeds to the number of about
one hundred and fifty, at Camp Release. Our forces also had
about two thousand Indian prisoners. A military commission
recommended some three hundred of them for capital punishment, but President Lincoln allowed only thirty-eight to be
hung.

GENERAL SIBLEY'S ACCOUNT OF THE CAPTIVES AT CAMP RELEASE.

" I entered with my officers to the center of the circle formed
" by the numerous lodges, and seeing the old savage whom I
" knew personally as the individual with stentorian lungs, who
" promulgated the orders of the chiefs and head men to the

" multitude, I beckoned him to me and, in a peremptory tone,
" ordered him to go through the camp and notify the tenants
" that I demanded all the female captives to be brought to me
" instanter.   And now was presented a scene which no one who
" witnessed it can ever forget.   From the lodges there issued
" more than one hundred comely young girls and women, most
" of whom were so scantily clad as scarcely to conceal their
" nakedness.   On the persons of some hung only a single gar-
" ment, while pitying half-breeds and Indian women had pro-
" vided others with scraps of clothing from their own little
" wardrobes, answering, indeed, a mere temporary purpose.
" But a worse accoutered or more distressed group of civilized
" beings imagination would fail to picture.   Some seemed
" stolid, as if their minds had been strained to madness and
" reaction had brought vacant gloom, indifference, and despair.
" They gazed with a sad stare.   Others acted differently.   The
" great body of the poor creatures rushed wildly to the spot
" where I was standing with my brave officers, pressing as
" close to us as possible, grasping our hands and clinging to
" our limbs, as if fearful that the red devils might yet reclaim
" their victims.   I did all I could to reassure them, by telling
" them they were now to be released from their horrible suffer-
" ings, and freed from their bondage.   Many were hysterical,
" bordering on convulsions, laughter and tears commingling,
" incredulous that they were in the hands of their preservers.
" A few of the more attractive had been offered the alternative
" of becoming the temporary wives of select warriors and so,
" helpless and powerless, yet escaping the promiscuous atten-
" tions of a horde of savages bent on brutal insult revolting to
" conceive, and impossible to be described.   The majority of
" these outraged girls and young women were of a superior
" class.   Some were school teachers who, accompanied by their
" girl pupils, had gone to pass their summer vacation with rel-
" atives or friends in the border counties of the state.   The
" settlers, both native and foreign were, for the most part,
" respectable, prosperous, and educated citizens whose wives
" and daughters had been afforded the privileges of a good
" common school education.   Such were the delicate young
" girls and women who had been subjected for weeks to the
" inhuman embraces of hundreds of filthy savages, utterly

OF MINNESOTA AND ITS PEOPLE.

"devoid of all compassion for the sufferers. Escorting the
"captives to the outside of the camp, they were placed under
"the protection of the troops and taken to our own encamp-
"ment, where I had ordered tents to be pitched for their
"accommodation. Officers and men, affected even to tears by
"the scene, denuded themselves of their entire underclothing,
"blankets, coats, and whatever they could give, or could be
"converted into raiment for these heart-broken and abused
"victims of savage lust and rage. The only white man found
"alive when we reached the Indian encampment was George
"H. Spencer, who was saved from death by the heroic devo-
"tion of his Indian comrade, but yet badly wounded. He
"said to me, 'It is God's mercy, that you did not march here
"on the night after the battle. A plan was formed, had you
"done so, to murder the captives, then scatter to the prairies,'
"thus verifying my prediction of the course they would pur-
"sue. I bless God for the wisdom he gave me, and whereby,
"with the aid of my brave men, in spite of all slander and
"abuse, I was enabled to win a victory so decisive, and redeem
"from their thraldom those unfortunate sufferers who were a
"burden on my heart from the first moment of my campaign."

Some two thousand Indians were taken from the state
and removed far from the borders of Minnesota. The expedition of 1863 against the scattered bands of Sioux that still
remained on the borders of the state, or were still further
removed into Dakota, gave some assurance of protection and
security against further disturbance from the Sioux.

On the 16th of February, 1863, the treaties before that
time existing between the United States and these annuity
Indians were abrogated and annulled, and all lands and rights
of occupancy within the State of Minnesota, and all annuities
and claims then existing in favor of said Indians, were
declared forfeited to the United States.

DEATH OF LITTLE CROW—KILLED BY MR. LAMPSON.

On Friday evening, July 3, 1863, Mr. Lampson and his son
Chauncey, while traveling along the road, about six miles
north of Hutchinson, discovered two Indians in a prairie
opening in the woods, interspersed with clumps of bushes and
vines and a few scattered poplars, picking berries. These
two Indians were Little Crow and his son Wowinapa.

" I am the son of Little Crow. My name is Wowinapa. I am sixteen years old. My father had two wives before he took my mother ; the first one had one son ; the second one son and daughter ; the third wife was my mother. After taking my mother he put away the first two. He had seven children by my mother—six are dead ; I am the only one living now. The fourth wife had four children born ; do not know whether any died or not ; two were boys and two were girls. The fifth wife had five children—three of them are dead, and two are living. The sixth wife had three children ; all of them are dead ; the oldest was a boy, the other two were girls. The last four wives were sisters.

Father went to St. Joseph last spring. When we were coming back he said he could not fight the white men, but would go below and steal horses from them, and give them to his children, so that they could be comfortable, and then he would go away off.

Father also told me that he was getting old, and wanted me to go with him to carry his bundles. He left his wives and his other children behind. There were sixteen men and one squaw in the party that went below with us. We had no horses, but walked all the way down to the settlements. Father and I were picking red-berries, near Scattered Lake, at the time he was shot. It was near night. He was hit the first time in the side, just above the hip. His gun and mine were lying on the ground. He took up my gun and fired it first, and then fired his own. He was shot the second time when he was firing his own gun. The ball struck the stock of his gun, and then hit him in the side, near the shoulder. This was the shot that killed him. He told me that he was killed, and asked me for water, which I gave him. He died immediately after. When I heard the first shot fired I laid down, and the man did not see me before father was killed.

A short time before father was killed an Indian named Hiuka, who married the daughter of my father's second wife, came to him. He had a horse with him —also a gray-colored coat that he had taken from a man that he had killed to the north or where father was killed. He gave the coat to father, telling him he might need it when it rained, as he had no coat with him. Hiuka said he had a horse now, and was going back to the Indian country.

The Indians that went down with us separated. Eight of them and the squaw went north ; the other eight went further down. I have not seen any of them since. After father was killed I took both guns and the ammunition and started to go to Devil's Lake, where I expected to find some of my friends. When I got to Beaver creek I saw the tracks of two Indians, and at Standing Buffalo's village I saw where the eight Indians that had gone north had crossed.

I carried both guns as far as the Sheyenne river, where I saw two men. I asw scared, and threw my gun and the ammunition down. After that I traveled only in the night ; and as I had no ammunition to kill anything to eat, I had not strength enough to travel fast. I went on until I arrived near Devil's Lake, when I staid in one place three days, being so weak and hungry that I could go no further. I had picked up a cartridge near Big Stone Lake, which I still had with me, and loaded father's gun with it, cutting the ball into slugs. With this charge I shot a wolf, ate some of it, which gave me strength to travel, and went on up the lake until the day I was captured, which was twenty-six days from the day my father was killed."

The removal of the Indians from the borders of Minnesota, and the opening up for settlement of over a million of acres of superior land, was a prospective benefit to the state of immense value, both in its domestic quiet and its rapid advancement in material wealth.

LETTER FROM GEN. H. H. SIBLEY, DATED SEPT. 24TH, 1889.

Col. J. H. Stevens—My dear Sir : I would cheerfully comply with your request, to furnish you with an account of the release of the captives, and incidents connected therewith, over my own signature, but unfortunately I cannot, after the lapse of so many years, trust my memory to recall the details of that most important and interesting episode in our history. If I can find the article I furnished years ago to some magazine or newspaper, and to which you refer, I will send it to you without delay. It would give me much pleasure to contribute to the success of your enterprise. With loving regards to Mrs. Stevens, believe me to be your sincere friend, HENRY H. SIBLEY.

CHAPTER XLIX

The autumn of 1862 was dreary to citizens of Minneapolis and St. Anthony. The Indian war had brought sorrow to many households in the two cities. Currency was so scarce that the town of Minneapolis issued scrip redeemable in bank notes in sums not less than five dollars. This script was signed by S. H. Mattison, president, and Geo. A. Savory, secretary. It was endorsed by R. J. Mendenhall, treasurer, which gave it a good standing in the community. Messrs. J. E. and D. C. Bell, Benj. F. Bull, and other merchants, exchanged their goods for the script. Most of the teams in the two cities were pressed into the service of the state for the Indian war.

Sidney Smith, a resident of Minneapolis since 1854, and one of the most reliable, respected citizens, became interested in the freighting business, but there was little work in that line this fall for want of teams.

The fall election passed off very quietly. John A. Armstrong was elected sheriff, Harlow A. Gale, auditor ; Geo. W. Chowan, register of deeds ; John B. Gilfillan, county attorney; A. Blakeman, county commissioner ; and F. W. Cook, surveyor ; A. C. Austin and R. B. McGrath, members of the house. R. J. Baldwin, senator, held his office for two years, as did David Heaton, in St. Anthony.

Rev. D. Cobb became pastor of the Methodist church in Minneapolis, this fall.

Anson Northrup and Simon P. Snyder raised a company of men to defend the unprotected settlers on the frontier from the depredations of the Indians ; while Eugene M. Wilson had no difficulty in organizing a company of mounted rangers. October 15th, the company was mustered into the service with Mr. Wilson, captain ; E. A. Goodell, first lieutenant ; and James M. Paine, second lieutenant.

Hon. H. E. Mann, a prominent attorney of Minneapolis, received the appointment of clerk of U. S. court at St. Paul.

David C. Bell was married this fall to Miss Lina Conklin at her family home in Richburg, Alleghany county, New York. The couple came directly to Minneapolis and have resided here ever since.

W. W. McNair of Minneapolis was married to Miss Wilson, daughter of Edgar Wilson of Virginia.

Harrison's block, the most commodious house up to this time in Minneapolis, was completed in October of this year.

The State Bank of Minnesota, with R. J. Mendenhall as its president, was organized in November.

The county commissioners followed the example of the town board and issued scrip for a circulating medium.

As winter approached it became necessary to renew efforts in behalf of wounded and sick soldiers. The soldiers' aid society was reorganized with Mrs. D. Morrison, president ; Mrs. Geo. W. Chowan and Mrs. George Godley, vice-presidents ; Miss Abby Harmon, treasurer ; Mrs. E. Harmon, secretary ; with Miss Nellie Elliot, Mrs. Case, and Mrs. H. O. Hamlin, managers. This organization, like the previous one, accomplished a good work in behalf of the soldiers.

November 19th Thos. S. King, recently from New York, assumed editorial control of the Atlas. Mr. King wielded an able pen, and for many years was one of the ablest newspaper men in the city.

Late in November D. Morrison & Co. opened a large store in Minneapolis. Messrs. Mat. Nothaker and Henry Oswald also successfully engaged in the mercantile business.

All agricultural products ruled low in prices this fall ; wheat was only worth sixty cents per bushel.

Rev. C. C. Salter was called to the pastorship of the Congregational church, which position he occupied many years· He was one of the most popular pastors of the city.

The Hennepin county medical society was organized in December. Dr. A. E. Ames was elected president, Dr. R. H. Ward, secretary ; and Dr. A. E. Johnson, librarian.

Dr. J. J. Linn became a resident of Minneapolis in 1857, and aided in the organization of the Hennepin County Medical Society that year. He was influenced in coming to Minneapolis by his nephew, Hon. E. M. Wilson. He has been and is a successful physician.

YOUNG MEN CONNECTED WITH THE PRESS.

The Press of those early times sent out several young men from the Falls of St. Anthony who have become distinguished. Among them was Hon. Erastus Timothy Cressey. He was the first printer's devil in the old St. Anthony Express office, soon after that paper made its first appearance. Daniel L. Paine is another man who was in the Express office in 1851, who has made his mark in the world. Joseph A. Wheelock, the veteran editor-in-chief of the Pioneer Press, was never connected with the newspapers at the Falls of St. Anthony, but he was a pioneer resident of the county as early as the fall of 1850. From several letters written to me in those early days it is easily seen that he wielded a powerful pen. At a later period Colonel Levine P. Plummer, Willard S. Whitemore, Colonel Charles W. Johnson, and Fred. L. Smith graduated from the printing offices in either St. Anthony or Minneapolis. They attained high places in the estimation of the community. Colonel Plummer died several years since. Colonel Johnson is Secretary of the United States Senate. C. H. Slocum is another worthy of mention in this connection. These facts are additional evidence that the composing-room of a printing-office turns out many of the best men of the country.

THE COUNTRY WEST OF MINNEAPOLIS.

In the fall of 1856 I resided with my family on my farm at Glencoe, where I remained for several years, and was interested in the settlement of the country west of Minneapolis. After my farm in Minneapolis had been laid off into lots, and covered with houses, I found if I was to "follow the plow" it would be necessary to select a new home. In doing so I experienced the pleasing senation of pioneer life over again. Carver, the intermediate county between Hennepin and McLeod counties, was being rapidly settled by a thrifty people, many of them from Germany. Several villages were springing up along the line of the road from Minneapolis to Glencoe.

The first settlers in Chaska were Judge Jacob Ebinger, T. D. Smith, Fred Greiner, Fred DuToit, John Lee, E. Ellsworth, G. Krayenbuhl, and Thomas B. Hunt. Carver was the river depot for Glencoe. Its first settlers were Axel Jorgenson and John Goodenough, in 1852. In February, 1854, Levi H. Griffin and associates purchased Jorgenson's claim and laid out the town. Mr. Griffin was a printer, and previous to his location in Carver had been to California. He erected a large hotel, and was energetic in building up the town. He was followed by Stephen Holmes, Anton Knoblaugh, Walton Bros., John O. Brunius, Charles Johnson, A. G. Anderson, Herman Muehlberg, Enoch Holmes, Charles Basler, J. S. Letford, J. W. Hartwell, C. A. Bloomquist, W. A. Griffin, J. A. Sargent, Dr. E. Bray, and other enterprising citizens.

Young America, midway between Carver and Glencoe, was a beautiful village laid out in the "deep green woods", by Dr. R. M. Kennedy and James Slocum, worthy pioneers. Dr. Kennedy died in 1862. His widow became the wife of Enoch Holmes, then a pioneer merchant of Carver, now a citizen of Minneapolis.

The first settlers of Glencoe, Hutchinson, and McLeod county generally, were pioneers of an excellent race of men. The names of W. S. Chapman, John V. McKean, Henry Little, L. G. Simons, A. J. Snyder, C. L. Snyder, B. F. Buck, James Phillips, John Smith, Lawrence Gillick, Henry Elliott, Prentice Chubb, John Folsom, G. K. Gilbert, A. H. Reed, Isaac W. Cummings, James B. and Thomas McClary, Bradbury Richardson, E. W. Richardson, F. B. Dean, A. H. Rouse, George Harris, J. R. Louden, F. W. Hanscomb, the Langley Bros., Peter Durfee, C. Chandler, the McDougal Bros., W. W. and J. H. Getchell, and others around Glencoe ; the Hutchinsons, R. E. Grimshaw, Wm. White, Lewis Harrington, B. E. Messer, W. W. Pendergast, J. H. Chubb, the Chesley Bros., the Pollock Bros., with others at Hutchinson and Lake Addie ; J. S. Noble, A. H. and C. Jennison, Daniel Nobles, A. S. Nobles, L. Guard, in the interior of the county, and E. Lambert, John and H. C. McClelland farther north, with other equally good men scattered throughout the county, was a sure guarantee that it was destined to be one of the best counties in the state.

REPRESENTATIVE MEN AT THE FALLS OF ST. ANTHONY.

Among the most persistent men at the Falls of St. Anthony during the hard times of the late fifties and early sixties were those engaged in an effort to make Minneapolis and St. Anthony the head of navigation. It is true every man, woman and child at the Falls fully believed in the wondrous future of the Twin Cities, and their faith therein was never clouded by a doubt; but Captain John Martin, Captain John C. Reno, Captain Edward Murphy, and Captain J. B. Gilbert, and some others, thought that steamboats would greatly assist in the development of their greatness. These gentlemen backed their belief by investing heavily in steamboats. Captain Martin seldom failed in any of his business pursuits. Excellent judgment with a clear head were his chief characteristics, and with promptness and integrity he has led a successful life.

Another gentleman who came to St. Anthony during the financial crisis, in 1859, is Henry F. Brown. During the so-called hard times he never for a moment became discouraged. His life is an illustration of the results of industry, thrift and energy. Following in the path pursued by Col. W. S. King, Mr. Brown earnestly engaged in breeding rich strains of thoroughbred stock, and like Col. King became a public benefactor to the whole northwest by the introduction of a superior quality of stock among the farmers.

Still another who came to Minneapolis during the hard times of the late fifties whose life has been a marked success financially and in his profession is Levi M. Stewart. By strict attention to the profession of law and by wise investment he has attained more than a competency, a portion of which he distributes in unostentatious charity.

No one has been more loyal to the interests of Minneapolis than Washington Pierce. He came here in a very early day, and has for many years been intrusted with different offices, which he has filled with credit.

John Ludlum, a brother-in-law of N. E. Stoddard, a pioneer of the early fifties, always commanded the respect of the whole community. His home is near where he first settled when he came to the territory. It is seldom even in this comparatively new country that the first homesteads remain in the same family more than one generation, in many instances

only a few years. I will give the names of a few of the many
early and valuable pioneers in this section whose homesteads
are in the hands of strangers.

REMOVED FROM THEIR OLD HOMESTEADS.

Luther Patch came to St. Anthony in 1847. His family
consisted of four boys and two girls. The former are Edw'd,
Wallace, Lewis, and Gibson S. Patch ; the latter Mrs. R. P.
Russell and Mrs. J. M. Marshall. Mrs. Russell is the only
representative of the family left.

The late Phineas B. Newton settled on his farm in Maple
Grove township in October, 1855. He and his family were
unusually respected. His boys, Wm. I., Frank H., Thos. R.,
and I. C. Newton, were of much promise. Their home was a
pleasant one, but the old farm is in the hands of strangers.

Isaac Hankinson settled in Helen, McLeod county, in 1856.
He was an industrious, respected citizen, and had a house full
of children who were esteemed by the whole community. A
good sized homestead made them happy and prosperous.
The boys, Thomas, James, Joseph, and John, aided their
father in raising large crops on the farm. The girls married
and settled in the neighborhood. The old homestead has
passed out of the hands of the family—not a representative
left on it.

In the very early days at the Falls no one wielded greater
influence than Pierre Bottineau. He has moved away—has
only one representative, the well-known lawyer John B.
Bottineau.

Not a descendant of John Jackins, one of our first county
commissioners, is left. Mr. Jackins and family are west of
the Rocky mountains. Only a few remain of the descendants
of our second county commissioner, Washington Getchell,
who went to Oregon long ago. Levi Longfellow, a respected
citizen, and a successful business man, is a grandson of Mr.
Getchell.

Ralph T. Gray, the first actual resident barber in St.
Anthony, still resides in Minneapolis, and is held in high
esteem by the people.

John Dudley has always lived on the east side of the river,
but his extensive mills were at the junction of the St. Croix
with the Mississippi.

CONCLUSION.

With the close of 1862 this record of pioneer events ends. In a feeble way, inadequate to the occasion, I have performed the duty I have felt that I owed to the Pioneers of Minnesota, and especially to Minneapolis, by willing testimony as to their sterling worth and generous deeds. They worked for the good of those who were to follow in their footsteps, inherit this glorious land, and possess the institutions founded in intelligence, and fostered with care. With prophetic eye they viewed with pride the blessings that would be showered upon generations that were to follow. Only a few of them were permitted to reap great personal and material benefit from the ripening harvest that follows the seeds they planted ; and comparatively few of them remain to clearly see, and fully comprehend, what has been accomplished, and realize the glories that will indefinitely increase after their eyes are closed in eternal sleep.

While to a limited extent this record is historical, it lays no claim to the dignity of history. It would be presumptuous in me to assume the importance of historian. That I am partial to the old settlers, is as natural as the love of a parent for his children, or the affection of brothers and sisters. I simply offer a tribute of love and respect to my old associates, which I know they richly merit. The record is by no means complete. In such a multitude of events, many as worthy or more worthy, with the most careful attention, in a work of such limited scope, must pass unrecorded.

With regretful eye, sad heart, and steps willing only as they performed a duty, I have aided in placing a large number of whom I have written, in the silent tomb. The open grave is familiar to me, and a frequently-recurring sight. But the limit will soon be reached. May fresh eyes, joyous footsteps, and loving hearts, ever inherit this land. I dedicate the record contained in this book to those who know me well, and I feel sure they will be lenient to its faults if they experience the pleasure in reading that I have felt in writing it. It is also hoped that more recent dwellers in this fair land, if they peruse these pages, will find some interest in comparing the present with the past. And may some abler pen trace their good deeds, with as good intentions, as I have recorded those of their immediate predecessors.

CHAPTER L.

Elsewhere I have written of Rev. Gideon H. Pond, one of the earliest missionaries to the Dakotas in Minnesota, and of his appointments to preach at my little house under the bluff, just above the Falls. And now, by the courtesy of his nephew, S. W. Pond, jr., of Minneapolis, I am enabled to present a glimpse of his life here at an earlier day, even half a century ago. The views are given by himself in extracts from his journal, commencing in 1837. To me it is the life of a noble, self-sacrificing man, devoted to an almost hopeless mission of mercy to the heathen, but not less interesting on that account.

EXTRACTS FROM THE PRIVATE JOURNAL OF REV. GIDEON H. POND.

Lac-qui-parle, June 30, 1837.—To-day I enter upon my twenty-eighth year, and for my future benefit commit to writing my determination to endeavor to deny myself ungodliness and follow after peace, seeking to be meek and lowly in mind and to exhibit an humble, unassuming character, striving at all times to look at myself in the glass of truth, as a rebel by nature against the government of the blessed God, and in myself entirely destitute of worth, but yet a child of God through the grace of Jesus Christ, as not my own and as having nothing which I can call my own ; that I will endeavor to improve my time diligently, remembering that it is short and precious, and that I can do nothing without exertions, and that I will most assuredly be doing wrong unless I make exertions to do right ; that I will endeavor to keep an account of the manner in which I spend each day, and strive to improve, to-morrow, in that wherein I fail to-day.

As all before me is dark, so that I can plan nothing for the future, I will endeavor to live by faith and cast all my care on God and seek His special guidance continually, through Jesus Christ : and

O may the blessed God, by His spirit through Jesus Christ, and for the sake of His own glory among these Indians, help a poor, weak and faithless sinner to be faithful through the year and till death. Amen.

July 3. Spent from eleven until half-past one looking over with Wamdiokie some simple translations I made Saturday. [The following days are filled with labors in fitting up the house, and improving every opportunity for learning the Indian language, and for conversing with the Indians on religious subjects.]

Friday, 7th—Have felt disposed to be a little impatient with an Indian to-day— Seca-duta. I am in want of a disposition to compassionate them as I should. May Christ sit in my heart as a refiner and purifier of silver until his own image shines bright in me.

Thursday, 13th.—I ought to feel very thankful that God has given me the opportunity to collect two or three words to-day. I feel that my responsibilities increase with every word which I learn, or which I might learn and do not. Will the Lord forgive me that I have been so negligent, and sanctify my heart through the truth by giving me a lively faith through Jesus Christ by the influence of the Holy Spirit, that I may love and serve Him only, and be faithful unto death.

Friday, 14th.—Preparing boards for floor. Though it is, in itself, most disagreeable, trying and tedious, yet I feel grateful because I have been favored with the company of Indians ; and though I have been engaged in manual labor, have, I hope, been able to learn some.

Monday, 17th.—Laying floor in chamber this afternoon. I commenced an attempt to translate the 31st Psalm into Dakota.

Monday, 31st.—This morning wrote a letter to brother Samuel, and went to Mr. R.'s with it. Have spent most of the day with the Indians. Had a long interview with Wamdiokie, and tried to tell him why Christ died, and why it is necessary that men should be made new, in the temper of the mind, the danger of self-deception, the wickedness of forsaking God, and some of his attributes. A miserable "guide of the blind," because my own eyes are so near shut. Lord that my eyes may be opened, and his too, that we may be renewed in the spirit of our minds.

Wednesday, 2d. Taoyateduta [Little Crow] came here this afternoon to read. I have some hope that he will apply himself ; if so, I shall endeavor to assist him while he stays.

Saturday, 5th. I have for two or three days felt more than commonly disposed to weep on behalf of the Indians, and especially Wamdiokie. They are blind and dead. Lord that their eyes may be opened.

Friday, 11th. The Indians came to dance to us to-day, and we considered it to be our duty to offend them grievously by disregarding them. The house, however, shook to their praise.

Monday, 14th.—To-day we have had a new exhibition of the gratitude of these degraded heathen by a letter from the principal chief at this village, written by Wamdiokie, reproaching us, not in anger, but with savage mildness, because we teach that we should love others as ourselves, and do not share with them what we ourselves possess. May I have grace to count the reproaches of Christ among these heathen greater riches than the pleasant society of New England Christians, and give them no occasion justly to reproach.

This afternoon the Indians are much terrified, supposing a man and woman will come here who have had the smallpox.

October 31, Tuesday.—I felt disposed to invite the blessed Savior to the marriage. I felt an earnest longing that He should rather come than any person in the world. O may the blessed presence be with us.

Nov. 1, 1837.—I was married this afternoon at 3 o'clock, to Miss Sarah Poage, by Rev. Stephen R. Riggs. The guests were the members of the Mission, Mr. Renville's family, and a number of Indians, and I trust our Savior was with us by His spirit in our hearts.

Saturday Minnie-apa-win and To-te-duta-win were examined for admission to the church, and received with hesitation. Sarah and Catharine were baptised. Perhaps more Indians have attended meeting to-day than have ever attended at once. O that their eyes may be opened.

Sunday seven made a profession of their faith, in church, and received the sacrament of the Supper.

Sixteenth.— All the week has been as Monday, except that I got one word, and do not yet know what it means.

Sunday, 17th.—Dr. Williamson read some translations he had prepared to six women and a few children in the morning. In the afternoon he read a sermon in English. We went to Mr. R.'s in the evening to sing. Several of the women came together. We sang three or four Dakota hymns. I spoke to them a little of God's urging us to seek the salvation he has made ready, and which is waiting for us, by the considerations of heaven and hell. The meeting was closed by a short prayer by myself in Dakota. The Indians have planted, I suppose, about thirty acres of corn at this village.

July 16th.—Spent most of the forenoon in reading the translation of the story of Joseph by my brother, which Mr. Rigg's brought up, with him, and in conversation with Wamdiokie, who says he believes now that all men are sinners, or have hearts inclined to evil, though he did not believe it, he says, "when you first told me so." So I was better able to tell him why Christ died, and the necessity of believing in him in order to be at peace with God.

Wednesday, 18th.—I had a visit this afternoon from Wamdiokie, who had much to say about our labors here, other missions, wars, etc. One fact worthy of particular notice he confessed concerning the nation of the Sioux, that "They are wicked exceedingly ;" to use his own expression, "What God loves is good, and men are commanded to do, they have gathered all together, hated and destroyed ; and what God hates and disallows, they have gathered all together, and love and do that only."

Saturday, 26th.—Dr. W. returned to-day from his visit to Big Stone Lake with Mons. Nicollet.

Twenty-sixth. This afternoon I had some conversation with Kayan Hotanka, who is strongly of the opinion that their religion and that of the Bible are the same, and that he has been a Christian twenty years. Deluded man! Can these dry bones live ?

Wednesday, 17th. The Indians are making the valley ring with their yells at scalp-dance, but I hope their time is now short, as they will bury the scalp as soon as the leaves are all fallen off.

Lac-qui-parle, February, 1839.— Heard that Cunagi was left thirty-five miles northeast of here to die of hunger, by her mother. A few days later heard that Intpa left his mother and aunt ten days away to die of hunger because they were unable to walk.

AT LAKE HARRIET (NOW IN HENNEPIN COUNTY) IN 1839.

July 1839. Sioux killed sixty Chippewas at Rum river. Names of Indians who raised corn at Lake Calhoun, and amounts raised by each : Canpuha, 100 bushels ; Xarirota, 50 bushels ; Hoxidan-sapa, 50 bushels ; Ho-waxte, 20 bushels, Karboca, 240 bushels ; Ohin,-paduta, 440 bushels. In all, 1,300 bushels.

Sunday, January 13th, 1840. To-day talked myself tired with some Indians who came after corn, and was able to tell them what I thought, so that they might, if they would, understand what they must do to be saved. One said, as they frequently do, that if the Dakotas could hear these things they would think of them ;" another said, "Nobody would think even though they might hear." At their request we sung two or three hymns in their language. They then said, " Now if you would give us a good supper then we should like it." They are sensual, and only God can make them spiritual.

In 1841 the Indians sell their land for $555,000.

February 10, 1844. —The ninth coffin I have made since October. In March the Indians were all convinced it was April, and near the close of the month the mercury fell to three degrees below zero. The lowest of the winter was ten below. April 1st, heard that an Indian perished with cold.

In 1847 some of the Indians had a drunken frolic, and one bit off the nose of another, which some say he swallowed, and others that they found it near the house the next day. The son of the one who lost his nose shot the one who bit it off in the face with shot, but probably did not hurt him very much. I am acquainted with some who have had their fingers and thumbs bitten off on such occasions. Fine sport, but it sometimes causes unpleasant feelings among them, but that is more than overbalanced by affording an interesting subject of conversation.

The Indians have had high times to-day. I am more and more confirmed in the opinion that as a general thing they

are extremely glad when one is killed by an enemy. A great
parade is always made at the burial. To-day has been peculiarly interesting. What made it highly so, they killed a beef
weighing between 800 and 900 pounds, and have eaten most
of it. In addition to beef they had a keg of whisky, which
would greatly enhance the interest of an event in itself interesting. Those who have killed an enemy were permitted to
sit together and one by one relate their stories and have it
pictured on a great long board previously procured and
planed for the purpose. This afternoon a neighboring Indian
brought a keg of the stuff to our village and invited the chief
and chief soldier to drink. The invitation was refused, which
so angered them them that now about sunset they are about
killing Marpi-wicaxta, and are running about the village and
howling. The women and children all fled and hid. I conclude no one was killed, as they are all quiet and no coffin is
wanted.

An affair came off this afternoon, not a very uncommon
occurrence among the Indians. Karboka's daughter got into
a quarrel with her little brother, and as her father could not
stop her without, he whipped her. The girl being very angry
came over to the hill by our house, where the dead are laid
upon a scaffold, to bewail her misfortune. Her grandmother,
hearing her from the field where she was picking corn, left
her work and came over to see what was the matter with her
granddaughter. Like all good grannies, on hearing from the
girl that her father had punished her, she became enraged,
and in revenge hung herself by a portage collar to the scaffold on which the corpses lie. The little girl, seeing her
sympathetic grandmother in such a predicament, was so terrified that she set up such a screaming that it called us out.
It was in sight of our door. Jane was first on the ground and
had the old woman loosed before we arrived. Even with
their views of futurity, the old woman acted a very foolish
part, for when one hangs herself, as a punishment for the act
she will have to drag through eternity that which they hang
themselves to and be driven about by others. Now the old
woman would have had the whole scaffold, which would have
made her a severe load. She is the same woman who over-
came her husband a short time ago.

Another man's nose gone! At Little Crow's village after they had drank themselves to the brave point one of the sons of the chief showed himself to be a man by biting off the nose of another man. It is thought that it will lead to murder, as the sufferer has declared himself ready to die—an expressive way of making known their intention to revenge an injury by taking life.

May 13th, 1850.—Last week the Indians renewed their threats against those who are disposed to come to our religious meetings ; the fact that two or three women who have never before attended have been attracted to us a few Sabbaths of late is the occasion of it. The great men appear to fear that if they let them alone all the common people will go away and believe on Jesus. It is reported that Red Boy said that whereas the missionaries were getting away all the money, the clothes should be torn from all who came to our meetings on the Sabbath.

Nov. 4th, 1850.—Went to St. Paul with a manuscript copy of the Dakota Friend, and put it into the hands of the printer. It has been with great reluctance that I have attempted the work of editing this little paper. It has been laid upon me by the missionaries under God. If I must perform this service ; if it is the will of God that I should ; He will enable me to do it ; without his assistance I cannot succeed. Lord I look to thee for strength as my day shall be, and may thy rich blessing attend this enterprise. O give wisdom and discretion that I may conduct this difficult and responsible work in thy fear and to thy glory. What am I that I should perform such a service.

November 27th. Started early for St. Paul and returned in the evening fasting. On my way home met Gov. Ramsey, who kindly invited me hereafter in my visits to St. Paul to stop at his house and have my horse put in his stable. Last week I fastened a bundle of hay on behind me for the poor beast, which had to stand the whole day and wait for me. It is no hardship to fast myself. It was with great anxiety that I waited to see the first number of the Dakota Friend. It made a more creditable appearance than was anticipated, and yet there was sufficient in it to mortify me. The blunders of the compositor added to my own inexperience.

CHAPTER LI

The Old Settlers at the Falls of St. Anthony, and Pioneers of Hennepin county, who were here before the first of January, 1853, formed an Association in 1867, for the preservation of a record of the incidents of their early settlement, and for the purpose of cherishing and perpetuating the friendships formed in pioneer days. The articles of association were signed by Isaac Atwater, Joseph Canney, William Hanson, B. B. Meeker, L. N. Parker, J. B. Bassett, R. P. Russell, Edwin Hedderly, Samuel Stanchfield, James Hoffman, James Sully, Waterman Stinson, Alvin Stone, Isaac E. Lane, Alonzo Leaming Sr., James Shaver, William P. Day, James A. Lennon, William Dickie, John Wensinger, Samuel Stough, Calvin Church, Charles Hoag, Allen Harmon, S. W. Case, Edward Murphy, Thomas Chambers, A. E. Ames, John H. Stevens, A. K. Hartwell, Anson Northrup, A. D. Foster, W. A. Rowell, Emery Worthingham, Calvin A. Tuttle, W. G. Moffett, L. W. Stratton, F. C. Coolbaugh, J. P. Miller, Geo. E. Huy, Geo. W. Chowen, Isaac I. Lewis, Pierre Bottineau, John B. Bottineau, and Edgar Folsom.

At the first banquet about two hundred signed the roll, giving the date of their arrival. At this meeting, (twenty-two years ago) Dr. A. E. Ames said : " When General Grant "paid a visit to this city, not long since, he remarked that the "Falls of St. Anthony was the great workshop of the North- "west. I have no doubt this great workshop, in a few years "will contain fifty thousand inhabitants, and there are some "in this room who will live to see it contain one hundred "thousand industrious citizens."

John H. Stevens delivered the first annual address. The second annual address was delivered by Isaac Atwater in 1868. In it he said : "It is given to but few in a lifetime to see "what has been revealed to us in less than a score of years. "If to others has been granted the reaping of the full harvest, "to us has been vouchsafed the first, and perhaps noblest "duty, of sowing the seeds, and the exceeding pleasure of "watching the early growth and increasing luxuriance of "judicious plantings."

Referring to those races which preceded the old settlers in the occupation of this soil, Judge Atwater related an incident : "It was in May, 1851. The day was warm and bright, the grass already green and luxuriant, and many prairie flowers in bloom, and it seemed one could hardly desire a more lovely prospect, from the bluffs just below the old stone mill on this side of the river. As I came in sight of the falls I observed six Dakota warriors standing on the bank gazing intently at the rapids. Four of them had firearms, and two bows and arrows. How long they may have been there I know not, but I watched them for more than an hour, scarcely changing their position, but ever gazing earnestly on the beautiful cataract, and also doubtless on the few buildings that were to be seen on the other side of the river. I then passed on by them, and observed that one of their number was evidently very old. I again passed on the bluff this side of the falls and watched them an half hour longer until they started slowly down the stream. At the foot of the bluff near where is now the lower end of the canal, they turned and looked upon the falls some minutes, and again still longer when they reached the top of the bluff, and then slowly turned their faces toward the setting sun and departed. More of them I do not know ; but who can doubt but that they were taking their last inexpressibly sad farewell of their lovely and loved laughing waters, which they saw were to fall into the hands of the pale-faces. That the Indians are capable of appreciating the beauties of nature cannot be doubted, and to see this glorious heritage of their fathers slipping from their grasp by a stern, irrevocable fate, must fill their breasts with poignant anguish."

Of one of the old settlers, Pierre Bottineau, whose life has perhaps been more full of thrilling adventure and romantic

interest than that of any other individual save the renowned
Kit Carson, the speaker, in the same address, said : "Born
"half a century since, within the limits of Dakota Territory,
"spending his whole life on the frontier, speaking with fluency
"five different languages, familiar with the habits and customs
"of several different tribes of Indians, renowned as a guide,
"hunter and voyageur, intimately acquainted with the whole
"vast country north and west of us to the Rocky mountains,
"and once the owner of the soil where a portion of the city of
"St. Anthony now stands, his life affords the richest material
"for the pen of the biographer, and merits a place in our rec-
"ords, and even a wider publicity than it would there obtain."

The third annual address was delivered by Charles Hoag,
the fourth by R. M. Johnson, and the fifth by William R.
Marshall. The last named gentleman, in 1871, said : "Almost
a quarter of a century ago, I stood on the banks of the grand
old river, and in hearing of the great falls. On a beautiful
September day I followed the winding trail from the little
French settlement that clustered around Father Galtiers'
log church which gave the name of St. Paul to the the present
city—across the beautiful prairie and over the wooded hills,
to what my French guide called San Antoine. And when
with weary feet I stood at last, in the afternoon of that day,
on the brink of the falls, I saw them in all their beauty and
grandeur, unmarred by the hand of man—in such beauty of
nature as no one has seen them in the last twenty-two years.

"The falls were then almost perpendicular ; that of the
main channel many hundred feet lower down than the present
falls. Spirit island, now almost wasted away, was then a
considerable wood-crowned island, just a little below the main
falls. Cataract and Nicollet islands were densely wooded.
The smooth river gliding over its sloping bed of limestone
from near midway of the upper island, plunged over the broken edge of its rocky bed much nearer the lower end of
Cataract island, on both sides, than it does now.

"Save the old government mill on the west side, so small
as to be half hidden among the rocks and trees of the river
bank, there was only the habitation that belonged to it. A little
further back there was only a state of nature on that side.

"On this, the St. Anthony side of the river, there was an

old log house opposite the falls, by which Mr. Steele held his claim to the lands, with a little field of corn attached covering a few acres of the plateau where Captain Rollin's house and the Tremont house now stand. A log house was then being built under the hill above the present mill, to be used for the men who were soon to commence work putting in the mill dam. These, with Pierre Bottineau's house on the bank above the head of Nicollet island, Calvin A. Tuttle's claim shanty near the brook this side of the State University, and two or three French squatters' cabins, were all that marked the presence of man on the east bank of the Mississippi.

As the light of the fast declining sun of that autumn day bathed the tops of the trees and the summits of the gentle hills, and as the plunging, seething, deafening falls sent up the mist and set its rainbow arching the same, I was filled with a sense of the beautiful, and somewhat of the awe-inspiring, in nature, such as I have rarely since experienced."

ADDRESS BY REV. E. D. NEILL.

In 1872, Rev. E. D. Neill delivered the sixth annual address, which contained : " Whenever we witness growth, we desire to know something of what was in the beginning. In all ages men have looked back with reverence to the origin of things, and have loved to compare the time that was with the present hour the then with the now. To gratify this desire the Hebrew lawgiver, Moses, was inspired to write the opening sentences of the earliest historical record, which the old Greek lawgivers pronounced sublime.

The patriot is always refreshed by tracing the successive stages of the development of national life and power ; and so the dwellers of particular neighborhoods are strengthened by coming together and remembering the days of old.

In this new city of the upper Mississippi, Neapolis, as the ancient Greeks would have termed it in their beautiful and flexible language, we are forcibly reminded of growth. It is difficult to realize that a busy population of twenty thousand occupy the ground that so many of us remember as the land of the Dakotas and an uncultivated prairie.

Imlay, a British subject, visited the valley of the Mississippi before the close of the last century, while Congress held its session in Philadelphia, and in his book upon the Western

Territory, published in London in 1797, he wrote that he
thought it was rather puerile in the United States to think of
making their seat of government upon the Potomac ; and at
that early date expressed the opinion that in the course of a
century the vicinity of the Falls of St. Anthony ought to be
the permanent seat of government.

I can but feel that it would be injurious to the dignity of
the American citizens ever to abandon the magnificent capitol
at Washington, whose lofty dome was being completed
while a vast army of insurgents were camped on adjacent
hillsides, and whose solidity and simple adornments are typi-
cal of a Republic whose President is elected from the people ;
and yet when I witness the city that has developed at the
Falls of St. Anthony, within the last ten years, and consider
the population that must follow the line of the Northern
Pacific railway for the next twenty-five years, I am inclined
to believe that Mr. Imlay's prediction may prove true, and
that before A. D. 1900 the center of population of the American Republic may be in the Northwest, and perhaps, as the
Hon. W. H. Seward said, in his Minnesota address, ' The
ultimate seat of government on this great continent will be
found somewhere not very far from the head of navigation of
the Mississippi river.

On the 15th of August, 1829, Agent Taliaferro established
an Indian agricultural school at Lake Calhoun, which he
named Eatonville after the Secretary of War, whose wife
caused so much disturbance in Washington social circles
during the days of President Jackson. The surgeon of the
Fort in 1829 was a young man, a native of Rhode Island, Dr.
R. C. Wood, and while there he went down to the garrison at
Prairie du Chien, and married the eldest daughter of Zachary
Taylor, the officer in command at that post. In an open boat
he returned to Fort Snelling with his youthful bride. How
wonderful the changes witnessed by that family in forty years !
The father of the bride became President of the United States
and lived long enough to see the clouds of rebellion gathering
in the South, and to abhor the plotters for disunion ; while
Jefferson Davis, a son-in-law of General Taylor, became the
President of the so-called confederate states. Dr. Wood
proved true to the government, and during the war was ·

assistant surgeon general of the United States army ; but his son followed the South, and was the commander of that noted rebel privateer, the Tallahassee.

Among the few slaves ever brought within the limits of Minnesota several belonged to Major Taliaferro. Under date of the 26th of May of the same year, we find in his journal this entry : 'Captain Plympton wishes to purchase my servant girl. I informed him that it was my intention to give her freedom after a limited time, but that Mrs. Plympton could keep her for two years, or perhaps three.

In 1836 Dred Scott, whose name has become historic, came to Fort Snelling with his master, Surgeon Emerson, and fell in love with Taliaferro's slave girl, Harriet, and in due time the marriage agreement was made in the Major's presence, and was duly certified by him as a justice of the peace. Two years after this Mr. Emerson left the Fort, taking with him Dred Scott and his wife, and while descending the river on the steamboat Gipsey the wife gave birth to her first born. The decision of Chief Justice Taney relative to the right of Dred Scott as a citizen led, as we all know, to acrimonious discussions between the friends of freedom and slavery, and was one of the causes that led to the fratricidal war which wiped out with much precious blood the 'sable spot' upon the escutchion of American liberty, to which Moore in one of his poems tauntingly alludes.

The earliest marriages in Hennepin county were declared in accordance with the forms of the civil law, before Lawrence Taliaferro, as justice of the peace. On July 3, 1835, Hippolite Provost was married to Margaret Brunell, and on the 29th of the same month a Mr. Godfrey married Sophia Perry. In February, 1836, Charles Musseau was married to Fanny, the daughter of Abraham Perry, a Swiss emigrant who came from the Hudson Bay Territory in 1827, and settled at first between the Fort and Minnehaha, and afterwards when the military reservation was defined, built a log house in what is now a suburb of St. Paul. On September 12th, 1846, at the house of Oliver Crattle, near the Fort, James Wells, who subsequently was a member of the territorial legislature, and was killed in the late Sioux massacre, was married to Jane, daughter of Duncan Graham, and on the 29th of November, at the quar-

398   PERSONAL RECOLLECTIONS

ters of Captain Barker, Alpheus R. French, the errly saddler
of St. Paul, was married to Mary Henry. One of the first
ecclesiastical ceremonies in the county took place at Lake
Harriet in 1839, when the Rev. Mr. Gavin was married to
Miss Stevens, a teacher in the mission school at that point."

ADDRESS BY GIDEON H. POND.

In 1873 Gideon H. Pond delivered an address at an Old
Settlers' picnic on the banks of Lake Harriet, in which reminiscent discourse he dwelt upon his pioneer experience of
savage life in what is now Hennepin county. It is now, 1889,
just sixty years since Major Taliaferro established an Indian
agricultural school at Lake Calhoun. This great northwestern territory, with its rivers, lakes, and plains, stretching out
to the east, west, north, and south, was a seemingly " intermin-
"able extent of earth, naked and empty of all traces of civil-
"ized life, (with few exceptions,) the abode only of savage
"beasts, wild fowl, and savage, pagan man. Little clusters of
"smoky wigwams along the rivers and around the lakes, con-
"tained the rude inhabitants of all the region."

On a July day in 1839, now just half a century ago, at Lake
Harriet, Mr. Pond says there was " a cluster of summer huts,
"constructed of small poles and barks of trees, the summer
"home of four or five hundred savage souls, surrounded by
"their gardens of corn and squashes. It was an Indian vil-
"lage. The five hundred had swarmed out into and around
"the shores of the lakes. Men, women and children were
"all engaged in hunting, chopping, fishing, swimming, play-
"ing, singing, yelling, whooping, and wailing. The air was
"full of all sorts of savage sounds, frightful to one unaccus-
"tomed to them. The clamor and clatter on all sides made
"me feel that I was in the midst of barbarism. And I was.
"Suddenly, like a peal of thunder when no cloud is visible,
"here, there, everywhere, awoke the startling alarm whoop,
"'Hoo, hoo, hoo!' Blankets were thrown in the air, men,
"women and children ran—they ran for life. Terror sat on
"every face—mothers grasped their little ones. All around
"was crying, wailing, shrieking, storming and scolding. Men
"vowed vengeance, whooped defiance, and dropped bullets
"into their gun-barrels. The excitement was intense and
"universal. The Chippewas! The Chippewas have surrounded

" us—we shall all be butchered ! Rupacokamaza is killed !

" Ah, yes ! just across there, on the other bank of Lake Harriet—there he lies, all bloody, the soul is gone from the body, escaping through that bullet hole, the scalp is torn from the head. A crowd has gathered, and every heart is hot with wrath. Ah, me ! what wailing ! what imprecation ! The dead one is the son-in-law of the chief, and nephew to the medicine man, Redbird. Every warrior, young and old, utters his determined vow of vengeance as Redbird stoops to press his lips on the yet warm, bleeding corpse, cursing the enemy in the name of the gods. Now see the runners scud in all directions. In an hour or two the warriors begin to arrive, painted, moccasined, victualed, and armed for the war path. Indian warriors are all minute men. Come with me to St. Anthony Falls. Here is the unspoiled river, rushing unhindered down his rocky bed —naught else. We will stand on the rocky bluff. Now come the avengers of blood ! They come from Shakopee, from Eaglehead, from Goodroad, from Badhail and from Blackdog. All the hot afternoon of this July day they cross and recross their canoes over the bosom of the river at the head of the island. The sun is just ready to sink, as we look at the long row of warriors, seated on the east bank. That tall form, dressed not much unlike Adam before the fall, save war paint, at the head of the line, is Redbird. One long wail goes up from three or four hundred savage throats, as Redbird utters his imprecatory prayer to the gods. He presents to them the pipe of war, and it goes down the ranks, as he follows it, laying his hands on the head of each, binding him by all that is sacred in human relationships and religion, to strike for the gods, and for Redbird.

The next evening the dusky runners begin to arrive at Lake Calhoun from the battle-ground at Rum river, where Redbird is killed, his son is killed, a dozen other Dakotas are killed, and the Chippewas are nearly all killed ! Seventy scalps dangle from the poles in the center of the village, close by the tepee of the father-in-law of Philander Prescott. The scalp-dance lasted for a month. It seemed as if hell had emptied itself here.

" Glorious contrast ! Cities now stand thick along your rivers, Civilized man everywhere. Schools, academies, colleges, and churches fill the land. Grace, mercy and peace !"

LETTER OF DR. CHAS. L. ANDERSON, WRITTEN ON SOLICITATION.

Old Settlers : Dear Friends : Almost half a century ago I began pioneering, and I have been a settler from the Alleghany mountains to the Pacific Ocean, taking a swath of latitude nearly ten degrees wide. After helping you, in my humble way, to plant the Garden of Eden, I have left you in the midst thereof and gone out of Paradise on the west side, following the river "that went out of Eden," up the branch Pison, "which compasseth the whole land of Havilah, where there is gold." I have followed the evening star to the orchards of the Hesperides, in search of golden apples, and have found none ! Whilst you who have remained to dress the garden have eaten the fruit and become wise. May the curse that followed Adam and Eve never be pronounced against you. And may you be the recipients of that promise made to Abraham and the faithful when your days of pioneering are over, "a city which hath foundations whose maker and builder is God."

But you do not all remain. Now and then I hear of some of your pioneer bands crossing a dark valley, leaving tears and sorrowings behind. We do not hear from them again, but we have the assurance that we shall see them when we reach the beautiful gate that bounds the Elysian shore.

Happy Old Settlers ! it would delight me to take you each one by the hand and look into your faces. I think that notwithstanding the few wrinkles and gray hairs gained I should be able to read a bright page of happiness set in bold type and ornamented by these blessed signs of age. So long as our bodies are free from disease we should be thankful and happy, and as we grow old strive to grow better. Should affliction be ours there is a consolation that trial only can purify and make our souls beautiful. Although literally speaking I have found no "golden apples" on this shore, yet I feel tolerably well contented, and that is worth something, however difficult it may be to estimate its value in gold or greenbacks.

Some of my friends have found golden bonanzas. We ought not to think less of them for their good luck, and I hope we do not ; but bonanzas are not the best things to be found, especially when they are alloyed with much base metal, which often has a contaminating effect upon the finder. Your Friend,

Santa Cruz, Cal., Jan. 22, 1876.   C. L. ANDERSON.

BIOGRAPHICAL MEMORANDA—WITH LETTERS TO
COLONEL JOHN H. STEVENS.

SELECTED BY MARSHALL ROBINSON.

The author of the foregoing "Personal Recollections of Minnesota and its People" would seem to merit a more extended
personal notice than appears therein.   He has so kindly written of many persons that it seems appropriate here to embody
their views in relation to him as expressed during an intimate
exchange of correspondence from fifty years ago to the present.
A few preliminary facts only will be given.

John Harrington Stevens was born in Lower Canada June
13th, 1820.   He is the second son of Gardner and Deborah
Stevens.   His parents were natives and citizens of Vermont,
and their ancestors were also New England people, many of
whom occupied positions in the councils of the national and
state governments.   The mother of Mr. Stevens was the only
daughter of Dr. John Harrington, a surgeon in the war for
Independence, who died in Brookfield, Vermont, in 1804.   His
grandfather also served throughout the Revolutionary war.
Gardner Stevens, his father, was a man of wealth and influence.

In very early manhood Mr. Stevens went to Galena, Illinois,
where he lived for several years.   He then entered the United
States military service in the war with Mexico, serving in the
Quartermaster's department.   Leaving Mineral Point, October
1846, for New Orleans, he sailed thence, November 1st, for
Brazos Santiago, near the mouth of the Rio Grande, and proceeded thence to Matamoras, Mexico.   On Christmas morning of that year he left Matamoras, with General Pillow's
command, for Victoria via San Fernando in the State of Tam-

aulipas. At Victoria he met General Zachary Taylor's command, and was sent to Tampico, and from there to Lobos Island, Vera Cruz, Puebla, and the City of Mexico. He was present at the battles of Contreras, San Antonia, Churubusco, Molino del Rey and Chepultepec. After the occupation of the City of Mexico he was sent to the National Bridge, in the state of Vera Cruz, where he remained during the winter. His retirement from the army is indicated by the following official correspondence :

RESIGNATION TENDERED.

Ass't Q. M. Office, National Bridge,
Mexico, May 13, 1848.

Colonel George R. McClellan, Commanding
Department, Point National, Mexico :

Sir—In consequence of being afflicted with sore eyes, I am reluctantly obliged to resign my office in the Quartermaster Department of the United States Army ; which berth it will be impossible for me to fill in consequence of the above-stated reason.

I hope you will be so kind as to accept the resignation, which I now tender, and I can assure you that it is done with much regret on my part. With great respect, I am, Sir,

Your obedient servant,   JOHN H. STEVENS.

RESIGNATION ACCEPTED.

Headquarters Department of National Bridge,
Mexico, May 14th, 1848.

Your resignation is accepted on the grounds given by you. The probability is that peace will soon be made and the troops moved out of Mexico.

In accepting your resignation I know that the government is about to lose the services of one who has faithfully discharged the arduous duties of his stations with credit to himself and the entire satisfaction of that portion of the army that it has been his fortune to serve with in the tented field.

GEO. R. McCLELLAN, Colonel Com'g Post.

Captain John H. Stevens.

National Bridge, Mexico, May 30th, 1848.

The above are recorded in the Colonel's Register.

COUNT DE LARN, Acting Secretary.

Quartermaster's Department, Assistant Office,
Puenta National, Mexico, May 30th, 1848.

My Dear Sir : You will leave this evening in charge of the train for Vera Cruz, and will be constantly on the alert, being sure to enforce good order with the escort and guard against any attack that may be made by the enemy.

On your arrival at Vera Cruz you will immediately embark on a government transport vessel for New Orleans, at which place, by your own request, you will be mustered out of service.

The department cannot allow you to retire to private life without expressing deep and sincere thanks for the valuable services you have rendered to it for the last two years. You justly merit the approbation of your brother officers and of every soldier in the American army, and it affords me much satisfaction to say that the whole command sees you retire with sorrow and regret, all hoping that you will have a happy and prosperous journey home, and that you may hereafter enjoy the society of your friends in that degree of happiness which exalted worth always surrounds the honest and noble of mankind.   SAM'L G. McCLELLAN, A. Q. M. and A. A. C. S.

To. John H. Stevens, U. S. C. Q. M. and P. Master.

On the 1th day of May, 1850, Colonel Stevens was married at Rockford, Illinois, to Miss Frances Helen Miller, daughter of Abner Miller, of Westmoreland, Oneida county, New York. Mrs. Stevens' parents were from New England, of Puritan ancestors. Her mother, before marriage, was Sallie Lyman, of the Lyman Beecher branch. Her grandfather and the grandmother of Henry Ward Beecher were brother and sister. Mr. and Mrs. Stevens have had six children. Mary Elizabeth, the first white child born in Minneapolis, died in her seventeenth year. Catharine Duane, their second child, is the wife of Philip B. Winston, a native of Virginia, now a wealthy and prominent citizen of Minneapolis. Sarah, the third child, died when a young lady. Gardner, their only son and fourth child, is a citizen of Minneapolis. Orma, the fifth child, is the wife of W. L. Peck of Minneapolis, a railroad contractor with Winston Brothers. Frances Helen, the youngest daughter, is at home in Minneapolis. Mr. and Mrs. Stevens have numerous relatives in Minnesota, and relations in other states occupying positions of prominence.

Colonel Stevens was a member of the first Minnesota house of representatives, of the second state senate, of the fourth legislature, and of the legislature of 1876. He has been brigadier-general of the state militia, and held many other civil and military offices, as will appear by extracts given from letters of his correspondents. Letters received by him for nearly half a century have been preserved almost entire, and number thousands. Many of them are of the most confidential character. Extracts from such only as might seem to be given with propriety are here presented as interesting reminiscences of the times in which they were written, and as illustrative of the estimation in which Colonel Stevens was held :

LETTER FROM HORACE GREELEY.

Office of the Tribune, New York, August 16, 1863.

My Dear Sir : It is now some two years and a half since I accepted an invitation to visit Minnesota and speak to her farmers at her State Agricultural Fair an invitation which gave me pleasure in the reception, and still more in the anticipation of its fulfillment. I am still anxious that my life and the patience of my friends in Minnesota may both hold out until I can be permitted to fulfill that engagement.

But those I (with all respect to others) most wish to meet when I shall visit your state are to-day in the National armies, braving exposure, fatigue, privation and death for the life of their country. I begin to grow old. I shall probably never traverse your state but this once : and I want to be at leisure to do it with some deliberation. But still more do I wish to meet and thank the noble Minnesotians—no matter where they were born or what have been their affinities or antipathies to me who have consecrated their lives to their country's salvation. You probably have noted that I have not always felt so sanguine of a happy issue from our present troubles as many if not most other loyal Americans have done. I have too often feared that disloyalty at the North would complete the ruin plotted and inaugurated by open treason at the South. It is possible, therefore, that I enjoy the brighter prospects that have recently opened before us more keenly than those who receive them as a matter of course. I now feel more than hopeful that the Rebellion will be put down and the Union preserved. But the struggle is not yet over, nor is the result absolutely sure. And, so long as there is anything to be done or to be feared on the side of the Union, it seems to me that my post, whether of duty or danger, is here, more especially while the greatest remaining and now most imminent peril of the National cause is that of Northern defection and hostility rather than of Southern treason. Let me once more, then, beg the Farmers of Minnesota to have patience with me and to excuse my absence from their Fair this Autumn, in the sanguine hope that the next Summer's sun will smile upon our country reunited, peaceful and secure, and that I may visit you next Autumn in the hope of meeting many of the heroes of our great struggle, safely returned from the bivouac and the battle-field, rejoicing in the grateful appreciation of their countrymen and in the proud endearments of their happy wives and children.

Yours truly, HORACE GREELEY.

John H. Stevens, Esq., Sec. State Ag. Soc., Minneapolis, Minn.

State of Minnesota, Executive Department,
St. Paul, September 21st, 1863.

To Whom it may Concern : This is to certify that pursuant to the provisions of the law of this State to enable citizens engaged in the military and naval service of the United States to vote in their several election districts, John H. Stevens, the bearer hereof, has been duly appointed and qualified as one of the Commissioners duly appointed to visit and receive the votes of such of the soldiers of Minnesota as are in the Southern and Western states lying west of the western line of the States of Virginia and North and South Carolina.

It is earnestly desired that the military authorities will respect Mr. Stevens as such Commissioner, and allow him free access to the soldiers of this state for the purpose designated. In testimony whereof I have hereunto set my hand and caused the Great Seal of the State to be affixed the day and year aforesaid. HENRY A. SWIFT.

[Seal.] By the Governor : D. Blakely, Sec. of State.

IN RELATION TO THE INDIAN WAR.

Governor Alex. Ramsey writes, Sept. 2, 1862 : " My dear " Col. I am pleased to learn that by your energetic measures " quiet has been restored to the country about Glencoe. I " wish Captain Strout to remain in the eastern counties where

" he now is until further orders. Our forces have relieved
" Ridgley, and on Sunday Col. Sibley with a portion of his
"command, moved towards the Lower Agency. The Chip-
"pewas are quiet, and we are sending relief to Abercrombie,
" so I hope in a short time we will return to a quiet condition.
" But the Sioux must leave the state."

Senator Henry M. Rice writes Oct. 12, 1862 : "Dear Col.:
What's in the wind ? Are the Indians again to be placed
upon their reservations, and their crimes go unavenged ?
God forbid. Who can care for Minnesota, or who can sympathize with those who have suffered worse than death, and
the relations of the dead, that will for a moment think of
keeping those fiends within our state ? The people of your
county have all at stake. You can help them, and I know
will. My all, life itself, will be given to save Minnesota."

Governor Stephen Miller writes, June 16, 1863 : " My dear
Sir—I have strong hopes that the days of panic have comparatively passed, and that the good citizens upon the frontier
will, like our old ancestors in Pennsylvania, Ohio, Kentucky,
and other states, pitch in on their own hook, and scalp every
hostile Sioux that by any possibility passes the military line.
So far as I can learn only about eighteen hostile Sioux, all
told, have visited the state this spring, and yet we learn that
grown up men talk of leaving the state. Let us, my good
friend, stand our ground at all hazards, and infuse such a
spirit of gallantry in our good citizens as will make our soil
the tomb of every redskinned demon that dares to approach
it. The military will be urged by every possible consideration to perform their whole duty."

On the 25th of the same month, Governor Miller writes :
" I know that in everything that tends to the promotion of the
great object in view I may rely upon the cooperation of yourself and a number of other worthies upon the frontier. Including Abercrombie, I have but two thousand troops, all told,
with which to protect four hundred miles of frontier. But
with the aid of yourself, and with other good citizens, who
greet me with kindly words, though they do not in all things
agree with me, I trust that reason will yet prevail. Help me,
I beg of you, to get our good citizens inspired with the hero-
ism which distinguished the early pioneers of the Northwest.

As a general rule they did their own fighting ; assistance by government troops was the exception. I would not, if I could, place so heavy a burthen upon our frontier now ; but is it too much to ask them to let us throw our strength upon the frontier line ; while they keep themselves ready to act as a reserve in case of an emergency ? It other words, while they trust in God and the soldiers, can we not persuade them to keep their arms convenient, and 'their powder dry' ? But let the red demons once know that soldiers and citizens alike have scouted panics, and sworn death to every savage invader, and my life for it, they will very soon let us alone. I am using every effort to establish the line and to make it efficient. I am terribly in earnest. I am applied to for hundreds of troops daily, from St. Croix via Lake Superior, Crow Wing, Otter Tail, &c., clear to the Iowa line and must needs reply to all, but certainly to none more cheerfully than yourself."

On the 22d of July, 1863, Governor Miller writes, dating from " Headquarters of the Forces in Garrison, District of Minnesota, Department of the Northwest. St. Paul, Minn. My Dear Col.: Your kind communication of a few days since found me greatly afflicted by the intelligence that my eldest son, a first lieutenant in the Seventh U. S. Infantry, had fallen at the battle of Gettysburg. It is a sad, sad blow ; but he died at his post ; and I bless his memory. Better that my entire family should perish than one star be erased from the old Flag.

" I am gratified to learn that you are likely to remain in the infected district for a time. I always feel much easier when you are there. Your paper too, I am happy to see, is distributing the best possible counsel to our panic-stricken citizens ; and will, I hope, bring them to see that a dozen or twenty Indians are not likely to depopulate a half-dozen counties if we do our duty.

" If the Democratic organization know their duty and consult their interests, and can elect any candidate, they will give you the gubernatorial nomination whether you want it or not. I am sorry to say that your party, as well as another I could name, too often reserves its nominations for 'pigmies,' instead of conferring them upon its best men. Ever your friend,

S. MILLER.

IN THE TREASURY DEPARTMENT.

Washington, May 17th, 1864.

My dear Col.: Whenever a vacancy in any place at Natchez occurs, and for which you desire to be a candidate, send me an application for the place and I will at once present it.

As Mr. Chase has a general agent for the business of his department in the southwest, it would be well to have his endorsement of the application. Very truly yours, &c.,

ALEX. RAMSEY.

Col. J. H. Stevens, Natchez, Miss.

From the Room of Claims Commission, Department of the Gulf, New Orleans, La., May 15, 1865, Brigadier-General M. Brayman reports : "Hon. John H. Stevens of Minnesota was, for several months during my command at Natchez, Miss., an officer of the Treasury Department at that place.

"He came, a stranger, highly recommended by men distinguished in civil and military life. I found him an upright, honorable and true man, and worthy my highest respect and confidence.

"So far as I know, (and I had good means of knowing,) his official duties were performed intelligently, honestly, and for the good of the service, and when he took responsibilities or used discretionary powers, it was done wisely, and with few mistakes.

"In my efforts to correct the gross iniquities which disgraced the public service at Natchez, and in the laborious investigations made under my direction, I profited much by the wise counsel and ready assistance afforded by Mr. Stevens."

LETTERS FROM GOVERNOR SIBLEY.

"Mendota, Feb. 22, 1862.—Hon. John H. Stevens, H. of R., St. Paul : My dear Sir There is a poor widow woman named Ellen Langford, for whose relief a bill was passed in '58 or '59, by the legislature, which gave her the preference in the purchase of the 160 acres on the school lands where she lived and still lives. A bill for the repeal of that act was introduced into the senate and passed while the woman was sick in bed, and she knew nothing of it, until within the last week. She is in great distress about it, and as the grant was made to her in good faith after the case had been thoroughly examined upon its merits, I trust the house will not concur in the repeal.

It is evident there has been some underhanded move against her, and I hope you will feel it to be your duty to defend her rights, with your vote and influence. I hope soon to see you and talk over matters in general."

St. Paul, Feb. 12, 1876.

My dear Colonel : Mr. Horace Thompson and myself were at the capitol yesterday, intending to call on you, but the house had adjourned before we could do so. Our object was to consult with you in relation to a joint resolution drawn by us, and now in the hands of Senator Wilkinson, providing for the formation of a commission of thirteen of the most prominent and reliable men in the state, geographically distributed, who shall have power to send for persons and papers, and examine witnesses under oath, and report to the next legislature their facts and conclusions as to the legal and equitable liabilities of the state in connection with the state railroad bonds. Every fair-minded man must feel the necessity in this centennial year of something being done to show to the outside world that Minnesota intends to ascertain what her status is, so far as those bonds are concerned, with a view to proper action in the promises. Minnesota is now suffering financially, as well as in character, and you will doubtless feel as we do, that the time has arrived for the state to take up this question and dispose of it upon equitable and honorable terms, and thus free herself of the stain which rests upon her. You can effect much in procuring the passage of the joint resolution through the house. You and I feel alike that the question should be adjusted on an honorable basis, and I hope that will be done during my lifetime. Your old friend. H. H. SIBLEY.

St. Paul, Nov. 10th, 1884.

My dear old friend : I feel deeply grateful to yourself, and the many friends I am fortunate enough to have among the old settlers of Hennepin county, for the kind and flattering greeting I have received from them, through you, on the fiftieth anniversary of my first advent to what is now a great and prosperous state.

The occasion was, nevertheless, somewhat tinged with melancholy, when my mind reverted to the long list of those who with us had "borne the burden and heat of the day," but had been "gathered to their fathers," leaving but a remnant of their co-laborers to survive them. God grant to you all a lengthened term of years, and a happy end.

Please give my warm regards to all the members of your honored Association, and believe me as ever, yours sincerely.

H. H. SIBLEY.

LETTERS FROM H. M. RICE.

Senator H. M. Rice, under date of Washington, Feb. 4th, 1855, writes : "My Dear Sir: Ere this reaches you, you will have heard of the passage of the Reserve Bill through the House, and ere to-morrow night I hope it will pass the Senate. Don't Ames feel good ! I hope you will all feel relieved. You do not know how much I have to do. The only reward I hope for is that my work will produce a good yield of rich fruit. The doctor has worked well, and I like him much. Soon as the Reserve Bill becomes a law I will start for home."

"Washington, April 1st, 1858.—Steele is here, but the death of one of his children, and the present illness of his entire family, has necessarily made him apparently neglectful of his friends. I intend to support the Administration, believing that in so doing I am protecting the best interests of our gloriour state, upon which nature has lavished so much that is good. In regard to the loan bill : I am a warm advocate of its ratification by the people. Upon its adoption consequences of the highest moment to the state depend. We must keep pace with the progress of other portions of the country. That a network of railroads in our state is imperatively demanded, no one can deny. And I believe the only feasible and sure method of accomplishing this result is the one adopted by the legislature. I trust the amendment will be adopted by an almost unanimous vote."

"Washington, April 16, 1858.—Steele left here to-day for New York. He is right all the time. We do not admit a constitution- we admit a state. The people can, after admission, fix up their own matters, as they please. How ridiculous this eternal quarrel about a few negroes, and at the expense of twenty-five millions of white people."

"Washington, April 24th, 1860.—The accounts from Pike's Peak are conflicting. Were you a single man, I might advise you to go there, but when I think of your wife and little ones that must be left behind, I cannot do it. You ought to have an appointment in our state where you have done such good service. I hope the time may come when you will be rewarded for your labors, not only for the party and your friends, but for services rendered the new comers."

"St. Paul, October 3d, 1860.— I went to the Fair for the purpose of meeting you, but you had left. I did wish to have a long talk with you. You are one of the old guard you who have sacrificed much for the good of Minnesota. I did wish to see you to ascertain what has caused a separation between us. My conscience tells me that I am right. I know that I am in the minority—but were I alone, and yet sustained by conscience, I would fight to the last. Political ties are strong but personal ones are stronger. A thousand new-comers may, disagree with me, and not a sleepless night will I psss—but when one of the old guard says I am wrong, I cannot sleep. Now, my friend, if your heart says that Douglas is right, that he has been consistent, continue to support him. I think Breckinridge is right—I shall support him. This is a private letter, written to a friend, in a friendly spirit. I say to you that a Douglas organization cannot be kept up ninety days. He has gone—he is working with the South Americans—and they cannot stand the light of day. Douglas now occupies the sixth position upon the subject of Slavery. Douglas is out of the question, and why waste powder upon him. Lincoln I do not believe can be elected. Therefore let us keep our forces together. God bless you."

"St. Paul, April 9, 1876.—Yours of the 7th came yesterday. Its tone struck a chord that has been dormant a long time. By it I can see that in you the milk of human kindness is as fresh and copious as in times long past. I thank you for it, and will try and visit your place this week. HENRY M. RICE."

FROM HON. IGNATIUS DONNELLY.

"Nininger, Minn., August 8th, 1859.—I perfectly agree with you, that politics should not make us lose sight of our material interests. Honor and wealth are two very distinct things, and one cannot supply the want of the other.

" Is there no way of trading lots in Nininger, or Louisville. for five hundred or one thousand acres of land, timber, lake. etc., near Glencoe ? I could throw in five hundred dollars in money. If so, I would improve the whole tract, and move on to it, and then set myself to work to advance the interests of McLeod county with all my strength and will. I want to get a good big farm. We could lay our heads together and either build a tram railroad from Carver or a plank road. That thirty miles of timber is the curse of McLeod county at present. It takes considerable hardihood to travel through it twice. You will never advance rapidly until you have a good road.

"By all means go into the legislature. I think there is a future of prosperity before both of us ; there are new towns to be laid out, and new counties to be settled.

"A poverty-stricken politician is one of the most miserable objects alive ; and it is the duty of every sensible man, by all means to place himself beyond the reach of want. There is no degree of intellect that can resist the deadening influence of an empty pocket."

"Nininger, Dec. 20, 1873.—If you had not made that unfortunate protection speech we could have nominated you for Governor and have elected you. But there is a future in which we can all correct our mistakes.

"Be assured that although compelled to opposed you then, it was on no personal ground, and I shall seize the first opportunity to show you how sincerely I am your friend.

IGNATIUS DONNELLY.

AN EARLY BOOM—WITH A PROTEST—FROM FRANKLIN STEELE.

"Fort Snelling, August 20th, 1854.— Dear Stevens : I have received your two letters, and write this with the hope that it may reach you in Galena. We have had our own troubles since you left, with the people claiming to have purchased lots from you, to the extent of about half of all that is valuable. Mr. Sampson returned from St. Paul the day that you left, and told everybody that you had authorized him to say that any one could go and select a lot where they pleased at one hundred and fifty dollars per lot. The consequence was that half the town was claimed, and they began to haul on the lumber to build. Northrup came down for me when, with the assistance of Mr. Lewis and Mr. Case, most of them were induced to desist until you should return. Some of them, having deeds from you, remained. Now it is absolutely nec-- essary that we should refuse to sell or permit a single indi vidual to come on to the premises before the day of sale. Upon your return you will be beset on all hands, but you must make but one rule to all, to refuse to do a thing before you get a title. In this way you will escape a world of trouble. I have taken the advice of our mutual friends, Case and Ames, and have acted as your agent in the affair."

"Fort Snelling, Sept. 22d, 1854.—Dear Stevens : Now for your own sake and mine, remember our arrangement and do not give away all you have or expect to get. I may be doing you an injustice ; if so, what I now write will go for nothing. Now I implore you not to promise a single lot before a title accrues.　　　　Your friend,　　　　FRANKLIN STEELE."

"Fort Snelling, Dec. 11, 1859.—Dear Col.: I shall ever cherish the most grateful feeling toward you and our mutual friends Cowan and Adams, for honest effort to promote my interest, although not successful. If all who have made professions of friendship had acted as you have done, I might have been gratified to the full extent of my ambition, and have been in a position to help my friends ; but I have found that those I have served most faithfully have been the first to desert me when I required their assistance. I will leave for the East immediately and obtain all the information possible in regard to Pike's Peak, and other places now resorted to for recuperation. I am of the opinion that a very large emigration will set in toward Minnesota in the spring, and that affairs will improve. If I did not entertain this belief I should take my final departure immediately, for I would not go through for another year what I have the past for any consideration. If I can find any place in which you can do better than at home upon your farm, I will write you. Your old and faithful friend,　　　　FRANKLIN STEELE."

FRATERNAL LETTERS FROM DR. ALFRED E. AMES.

Dr. Alfred E. Ames was one of the earliest and most prominent pioneers of Minneapolis. From notes made at the request of his children, it appears that he was a native of Vermont. His grandfather Ames had fourteen children, his father eight, and the doctor himself seven. In youth he struggled for an education, taught school, studied medicine, and worked incessantly. In boyhood, on his way from Vermont to Ohio, by the Erie Canal, at Schenectady he first saw a railroad train.

"A rude engine, with three cars attached, made several efforts "to start, when bystanders pushed, and off it went." He rode from Detroit to Chicago in a stage. "Chicago then had 3,000 "inhabitants of half breeds and all others." From Chicago he followed an Indian trail sixty-five miles northwest to Boone county, Illinois, where he made a claim of one hundred and sixty acres and built a log house ; passing through severe trials, in relation to which he says "there is nothing so good "for such dark days as a firm resolution—a sure determination "and reliance upon God." Putting a pack on his back, he " took an Indian trail and went to Vandalia, then the seat of "government. Thanks to Heaven," he writes, " I soon found "employment. Hon. Stephen A. Douglas and Captain James " Craig interceded and introduced me to Alex. B. Field, who "was then secretary of state, who employed me as his deputy, "and Governor Thomas Carlin made me his private secretary." He afterwards went to Springfield, Illinois, and was employed by Stephen A. Douglas as his deputy secretary of state. About this time he was " raised to the Sublime degree of Masonry," and also gave medical lectures. He was elected first to the house and then to the senate of Illinois. In 1851 he came to Minneapolis, and in 1852 brought his family here. He records that " Minneapolis was then called and known as All Saints." He was present at the organization of Hennepin county, and was the first physician in Minneapolis. In 1854, his journal says, " an effort was made to sell the Reserve to the highest "bidder, but the plats did not arrive in time to make the sale. " By the request of friends I went to Washington, took an "appeal from the Commissioner to the Secretary of the Inte- "rior, which stayed proceedings until the meeting of Congress, "when a law was passed giving the settlers a preemption." Dr. Ames was a member of the Minnesota Constitutional Con- vention. During the civil war, while his sons were enlisting, he recorded his "hope and trust that God would overrule the "storm and again bring our fair land to rest and our people to "peace and happiness." He died in 1874. Some character- istic letters of his are given :

Washington, Jan. 5, 1855.—Dear Col.: To-day Rice and myself will go all around and see how the boys feel. Be assured that it is up hill work. My communications are not for the public eye. Henceforth let me only be known in quiet life. I have already met with too many besetments on life's journey. Illy am I prepared for vexations and troubles. At my period of life, I am weary, and rest would not be distressing to my thoughts. Speak not of me to any but my friends. To my friends I am indebted for what life is to me.

Washington, Jan. 7, 1855.—The chiefs of the Winnebago tribes and the upper Chippewa chiefs have been ordered on here to treat with them. So you see there will soon be more public land in Minnesota for settlement and cultivation. We are going at a snail's pace. I have been here a week this evening. The way looks dark and doubtful. Keep shady. Don't let our enemies know what our thoughts are. I hope Steele and Case will be here this week. Steele's procrastination endangers our equities. When Case, Steele and Smith get here we will do something or die.

Colonel, tell our enemies that the Reserve will be sold under the direction of the War Department. Tell them anything but the facts. But stick to what you tell them. Fraternally.

Washington, Jan. 14.—Dear Col.: To-day has been a lonesome day to me. The mind has viewed the panorama of my life and prognosticated the future. Nothing in the past very interesting or useful ; in the future much darkness and confusion, judging from the manifestations. Your expectations of me are too high. I am but a feeble man. However, I am always ready to labor for the best interests of my friends and Minnesota. I cannot yet make a favorable report to you. During the week there will be something done, but I fear and tremble for the result. Our hopes are very low. For God's sake and our interests, don't drop a word that I write to you ; it would be hazardous. Our enemies have injured us much, and stand ready at their posts to carry forward their __ael work. So soon as there is anything final had as to our interests you shall be advised. Your brother.

Washington, Jan. 21.- My dear Col.: This is the tenth letter I have written to you. Why I write, can't say, only that you are often in my mind ; also my regard for you and the recollection of the many kindnesses that have been bestowed upon me by you and yours makes the impression and demands a manifestation of recollection. My mission here has not yet manifested anything good for us. We shall make big efforts, the coming week. All is darkness and doubt to me. Keep my letters from the public eye. Faithfully and fraternally.

Washington, Jan. 31, 1855.—My dear Brother and Com.: You speak of an excitement—political, postoffice, &c. Little do I care for such storms ; give me a title to my claim, and everything else may go. Your attachments to your party— Whig—is known to me. Go it. I will not quarrel with you about that. Your labors in grand lodge will, no doubt, be approved by the overseer's square. As yet I know nothing of affairs in the Minnesota legislature—don't care to know.

You say that I must not show my head there again, if I fail in obtaining a law for the security of the settlers on the Reserve. Colonel, you are too stringent on me. You know very well that I will do all I can to secure our equities and those of our good neighbors. It is very little that an outsider can do. If nothing else, to promote my own interest would make me work. We have a bill in committee of the whole house ; if it passes it will go to the senate ; it will secure all the settlers on the Reserve in their equities.

Washington, Feb. 28th, 1855.—Col. Stevens : The Reserve bill passed this morning without amendment. We are safe. All is well. Rejoice ! We have great rejoicing here to-day. Mr. Rice has worked hard for us—don't forget him. Our people are under great obligations to him.   A. E. AMES.

Minneapolis, M. T., March 11, 1857.—We are glad to hear from you and your dear family. May our God ever bless you and yours at the "Monticello" of your soul, alias the "Home farm" of comfort and happiness. I have nothing to communicate that will be interesting, excepting the glorious intelligence, the passage of the Railroad bill. It passed Congress on the 3d inst. A new day has dawned on this fair land. The most sanguine expectations of the sons of Minnesota will be more than realized. Our fair maiden will soon put on her attire of sister. Her chains are already being designed. She will be the fairest of the family. Blessed be God, she has not a blemish, and will never grow old. How often we have talked over her graces and future wealth. Beautiful landscapes, and running, laughing waters. How inviting. "Say on, brother!" Fraternally.   A. E. AMES.

Bradley B. Meeker was one of the first Federal Judges in Minnesota, and in 1849 held the first court in Hennepin county in the old government mill on the reservation (now Minneapolis), and appointed Franklin Steele foreman of the grand jury. He was one of the organizers of the old settlers' association. Here is a letter from him dated

Terra Haute, Nov. 7th, 1857.—Col. Stevens : Dear Sir - I intended to have made you a visit passing through Clearwater and Forest City to Glencoe, but pressing engagements will make my absence necessary. I congratulate you on your election. It was a just tribute to a worthy, warm-hearted old pioneer that has done as much to settle Hennepin as any fifteen men that can be found within her borders. You are now in a position to do Minnesota good service, and I know you well enough to know that you will do all in your power to promote her best interests. Now something has to be done, can be done, and must be done, or northern Minnesota will be a pauper country in two years. I have thought much about the matter, and have at last fallen upon the following relief measures :

In the first place, I want you to pass a law prohibiting all our courts of justice rendering any judgments for debts due by contract or judgment contracted or rendered out of Minnesota for the term of five years from the passage of such law. Now the effect of such a legislative act would be this : all the embarrassed men of business, whether manufacturers, merchants or mechanics, would wend their way with their families and friends to Minnesota in the spring, where they could enjoy legal repose from the clamors of their creditors until they had had an opportunity to establish themselves anew. This step, so merciful in these days of pecuniary depression and oppression, would revive immigration again to Minnesota, and fill it with enterprise and money. Your friend.

Judge Andrew G. Chatfield was appointed associate justice of the supreme court of Minnesota in 1853. His first appearance in a judicial capacity in Hennepin county was at a special term of court held that year in the parlors of Col. Stevens' house. From the town he laid out and named he writes : ·

Belle Plaine, Jan. 12th, 1860.—Col. Stevens : Dear Sir—
While I was in Mankato, a few days ago, Mr. C. L. Taylor of
Shelbyville called on me and requested me to write to some
member of the legislature, in his behalf, which I promised to
do ; and to that circumstance you must charge the trouble
that this letter will give you.

Mr. Taylor has a little daughter about twelve years old who
is a deaf mute. He says she is very bright and intelligent,
and spoke with much feeling of his inability to send her
abroad to be educated. He is poor. Though the state is
deeply embarrassed, cannot some plan be devised by which
the incipient or preparatory steps towards the establishment
of an institution for the education of deaf mutes may be taken?
Cannot a school, even on a limited scale, be opened ? Such
an institution the state must have, sooner or later, and this
one case impresses upon the legislature the necessity of commencing now, if any plan can be devised.

I write to you because I know you are always ready to listen
to appeals from the unfortunate, and that if there are any
means of relief within your reach, relief will be had.

FROM MRS. E. E. CHATFIELD.

Belle Plaine, Dec. 1875.—Col. Stevens : My dear Sir—The
only light which has dawned above the thick darkness which
has surrounded me, since my dear husband's death, has ema-
nated from the beautiful tokens of respect and esteem which
his friends have paid to his memory ; and foremost among
those, I place your beautiful tribute published in the Press.
From my sad heart I thank you ; and at this festival season
beg your acceptance of the accompanying photograph, as a
memento of your friend, and an acknowledgment of my gratitude to you for your fidelity to him. I am truly your friend.

JUDGE ATWATER'S TESTIMONY AS TO THE HARD TIMES OF '57.

St. Anthony, Oct. 31, 1857.—Dear Colonel : I am rejoiced
that you are elected. With you there, things will go right.
Such old wheel-horses are just what we need in such a body.

Martin has returned dead broke. Instead of bringing out
more money, he has been obliged to borrow money to send
there. It is utterly impossible to collect a dollar. For my
own part I have entirely suspended. I have between two and
three thousand dollars now due on the last payment on my

house, and where it is to come from I don't know. I cannot get money enough to buy provisions for my family. You are a lucky dog if you have raised enough to eat to get you through the winter. It is because I have been so harrassed about money matters that I have not been out to see you.

FROM H. T. WELLES.

Minneapolis, April 30, 1860.—Dear Colonel : I thank you very kindly and am grateful for the interest you manifest in Mr. Steele and myself in the sore troubles that are now upon us. Both of us would be glad to reciprocate this feeling by something more substantial than words.

No man can be named in this state whom I should prefer to you for representative in congress. I know all men do not want that position, but then some one must take it, although he does so at a sacrifice. If you can make up your mind to run for the nomination, it is my earnest desire, and will be Steele's, that you should do so. Most truly yours.

February 1st, 1881.—Dear Sir : Before I left home, the gentlemen who are compiling a history of Hennepin county called for my subscription, and for a brief notice. I do not know much about the book, but so far as any notice of myself is concerned, I propose to have you prepare it. In fact you ought to have put out the proposed history yourself, and under your own name. No stranger can do that work as well as you can. Better if you had been the father of the whole of it. You will do me a favor if you will say what is to be said about me exclusively.

Hennepin county owes as much to you, if not more than to any other man. You were the corner-stone on which Mr. Steele's fortune was built. You shaped the early beginnings of what is now the City of Minneapolis ; and in any history of the county you ought to have credit accordingly. Ever yours.

THE FIRST AND MOST NEEDY OF THE OLD SETTLERS.

St. Peter, Nov. 7th, 1875.—Dear Col.: You will recollect our old friend, John Bush, the old Indian farmer of Red Wing, and the oldest white settler in Minnesota—so says the Atlas. As you keep trace of all the early ones, you are probably aware that for many years he lived on the road between here and Fort Ridgely, at Lafayette. The Indian war ruined him financially, and after living on his place two or three years after, he bought a house in this place, and to assist a young man to secure his creditors, mortgaged his house. Of course this was the last remnant left himself and wife, and they were left with nothing—he too old and sickly to work, and she unable to make more than a bare living.

They removed to Redwood in '70, to New Ulm last fall, and now have brought up here again, in very straightened circumstances, with nothing to live on, and barely enough clothing for this mild weather. I have just been to see them. Of course the county will do something for them, if called on, but they will try to get through without this if possible ; and I write to ask you if among the old settlers and those who knew them formerly, you could not make up something for them. A little from a few would be a great deal for them.

Bush is eighty-seven years old, and has always been sick. His wife weighs about three hundred pounds, and of course don't get about as lively as a cricket by a good deal. It is of no use to quote scripture to you, but let me know if you think it is not a good object for charity.   B. H. RANDALL.

AN EARLY VISITOR'S VIEWS OF MINNESOTA.

August 3, 1849.—Mr. Stevens : From what I have seen and heard I have a few general objections to this country. The prairies are too large, timber too scarce, winters too long, and consequently summers too short. Yet it may be tolerably good to grow most small grain, as oats, barley, rye and wheat, but wheat will hardly do as well. The soil is rather too sandy, hence drouth soon effects vegetation. You have doubtless observed before this time the enthusiasm with which people in various parts of Minnesota Territory are engaging in the various enterprises ; she lives five years in one now ; the rush by and by will subside ; and how many will be astonished ; many will be or feel a little like Job's turkey—that had to lean against the fence to gobble.   M. KRIS KLENNER.

A VIEW TEN YEARS AFTER THE FOREGOING.

Cold Spring, July 6th, 1859.—Dear Sir : I earnestly and honestly believe that with your climate, and with your people, nothing is impossible. I see that you are pushing yourselves far into the wilderness, if that expression can be used of a people who plant their corn to-day and explore some untried field to-morrow. In the energy and enterprise of your people lies the gold already coined. It is this that forbids any limit to what you can accomplish. You laugh at impossibilities, and while mere supine men are conjecturing how a thing is to be done, you do it. I am yours truly. E. J. McGHEE.

KIND WORDS FROM AN OLD SETTLER.

Minneapolis, Feb. 1st, 1858. Dear Sir : We have the best feeling existing between upper and lower town. I have watched your course and action in the legislature this winter, and am proud to say that your positions are reasonable and just generally, and no man in that body would I sooner trust with important measures. Yours. EDWARD MURPHY.

"LO!"—WHAT WILL BECOME OF HIM ?

Itasca, March 16th, 1864.—Col. Stevens : Having a great desire to spread the glories of Minnesota far and wide, I have become a regular correspondent of the National Republican at Washington. Permit me to place your valuable correspondence on my list. Though I never met you, I claim you as an old acquaintance from reputation—just as a hawk claims a chicken. If nothing better crosses your mind, give me your opinion as to the best method of Christianizing and civilizing the Sioux—or any other red men. Eastern philanthropists are in a peck of trouble as to the proper manner of putting them on the track to kingdom come and letting white folks occupy the whole of the continent—and the question pops up "what will become of the poor Indian ?" O. H. KELLY.

HAZLEWOOD REPUBLIC.

Oomahoo, Minnesota, Pajutaze P. O., Nov. 11, 1859.—Hon. J. H. Stevens : My Dear Sir—I take the advantage of my slight personal acquaintance with you, to make an application, in which I flatter myself you will feel some interest. I refer to the passage of such a law as is contemplated by the constitution in reference to admitting to the rights of citizenship such Indians as may have made some progress in the track of civilization. You have probably heard something of the Hazlewood Republic. As an index of the progress made here, I send you a copy of the Constitution of Minnesota in the Dakota language. You are aware that in order to have any Indians raised to the status of men, there must be a law of the legislature regulating the mode. I have written to Governor Sibley, who will doubtless recommend the requisite legislation. May we depend upon you to initiate and advocate such a measure in the senate ? I need not say that I am much interested in the speedy passage of whatever act is necessary in the case. And I would fondly hope that the members of the legislature will all be disposed to do what can be done for the advancement of these " old settlers" of Minnesota in civilization and Christianization ; and that it will not be made a party question at all. Yours very truly.   S. R. RIGGS.

PROPOSED CAPITOL REMOVAL.

St. Paul, April 18, 1857.—J. H. Stevens, Glencoe, Dear Sir : I want your help in the matter of locating the Capitol by a vote of the people on the Big Peninsula in Lake Minnetonka. The scheme is pretty well under way. I can get over four thousand acres of land from the settlers on the lake in the way of donations to aid in the project.   W. P. RUSSELL.

JUDGE GOODRICH.

St. Paul, July 4th, 1857.—Dear Col.: I am not unmindful of your kindness to me as a citizen and legislator. I hope that you will never have cause to regret those kind offices. I shall always strive to continue the friendly relations that exist between us. We have generally taken better care of the interests of others than of our own. All that you and I need to make us popular men, is ample fortune. That I shall never have, so I make no calculations upon being a great man either in my own estimation or that of any one else. I am your friend.   AARON GOODRICH.

ON COLONEL BENTON.

St. Paul, April 30th, 1858.—Dear Col.: You speak of that great man, Colonel Benton. Yes, he is dead. We have no other Benton to die. It is no ordinary grief that can or should express the nation's sorrow. He has gone down to history with a more enduring page than any man in our country's history. Extracts from his speeches, and his thirty years in the senate, will be read as long as the language shall endure. Well may he exclaim, " What is a seat in congress to me ? I who have sat for thirty years in the highest branch of the national councils." But enough. I have never experienced feelings of envy for great men. I think I can honor all. I wish I was the only small man in the land ; I could then leave. But I must close.   AARON GOODRICH.

THE HUTCHINSONS.

Hutchinson, Minn., Feb. 23, 1876. Col. J. H. Stevens : Dear friend and brother- Knowing your love for music, and your willingness to aid every good word (song) and work, in behalf of the musical fraternity I have this first and only favor to ask through you of the legislature of our adopted state, viz : that before the close of the present session you will form and pass a bill in the interest of free singing, as well as free speaking, granting to any person or persons the right to hold public concerts of music anywhere in the state without license or penalty. The present infamous license is frequently perpetrated in our own adopted state upon those messengers of peace and good-will, the musicians, hindering their usefulness in disseminating a higher civilization through the divine medium of song. ASA B. HUTCHINSON.

Hutchinson, July 8, 1886.—Col. J. H. Stevens : My good old friend 1 was much pleased to receive a word from you, and it set me thinking of the past when, thirty-one years ago, we first came up the river to St. Paul to see the country, and give our concerts On one occasion in the corridor of the church we met two enthusiastic men who besought us to come to St. Anthony and Minneapolis. We kept our promise and were entertained at the cottage under the hill near the bridge, and met other good friends, and were treated to milk and honey. Then the getting away to the Fort for supplies for the journey through the big woods to the grand prairie ; the impromptu concert at Shakopee ; the camping in the woods en route to Glencoe ; the foraging among the Dutch settlers; the welcome reception by Bell & Chapman ; the social gathering and songs at the little hotel ; the tour over the prairie to the valley of the Hassan ; the campfires, the game, the Johnsons, Pendergasts, Messers, and Harringtons, all sleeping by the blazing log fire, and the mercury falling ; the early risers with axes, chopping for the morning meal ; the prospectors, returning in the evening delighted with the lay of the land and richness of the soil ; the farewell, and ride down the river. My dear brothers are now all sleeping their last sleep, having proved all things earthly full of vanity and vexation. Glad, dear man, you survive the wreck, and still can hold the pen. JOHN W. HUTCHINSON.

Colonel Stevens and Jacob Schaefer were socially and financially intimate as early as 1849, when the former came to Minnesota, and the latter went to California. Their wives were
sisters. Later Mr. Schaefer was well known in Hennepin
county, as auditor, commissioner, and business man. He was
born in Baeruth, near Strasburg, then France, now Germany,
at which last-named place he was educated, and then came to
the United States. He was four and a half months on the way
overland to California, where he quickly won and lost a fortune,
and then made his way to Central America, being taken ill with
yellow fever on the route. He lay unconscious, with several
other patients, in an illy-ventilated room, and the doctor said
he would die. Two friendly sea-captains had him removed to
airy quarters, and he recovered, to the surprise of the doctor,
disappointment of the undertaker, and delight of his seafaring
friends. He took a look at the coffin provided for him, and
though it was of beautiful redwood, he declined its use, in favor
of somebody seemingly less fortunate, and proceeded on his
way, buoyant with hope, and courageous to work. Going home
to the United States, he was shipwrecked on the way.

Mrs. Schaefer returned with him to his silver-mining camp
in Honduras, and for five or six years was the only white woman
there, a wonder to the dusky natives. Their daughter Francisca,
now wife of W. O. Winston, of Winston Brothers, of Minneapolis, was born at Yuscaran. The Catholic natives accomplished by strategy what they could not with consent of parents,
and the little white native of the tropics was baptised in their
church, near the mining town of Depilto. Coming North from
that country of tropical scenery, fruits, and flowers, where
there were no wheeled vehicles, and all conveyance was on mule-
back, the little Central American brought with her a young pet
tiger, and a bird of rare plumage ; but was nevertheless home-
sick to return, preferring Spanish as more pleasing to her ear,
and more yielding to her tongue.

Mr. Schaefer was of a brusque cheerfulness, that was like a
tonic to those with whom he came in contact. He was fond
of children, and was their popular friend. During the late war
he was regimental, then brigade quartermaster, and was called
to the staff of a division quartermaster. He experienced financial reverses from fire, flood, and shipwreck ; but was honored

with military and civil offices; and blessed with friends. A characteristic letter is given from --

Truxilo, November 28, 1855. As you were somewhat uneasy about our safe arrival here, I must inform you that Sunday last, the 25th instant, we landed safe, after a very pleasant voyage of only sixteen days, at this seaboard town in Honduras. Our captain was a gentleman, and we had a good crew. Mrs. S. was sick for five days, after which she was able to beat the captain at chess almost every day. We have excellent health, and are in first-rate quarters, with an Englishman who has a pleasant house and sets a fine table, with fruits and wines.

My machinery, trunks, and goods, are already on their way to the interior. We shall leave the 30th with our servant. We have native visitors every evening. Mrs. Schaefer is the first American lady who ever traveled into the interior. This evening we took a walk. A boy came running after, and presented a rose, saying his mother sent it to the lady. Flowers in the gardens this 28th of November! We visited a Carib village near this place. They are a black race, strong and well built. Each man has as many wives as he can build huts for. Each wife must have her own dwelling. The man clears a piece of ground for her, which she must cultivate as long as he is with her. He goes a fishing, and for a few months each year cuts mahogany. Happy race! We entered several of the houses. In one of them we found a young woman who was very happy. She said she had been very busy all day, and was going to be married to-morrow.

We expect to be in Yuscaran by the 18th of December. The revolution is ended. I hope it will not revive until the Yankees occupy the land. Then the country will improve, and it will be the garden of the world.   J. SCHAEFER.

Col. Stevens—Dear Sir : He that doeth well ought to be commended, and I feel privileged to say, that in the legislature your willingness to undertake, and efficiency in carrying through what you did undertake, whether for constituencies you immediately represent, or those more remote, make you a model legislator. You have done the whole state a great service in procuring the establishment of an institution that will be a lasting honor and glory to our commonwealth. Your obliged follow-citizen.   T. ELWELL.

Oak Grove, March 11, 1852.

Dear Sir : Before I take up my weary way to resume the shackles of bondage imposed upon me by the most trying of all callings, the Indian trade, I will drop you a line. Mr. Pond was here this morning, and said that he thought Mrs. P. would not recover, but linger on, perhaps for some months yet. She is wearing away from this frail abode, to the quiet repose of a future and better hope, than aught of earth. Happy those who are prepared for the change.

Granby, C. E., April 25, 1854.—Dear Sir : After twenty years absence from ones native land it is no easy matter to get away to return to that of our adoption. I have been staying here for some time with the dearest of my brothers, Rev. Norman McLeod, and will quit his most agreeable and instructive society with deep regret. He is highly esteemed in the region round about, and has been of much usefulness. You would like him. I hope we will have him one of these days, with us in Minnesota. He is anxious to go west. Indeed every one is. Westward the star of empire holds its unwavering course. Minnesota has incalculably advanced in my estimation since I started on my journey. Having seen such an extent of country in the United States and both the Canadas, so far inferior in every respect to our Territory, I am now without a ray of doubt, sanguine that it will very soon be settled, and well settled, with an industrious, thriving and happy population. There is no place I have seen since I left I prefer to Minnesota—none that I like so well.

Oak Grove, Hennepin county, Jan. 20, 1857.—Dear Col.: What about that draft for the University ? We can get the charter through without difficulty, I think, but the question is about the grant to endow it. You will have perhaps seen by the papers that Rice has introduced a bill providing for state organization, making a north and south line. I do not know what your views are as to the boundaries ; mine are for the north and south line. I know the west, and the utter worthlessness of a great portion of it toward the Missouri. I also know and have traveled in the Lake Superior region in many directions. We want the minerals, pines, fisheries, and the outlet by the great inland sea. We do not want the muddy and turbulent Missouri, with its still more dark and turbulent tribes, its gravelly hills, its sterile prairies without a tree, "its deserts vast and idle". For all these reasons, and more, I am now, and always have been, for the north and south line, which will make Minnesota a magnificent state with great and diversified resources, leading to boundless wealth, and all the mighty results which follow in its train, and the interminable blessings also, when properly applied, as let us hope they will be in the brighter and wiser future. We belong to the past, but let us embrace our little share, prospectively.

I most heartily agree with you as regards keeping some mementos of the poor disappearing aborigines, but also have to thank you for your compliment to my individual name. I am fully impressed with all that appertains to the future of Glencee. The Creator has done his great part, but there is always something left for man to do.

April 4, 1858.—The proposed cemetery is too near Glencoe. What is needed of a ten acre cemetery, which would be large enough for a place of burial—a Necropolis for a city of half a million of inhabitants. Why, ten acres would be large enough for the whole county, for generations yet unborn, with room and verge enough for all the ghosts and ghostesses in the Northwest to pace their weary rounds, above ground by the pale light of the moon, or the flickering glare of the aurora boraelis. And the day, the barberous age, of burying the dead at our doors, is past. Surely this insane relic of anti-sanity will not be resuscitated at Glencoe.

July 23, 1859.—I regret to see in the New York Herald that poor Judson Hutchinson has, in a state of mental derangement, hung himself at Lynn, Massachusetts, his residence. What a poor, uncertain, probationary state, this life is, at best, but ah! how miserable when the end is so gloomy and deplorable.

Be fearless for the people in your Register. It is a sacred duty you owe to your adopted country as a man and a journalist. It matters not whose toes you may tread upon. It is only rogues, not honest men, who will fear you, and that is the proudest position any paper or public exponent can attain to.   MARTIN MCLEOD.

DEATH OF MARTIN MCLEOD — LETTER FROM WM. S. CHAPMAN.

Minneapolis, Nov. 23, 1860.—Dear Colonel : I have just returned from paying the last tribute of respect to Hon. Martin McLeod. He was at my house the day I wrote you last, took dinner with me, was unusually jovial, and spoke of his excellent health. He asked me to rent a house here for him, and said he would bring his family here and send his children to school this winter. He went home to Oak Grove late in the evening, attended church the next day, and in the evening was taken quite unwell. Wednesday he wrote in for medicine, which I sent him. The next day Dr. Boutillier visited him, and thought he would be better in a day or two. He grew worse, and I sent Dr. Anderson out. He was deranged, and talked incessantly. He told Mr. Pond, who called the day he died, that he was too young a man to die, and that he put his trust in the Savior. He died Tuesday. Mr. Pond preached the sermon.   W. S. CHAPMAN.

REMINISCENT.

Department of Agriculture, Washington, July 5th, 1877. – Old in our friendship, and growing old in years, what vital changes have taken place since we discussed the agricultural possibilities of Minnesota, twenty-seven years ago, sitting on the bank of the Mississippi above the Falls, or wandering from your little claim-house across the virgin prairie which is now adorned by streets, houses, and mills, of this wonderful city of Minneapolis. Enthusiastic and imaginative as we were, the facts accomplished have outrun all prophecy and hope, and our state to-day leads in the production of man's first necessity, bread. What are the changes for the next twenty-seven years ? Who can tell ? You and I may not be here to know ; but let us do our earnest part in the right direction for the glory of the present, and the benefit of the future. Your friend.   WM. G. LEDUC.

COMING TO THE POINT—AND TO MINNESOTA.

Salem, Ohio, 3d Month, 11th, 1852.—Dear Friend : I have very often thought of you with feelings of near affection, strangers though we are to each other, and have often been led to sympathize with you, in your isolated situation ; and yet in view of the difficulties in our once peaceful Society, perhaps it would be more appropriate to rejoice on your account, that in respect to these things you are not as we are, "Tossed with a tempest and not comforted." There is no doubt in my mind that there is a disposition in many to give encouragement, either directly or indirectly, to views approximating more nearly to the doctrines of other professors of the Christian name, than those of our early friends did ; but there are many who feel bound to " contend earnestly for the faith once delivered to the saints." In all our travels we saw no place we liked so well as Minnesota, and I believe if it should prove to be adapted to Agricultural pursuits there are several families of friends in the neighborhood that will turn their steps thitherward ere long, perhaps myself and family among the rest. Hoping to hear from thee soon, I conclude with much love to thee and thine. JOSEPH BRANTINGHAM.

Amasa Cobb, once a messmate of Colonel Stevens in the lead mines at Galena, Illinois, and afterwards a general in the army, now Chief Justice of the Supreme Court of Nebraska, recently visited his old friend in Minneapolis, and heralded in a pleasant way his coming by a letter dated—

State of Nebraska, Supreme Court, Lincoln, July 11, 1888. My dear old Friend and Compatriot : I am making calculations to invade your city the last of next week or the week following. The ostensible object of this movement is to take my wife to visit her brother, Dr. Moffet, of Minneapolis, but my real purpose in making the campaign, is that I may have another meeting with you, before one of us is mustered out. I write this to inquire whether you will probably be in the city at or about the time above indicated. As the fellow said when his lawyer advised him to run away from Texas, " I don't know where you would go to" from cool Minnesota such weather as this ; and still Minnesota is a large state, I am advised, and I might not be able to find you among the lakes and cool recesses without information or a guide. Your old friend. AMASA COBB.

St. Paul, Sept. 28, 1849.—Mr. Steele's ferry bill was up in the Council yesterday, and they have made the most complete humbug of it you can imagine. The time is reduced to five years. Foot passengers pay six and-a-fourth cents, the rest in proportion, and he is bound in $1,000 to keep his ferry open day and night, &c. JOSEPH R. BROWN.

AN ELECTION IN YE OLDEN TYME.

October 7th, 1852.—I wrote you a note two days since informing you and our friends that the people at Little Crow's village had held a meeting and nominated J. W. Brown of Dakota county for their representative, Mr. Robertson and Mr. Cook both having refused to run. Mr. Brown is a member of the Methodist church in good standing, and a good Whig, and will support the People's ticket, and I hope all good citizens will support him.

I would like to get my house at Little Falls insured for about $350, but wish to know your rates of percentage before I conclude to do so.   P. PRESCOTT.

Executive Department, Idaho Territory, Boise City, June 21, 1878.—My dear Friend : Like a pleasant echo from the chamber of pleasant memories, comes your very kind letter of the 10th. Very happy am I to hear from you. I have thought of you a thousand times—wondered if you still lived, and where ? whether you still thought of me ? whether we should meet again ? and often thought of writing to you. For of the many good and true men it has been my fortune to know, you hold a sacred place.   M. BRAYMAN.

Minneapolis, March 17th, 1855.—I beg leave to resign the position to which your kindness called me, that of Teacher of the Public School of Minneapolis. The reason which induces me to this step is the perplexities surrounding us pertaining to the entry of homes at the Land Office, which will necessarily draw much upon our time and attention. I thank you for the uniform kindness and attention you have shown me since my service under your direction.   CHARLES HOAG.

Princeton Mills, Preston county, Virginia.—Brother and friend—Permit me thus to address you, for so I esteem all who work upon the square. News from Minnesota is like good news from a far country. I now feel interested more in that far-off territory than in the old tobacco fields of Virginia. I will resign the office of surveyor and take my little family to Minnesota in the spring. I would rather live in snow a foot deep than in this rainy climate in the winter. Could I sell a few dozen first-rate rifles, also a few hundred good chopping axes ? and I think of taking out a pair of good horses and a buggy. Give me your opinion.   A. J. BELL.

CARVER'S SKETCH OF THE FALLS OF ST. ANTHONY. 1766.

Washington, Feb. 14, 1867.—I have been here about ten days, and have done but little towards making a treaty with the Indians. There are a dozen or more delegations of Indians here from different parts of the country, all pressing their claims for precedence at the department. Congress is growing more radical every day. Even Reverdy Johnson is in favor of the constitutional amendment and negro suffrage. So you see the political world moves. I am satisfied the next congress will insist on universal suffrage.   J. B. BASSETT.

AN INFANT PIONEER—AN OLD SETTLER.

A grand woman of this century, identified with the history of Minnesota, is living in Minneapolis, at the age of "three score years and ten." Of romantic birth, she was here in infancy and during early childhood, when Minnehaha, and the Falls of St. Anthony, were in their natural glory ; and she saw them with fresh young eyes undimmed to their beauty and grandeur. She was here with her parents when Fort Snelling was Camp Coldwater. Outside the Fort, the nearest neighbors were three hundred miles away, and the mail was received only once in six months. She witnessed the arrival of the first steamboat at the Fort. The Dakota language was familiar to her. She has been intimately acquainted with our great statesmen, brave generals, grand philanthropists, and identified with the nation's progress and glory. The infant pioneer of 1819 is in 1889 one of the oldest settlers. Incidents of her life are autobiagraphically told by Charlotte Ouisconsin Van Cleve, wife of Major-General Horatio P. Van Cleve, and are of great interest.

The Two Hundredth Anniversary of the Discovery of the Falls of Saint Anthony was celebrated by the Minnesota Historical Society, at the University Campus, Minneapolis, Minnesota, on the third day of July, eighteen hundred and eighty. Articles were requested to be prepared for a Memorial Volume on the Life of Hennepin and Establishment of Catholic Missions, by Bishop John Ireland ; Indian Trade, by Hon. H. M. Rice; Military Occupation, by T. V. D. Heard, Esq.; Protestant Missions, by Rev. S. R. Riggs, D. D.; Education, by Rev. E. D. Neill ; Civil Government, by Gen. H. H. Sibley ; Our Commercial Interests, by Capt. R. Blakely ; Agriculture, by Col. J. H. Stevens ; Early French Explorers, by J. E. Ferte.

1680. In September, DuLuth and Hennepin were at the Falls of St. Anthony.

1700. LeSueur ascends the Minnesota River.

1766. Jonathan Carver, on November 17th, reaches the Falls of St. Anthony.

1817. Major Stephen Long, U. S. A., visits the Falls of St. Anthony.

1819. Colonel Leavenworth arrives on the 24th of August, with troops, at Mendota.

1820. Laidlow, superintendent of farming for Earl Selkirk, passes from Pembina to Prairie du Chien, to purchase seed wheat. Upon the 15th of April left Prairie du Chien with Mackinaw boats and ascended the Minnesota to Big Stone Lake, where the boats were placed on rollers and dragged a short distance to Lake Traverse, and on the 3d of June reached Pembina. On the 5th of May, Col. Leavenworth established summer quarters at Camp Coldwater, Hennepin county. In July, Governor Cass, of Michigan, visits the camp. In August, Col. Snelling succeeds Leavenworth. Sept 20, corner-stone laid under command of Col. Snelling. First white marriage in Minnesota, Lieutenant Green to a daughter of Captain Gooding.

1821. Fort St. Anthony was sufficiently completed to be occupied by troops. Mill at St. Anthony Falls constructed for the use of garrison, under supervision of Lieut. McCabe.

1823. The first steamboat, the Virginia, on May 10th, arrived at the mouth of the Minnesota river.

1824. General Winfield Scott inspects Fort St. Anthony, and at his suggestion the War Department changed the name to Fort Snelling.

1826. January 26th, first mail in five months received at the Fort. April 5th, snow-storm with flashes of lightning.

1829. Major Taliaferro, Indian agent, establishes a farm for the benefit of the Indians at Lake Calhoun.

1833. Rev. W. T. Boutwell establishes a mission school for Ojibways at Leech Lake.

1834. In May, Samuel W. and Gideon H. Pond arrive at Lake Calhoun as missionaries among the Sioux. November, Henry H. Sibley arrives at Mendota as agent of Fur Company. In June, Presbyterian Church at Fort Snelling organized.

KIND WORDS OF COMMENDATION OF THE WORK.

Dated at the Rooms of the Minnesota Historical Society,
St. Paul, Nov. 13, 1889.

My dear Colonel Stevens : I have read the proof-sheets of your Reminiscences with great interest. It contains a large mass of valuable facts regarding the pioneer history of Minnesota, and about our old settlers, which have never been placed in print before, and every old settler will read the work with gratification and interest. It will prove a valuable addition to our materials for Minnesota history, more especially so if a good index is added to it. Yours truly.

J. FLETCHER WILLIAMS.

Minneapolis, December 5th, 1889.

Colonel John H. Stevens—My Dear Sir: I have read with great interest the proof-sheets of your forthcoming work entitled "Personal Recollections of Minnesota and its People." This book, I believe, is the result of the urgent request of many of our older citizens that the man who first settled with his family on the site of Minneapolis, and who preempted one hundred and sixty acres in its very heart—who knows every detail of the early beginnings here as no other man does, should put into permanent record all the things he could remember, both little and great, about these beginnings. This you have done, it seems to me, with eminent success. You have also included very much valuable historical matter pertaining to Hennepin county and the whole state of Minnesota. You certainly have furnished the treasure-house for all persons in the future who may undertake to write the story of Minneapolis in its early days. Yours very sincerely,

S. C. GALE.

The publishers of this book are indebted to D. D. Merrill, of St. Paul, for the use, kindly tendered, of illustrations of the early missionaries to the Indians in Minnesota, and for views of St. Anthony Falls of 1853, and of Minnehaha Falls. Also to Walter S. McLeod for the private journal of his father. Rev. S. W. Pond, of Shakopee, materially aided them by the loan of manuscript in relation to the early missionaries. To Chas. M. Foote, of Minneapolis, they are also under obligations for well-authenticated incidents of the Sioux Massacre.

Capt. John West came to the county of Hennepin as early as 1854; Capt. Daniel Day about the same time. Both of these gentlemen have rendered efficient and valuable service on the police force of Minneapolis. George McMullen followed in the footsteps of John L. Tenny, and to that gentleman are the citizens indebted for many of the beautiful stone and brick buildings in the city. Wm. T. Inks, another early contractor, kept pace with Mr. McMullen. Hon. Joseph Moody, Thos. Moulton, and Geo. D. Perkins, pioneers on the east side, rendered valuable aid in developing the resources of St. Anthony.

Albert W. Lawrence, who landed in St. Anthony in 1855, has always labored in the interests of good morals, and ever endeavored to elevate and better the condition of his fellow-men. In this he has always received the cordial aid of Calvin W. Clark, a resident of Minneapolis since 1860. James Patten, who made his home in St. Anthony in May, 1851, has gained a competency by industry in the lumbering business.

To Prof. C. A. Widstrand were the early settlers indebted for the education of their young ladies in the higher and necessary branches of everything that appertained to music. Most of these ladies are matrons now, and all cherish his efforts, so earnestly bestowed by him in their behalf. In the fall of 1856, I heard the since immortal Adelina Patti contribute a merited compliment to Prof. Widstrand. It was on the occasion of her visit to the then embryo city of Minneapolis. The Professor aided her in a concert she gave in the city. Neither of them expected that in their life time Minneapolis would expand into such a large city.

Since the closing pages of this work have been finished, many more of the author's kind and early friends have crossed the silent river. Among them are Hon. Eugene M. Wilson, Judge E. S. Jones, Joseph Dean, Benjamin F. Bull, A. D. Foster, and Richard Martin; all pioneers and men of great merit, whose memory will always be cherished by those who were associated with them in the early history of this country.

INDEX.

www.ingramcontent.com/pod-product-compliance
Lightning Source LLC
Chambersburg PA
CBHW022007110726
47901CB00006B/1435